About the A

Fiona Scott-Barrett grew up in Edinburgh and lives there now, but spent most of her working life abroad. She taught English as a Foreign Language in Italy, Indonesia, Germany and Greece, and has written more than a dozen books for learners of English. *The Exit Facility* is her first novel.

First Edition 2021

Published in the UK, USA & Europe by
Blind Bats Publishing

ISBN 9798481895345

A CIP record for this book is available from the British Library.

The
EXIT FACILITY

Fiona Scott-Barrett

For my daughter, who is absolutely not Alexandra

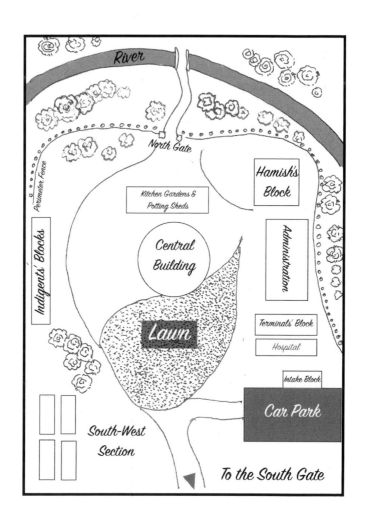

River

North Gate

Perimeter Fence

Indigents' Blocks

Kitchen Gardens &
Potting Sheds

Hamish's
Block

Central
Building

Administration

Lawn

Terminals' Block

Hospital

Intake Block

Car Park

South-West
Section

To the South Gate

Prologue

The noise of the weekly post being thrust through the letterbox and thudding onto the bare boards of her hall woke Elaine from her post-lunch nap. She got off the sofa and padded on bare feet through to the hall to collect it, rather hoping it might include a missive from a lawyer telling her she was the legatee of a long-lost, wealthy relative.

Instead it consisted of a sheaf of junk mail, a final demand from her power supplier and a postcard that showed a tropical beach, turquoise water and fantastically-shaped mountains in the background. Elaine guessed it was Thailand. She reached for her tablet, flipped the card over and photographed the back of it and then magnified the photo so that she could read what was written there. Yes, it was from Thailand, and Alexandra's exuberant handwriting was instantly recognisable. She was enthusing about the scenery and the fantastic hotel Ben had booked them into. This made no sense to Elaine, as, to the best of her knowledge, her daughter was currently at work in Hong Kong. Elaine enlarged the photograph even more until she could make out the postmark. It dated from almost a year before. Clearly the card had gone astray in the postal chaos that followed the pandemic. During that time Alexandra had ditched Ben, her wealthy expat boyfriend, and replaced him with Jason, an activist who took his life in his hands every time he walked out of his apartment block.

Elaine sighed. Their monthly video chats online were fun, but they didn't make up for Alexandra's absence, and written reminders of the distance between them only made things worse. Elaine stuck the postcard in a drawer and was reaching for the wad of junk mail to put into the recycling when the phone rang. The landline rarely rang these days and she kept it only because it was part of her comms package, costing her nothing extra.

She hesitated, aware that only health workers or government officials ever used that number and she wanted nothing to do with any of them. Then it crossed her mind that this was also Alexandra's emergency point of contact for her, and she picked up the receiver. A small cough greeted her, followed by a man's voice, the accent neutral and the tone business-like.

"Good afternoon. Is that Elaine Treasoner?"

"Who's speaking?" Elaine asked.

"My name is Roderick Payne. I'm calling from the Inland Revenue's Retroactive Investigations Office."

"From the Tax Office? I've already filed my self-assessment. Is there some problem with it?"

"Not as far as I know," the man replied, "but that's not my department. I'm with Retroactive Investigations. We have written to you twice and you failed to reply each time. That's why I'm calling you now."

This sounded suspicious to Elaine. "Look, I haven't had any correspondence from you or your office. I'm not answering any questions over the phone. You could be a scammer."

"You're right to be cautious, Miss Treasoner." A certain note of amusement seemed to enter the man's voice. "We like that in our dealings with the public."

"It's Ms Treasoner, not Miss." Elaine wasn't going to let some bureaucrat treat her like a bubble-headed youngster.

"Miss Treasoner, please go to your computer and log into your Citizens' Gateway account. You will find a message from me in your inbox. Access the secure link in that email and follow the instructions on the screen after that."

"You'll have to wait a bit," Elaine said. "I don't see well, and I probably haven't saved my Citizens' Gateway details."

"Don't worry, Miss Treasoner," the man said, "I have plenty of time." But Elaine could hear the drumming of fingernails on a desk as she stumbled her way through the security procedure.

"Right, done," Elaine said and the drumming stopped.

"If you are now satisfied about my identity, let us continue. You are currently the owner and occupier of the flat at 16/5 Melrose Wynd, are you not?"

"Yes."

"Did you ever let the said flat out?"

Taken aback, Elaine blurted out the truth. "Yes, but that was over a decade ago, and only for a very short period."

"The period of time is irrelevant. As you must know, under the terms of the recent Retroactive Tax Act, all citizens are liable for back tax on any unearned income they have had since April 2009."

"I've heard nothing about that. That's outrageous!"

"Miss Treasoner, I am not responsible for either the vagaries of the postal system or for your failure to keep up with important changes in legislation. According to my calculations, based on an average monthly income for the flat, post expenses, of £465 per month for the period in question, at the lower tax rate, and allowing for annual compound interest on that sum, you owe the Inland Revenue £4,180.86."

"You've got to be bloody joking!" Elaine roared into the phone. "Why don't you tax corporate fat cats instead of picking on poor pensioners? Where the hell am I meant to find that kind of money?"

"Please do not swear, Miss Treasoner."

"It's Ms, damn it! I'm neither a child nor a spinster. Stop patronising me."

"I must warn you that HMRC operates a zero tolerance policy with regard to anyone abusing its staff. Now can we discuss a payment schedule for this back tax?"

"No, we cannot. Firstly, I dispute the figure you have come up with and, secondly, I was resident abroad when I let out the flat, and I paid tax on it where I was living."

"Really? And where might that have been?"

"In Cyprus."

The tax official let out what sounded like a snort, then quickly masked it with a cough.

"Is that so? Then you must have been one of the few people in the country who did pay any tax."

"Cyprus is no longer a tax haven, Mr, Mr ehm, and I must warn you that I have zero tolerance for sarcasm on that subject."

"Payne."

"Yes, it caused me a lot of pain when I had to…."

"My name is Roderick Payne," the man snapped.

"Ah, I remember now. How appropriate. And where did you get these figures from, Mr Payne?"

"From the lettings agency that you placed the flat with."

"I see. So why bother to phone me, since you are so sure you know the facts already?"

"For the purposes of corroboration. Like you, many citizens try to deny they had undeclared income in the past. The recordings of the phone calls are acceptable as evidence in court."

"You can't do that! It's illegal to record calls to be used as evidence without informing someone of the fact first."

"Not anymore, Ms Treasoner. Not since the repeal of the Human Rights Act. You really should keep up with the news. Once more, may we discuss a payment schedule?"

"There's nothing to discuss. I'm broke."

"In that case, the state will be entitled to seize your assets – jewellery, electronics, vehicles, any other valuables – and auction them to pay off your tax bill."

"Mo'lon la've!" Elaine said.

"I warned you not to swear, Miss Treasoner."

"I'm not swearing, Master Payne. $Μολ$ '$ν$ $λαβέ$ is Ancient Greek. It was reputedly said by Leonidas, King of Sparta, to the invading Persians when they asked him to lay down his weapons. It means: *Come and get them*!"

"Don't worry, Miss Treasoner. We most assuredly will. Some members of my team will be round to visit you very shortly. Good afternoon to you."

Elaine heard the click as Payne hung up, threw the handset across the room and watched as it bounced off the wall.

"Fuck! Smarmy little jobsworthy git! Retroactive tax, my arse," she yelled. "Bastards, the lot of you!" Elaine retrieved the handset from the floor. It fell into two pieces in her hand.

"Bugger!" Elaine screamed, dropping the pieces into her wastepaper bin. "Now I'll have to replace the bloody phone!"

Shaking, she began venting her fury on the junk mail, ripping the takeaway menus, pizza delivery offers and loft insulation adverts into shreds. A gushing offer of grants available for installing double glazing fed her rage – she'd tried that one and discovered that the small print carefully excluded everyone who might actually need a grant to get the work done. It was printed on shiny card and she snagged three nails painfully in her mission of destruction but finally converted it into a heap of gloss-finished confetti.

A final piece of junk mail caught Elaine's attention. It wasn't so much the words *PEACE AT LAST* that appealed, it was the restraint of the graphic design that had gone into the cover of the A5 leaflet – a tasteful abstract design in dark charcoal, lemon yellow, pastel pink and a light teal. Staring at the soothing colours slowed her racing pulse. Despite the tag line, it didn't have the look of a religious group trying to recruit new members. Elaine turned the leaflet over. It was printed in a typeface that was easy to read, with clear colour contrasts that would work for people with dyslexia or, like her, macular problems. She could read the text without magnification but, in contrast to the clarity of the design, the message was couched in vague euphemisms that hindered understanding. On first glance, it seemed to be promoting a UK organisation similar to the ones in Switzerland that offered assisted suicide. Along with tax changes, had she missed a change in the law for the terminally ill? Whatever it was – care home, sheltered housing, euthanasia clinic, gated community – it would be beyond her budget. She was smart enough to know that everything, peace especially, usually came at a price.

A Year Later

Chapter 1

Sunday 1 - Monday 2 April

Elaine closed the tenement door behind her, careful not to bang it and make the building judder, then walked towards the park that had been a backdrop to two separate stages of her life. The first had been her schooldays, when she and her world had been young and full of the promise of adventures to come. Latterly, the park had been a silent witness to her return to her roots, when she and her world had felt older and smaller and almost devoid of hope.

The illusion that had haunted Elaine when she first returned crept up on her now, for the first time in ages. Surely, at some corner of one of the transverse paths she would encounter a group of her friends sauntering home from school, their caps in their pockets, ready to be whipped out and put on if a prefect came into sight, their skirts rolled up at the waist to bring the hems above the regulation inch above the knee? But now, as in the early days of her homecoming, the ghosts resolved themselves into gaggles of strangers as she grew closer – girls of the right age, but clad in smarter uniforms, with better-groomed hair and more confident swaggers than she and her peers had ever had. For all she knew, some of them could be the grandchildren of her former classmates.

Elaine passed the tennis courts where once, almost half a century ago, the weather had been so hot that the tar surface on the courts had melted and ruined her new tennis shoes. The stuck-on tar had then dried, and she had click-clacked home along the pavement, embarrassed by the noise and apprehensive about her mother's reaction. Now the thwack of rackets on balls was as rhythmic and hypnotic as ever, but the memory of that hot day was dissonant, bringing her nothing but regret that she had long since ceased to be able to see a tennis ball in flight.

Elaine walked on, skirting the play park – no memories there, thank goodness – and passing the free pop-up library, an initiative she applauded, but which had arrived several years too late for Elaine to benefit from; large print books were never deposited there and, anyway, even those were too difficult for her to read these days.

She turned onto one of the tree-lined paths that criss-crossed the park. The cherry trees were in full blossom, as they had been three years or so ago when she and Alexandra had walked there together. Her daughter had been happy, but strangely nervous too. They had sat on a bench and, twirling a strand of her long hair round one finger, Alexandra had suddenly announced: "I've got news, Mum."

"Good or bad?" Elaine had asked, bracing herself for the latter.

"Both," Alexandra had replied. "I've found a job, and it's well-paid." Elaine had relaxed a little, but not entirely – that both was ominous – and then the blow had come. "It's in Hong Kong, and I leave in five days."

Elaine had chosen this path today in the hope that walking along it would be a cathartic move, a symbolic act that would give her some kind of closure. Now she felt it had been a mistake; she had merely stuck a knife in an old wound and turned it. She abandoned the path and headed westwards across the grass, walking rapidly and counting her steps to prevent herself from thinking.

After half an hour, a nagging pain in her hip caused Elaine

to turn back towards home. The most direct route took her past the café where Gary had loved to sit at a pavement table under the canopy in all weathers, drinking over-priced coffee and seeing and being seen. This reawakened Elaine's old fury at his parsimonious behaviour with her, coupled with his extravagance and glad-handing whenever he went out. She put her head down, and headed on to her house.

Elaine stuck her key in the door to the tenement stair and jiggled it about until it consented to turning. The recent rain had swollen the door and the lock would benefit from adjustment again, but it wouldn't be she who had to organise it this time. The thought that she was escaping the burden of finding tradesmen and harrying fellow residents for their share of repair costs brought a small smile to Elaine's lips. She limped up the stair, sore from her walk. As she approached her own door, the stair light beside it, which had been flickering and fading for weeks, gave a final burst of light and then went out. Considering the choice she had made, it felt like a metaphor to Elaine. She unlocked her own door by feel, went into her flat and sat down on the sofa.

Her packing was long since done, the letter to Alexandra was nestled safely in a drawer; now there was nothing to do but wait until an official arrived.

+++

"Is that all you're taking?" the uniformed woman asked, casting a glance at Elaine's small holdall. A large badge on her chest proclaimed 'Emily, Dispatch Facilitator' in big, low-vision-friendly navy blue letters on a yellow background. Elaine wasn't fooled by the job title – Emily was a guard, and guards were rumoured to carry Tasers. Still, Emily seemed nice enough.

"Go on, you're allowed more," Emily said. "Lots of our

clients like to have a few little keepsakes with them."

Elaine took another look around the small, bare room that had served as her living room, dining room, office and studio. Her books and paints and CDs had gone. Every flat surface, from the wooden floor to the top shelf of the bookcase, was scratched, stained or chipped but impeccably clean; she'd made sure of that.

A slit of orange light from the streetlamp was visible between the curtains. They'd never hung well since she'd decided to break their beige blandness with a Jackson Pollock splatter theme. She should have known better than to use the gloss paint left over from her front door; inevitably the fabric had ended up stiffer in some patches than others. Elaine crossed the room and tugged at the left curtain until it fell into place, closing the gap that always irritated her. A needle of pain shot through her hip as she did so. She leaned on the back of the sofa bed to support herself.

"Little keepsakes, eh? What for? It's not like I'll be staying long," Elaine said.

The sofa bed, now an irregular shade of old rose, once a funky fuchsia, held more memories than any trinkets or souvenirs could. That was something she'd have liked to take with her.

"How about the painting?" Elaine asked, indicating the life-size portrait she'd done of Alexandra in her graduation robes, her long pink hair incongruous with the mortarboard and gown, but a perfect match for the sofa bed in its heyday.

"I am terribly sorry, but that is way outside the regulation size. Is she a family member?"

"My daughter. Never mind, it's better if she finds it here when she comes back."

"How about a photo of her instead? Have you packed one?"

"It's OK, I've got lots on my tablet."

Elaine picked up her holdall as she spoke and looked inside, checking once again that her old but ever-reliable Nexus 7 was in there. A thought struck her.

"I will be able to charge a tablet, won't I?"

"Don't worry. The rooms at the facility are old. I mean, they're comfortable, of course, but they haven't been rewired for the new system yet, so you'll be able to use your charger."

"Then I'm ready to go." Elaine walked to the door without risking a backward look. It hadn't been the most luxurious or the best-loved of the places Elaine had lived in, but she had called it home for the last twelve years.

An unmarked black van with smoked glass windows was waiting on the street outside Elaine's tenement door. Emily unlocked the back doors, put Elaine's holdall on the floor and then helped Elaine up the step. There were two beds in the back of the van. Elaine sat down on one while Emily pulled the doors shut, turned on an overhead strip light, and then perched opposite Elaine.

"This is where I say goodbye," Emily said. "You'll be met by one of my colleagues at the other end. It's a longish journey, so we generally offer our clients a mild sedative to help them sleep. It eases the transition, as it were. You don't have to accept it, of course, but …"

"That's OK," said Elaine. "Bring it on."

"Take off your coat and roll up your sleeve," Emily instructed, unlocking a metal cabinet bolted to the partition between the driver's compartment and the passenger area. She took out a syringe and slid the needle into Elaine's forearm.

"Have a good journey," Emily said, and climbed out of the van and locked the doors behind her.

+++

Elaine awoke to the sound of bolts being drawn and doors clattering open. A pale grey morning light barely illuminated the space she was in. Her head felt foggy and her tongue was dry. At arm's length from herself she could see a pinched face, its toothless mouth open and a ribbon of drool connecting it to a pillow. Where the hell was she?

She could hear two voices somewhere beyond her feet.

"Same procedure as usual, boss?" asked a rough male voice.

"I told you before, Brendan," a female voice said. "We use first names around here. So you call me Ashley, OK? But that doesn't give you the right to be disrespectful just cos you're using my first name. Got that?"

"Yes, boss. I mean Ashley," said the male. "So is it the usual procedure – searching, tagging, shooting?"

"No, we don't need to tag them," the woman replied. "The old one's a T and the female is a V, so tagging isn't needed. We'll just do the basic search and shoot."

The fog in Elaine's head suddenly cleared and was replaced by a nasty void in the area of her stomach, and a rapidly increased heartbeat. She sat up abruptly, causing her heart to race even faster. She could see a figure standing by the open door of the van.

"What's going on here?" Elaine asked. Her voice sounded faint and croaky.

"Oh, you're awake. Good morning, Elaine," the woman said. "You've arrived safely at your destination. I'm Ashley, your Intake Facilitator."

"What's all this about shooting?" Elaine pushed a blanket aside and struggled to get to her feet. Her hips groaned after hours on a narrow pallet bed.

"Nothing to worry about, Elaine," Ashley said, "It's a mere formality, a standard part of the Intake Procedure." As she spoke she looked down at something in her left hand, a clipboard perhaps, and wrote on it with her other hand. Her indifference fuelled Elaine's fear and indignation.

"No, this is not what I agreed to. I have rights. I am a free citizen. At the interview they spoke to me about dignity, they said …"

"Shall I subdue her, boss?" A large orange-clad figure entered Elaine's line of sight, its hand apparently straying towards its pocket.

"It's Ashley, I told you! And no, the situation is under control. Elaine, pick up your bag, get out of the van, and get into this wheelchair, please."

"I don't need a wheelchair!" Elaine said, the hysteria in her own voice embarrassing her. This could not be happening, not this way.

"Alright, then," Ashley said. "Just pick up your bag, slowly now. That's it. Good, well done. Now get out of the van. Do you prefer to walk?"

"I'll walk," Elaine said, "But I protest! I wasn't told it would be like this. I need time to prepare!"

"Oh, want to get your lipstick and mascara on first, do you, love?" said the orange-clad figure.

"That's enough, Brendan!" snapped Ashley. "I am in charge

here. And these are clients. We treat them with respect, didn't they tell you that in your training? Now get the T out of the van and follow on behind us."

Elaine stood on the tarmac, shaking and diminished. She'd imagined the final moment many times, but not this way. She'd pictured herself, chin up, proud and impressive, striding to the fate she had chosen, not caught short and unprepared like this.

The orange-clad thug was manoeuvring Elaine's ancient co-passenger into a wheelchair. The old man was still asleep – at least he wasn't aware of his imminent fate.

"Ready to go?" asked Ashley brightly, pointing at a heavy steel door fifty metres away.

"Move!" snarled Brendan. This time Ashley didn't rein him in.

Elaine fixed her eyes on the steel door and began walking, counting her steps silently in an effort to keep calm.

... eleven, twelve, thirteen ...

What the fuck had she been thinking of? There was no dignity in this.

... eighteen, nineteen, twenty ...

This was awful, ridiculous, it couldn't be happening.

... twenty-five, twenty-six, twenty-seven ...

She'd been sold an image of choice and peace, but was this really just a slaughterhouse?

... thirty-three, thirty-four, thirty-five ...

She was a fool, she'd let herself and Alexandra down, she should have hung on for her just a little bit longer.

… forty-two, forty-three …

A seagull wheeled overhead, screeching, then landed on an overflowing wheelie bin near Elaine, causing her to jump.

… forty-nine, fifty, fifty-one …

She was nearly at the door now.

… fifty-seven, fifty-eight, fifty-nine …

Alexandra, I love you … be safe … prosper and be happy!

… sixty-six … sixty-seven …

Ashley wrenched the steel door open and stood back to let Elaine in first, followed by Brendan and his wheelchair passenger. The room they had entered was small and dominated by what looked very like an airport security luggage scanner. Elaine's heart was thumping and the lower half of her vision was populated by fluorescent green, orange and pink worms wriggling frenetically. *Great – a visual migraine, just what she needed.*

Elaine was vaguely aware of her bag being passed through the airport-style scanner and of then being ushered into a brightly-lit room with a curved back wall, painted white. She complied with Ashley's instructions to stand on clown-sized footprints marked on the floor and Ashley then stepped behind a partition.

Elaine thought she could see a small red light moving up and down behind the partition and finally coming to rest around the level of her nose.

"Stand absolutely still, please," called Ashley, sounding positively cheerful. "This won't take long!"

A sudden bright flash emanated from a slit in the partition and Elaine flinched, but she was still standing after the light disappeared, still apparently alive.

"You moved," said Ashley. "I'll have to do it again. Holographic cameras are very sensitive."

"A camera?" Elaine stuttered.

"Yes," Ashley answered, oblivious, "now, hold it there for me …"

The torture lasted another five minutes, as Ashley shot take after take, moving Elaine on a turntable beneath the clown feet to get right and left profiles as well as full face. Ashley was either a perfectionist or a sadist, but Elaine couldn't make out which. By the time the ordeal was over, Elaine was half-blinded by flashing lights and drained by terror, but still standing and breathing.

"That's fantastic," said Ashley, emerging from behind the partition. "Search and shoot complete. Your ID card will be ready before lunchtime. Someone will bring it to you, as you won't get lunch without it. Now, let's collect your bag and I'll show you to your room. Brendan, you can deal with your client now."

Elaine was barely aware of where she was being taken, her mind numb, her legs shaky and her eyes unfocussed as she followed the Intake Facilitator out of the building and along a path. Ashley thrust open the large glass front door of a two-storey building, then led Elaine through an internal door to their right.

"This is your unit," said Ashley. "Six bedrooms, all with ensuite toilet and shower, but you can use the old bathroom at the end of the corridor once a week if you prefer a bath. There's a kitchen at the end of the corridor too – tea and coffee-making facilities only, though. Breakfast, lunch and dinner are all served in the central building – a map and the opening times of the central building are in your room. And this is you in here."

Ashley pushed open the second door on the right hand side of the corridor, carried Elaine's holdall in and dumped it on the bed.

"So, I'll leave you to unpack and settle in," Ashley said. "Oh, and your Intake Interview with the Facility Administrator will be after breakfast tomorrow. We normally do that on your intake day, but there's a bit of a backlog at the moment."

Ashley bared her teeth at Elaine in the semblance of a smile, and left.

The room was small and narrow. The furniture consisted of a single bed bolted to the floor, a desk ranged along the opposite wall and attached to it in a similar manner, a narrow wardrobe at the foot of the bed and two shelves above the desk. The walls were an insipid shade of beige and the serviceable twisted pile carpet was a muted brown. Brown and beige curtains flanked a window with a safety catch that permitted a maximum opening the width of Elaine's fist. It reminded her uncomfortably of a university hall of residence she'd briefly stayed in over forty years earlier, before escaping to the more congenial environment of a shared student flat.

She opened a plastic door beside the wardrobe and revealed a tiny capsule bathroom. When she stepped in to use the moulded plastic loo, the floor bounced gently beneath Elaine's feet, triggering memories of being in the toilet of an aircraft or a second class cabin on an island-hopping Greek ferry.

Elaine dried her hands on a scratchy, threadbare towel and removed the tablet from her holdall. Emily had been right –

the sockets were for three-pin plugs. Elaine plugged the Nexus in, propped it up on the desk, selected 'gallery' and set it to 'slideshow'. She then sat on the narrow bed and wept while images from her past flitted in front of her.

Chapter 2

Monday 2 April

Elaine awoke to the sound of thumping, and her name being shouted. She was lying on a narrow bed, her face on a blanket which smelled vaguely of bleach, her feet on the floor.

Ah, yes. The Exit Facility, Elaine remembered. She got to her feet, walked the two steps to the door, fumbled with the lock and yanked it open. Brendan was there, his fist raised for another assault.

"Oh, there you are," he snarled. "About bloody time. I've got your ID card, and I have to take you over to the central building for lunch."

Brendan handed Elaine a printed ID card attached to a dark blue lanyard. Her perfectly scaled-down holographic image alarmed her. She looked white and tense, her eyes staring, her hair spiky and unkempt. Her first name was emblazoned in large black letters across the middle of the card. At the top right were the letters 'VD', followed by a digital display set to 000. She laid it on the desk.

"No, you've got to keep it on you," Brendan said. "At all times. You'll have to scan it to get into the dining hall and any of the other facilities in the central building."

Elaine picked up the ID card and put it in her trouser pocket.

"No, not in your pocket!" Brendan snapped. "Wear it! Round your neck. That's what the lanyard's for. Duh!"

The words 'Fuck you' rose to Elaine's lips and she suppressed them with difficulty. She then slipped the lanyard over her head and limped to the door, her hips aching from the unscheduled and ungainly nap.

The short walk to the central building was carried out in silence, Brendan striding impatiently five paces ahead. As far as Elaine could make out, the building was circular and one-storeyed, with glass walls. Brendan led her through a double door into a hallway, then pointed.

"Scan your ID card over that console, there," he instructed. "Then walk through the arch. You're not carrying anything metal, are you?"

"Take me closer," Elaine said. "I'm partially sighted, I can't see a console from here."

Brendan sighed theatrically and led her forward, his grip on her elbow tight. "See now – that blinking red eye? Scan your card over it. Got it?"

"Got it," Elaine replied. The glass door beside the console slid open and she stepped through it then passed under another arch that looked straight out of airport security. As she stepped forwards she realised she was now in a self-service dining hall. Elaine took a tray from a pile to her left and advanced across the grey lino towards a row of glass-fronted cabinets.

"Hello!" said a young girl in a white uniform, who was standing behind the cabinets. "I haven't seen you before. I'm Siobhan. What's your name?" Her voice was kind and cheerful.

Elaine smiled back. "Hi, I'm Elaine. I arrived this morning. Can you explain what I do?"

"Sure, it's easy! Just tell me what you want. There's haddock and chips with salad or the vegetarian option, which is vegetable lasagne with salad. I'm afraid the third lunch option today, the beef stroganoff, is only for the party guests. Where drinks are concerned, help yourself to any soft drinks you find at the end of the counter. If you want wine or prosecco, you need to pay for it."

"Party?" said Elaine. "What kind of party?"

As she asked, she became aware of a song playing in the dining hall that she hadn't heard since her early childhood. *Bye, bye, love, bye, bye, happiness …*

"Good Lord, what's that song? It sounds like the… the whatsit brothers!"

"Yes, the Everly Brothers," Siobhan said happily. "It's Ernie's favourite! He requested it specially for his Last Lunch today."

"I see," said Elaine, feeling the little appetite she'd had fading rapidly, "And who is Ernie?"

"He's one of the clients scheduled for Exit later today. See – the old gent over there in the wheelchair." Siobhan pointed to the far corner of the dining hall where Elaine could just make out a group of five or six people clustered round a person in a wheelchair.

"So, what'll you have?" Siobhan continued.

Elaine took a tray with lasagne and salad, a glass of mineral water and plastic cutlery over to the nearest table. A woman with short steel-grey hair and bottle-bottom glasses was the only other occupant of the table. She was eyeing her fish and chips aslant, apparently having some trouble dealing with the fillet of haddock.

"Can I help you?" Elaine asked, as the woman slowly

dismembered the fish fillet with her plastic implements, peering sideways at each piece before she put it in her mouth. "I think the bones have been removed already, actually, but I can check for you."

It would be a case of the blind leading the blind, Elaine knew, but this woman seemed to be considerably more visually challenged than Elaine was herself. But her offer was ignored, so perhaps the woman was deaf as well as nearly blind.

Elaine toyed with her lasagne in silence until a voice interrupted her.

"Hello, there! Did you, or rather, I suppose I should still say, do you, know Uncle Ernie?"

A brassy blonde woman in a black lacy dress was hovering nearby, a nervous smile on her face and a bottle of prosecco in her hand.

"I'm afraid not," said Elaine.

"Oh, that's a pity," the woman said, moving closer to Elaine. "You see, it's like, we'd kind of expected more people for his party, and there's a lot of prosecco left, and he's feeling a bit nervous, you know what I mean? I thought, maybe, you'd like to, you know, join us, for a last drink? To his health, or more like to his passing, you know?"

"Thanks, but I think not," Elaine said firmly. "I've only just got here and we never met, I don't think it would be appropriate."

The woman's face crumpled. "Please," she said. "He won't remember if he knew you or not. But Uncle Ernie always loved a party, he liked to be popular, you know what I mean? The more the merrier and all that," she continued, as a fat tear coursed down one cheek, leaving a track mark in her blusher and powder.

"Very well," replied Elaine, rising to her feet and abandoning her barely-eaten lasagne and salad.

Ernie was semi-slumped in his wheelchair, apparently drunk, doped up, despairing, or a combination of all three. He was wearing a dark blue jacket with a black velvet collar and lapels. His hair, still thick, had been combed into a quiff and dyed the colour of tobacco-stained fingers to match his generous sideburns. He perked up at the sight of a new arrival and proffered a skeletally thin, liver-spotted hand for Elaine to shake.

"Hi babe," Ernie said. "Nice to see you again. You're looking good."

"Thank you, Uncle Ernie," Elaine replied. "You too."

"Don't be crazy, kid. I look like shit and I know it. Can't beat cancer, no matter how hard you try. But I'm going out in style – music, booze, pretty women. What more could I need?"

"Sure, Uncle Ernie," said Elaine. "You always had style."

"Good on yer, kid," replied Ernie. "Got a glass? Hey, somebody give Nancy a drink! You like bubbly, don't you Nancy?"

"Of course I do," said Elaine, accepting a glass of prosecco along with a new persona. "Here's to you, Uncle Ernie. Safe journey."

The small cluster of Ernie's friends and relatives clapped enthusiastically and poured a fresh round of prosecco while Elvis sang *Heartbreak Hotel* in the background. Two of the women tried to persuade Ernie to sing along. Elaine downed another two glasses of prosecco and, with mumbled apologies, escaped from the dining hall.

She walked back to her block and headed down the corridor to the room Ashley had indicated was the communal kitchen. It was a small room bereft of tables or chairs; instead there was a high counter with six bar stools ranged in front of it. From behind it came some scuffling sounds that Elaine hoped did not emanate from mice. She stepped round the end of the counter and saw a tiny lady, bent like the hook of a coat hanger with age, shuffling about with a teapot in one hand. She was so small that her head did not protrude above the counter, which was about bust height on Elaine. Four or five drawers below the worktop stood open, as did two low cupboards, into one of which the old lady was peering.

"Can I help you?" Elaine asked.

The old woman turned round, her free hand on the worktop to balance herself, and her face broke into a smile.

"Oh, there you are my dear! Just in time. I can't seem to remember where I left the tea. Do you recall where I put it?"

"I'm afraid not," said Elaine "I've only just got here."

"Oh, aren't you Daphne? I'm so sorry. You look a bit like her. No, of course, I remember now. Daphne has gone. In fact, I think I attended the party beforehand. Did you attend it, my dear?"

"No, I didn't. You see, I've only just, um, checked in."

"Oh, you're the new girl! Yes, one of the morning staff said we'd be getting a new girl today. Silly me. So pleased to meet you, my dear. I'm Miss Latimer."

She extended her right hand, seemingly oblivious to the china teapot dangling from it at a dangerous angle.

Elaine removed the teapot and placed it on the counter, then shook Miss Latimer's hand.

"Pleased to meet you too. I'm Elaine. Elaine Treasoner."

"Elaine. Are you French? They used to say that was a French form of Helen. You don't look very French, though," said Miss Latimer, scrutinising Elaine's faded black jeans and spiky burgundy-coloured hair. Clearly there was nothing wrong with this old lady's eyesight.

"No, I think my mother just liked the name. It was quite popular at the time."

"Yes, I remember there was a time when I had two or three of them in my form." The old lady put a hand to one side of her head and patted her permed silver hair. "It's funny how these things go in cycles, isn't it? Then we had all those awful names – Kylie and Chelsea and Courtney and nonsense like that. And then all those old names like Sarah and Emily and Rachel came back into fashion."

"You're right," Elaine said. "Now how about the tea? Perhaps I can help with that?"

"Thank you, my dear. I can't find it anywhere."

Elaine opened a corner cupboard at her eye height and found an array of Nescafé jars, cartons of tea bags and bags of sugar. Each had a white adhesive label on it bearing a handwritten name in large black capital letters. A packet of PG Tips stated 'Dorothy', but that didn't seem to be quite Miss Latimer's style, Elaine felt. A carton of loose Assam tea with the label 'Violet' seemed more likely.

Elaine turned to the old lady. "Is your first name Violet?"

"Yes, it is, my dear," said Miss Latimer. "Aren't you clever? But I feel more comfortable being known as Miss Latimer.

Habits of a lifetime die hard."

"I've found your tea. Let me make it. I'll take you to your room and then bring the tea," Elaine suggested.

The two of them shuffled down the corridor, Miss Latimer leaning on the crook of Elaine's arm.

"Here I am." Miss Latimer stopped outside the door directly across the corridor from Elaine's. "It's easy to remember – it's opposite Daphne's room."

Elaine returned to the kitchen and made the tea. She wasn't a tea-drinker herself, but her mother had administered rigorous instruction in the art of proper tea-making. A further rummage in the cupboard turned up a small tin of Nescafé with a sticker inscribed 'Daphne'. She dumped a teaspoon of it in a cracked mug and added the last of the boiling water. It sounded like Daphne wouldn't be needing her Nescafé where she was now.

Elaine left the coffee in her own room and knocked on Miss Latimer's door. There was no reply. She pushed the door open gently. The room was a mirror image of the one she had been assigned, apart from the large wing chair jammed between the bed and the desk. Miss Latimer was ensconced in the chair, her hands neatly folded on her tweed-clad lap, her head nestled against one of the wings and her single string of pearls rising and falling gently on her pink cashmere jumper as she dozed.

A silver tray on the desk had a single tea cup and saucer, a matching sugar bowl and milk jug and a large silver cake slice sitting on it. Flanking the tray were a bottle of well-aged malt whisky, and two cut glass tumblers.

Elaine laid the teapot on the tray and cleared her throat. Miss Latimer's eyes opened.

"Oh, there you are my dear! How are you?"

"Fine, thank you. I've brought your tea, Miss Latimer."

"How kind of you. Are you a new helper?" asked Miss Latimer. "You're very polite compared to the other one."

"No, I'm your new neighbour. I'm in the room opposite."

"With Daphne? Surely not."

"No, you told me that Daphne has departed. I mean passed on."

"Of course, silly me. I remember now." Miss Latimer sat up a little straighter in her chair and patted her hair again. "You're the new girl. Would you care for some tea?"

"No, thank you. I'm not very partial to tea," said Elaine, suddenly aware that her phraseology had changed to mirror Miss Latimer's. She hoped she wasn't parodying the old dear.

"Very well. How about a small whisky then? I must confess I do like a little dram now and again myself. It warms the bones."

"Indeed it does, but I've already had three glasses of … I mean, it's a bit early for me."

"Very wise. Freddie always used to say one should wait till the sun was over the yardarm. Did you know Freddie?"

Elaine shook her head.

"Pity. He was such a nice chap. He was killed in Korea, you know. Terrible shame." Miss Latimer removed a tiny white handkerchief from the sleeve of her jumper and dabbed delicately at her nose.

"I'm sorry to hear that. Miss Latimer, I wondered if I could ask you something. You mentioned earlier that Daphne had finally departed. Does that mean she had been here for a long time?"

"Daphne? I'm afraid I don't recall a Daphne here. My memory's not quite what it used to be, you know. But I do try to keep it lively. I'm rather fond of Scrabble. Do you play?"

"Well, I haven't played for years, but I do know the game," said Elaine.

"Excellent! Then come back later and we'll have a little whisky and a game of Scrabble. How about that?"

"I'll do that. Thank you, Miss Latimer," said Elaine, backing towards the door.

"And thanks to you for the tea, my dear. I'm sorry, what was your name again?"

Elaine let herself back into the room that had so recently been Daphne's and sat on the bed again, cradling the mug of coffee. The slide show on her Nexus had frozen on a picture of Alexandra, gap-toothed and dungareed, her arms cradling the neck of a white nanny-goat that had belonged to her great aunt. She picked up the tablet and tapped it on the side to make the display move on, but Alexandra and the goat remained stubbornly in place. The Nexus 7 was old and temperamental, just like her.

Through the wall between her room and the one located between hers and the main door of the unit came a low, whimpering moan. Between the moans a voice said: "Not again. No. Go away. Please, go away."

Elaine stood up and moved towards her door, then stopped. Compassion fought with an inner voice that told her she'd interfered enough in other people's lives for one day. She dithered for a while, and then cowardice and a gently incipient prosecco hangover won the battle.

Elaine had tucked a few sleeping pills in the gap in the lining of her holdall before the Dispatch Facilitator had arrived. She now unearthed two of these, washed them down with the coffee, set the alarm on her tablet for seven a.m., removed her shoes and lay down on the bed. Miss Latimer was a sweetie, but she wouldn't remember that Elaine had said she'd come back. Scrabble could wait; for now, temporary oblivion was a far more appealing option.

Chapter 3

Tuesday 3 April

Elaine rushed her breakfast and was waiting outside the Facility Administrator's office for her Intake Interview five minutes before her appointment. She paced up and down the corridor anxiously. Another five minutes passed. Eventually a young woman emerged from an adjoining office.

"Are you Elaine?" she asked. "Nicola's running a bit late, but she said you should go into her office and wait." Evidently the pervasive insistence on first names extended even to the Facility Administrator.

Elaine pushed the door and went in, leaving it open. The office smelt of cleaning fluids. There was little in it but a desk, with a chair on either side of it and a vast computer screen and slim console sitting on top of it. The screen and a free-standing engraved nameplate – *Nicola Pemberton, Facility Administrator* – were facing in the same direction, which confused Elaine. After due consideration, she decided the chair that faced the back of the monitor must be for guests and turned the nameplate towards it. Surely the Facility Administrator did not need to be reminded of what her own name was.

"How very kind of you," a voice said from behind her.

Elaine whirled round. A tall woman in a navy blue suit was standing in the doorway. "I do appreciate a tidy office." It was hard to tell if she was laughing at Elaine, or expressing genuine gratitude. "You must be Elaine. I'm Nicola, the Facility Administrator."

Nicola walked over and shook Elaine's hand, then gestured for her to sit down.

"So, Elaine. I must apologise for keeping you waiting, both yesterday and this morning. I'm afraid we've had an unusually high intake of Terminals this week and that has disrupted our usual routine."

Elaine glanced at the large monitor on the desk. "Computer terminals?" she asked.

"Oh no!" The Facility Administrator sounded vaguely amused again. "I'm sorry, of course you wouldn't know our terminology yet. Let me explain. We have different categories of client here. The first are the Facility's original category, terminally-ill clients who are in urgent need of Compassionate Closure. Then we have the voluntary clients – people such as yourself who have chosen Closure for their own personal reasons. So we talk about Terminals and Voluntaries, or Ts and Vs for short."

"What about the third category?" Elaine asked.

Nicola opened a drawer in her desk and searched inside it.

"There is no third category," she said.

The Facility Administrator drew what looked like an ID badge out of the drawer and waved it over the console. The computer screen lit up, bathing one side of Nicola's face in a greenish-blue glow that made it hard for Elaine to make out her facial expression.

"You surprise me," Elaine said. "I heard two of the staff mentioning tagging when I was brought in. They said I was a V and the old man who arrived with me was a T, so we didn't need to be tagged. That implies there must be at least one other category of inmates, or, rather, clients, that does need to be tagged."

"You must have been mistaken. I expect you were still under the influence of the sedative you were given on departure," Nicola said. "So, let's proceed to the Intake Interview, shall we?"

"You may be right," said Elaine, sensing that she would get no more out of Nicola on this topic now. "The whole arrival experience was, shall we say, a little disconcerting."

"I'm sorry to hear that," said Nicola. "Did the staff mistreat you in any way? Do you wish to lodge a complaint?"

"No, it's fine. It was more a matter of my own misconceptions."

"Then, let's get started." Nicola swung the computer screen fully towards herself so that Elaine no longer had a side view of it. "As I explained before, we have recently had an unexpectedly high intake of Terminals. This means that the waiting times until Closure have, regrettably, been extended for those, such as yourself, whose needs are not urgent as they are not in extreme physical pain."

A jolt like an electric shock hit Elaine in the solar plexus, setting her pulse racing. "Extended? By how much?" she said. "I was told at my Pre-Intake Consultation that seventy-two hours would be the maximum interval between Intake and Exit."

"I'm afraid it will be rather longer than that, given the current pressure on our resources," said Nicola. "Each client's Exit Date, or Closure Date, as we prefer to put it, is calculated on an individual basis using a rather complex algorithm. If you could pass me your ID card, I will swipe it and access your details."

Elaine slipped the lanyard over her head and gave the card to the Administrator. "Oh, that reminds me," she said. "Why does it state 'VD' on the card? I find that somewhat offensive."

"Offensive? Why so?"

"Well, I'm sure you're aware of what the letters 'VD' stand for, or at least used to stand for in my day," said Elaine.

The Facility Administrator stared at Elaine and tilted her head slightly.

"I'm talking about venereal disease, what people nowadays call STIs or STDs. I object to having that emblazoned in huge letters on a badge I wear around my neck. I haven't had a sexually transmitted infection since I was a student at art college, I'll have you know."

Nicola gulped, coughed and then cleared her throat. "Oh, I see what you mean now," she said finally. Elaine was pleased to notice this small crack in the woman's veneer of polite but distant efficiency.

"No, no, nothing of that nature," Nicola continued, having recovered her poise. "The 'V' is, of course, for voluntary, and the 'D' stands for disabled."

"But I'm not classified as disabled," said Elaine.

"Really?" said Nicola, who had swiped Elaine's ID card and was looking at the computer screen. "It mentions rheumatoid arthritis here."

"Yes, I do suffer from that intermittently, but not to the extent that I would describe myself as disabled."

"It must refer to something else, then. Ah, here we go. Best disease. That's a new one on me. I haven't seen diseases being classified as good, better or best before."

Elaine smiled wryly and nodded. "Yes, it's singularly badly named, I have always thought. Best disease is a hereditary condition that affects the central part of the retina. It causes visual impairment."

"I see," Nicola said. "Yes, the form states that you are partially-sighted and that you therefore qualified for disability benefits a decade ago. That explains the 'D' on your badge. And that means that your waiting time until Closure will be twenty-three days."

"What? But I never did receive any disability benefits," Elaine said. "I lived abroad for many years. When I returned to this country I was refused disability benefits until a period of three years had elapsed. A week after I reached that deadline, the government abolished the benefits that should have applied to me."

"That was unfortunate," said Nicola, "I'll correct your data in that case." She typed rapidly. "So, that gives us an adjusted waiting period of thirty days."

Elaine could hear the blood pounding in her ears. She clasped her hands tightly together to prevent herself from hammering on the desk in front of her. "Thirty days! That makes no sense!"

"On the contrary, it makes perfect sense. You have, in the past, consumed fewer state resources than we thought was the case, and thus you are entitled to more time in this Facility at the state's expense."

"But I don't want more time! I want to get it over with. Surely you realise how difficult a decision this is to make? Having made it, I don't need a thirty-day cooling off period. It's not as if I was buying a new fridge and decided I'd chosen the wrong bloody model. I'll go crazy if I have to wait that

43

long. It's not possible," said Elaine, aware of the rising hysteria in her voice.

The Facility Administrator reached underneath her desk with one hand, and Elaine heard a buzzing noise outside in the corridor.

"I appreciate your concern," said Nicola, "and I regret the inconvenience to you. Please rest assured that we will do our best to make your unavoidably extended stay as comfortable as possible."

She handed the ID badge back to Elaine, whose hand shook as she grasped it. The digital display, previously set to 000, now read 030 in red figures on a grey background.

"Ah, here's Brendan," Nicola continued, as there was a knock at the door. Brendan came in, his right hand once again hovering in the vicinity of his pocket.

"Brendan," said Nicola, "would you please show Elaine some of the amenities we have for our clients' spiritual and mental relaxation? Elaine, I believe snorkelling in the Maldives is a particularly popular option in the VR room."

"VR?" said Elaine. "What's that? Voluntary Recidivist?"

"Oh, no! Virtual reality. Absolutely state of the art, I'm led to believe," replied Nicola, "though I've been far too busy to try it myself."

"I see. Didn't the Maldives disappear a year or two ago? Totally submerged, I heard," Elaine said.

"Sadly, I think you're right. But the good news is that the camera teams got there in time, so the VR experience is thoroughly documented and very authentic." The Facility Administrator rose to her feet, dusting invisible fluff off the sleeves of her suit jacket. "It was a pleasure to meet you,

Elaine," she said. "Feel free to make an appointment if you want to discuss anything else with me at a later date."

Brendan led Elaine from the administration block to the central building, entering this time through an entrance diametrically opposite the dining hall. They turned left into a corridor that led clockwise round the glass wall of the building. Brendan threw open the door of the first room on the right.

"Media room," he said. "You can use this any time between breakfast and ten p.m."

A dozen unoccupied armchairs were placed in a semi-circle in front of a large wall-mounted flat-screen TV at the far end of the room. In the centre of the room four computer terminals were ranged back to back on a large square table. They looked at least ten years older than the equipment in the Administrator's office.

"You're a V," said Brendan, "so you're allowed internet access for up to four hours a day. Just scan your card over the access pad."

"You'll have to show me," Elaine said. "I don't see well, remember?"

"Oh, yeah, right. Give me your ID card." Brendan led Elaine to the nearest terminal and showed her a small pad attached to one side of the screen. He scanned her card over it and the screen lit up. "So, you've got all the usual search engines. Can you see those icons, there?"

Elaine bent closer to peer at the screen, leaning on the back of an office chair as she did so. It didn't budge an inch. Looking down, she was able to make out that the normal castor wheels had been replaced with bolts that attached the chair to the floor.

"What's with all the furniture in this place, Brendan? Why's it all bolted to the walls or floors?"

"I dunno. Some kind of safety measure, I guess. Not my job to ask. Now come on, this is meant to be a quick tour. I've got other work to do, you know."

The games room next door appeared to offer little but a table tennis table. Brendan rapped his knuckles on it as if to prove it was genuine.

"Where's the VR room?" Elaine asked.

"Next door along. But it's popular, you need to book it. Clients with a Closure Date less than ten days away get priority." Brendan glanced at the ID card on Elaine's chest. "Oh, you've got thirty days. Not much chance for a while then."

"Right. Great. What about the spiritual solace?"

"You what?"

"The Administrator mentioned spiritual relaxation. What do you offer? Yoga classes? Group meditation? Mindfulness training? Bible readings?"

Brendan scratched his head. "Maybe she meant the Non-Dominational Chapel. Can't think of anything else. Hey, what are you laughing at?"

"Nothing," Elaine said, opening her eyes wide and shaking her head. "When it comes to religion, I'm all for non-domination."

"Are you taking the piss?" Brendan's hand was straying towards his Taser pocket again.

"Certainly not," Elaine said. "Do please show me the Non-

Denominational Chapel."

"No, it'll be shut now. It's only opened up for an hour or so before a Closure. Some people like a Closure Ceremony before they Exit."

"What if I want to pray now?"

"You can make a booking. Ask in the admin block. I've got to go now."

After Brendan left Elaine found four paddles and three balls in a box beneath the table tennis table. She bounced one of the balls on a paddle several times, then tried a serve. The ball overshot, not even touching the table on the other side of the net, and disappeared from her field of vision. She shuffled about the room bent double, looking for a white ball on an off-white tiled floor. A loud crunch indicated that she'd stood on it. *Shit, even if she had a partner, she wouldn't see well enough to play.*

Back to the media room – maybe she could watch some TV. *That was supposed to relax you, wasn't it?* There would be no point in emailing Alexandra – she'd be on a plane out of Hong Kong by now.

A grey-haired, whey-faced man with a sandy beard was sitting at one of the computers. Elaine had sat at the same table as him in the dining hall earlier, but they hadn't spoken. She nodded an acknowledgement and received a leaden stare in return. Elaine passed him, moved towards the TV and picked up a remote that was lying on one of the chairs. The symbols and numbers on it were small and worn, and she'd never been too smart with remotes anyway, having scorned TV most of her life. Random pressing evoked no response.

Elaine approached the man with the remote extended in front of her.

"I was wondering. Ehm, could you ..?"

The grey stare had a baleful quality now.

"No, actually, forget that. Thanks anyway." Elaine put the device on one of the chairs and headed for the door. Perhaps Miss Latimer would enjoy a game of Scrabble and she could find some solace in a glass or two of Glenfiddich. One thing was clear – if she couldn't find a way to unravel this bureaucratic mess, it was going to be a very long thirty days.

Chapter 4

Wednesday 4 April

"Can I ask you something?" Elaine said as she accepted a plate of vegetable lasagne from Siobhan.

"Sure," said Siobhan, "and help yourself to as much salad as you want. Nobody seems to have been in the mood for it this lunchtime."

"Thanks," Elaine said. She eyed the bowls full of pale iceberg lettuce and anaemic-looking tomatoes without enthusiasm, but took some of each so as not to upset Siobhan. "I was wondering how come the dining hall is always so empty. The Administrator told me yesterday there was a backlog."

"That's true, but it's a backlog of Terminals, you see," Siobhan said. "They're usually too ill to come here so they get fed in their rooms. Lots of the Voluntaries prefer to eat in their rooms too. They're pretty old. I don't mean you, of course. You look really young. Far too young to be exi-"

A scarlet blush, perceptible even to Elaine's pixelated vision, spread up Siobhan's neck and into her cheeks.

"I'm really sorry, Miss, I mean Elaine. I didn't mean …"

"It's OK, Siobhan, don't worry about it. Thanks for the food."

Elaine took her tray to a vacant table, avoiding the whey-faced man and the woman with the bottle-bottom glasses. She ate rapidly without really tasting her food. As soon as she was done, she put her tray on the conveyor belt and made her way out of the central building.

A thin shaft of sunshine was piercing the cloud cover as Elaine pushed open the double doors of the vestibule and stepped outside. A walk might clear her head and exploring the grounds would pass some time. She started out going clockwise round the circular building that housed the dining hall. About a quarter of the way round, a shoulder-high privet hedge planted at right angles to the building sheltered a paved seating area with a couple of wooden benches in it – like every other item of seating she had seen in the public areas, they were bolted to the ground. It was noticeably warmer there, so Elaine sat down on one of the benches, shut her eyes and raised her face to the sun, which had now fully broken through the clouds.

A light breeze carried the smell of tobacco to Elaine, not the chemical smell of a cigarette, but the more pleasant and full aroma of a pipe or rolling tobacco. She opened her eyes and saw a figure in a wheelchair at the far end of the seating area. With her vision it was hard to tell if it was a man or a woman, as their silver hair appeared to be full and quite long. As Elaine squinted while trying not to be seen trying to see, something fell off the person's knee onto the ground. He or she leaned out of the wheelchair and fished vainly in the direction of the fallen object, but couldn't reach it.

Elaine leapt to her feet and walked towards the person in the wheelchair, anxious to help before further efforts to retrieve the fallen object capsized the chair.

"Can I give you a hand?" Elaine asked.

"Actually, I'd rather you gave me a functioning pair of legs," came the reply, "but I appreciate the offer nevertheless."

Elaine was now close enough to see that the person was a man, in fact a strikingly good-looking man, with deep blue eyes and an aquiline nose, and a shock of silver hair that was swept back off his forehead and was long enough to curve over the collar of his leather flying jacket. One eyebrow was raised and one corner of his mouth was turned up in what seemed to be a self-mocking smile.

"Sorry," the man continued. "Old joke, but I couldn't resist."

Silently, Elaine bent down to retrieve the fallen object. It was a packet of Gold Leaf rolling tobacco. She picked it up and handed it to the man, aware, now that she was close to him, not only of the smell of tobacco that emanated from the packet in her hand and the lit roll-up in his, but of an underlying odour of fresh male sweat, no doubt generated by the effort of manually wheeling the old and heavy-looking wheelchair. Elaine breathed in appreciatively.

"Are you a smoker?" the man asked. "Shall I roll you one?"

"No, I don't smoke. Gave up twelve years ago," Elaine said automatically.

"Ah, still counting the years, though – that's telling," the man replied. "Are you sure?"

"Well, oh, OK, go on, then," said Elaine. "Why not? It's not as if there's any point in worrying about my health now, is there?"

"Indeed not, you're on Death Row already. And you look like you could use a smoke," he said, clamping his own roll up in a corner of his mouth and starting to roll another cigarette. "I'm Joe, by the way".

"Elaine Treasoner," said Elaine. "Nice to meet you."

"The pleasure is mine, Elaine Treasoner," Joe said, handing

the roll-up to Elaine. "I've got a lighter somewhere. Here we are."

Elaine put the cigarette in her mouth and bent in close to Joe as he flicked the lighter. The breeze blew the flame out before Elaine could draw. Absurdly, she found herself feeling glad that she'd dyed her roots again before leaving home. Joe cupped his hand round the flame and Elaine got the rollup lit this time, gasping as the smoke hit the back of her throat. Before she straightened up, Elaine noticed the badge slung from the lanyard round Joe's neck. Above the word 'Joe', the printed letters 'ID' were followed by the digits 000.

"Have you only just got here?" Elaine asked.

"No, I've been here for over two weeks, but I haven't been sorted yet," Joe said with another lopsided smile.

"Sorted? Oh, I get it. Yes, I suppose the Intake Interview is a bit like a macabre version of the Sorting Hat ceremony. How come you're a 'Harry Potter' fan? And how did you know I would be one?"

"Your age," Joe said. "There aren't many fifty-something women who haven't raised a Harry Potter devotee. And I'm a fan because I used to read the books to my niece."

Elaine decided not to mention that his age estimate was out by a decade.

"True. My daughter was … well, still is … a mad keen fan. So, why haven't you been sorted? And what's the 'I' on your badge for? I know, 'D' is disabled, 'cos I've got that too, but …"

"May I suggest that we move over to the benches?" said Joe. "Then you can sit down and stop towering over me as if you're interrogating me. Plus, there is the small matter of an open window behind us and you never know who's listening around here."

"Sorry, yes, let's do that. Shall I wheel you?" Elaine said.

"Absolutely not."

Elaine was glad to sit down as the tobacco was making her feel lightheaded. Joe positioned his wheelchair close to her so that they could speak without raising their voices too much.

"So what is the 'I' for?" Elaine asked again.

"Indigent. One of the poor, needy, dregs of society, that's me."

"Indigent. Really? So there is a third category, I wasn't mistaken. But the Administrator denied it when I asked her."

"Of course our delightful Lagerkommandant Pemberton would deny it. We – I mean the Indigents – are meant to be invisible," Joe replied.

"Are you tagged?" Elaine asked. "When I was brought in I heard two of the staff talk about tagging."

Joe lifted the blanket that covered his knees and pulled up the left leg of his jeans. He twisted his knee slightly inwards to display his calf to her. A livid red lump could be seen about two inches above the top of a very old and scuffed Dr Marten's boot.

"Christ, that looks painful," Elaine said. "What is it?"

"An implanted electronic chip," Joe said. "It hasn't fully healed yet."

"Right, I didn't imagine that either, then," Elaine said. "At least I'm not going mad. That Pemberton woman was trying to make me believe I was delusional."

Joe rolled the bottom of his jeans back down over the angry lump. "That's Psychology 101 for camp commandants," he said. "Make the punters believe they can't trust themselves and then feed them any bullshit you want them to believe."

"I guess so," Elaine said. "But why? I'm a Voluntary. Oh, for fuck's fucking sake, even her bureaucratic claptrap is catching! It really pisses me off when people murder grammar like that. Voluntary is an adjective, not a bloody noun, unless you're talking about church music!"

Elaine took a last drag on the roll-up, burning her fingers in the process, threw the stub end on the grass and ground it out. She turned to Joe and saw him grinning.

"Now you're laughing at me!" she said.

"Not at all. I'm just admiring the facility with which you swear," Joe said, raising one eyebrow at Elaine again. "Do go on."

"Yes, well, I was saying ..." Elaine had lost her train of thought, flustered by the intensity of Joe's gaze. "What was I saying? Ah, yes, I chose to come in, I wasn't coerced. So why should she lie to me? What is she hiding?"

"Well, the small matter of about sixty Indigents ... sorry, I mean poor and needy street people, who didn't choose to come in, perhaps?" Joe answered.

"Sixty? And you didn't come in voluntarily?" Elaine repeated. She was about to say more, but the sound of a bell ringing in the distance ahead of them interrupted her.

"What was that?" Elaine asked.

"Our lunch bell," Joe replied. "They feed us after you. We get the leftovers from the Voluntaries and the Terminals. Here's hoping you weren't very hungry today."

"Are you kidding?" Elaine said.

"Unfortunately not," Joe said, as he began to manoeuvre his wheelchair away from the bench where Elaine was sitting.

"Can we talk again?" Elaine asked, getting to her feet. "Can I wheel you to the dining hall?"

"Yes, to the first. No to the second. I told you, we're meant to be invisible."

"OK," Elaine said. "Where and when, then?"

"This evening, same place, around eight? But I'm on a curfew, so I have to be back in my unit at nine," Joe said.

"Great, I'll be here," Elaine said.

"Excellent. I'll look forward to our first date," Joe said. He winked at her, then propelled himself away. Elaine sat for a while, her thoughts churning, then headed back to her unit. She needed somewhere safe and quiet to process the information she'd been given.

+++

A pinkish glow was suffusing the horizon, but it felt much colder now in the outdoor seating area.

"So, what's a nice girl like you doing in a place like this?" said Joe.

"God, that's corny."

"I'll try harder next time. But seriously, why are you here? What made you suicidal? Have you been diagnosed with an incurable illness that is still in the early stages? Or been madly disappointed in love?"

"I'm not suicidal, nor am I suffering from a broken heart. I'm skint," Elaine said.

"Join the club. I've been skint for years. Try living on the street before you talk to me about being broke."

"OK, not flat broke," Elaine said, feeling defensive in the face of Joe's response. "But if I hadn't come here, I would have had to sell my flat to live, and the money wouldn't have lasted long. I checked in here so that my daughter can inherit the flat. It was a purely rational decision."

"Rational? Are you out of your mind? How old is your daughter? Twelve? Doesn't she work?"

"She's twenty-five and, yes, she normally works. But you know what it's like these days. Or maybe you don't if you don't have kids. You graduate, then you work as a volunteer for months on bloody end. After that, if you're lucky, you get an internship. But, as often as not, that's unpaid too. So your parents continue to fork out for you, or you take out another loan. Then what do you find? A fucking zero hours contract delivering boxes for an online retailer or some shit like that."

"Do you want a smoke?" Joe said quietly. He sounded like he was trying to pour oil on angry waters.

"Yes, why not? Thanks." Elaine was still feeling wound up and tetchy. "But you roll it, please. I'm half-blind and I can't see in this light."

"I'm sorry to hear that. So do you …?"

"I don't want to go into details now." Elaine was appalled at her own rudeness. She couldn't understand how this encounter with a man she felt drawn to had turned sour so suddenly.

"OK. So your daughter has an awful job. I get it. At least it's something."

"No, you don't get it at all." Elaine could hear herself becoming strident. She didn't like it, but she could never control it when someone seemed to be criticising her daughter. "She had a great job teaching English in Hong Kong. She was doing well in it. She thought she might stay there for several years and work her way up. I rather hoped she'd end up marrying the expat banker she was going out with. But then she left him for a local dissident."

"Oops, bad move," said Joe, passing a lit roll-up to Elaine.

"Very. She took part in a big demonstration with him. Two days later Alexandra's visa was revoked, and she was told to leave the country within twenty-four hours. She's now heading home, jobless. She's stopped off for a while in Goa on the way back."

"So this feckless daughter of yours is happy to let her mum go to the gas chamber to save her while she frolics on a beach in Goa?"

"It's not like that! She isn't feckless; she just fell in love with the wrong person. And she doesn't know I'm here. My whole idea was to have this over and done with before Alexandra got home, but Pemberton told me yesterday that I need to wait thirty days!"

Elaine inhaled too deeply, began coughing and suddenly the cough turned into hysterical sobs.

"Oh, God, sorry … I'm sorry … I didn't mean to dump all this on you … I actually … I really … wanted to hear … your story."

"Another time," said Joe. "I've got a curfew. See you around."

Elaine gulped on her tears and watched, bereft, as Joe

wheeled himself off in the direction of the darkening sky.

Chapter 5

Thursday 5 April

Elaine couldn't face going to the dining hall for breakfast. Apart from Miss Latimer, Joe was the only person who had been friendly to her, and she'd made an idiot of herself in front of him. There was no way she'd risk bumping into him on the way to the central building.

In the middle of the morning she knocked on Miss Latimer's door, hoping for a chat. There was no reply, so she peeped in. Miss Latimer wasn't there. Elaine panicked slightly, worrying that the old lady might have died in the night. Then she remembered Miss Latimer saying that her niece Betty was taking her out for a drive today. It had seemed like one of her fantasies at the time, but maybe not. An illicit slice of the fruit cake that was sitting on Miss Latimer's desk saw Elaine through the rest of the morning. A trip to the kitchen a couple of hours later yielded coffee and a half empty packet of Rich Tea biscuits labelled 'Daphne'.

As Elaine left the kitchen, the bedroom door closest to it opened and Brendan backed out, pulling a wheelchair that contained a woman Elaine had not seen before. The woman's lipsticked mouth was set in a tight line and she was dabbing at her eyes with a tissue. A young woman in a nurse's uniform closed the bedroom door and led the way down the corridor.

Brendan wheeled the woman out of the unit and the door banged shut behind her. Seconds later it opened again and Brendan stuck his head round it and shouted.

"You, Elaine! You wanted to see the chapel, right?" He jerked his thumb upwards and pointed behind him with it. "Well, now's your chance. This V and her husband are exiting together and there's a short service there first."

"Oh, I see. Well, thanks, Brendan, but I don't think that would be appropriate. We never met. I don't even know her name."

Brendan shrugged. "Suit yourself then. I was just trying to do you a favour, right?"

"Sure, I appreciate it. Thanks anyway, Brendan."

Elaine took the coffee and biscuits into her room, put them on the desk and glanced out of the window. A tall man in a grey suit was pacing up and down outside the door to the block. Brendan pushed the wheelchair outside and the man bent to kiss the woman sitting in it. The three of them and the nurse then made their way towards the central building, the man holding hands with the woman in the wheelchair.

Elaine turned round to find Alexandra's father staring out at her from a photo on the tablet – as in most of his photos, he had a glass in his hand and was toasting the camera and looking jovial. She remembered the occasion well – she'd been three months pregnant and he had just announced the fact to his friends and family. Six of his buddies had dropped in to celebrate the news, bringing masses of pork chops for her to cook while they drank. The smell of the chops had made her nauseous and she had gone to lie down. The father-to-be hadn't liked that one little bit and had berated her for hours about the importance of hospitality after the guests had gone.

Elaine picked up the Nexus 7, hoping that she might find a game or an old story of Alexandra's she'd forgotten to delete, anything to pass the time a little. The screen went black as she attempted to swipe it. Of course – she hadn't charged it since the day of her arrival, whenever that was. She yanked the drawer of the desk open to get the tablet's charging cord, and a pencil rolled towards the front of the drawer. Not hers; another posthumous gift from Daphne, maybe.

Elaine plugged in her Nexus then looked at her ID card. It now read 028. She drew thirty vertical lines on the wall behind the desk with the pencil, then crossed the first two out. The blackness of the lines on the bland beige gave her a guilty thrill. Apart from an ill-fated attempt at a fresco in her college days, she had never, and would never have, drawn on a wall. An image came into her head – Manet's *The Execution of Emperor Maximilian*. Elaine shut her eyes and pictured the painting – a bleak courtyard, a blank wall with a crowd of urchins peeping over it, the emperor to the left of the painting facing the firing squad, and a group of soldiers in the centre, shooting at him from almost point blank range. Elaine began sketching a large-scale copy of the painting on the wall behind her bed.

The whimpering from next door started an hour or so later. Elaine ignored it for as long as she could, but eventually it broke her concentration. She knocked on the door next to hers and the noise reached a crescendo of sobbing and whining. Elaine pushed the door open and found the bottle-bottom glasses woman sitting on the bed, her curtains drawn and her eyes fixed on a blank space on the wall. The sound of the door opening prompted her to moan "Help me, please! Make them go away!" but her gaze didn't leave the blank wall.

Elaine sat down beside her, and spoke softly. "What are you seeing?" she asked the woman.

"The man and the dog. They're here again."

"Can you hear them as well?" Elaine asked.

"No, they don't make a noise. They just look at me. Can you hear them?"

"No."

The woman finally dragged her gaze from the wall and looked at Elaine. "But you do see them, don't you?"

Elaine hesitated between brutal honesty and a reassuring, tactful lie. If her hunch was correct, the former would be more helpful. "No, I don't. There's nothing over there."

The woman's shoulders slumped, and she shifted her gaze back to the wall. "Then I am crazy, like the doctor says," she said.

"Hold on," said Elaine. She went to the window and pulled back the curtains, letting some light in. "Do you still see them now?" she asked.

The woman rubbed her eyes then looked back at the same section of wall.

"No, they've gone now, thank God."

"Good. I'm Elaine, I'm your neighbour, and I stay in the next room," she said, indicating the wall that the woman had been staring at. "What's your name?"

"Dorothy. Have we met before?"

"No, we haven't, but I've seen you in the dining hall a couple of times."

"I haven't seen you. I don't see well at all. I've got AMD. Do you know what that is?"

"I do, actually," said Elaine. "I've got macular problems too, but not age-related ones."

"Oh, and are you schizophrenic too?" Dorothy asked.

"Ehm, no. Are you?"

"That's what the doctor told me. I see things, and apparently they're not there. You didn't see the man and the dog, but I did."

Elaine moved back to the bed and sat down beside the woman again. She was almost certain now that her instinct had been right.

"Is it always the same man and dog you see?" she asked. "Or other things too?"

"Sometimes it's leprechauns. I don't mind them so much as they're smaller than me."

"Indeed. And do they speak to you?"

"No, never. They like dancing, though."

Elaine was certain now. "Did your doctor ever mention something called Charles Bonnet Syndrome to you, Dorothy?"

"No, I don't think so. Is that another mental illness?"

"No, absolutely not. It's actually a phenomenon caused by the brain not receiving sufficient stimu–".

Elaine was interrupted mid-stride by Dorothy tugging at the blanket beneath them. Her well-rehearsed explanation was eliciting no interest at all.

"What's up, Dorothy? You don't see the dog and the man now, do you?"

"No, I feel cold. I think I'll get into bed."

"Oh, I'm sorry," Elaine said. "Of course, after a shock, it's natural to feel cold. Can I get you something? A cup of tea, maybe?"

"Thank you. I have some teabags down in the kitchen. Milk, no sugar, please."

"OK, you get into bed and I'll be back shortly. Keep the curtains open. That's very important."

Elaine returned with a mug of tea and placed it on the bookshelf as Dorothy's desk was covered in clutter.

"I won't be able to reach it there," Dorothy said. "Make a space on the desk, please."

Elaine shoved skeins of wool and knitting needles, squares of felt, socks rolled into balls and piles of yellowing papers to the back of the desk and moved the tea to the corner nearest to Dorothy. Something fell off the pile of displaced objects onto the floor. It was Dorothy's ID card. Where Elaine's card had 'VD', Dorothy's said 'VM'.

"What does the 'M' on your card stand for?" Elaine asked.

"Sorry, I don't follow you."

"We've all got codes on out ID cards. I'm 'VD'. The 'D' stands for disabled. Yours says 'VM'."

"Is that so? In that case, I suppose my 'M' is for mad, or mentally ill, something like that." Dorothy squinted at her desk, located her mug of tea, reached over and picked it up carefully.

"And the 'V'? What do you think that's for?" Elaine asked.

"I don't know. I hadn't noticed any letters on the card. But the doctor said I was vulnerable when he signed the papers for me. He said I was a danger to myself and would be safer here. So, it could be vulnerable, perhaps? Vulnerable Mental,

I suppose?"

Elaine could hardly believe what she was hearing. "So, you didn't sign the papers to come in here. Is that what you're saying?"

"Yes, my doctor and a lawyer handled everything for me. I think it's called 'sectioning'."

There was silence in the room while Dorothy drank her tea, then she held her empty mug out to Elaine. "I think I'll have a rest now. Thanks for making the tea."

"You're welcome. Remember to keep the curtains open until you go to bed for the night. I don't think the man and the dog will come back as long as you do that. Bye for now."

Elaine rinsed out Dorothy's mug in the kitchen and rifled through the drawers in search of a sharp knife to whittle the pencil she had found. Nothing. As in the canteen, every piece of cutlery was made of plastic. She went into her own room to check the time on her tablet. Four thirty. She might just catch the Facility Administrator before she finished work for the day. She couldn't leave things as they were. Dorothy seemed pretty lucid and was displaying classic Charles Bonnet symptoms. It was sheer cruelty to let the poor woman assume she was suffering from a mental illness. And if she bumped into Joe on the way over to the administrative block, well that was just too bad. She'd smile and wave breezily and walk on by. See you around, indeed! A classic brush off, but two could play at that game.

As Elaine left the unit, Violet Latimer was shuffling towards the door, leaning heavily on a Zimmer frame. A middle-aged woman in a lilac crushed velvet tracksuit was walking behind her, carrying Miss Latimer's handbag.

"Oh, hello, dear!" exclaimed Miss Latimer. "I've been out for a drive with my niece. We had such a lovely time and the trees looked so beautiful with all the spring growth coming in! Would you care to join us for a cup of tea in my room? And I've got some fruit cake there, I do believe."

"Auntie Vee, we've just had afternoon tea at my flat. Don't you remember? It won't do your digestion any good at all to have more cake."

The woman was close enough now that Elaine could see her rolling her eyes behind Miss Latimer's back.

"Of course, you're right, Betty. Silly me. My memory's not what it used to be, you know," said Miss Latimer. Her niece's eyes rolled again.

"Come along, Auntie. Let's get you settled. I haven't got all day."

"That's fine," said Elaine. "I've got to get over to the administrative block now, Miss Latimer, but maybe I'll see you for some Scrabble tomorrow."

Miss Latimer's niece gave her a tight-lipped smile as she passed.

The Facility Administrator was in a meeting, but Elaine was lucky to get an appointment for the following morning thanks to a cancellation. The receptionist explained that a terminal patient had undergone an Unforeseen Natural Closure, and so Nicola Pemberton's diary had been freed up.

Suddenly aware of her empty stomach, Elaine headed to the central building to find out when the first sitting for dinner was.

Chapter 6

Friday 6 April

A ll the classic signs are there," Elaine said, leaning forward in her chair as she addressed Nicola Pemberton. "The hallucinations are purely visual, without any auditory element. They come on when the light is dim and stimulation of the visual cortex via the optic nerve is at its lowest. They disappear when the light changes. I'm pretty certain that Dorothy is suffering from Charles Bonnet Syndrome. As for the diagnosis of schizophrenia, well, it is quite common that …"

The Facility Administrator cleared her throat. Elaine paused, suddenly aware that her excitement about her diagnosis of Dorothy's problem was possibly not shared by Nicola.

"I do appreciate your concern for a housemate, Elaine. However, as you have been speaking, I have reviewed your records. I note that you are an erstwhile artist and intermittent office assistant. I can see nothing about your having trained either as a clinical psychologist, or as an ophthalmologist."

Elaine breathed in slowly and deliberately, counting inwardly as she did so. "Well, yes, you're right, but I used to volunteer with a helpline for macular patients. We were very well trained. I know what I'm talking about."

"Elaine, leave the diagnosis to the experts. Dorothy has been examined by our in-house team as well as by her own GP. There is nothing more to be said on the matter."

The counting wasn't working any more. "On the contrary,

Nicola," Elaine said, mirroring the Administrator's measured tone. "I have quite a lot more to say. There is also the fact that Dorothy seems to be unaware of her fate here. She thinks she has been taken into care because she is vulnerable. That does not constitute a voluntary Exit Agreement as I see it."

"How you see things is utterly irrelevant, Elaine. It is my job to take care of the administrative and legal aspects of each client's sojourn here, not yours." Nicola picked up a large glass paperweight, then replaced it on the desk with a thud. "What's more, did you notice Dorothy's Exit schedule while you were examining her ID badge?"

"No, I didn't actually."

"If you do so – and I'm sure you will want to verify this when you return to your unit – you will see that Dorothy has precisely nine days left with us. I think it would be cruel to upset her for the rest of her stay with wild notions that she might have been misdiagnosed."

"She's upset already. More than upset, in fact; she's terrified. She spends half the day whimpering or begging for help." Elaine was aware that her voice was getting louder, but she was now too angry to control it.

"I am sorry you are being disturbed by her, Elaine. I shall ask the doctor to prescribe an extra sedative to keep Dorothy calm. If you'd care to have a little sedation yourself, I am happy to arrange that too. But now I have another appointment, so you may go."

"But …"

"This interview is over." Nicola rose to her feet and opened the door, holding it and tapping one foot on the floor until Elaine left the office.

Fuming, Elaine stomped down two corridors before she realised she was heading away from the main entrance of the administrative block instead of towards it. As she stopped to get her bearings, Joe and his wheelchair emerged from a door several metres further down the corridor. He paused in the doorway and shoved his right hand inside the front of his flying jacket. He might have been holding something, but Elaine couldn't tell at that distance. He then withdrew his hand, turned the chair in the opposite direction from her and wheeled himself away.

As soon as he was out of sight, Elaine continued along the corridor and stopped outside the door Joe had emerged from. The word *Commissary* was written in black letters on the door. She pushed the door open and went in. The room was small, with a counter at the front of it, cupboards mounted on the wall behind the counter, and another door that appeared to open into a back room. Elaine could hear the sounds of a tap running and a voice humming a jaunty tune. A young man with immaculately highlighted hair and wearing a flamboyantly floral shirt came out of the back room, doing up the top button of his flies.

"Ooh, a newbie!" he said. "Sorry, darling, I didn't hear you come in. You snuck right up on me!"

"Sorry, yes, I suppose I did."

"What can I do you for then, darling?" he asked.

"I don't know. What have you got?"

"Fags – well of course, I would have those, wouldn't I?"

Unable to think of a witty response, Elaine nodded instead.

"And rolling tobacco and papers, soft drinks, biscuits, chocolate, gum, drugs. No, only joking, just paracetamol or ibuprofen, not serious drugs." The young man gave an exaggerated shrug and waited for Elaine's reaction.

There was something she really wanted. "Have you got a 2B pencil?"

"Ooh!" he squealed. "We've only just met, and you're asking personal questions already, you naughty lady."

This time Elaine tittered.

"Glad to see you've got a sense of humour. But sorry, no pencils. How about a black biro, instead?"

"No, that wouldn't do. I'm doing a drawing."

"You're an artist! How exciting! I'll tell you what, I can have one for you if you come by tomorrow. I'm not sure of the exact price, but around two to three quid, I guess."

"Oh, I'd have to pay? But I didn't bring any money in here with me. And that seems a bit pricey for a pencil."

"No money? You're joking! What do you think I'm running here – a charity?" The young man put his hands on his hips and scowled at Elaine.

Elaine felt disappointed and wrong-footed. "I'm sorry, I didn't mean to offend you or anything. I just assumed that since everything else is provided free … And I didn't think I'd be here long, you see."

"Well, I'm sorry, but I can't help you in that case. No money, no honey. It's the way of the world."

"Indeed," said Elaine. "Well, thanks anyway."

"My pleasure. Nice to meet you, darling. Come back if you find some money under your mattress."

Elaine went to the media room after lunch – Alexandra would have reached Goa by now and she'd probably have sent an email. The grey man was there at the same monitor as last time. Elaine sat down at the computer Brendan had switched on for her. It was still on, it seemed. She found the access pad and scanned her ID card over it. The computer switched itself off.

"Bugger!" she said out loud.

She scanned her card over the access pad again and the computer switched itself back on.

Elaine clicked in turn on three icons that she presumed were browsers, but none of them loaded.

"Oh for God's sake. Why the hell won't they load?"

"Can I help you?" asked the grey man.

"Oh, wow! Yes, that would be great. Do you know about computers?"

"You could say that," the man said and came round to her side of the table. "If I could sit down, perhaps? What are you trying to do?"

Elaine stood up to let him sit at her monitor. "I want to check my email. I'm sure I was told I had four hours of internet access per day, but I don't seem to be online."

The man typed rapidly on her keyboard then turned to look at Elaine. "The problem is you didn't log out the last time you were here," he explained. "You've used up your internet allowance for today, without even doing anything."

"Shit. How stupid of me. So what can I do now?" Elaine

asked.

"Nothing, you'll have to come back tomorrow."

"Oh no, that's no good. You see, my daughter's in Goa and I'm sure she'll have emailed me. And she'll worry if I don't get back to her. I don't suppose I could access my email via your log-in, could I? Just very briefly."

"I'm afraid not," the man said.

This day was going really badly, Elaine thought, but she made an effort to be civil. "OK, never mind. Thanks for your help anyway."

The man stood up and faced Elaine. "Don't get me wrong – I'd like to help. I wouldn't want your daughter to worry about you. Mums are special after all."

The man's voice cracked slightly. As Elaine looked at him, he raised one hand to his eye and rubbed it lightly, then looked away quickly.

"It's not that I don't want to help," he continued. "The thing is that I don't have internet privileges."

"Really? Aren't you a V? And what can you do on a computer all day if you haven't got internet?"

"I am a V, but I'm a special case. Long story. Here, look." The man ushered Elaine round to his side of the table and showed her his monitor. She bent down to scrutinise it from her standard distance of eight inches. The screen was full of random letters and symbols.

"I'm coding," the man said.

"Coding? Like computer programming? What for?"

"It's fun. It passes the time."

"I see. Hey, if you're a computer genius, would you be able to pick up email on my tablet? Piggy-back or hotspot or something?" Elaine had only a vague idea what the terms meant, but anything was worth a try.

"You've got a tablet here with you? That's interesting. Is it Android?"

"It's a Nexus 7. It's very old."

"Never mind. At least it isn't iOS."

"I'm sorry, I don't really understand what you're talking about. My computer knowledge peaked circa 2013 and never moved on much after that."

"That's OK," the man said. "Look, there's nothing you can do to get online today. But come back tomorrow and I'll help you if you need it. You could maybe bring your tablet as well. It would be useful as back-up."

"Really? OK, I'll do that. Thanks for your help."

"Log off."

"I'm sorry? What? Oh, yes, good thinking." Elaine swiped her ID card over the access pad and waited for the screen to go dark." I'll see you tomorrow, then. I'm Elaine, by-the-way."

"I'm Hamish. Nice to meet you. I hope your mum, I mean your daughter, doesn't worry too much."

When she entered her block, Elaine could hear the sound of a vacuum cleaner coming from her unit. She quickened her pace, hoping to reach her room before a cleaner entered it and discovered her drawing on the wall.

The sound was coming from Miss Latimer's room. Elaine knocked, then pushed the door open. A woman in a blue uniform was hoovering under the desk. Miss Latimer and her wing chair were missing.

"Excuse me, have you done the room opposite yet?" Elaine asked.

The cleaner waggled one hand near her ear, then switched the vacuum cleaner off. Elaine repeated her question.

"Nope," the cleaner said. "I start going up the left and come back down the rooms on the other side of the corridor after doing the kitchen."

"I see. Well, I don't really need my room cleaned," Elaine said. "In fact, I'd prefer to do it myself."

"My job sheet says all six bedrooms and the kitchen."

"How many units do you have to do this afternoon?"

"Let me see – I've got four units left, with six bedrooms in each, plus the kitchens."

"Wow, that's a lot," Elaine said, sounding as sympathetic as she could, "and you look pretty tired. Honestly, I'm happy to do mine, and the other two on the right hand side if you want. I actually like cleaning."

"Really? Well, if you're sure," the cleaner said. "But you mustn't tell anyone, or I'll get into trouble. And make sure you put the vacuum cleaner away when you're done. It lives in the cupboard beside the bathroom."

"Fine. Now, where's Miss Latimer?"

"The old lady? I put her in the empty room next door, along with the chair. I couldn't get at the carpet properly. That bloody chair weighs a ton."

"I can imagine. When you're done with this room, I'll help

you move them back."

Miss Latimer was sitting bolt upright on the bed in the adjoining room, her hands clasped in her lap.

"I don't care for this at all," she said as soon as Elaine entered the room. "It's really not good enough!"

As Elaine got closer, she could see Miss Latimer's cheeks were unusually pink and her lips were pursed.

"Don't worry, Miss Latimer. We'll take you back to your own room. It's nice and clean now."

"And so it should be at the prices I'm paying! I don't know what you're thinking about making me move rooms like that. And where are all my things? I wish to speak to the manager."

Elaine sat down on the bed beside her. "There's nothing to worry about, Miss Latimer, nobody's taken your things. If you could just sit here on the bed for two minutes longer, the cleaner and I will take your chair through and then get you back to your own room."

"That one's completely gaga," the cleaner said as they manoeuvred the chair back into the space between Miss Latimer's desk and her bed. "She seems to think she's in a posh care home or something and gives me a hard time about the service week in, week out. Can't say I'll be too sorry when her appointment comes up."

"I think she's a dear," Elaine said, "but she is a bit confused. Look, you need to get on and I have time to fill. Give me a shout when you're done with the kitchen and I'll take over, like I said."

Elaine settled Miss Latimer back in her room and r went to sit in her own bedroom until the cleaner left. As she was waiting, it occurred to her that Miss Latimer was the only person in the facility, staff or so-called client, who didn't wear an ID card on a lanyard round their neck.

Chapter 7

Saturday 7 April

Elaine put her Nexus in her jacket pocket and hurried over to the central building. An alarm went off as she walked through the archway into the dining hall.

Siobhan came running over. "Have you got something metal on you, Elaine?"

"Not unless the buttons on my jacket set it off."

"No, the scanner in here's not that sensitive. It must be something else. I'm sorry about this, but I need to search your pockets."

Siobhan fished the tablet out of Elaine's pocket. "Is this a mobile computing device? How did you bring that in?"

"Yes, it's a tablet. I've had it for years. It was in my bag when Ashley checked me in. She didn't say anything about it."

"Oh well, if Ashley doesn't mind, I guess it's OK. Just pop it back in your pocket and hang your jacket up in the vestibule. I'm sure no one will touch it."

"Thanks, Siobhan." Elaine was glad it had been her on duty, and not one of the other catering assistants, who were far less friendly.

She had a hasty breakfast, collected her jacket and went clockwise round the building to get to the north entrance and access the media room.

Joe was sitting in the same spot where they had first met

three days ago. Elaine rejected the fleeting notion of turning on her heel and going round the building the other way. Instead she sauntered over and stood beside his wheelchair.

"Hi, Joe. How're you doing?"

"Hello again, Elaine. I knew we'd run into each other sooner or later."

"Yes, inevitable really. Look, I'm sorry about the other night. I didn't mean to get so emotional."

"Don't worry about it. It's understandable in the circumstances. You hadn't been drinking by any chance, had you?" Joe asked.

"Drinking? Certainly not. And anyway, I tend to get happy or silly when I drink, not morose."

"Oh, good. I can't stand morose drunks. In that case, join me here tomorrow to watch the sunset again, and I'll see if I can get hold of a little something to oil the works."

Joe winked at her.

Elaine felt her neck and cheeks flushing and was furious with herself for her adolescent reaction. She stammered an acceptance, waved breezily and then walked off, cringing inwardly at her lack of cool. Why did this man with his ridiculous patter make her feel like a teenager? And why should she encounter the hottest man she'd met in a decade just as she was about to go to her death?

When she arrived in the media room and managed to log on, she found an email from Alexandra that had come in the previous day.

Hi Mum,

Goa is great – just what I needed after the stress of the last few days in HK! I had to abandon a lot of my stuff as I left in such a hurry, but I have shipped a big suitcase and am travelling just with hand luggage.

I have met a couple of really fun Australian girls who are doing the round the world thing. Their next stop is Rome, so I thought I might go with them and stay for a few days there. I can have one more stopover on my flight at no extra cost, which is good. If I do that, I'll be home a bit later than planned; I hope you don't mind. Don't worry – I still have money saved from the first year in HK and Goa is cheap, so I am not getting through it fast.

I hope you're getting some things sorted out financially. How did you get on with your pension appeal? Did they take your old Cypriot insurance contributions into account? Whatever has happened, hang on in there, Mum. I'll be back soon and we'll sort something out together.

See you in about three weeks. More news soon.

Love you lots,

Alexandra xxx

Elaine wiped her eyes on a tissue as she reached the end of

the email – hanging on in there was exactly what she had chosen not to do. She tucked the damp tissue in her pocket and calculated three weeks from the date of the email – it was better than she'd feared, but still too soon. Alexandra would be back before Elaine's Exit appointment. Once she found the letter Elaine had left for her, Alexandra would try to prevent her from exiting. It was time for some judicious lying.

Hi darling,

Sorry for the late reply – the internet was down yesterday. I'm so glad to hear you are enjoying Goa and have found new friends.

I think the idea of a stopover in Rome is great. In fact, since you'll be in Italy, why don't you extend your stay a bit longer? You and your Australian pals could maybe look up my old friend Katerina. Do you remember her? She lives in Bracciano, not far from Rome. We spent a week there with her when you were about seven, and you loved swimming in the lake. If she can't put you up herself, I expect she could find you some cheap accommodation for a week or so. I can't find her address, but ask in the bar *Il Trovatore* – they'll know where she is.

Not much news from here. The pension appeal hasn't gone through yet – there's a backlog apparently – but I don't hold out much hope, to be frank. I might have stood a chance before Brexit, but not now. Anyway, like you said, we shall work something out.

I miss you a lot, but am happy you are having fun.

All my love,

Mum xxx

Elaine re-read her message, then pressed SEND. She hoped it would work. If Alexandra took the bait and went to Bracciano, that would buy Elaine more time.

Hamish hadn't appeared yet, but a woman wearing a kaftan and a sort of turban was sitting watching the television with the sound down. Elaine sat down near her.

"Oh, hello," the woman said. "Have you finished on the computer? If so, do you mind if I turn the sound up now? I didn't want to disturb you."

"That was kind of you. By all means turn it up. I've finished now."

"I don't know why I'm bothering, really," the woman continued. "Habit of a lifetime, I suppose. But my companion and I are for the chop later today, so the news is irrelevant."

Elaine drew her breath in suddenly, wondering how to respond, but the woman spoke again before she could. "Sorry, I don't believe in mincing my words. I believe we are meant to call it Compassionate Closure or some such claptrap."

"No problem," Elaine said. "I prefer plain speaking too."

The woman turned the volume up and they were assaulted with a rapid-fire litany of teenage stabbings, budget deficits, social security cutbacks, floods and unemployment figures.

"Not much change from when I came in here," the woman said, staring at the screen. "I try to watch the news most days. I feel I ought to keep up with what's going on even though I haven't written anything new for years. But I don't think I'll miss it where I'm going. Do you?" She looked at Elaine's ID badge. "Oh, poor thing, you've got a while to wait yet. And you're here voluntarily, like Rose."

"Who's Rose?"

"My companion. I've got pancreatic cancer – no hope at all, and all the chemo did was destroy my best feature, my beautiful thick hair." She gestured towards her turban, and grimaced. "But Rose is perfectly healthy. She just says life wouldn't be worth living without me. So sweet, don't you think? Rose was always devoted to me."

"Still am, Olivia, for a few hours more at least," said a melodic voice behind them.

Elaine turned and saw a middle-aged woman smiling serenely at the turbaned woman.

"Hello, I see you've met Olivia," the newcomer said. "I'm Rose, her secretary, and companion. Olivia, I don't like to interrupt, but it's time for the service."

"Of course, dear, I'm just coming. Would you care to join us, ehm …?"

"Elaine."

"Would you like to join us, Elaine?" Olivia continued. "We're having a humanist service in the chapel."

"That's very kind, but I'm meeting someone in here shortly."

"In that case, have a sherry with us in the dining hall afterwards," Olivia said. "We're not allowed to eat much as it would interfere with the efficacy of the pills, but I expect there'll be something light to nibble on."

"Thank you," Elaine said, and watched the two women leave the room, Olivia leaning on Rose's guiding arm.

Hamish arrived a few minutes later.

"Good morning. How did you get on with the computer today? Have you heard from your daughter?" he asked.

"Yes, all well with both, I'm glad to say." Elaine smiled at him.

"That's good. So you don't need any help?"

"Not today, thanks. Oh, I brought the tablet."

Elaine pulled the tablet out of her pocket. It was displaying a photograph of her, scantily clad, lying on her fuchsia sofa bed and sipping a glass of wine. Her last boyfriend, Gary, and she had been celebrating a competition win and she had got rather frisky on Pinot Grigio.

"Oops, an old photo! You don't want to see that."

Elaine swiped wildly and ineffectively across the screen, feeling herself blush for the second time that day.

"Those old tablets are often sticky," Hamish said. "Try switching it off, wait ten seconds, then put it back on again."

Elaine followed his instructions. The Nexus went back on, she dismissed the photo and handed the device to Hamish. "Look after this carefully, please" she said. "It's my last link with home."

"Of course. I'll be very careful with it. I really appreciate your help. What I need to do is get a message out without it being traced," Hamish explained. "If your internet access hasn't run out for today, I shall use your computer as a hotspot, tether the tablet to it, access my email account from

83

the tablet, and then erase all traces of my activity before I give it back to you. If that's OK with you, of course."

"It sounds complicated. Why don't you just send a message from my email address?"

"I expect they're monitoring all incoming and outgoing traffic. Not in real time, perhaps, but they'll keep and check records. Be careful about what you say if you're emailing your daughter, or anyone else for that matter"

Hamish spent about fifteen minutes doing things on the Nexus 7 and the computer Elaine had logged into while she watched a very dull gardening programme on TV.

"That's it. Many thanks" said Hamish, handing back the tablet.

"You're welcome. If you need it again, just say."

"Well, it would be handy if I could do the same later. After lunch, maybe?"

"Sure. That's fine with me," Elaine said.

"Then log out, so you don't waste your access time."

"Right, yes. Are you ready for lunch? I'm going round there now because I've been invited for a drink beforehand with two people who are exiting later today."

"How macabre."

"I suppose it is in a way. Actually, it's my second pre-Closure party. You know, I've got a better social life here than I did in the outside world!"

Hamish did not echo Elaine's laughter. "I wouldn't know what to say to people in that situation," he said. "I'll see you in the dining hall later and we can come back here together after lunch."

The guests at Olivia and Rose's party were even sparser than those at Ernie's, but the atmosphere of drunken despair was replaced by one of determinedly upbeat decorum.

"Such a pity you missed the service, dear. Rupert was wonderful," said Olivia, indicating the man seated to her left. "I was so lucky to have a celebrant who's known me for decades. And this is Gerard, my agent, and his wife Alice. Darlings, this is Elaine. We only just met in the TV lounge, but she seems like a good sort, so I asked her to join us. Now, would you prefer a sweet or a dry sherry?"

"Dry, please," Elaine said.

"Jolly good. And the canapes are beside Rose."

The conversation ranged from Olivia's first book – a history of the Suez crisis, apparently – to current affairs and the recent currency controls, interspersed with gentle jibes about Rupert's taste in cravats. Olivia did most of the talking, pausing only to wince every so often, at which Rose would squeeze her hand and pat her on the forearm.

Finally, Rose whispered something in Olivia's ear.

"Rose tells me it's time for us to go. So a final toast to you all."

Olivia and Rose refilled their glasses, raised them and chorused 'Morituri te salutant'. Olivia looked almost cheerful as she did so and Rose exuded confidence and serenity.

Elaine bit her lower lip to stop herself from crying, whispered a word of thanks, and went over to look for Hamish at the other side of the dining hall.

+++

"Yes!" said Hamish, and punched the air. Apart from the tiny gesture yesterday that might or might not have been brushing a tear, it was the first sign of emotion that Elaine had seen from him.

"What's up?"

"I got the reply I needed. Excellent. So I'll clean everything up, and you're good to go. Oh, hold on." It was now Hamish's turn to tap and swipe in vain.

"Like I said, any time you need it... Oh, has it crashed again?"

"Possibly. It is very slow, isn't it?" he said.

"Like wading through mud most of the time. It's been like that for years."

Elaine moved closer to Hamish and glanced at the screen, praying it wasn't showing another inappropriate photo, but it was completely black.

"If you like, I can take a look at it. Try and clean some of the apps up and it may go a bit faster."

"That would be good. But leave the photo gallery, OK? That's personal."

"Of course," Hamish said. "How was your drinks event by the way?"

"You were right, it was a little macabre. But those women were incredibly calm and brave. I couldn't believe it. I hope I'll be able to muster a quarter of their courage when my appointment comes."

Hamish said nothing and looked away.

"How long have you got, Hamish? And how long have you

been here?"

"Twenty-eight days left, and I came in ten days ago."

"Wow, that's an even longer wait than mine. How come?"

Hamish shrugged. "I don't know. It's all in the algorithms."

"So have you had very little state support in the past, like me?"

"Not exactly."

A silence ensued. Hamish was clearly not going to elaborate. Elaine decided to push her luck.

"So what brought you in here?"

"My Mum had Parkinson's. Her care was expensive, and there were related problems. Look, if you want me to clean the tablet up, I'm going to have to remove and reinstall some programs. I need the internet for that and your access will run out fairly soon."

"Yes, of course, go ahead. But what about logging off when you're done? You'll need my ID card for that. I can't leave it with you."

"No, of course not," Hamish said. "Well, you could go for a walk, or stay and watch some TV. I'll use headphones so you don't disturb me."

Unwilling to bump into Joe again, Elaine opted to watch a contemporary art programme that made her itch to get her hands on a paintbrush again. The quest for a new pencil would have to continue tomorrow.

Chapter 8

Sunday 8 April

It occurred to Elaine while she was having breakfast that she hadn't seen or heard anything of Dorothy for the last two days. At least the moaning had stopped – that was a blessing – but Elaine felt guilty for not having checked up on her. In a spirit of neighbourliness, Elaine returned to her unit instead of going straight to the media room.

Dorothy was in her room and the curtains were open, allowing some morning light in. She was sitting at her desk attempting to darn a sock, her head cocked to one side to use her peripheral vision.

"Oh, wow! You've got a real darning mushroom – I haven't seen one of those for years!" Elaine said.

"Of course – is there any other way to darn socks?" Dorothy asked, sounding rather defensive.

"Well, actually, I don't think many people bother to darn socks these days. They just chuck them away when they get holes in them, and buy some more."

Dorothy tut-tutted loudly.

"Anyway, I admire you for giving it a go. I wouldn't manage with my vision, and I guess yours is worse than mine. So, how have you been feeling?"

"Who are you?" Dorothy asked. Her tone was sullen rather than curious.

"Sorry, I should have reminded you. I'm Elaine. I have the

room next door to yours, and I came in the other day when you were seeing … ehm, feeling unwell, you know?"

"Ah, it was you. Well, I have been sleeping better, and I haven't had any more visions I'm glad to say. I suppose I should thank you."

"You're welcome," said Elaine. "So tell me about yourself. Were you a keen needlewoman?"

"Oh, yes, I love sewing!" Dorothy's face lit up briefly then settled again into its usual dour expression. "Or at least I used to when I saw better."

Elaine ploughed on. "What did you sew?"

"Well, I used to make my own clothes, but I liked making stuffed toys best. I made lots for Binkie and Boxer."

"Are they your grandchildren?"

"Oh no, my cats. Binkie's a tabby and Boxer's a ginger tom, but I had them both done, of course. One day the minister came round on a visit and he saw the toys and said I should sell some at the village fete. They were a great success. After that I made cuddly toys for lots of the children in our village. In fact, I might have one here I could show you."

Dorothy got to her feet and rummaged in the wardrobe, eventually producing a small turquoise blue felt pony with enormous eyes and a hot pink mane. Elaine took it and examined it. The taste was execrable, but the workmanship was excellent – you could barely see the stitching. She was groping for a suitable compliment when Dorothy, whose head was in the wardrobe, let out a squeak of joy.

"Oh, here's my old sewing basket, the good one! I'd forgotten I brought that as well as the everyday one. Now just have a look at this."

Dorothy laid a rectangular raffia box on the bed and opened it. A tray contained a fantastic array of spools of thread arranged in colour groups, much as Elaine's acrylic paints had been arranged in her box at home.

"Oh, they're beautiful."

"Yes, aren't they?" Dorothy beamed. "And here are my tools."

She lifted the tray out and revealed a lower level of scissors, needles, threaders, pincushions, tape measures and something that made Elaine's heart leap.

"Is that a packet of watercolour pencils, by any chance?" she asked.

"What? Oh, those. No, they're fabric pencils, like tailor's chalk, you know."

"May I look at them?" Elaine asked.

"If you want to."

Elaine opened the packet. It contained a blue, a yellow, a red and a white pencil and, miracle of miracles, a sharpener!

"Dorothy, could I possibly borrow these for a while?"

"Have them, if you like. They were a gift from a customer, but I always preferred the traditional triangular blocks of tailor's chalk, to be honest."

"You're sure? That's fantastic, Dorothy. Thank you so much!"

"Do you sew too?"

"No, I'm an artist, but I didn't bring my equipment with me."

"Well, that was a bit silly."

"Yes, as it turns out, it was. Excuse me a minute, please."

Elaine took the packet next door and hid it under her mattress, then returned to Dorothy's room.

"Thank you again, Dorothy. Look, I've had a thought. Would you like to go out for a walk? It's rather a nice sunny day."

"Is that allowed?"

"Put it this way; I haven't been told it's not allowed."

They set out from the unit on a path that led in a northerly direction. It passed by a patch of sparse but mature trees, then continued straight on. To their left lay a line of accommodation blocks that looked older than the ones in Elaine's area of the grounds, and in worse repair. She wondered if this was where Joe and the other Indigents were housed.

"From what I can see," Dorothy said, "which isn't much, I suppose, it seems quite pleasant for a mental asylum. I never imagined there would be such big gardens."

"Yes, well it isn't exactly an asylum," said Elaine.

"What would you call it then?"

Mindful of Nicola's warnings, Elaine chose her words carefully. "A medical facility, of sorts."

"Same difference."

They walked in silence for a while. The path took a gentle turn to the right, leading them through an area of kitchen gardens, then turned sharply right. From the position of the sun, Elaine judged they were now walking due east, with a thicker copse of mature trees to their left.

"I want to discuss something," Dorothy said abruptly. "I'm worried about Binkie and Boxer. My cats. The lawyer said they'd be taken to a cat refuge and that somebody would adopt them. But I don't want them to be split up. They're brother and sister and they've never been out of the house, you see. They'll hate it in a new place with other cats, or if they're separated."

"Did you make that clear to the lawyer?"

"I tried to, but he sent me here because I'm crazy, so maybe he didn't pay attention."

"No, not crazy," Elaine said. "I think you told me the other day that he said you were vulnerable. So I am sure he'll follow your instructions. That's what lawyers are for."

Dorothy was not convinced. She stood still in the middle of the path and large tears started to flow down her cheeks.

"And there's something else. Maybe they'll put Binkie and Boxer down if they can't find a home that will take them both. That would be terrible!"

"No, surely not. Who would put someone, I mean, cats, down for no reason?" Elaine was struggling hard to think of a convincing lie while she fished in her pocket for a tissue.

"Here, take this, Dorothy. Wipe your face. It'll all be OK."

Suddenly Elaine became aware of a familiar voice coming from beyond the next bend in the path. It was definitely Joe, but Joe with a rather stagey Irish accent. Elaine grabbed Dorothy by the arm and hauled her into the copse.

"What are you doing?" Dorothy said.

"Sssh, there's a courting couple up ahead on the path. They'll be embarrassed if they see us."

"Why would there be a courting couple in an asylum?"

"Sssssh! Stay there and don't move or say anything!" Elaine manoeuvred Dorothy behind a tree and crept forward until she could see the stretch of path beyond the bend. Joe was clearly recognisable by his shock of white hair. A female wheeling a bicycle had stopped and was chatting to him.

"Thank you, darling, you know I appreciate what you do for me," said Joe.

"Sure and you deserve it after all you've been through. I'd do more if I could, but I'm off on my holidays from tomorrow, so there won't be anything for a while."

That voice was familiar too, but Elaine couldn't place it immediately.

"Going back home are you?" Joe asked.

"Yes. Not for long, sadly. I've got just over a week."

"Well, enjoy the craic, and give my love to Dublin if you pass through the old place."

"I'm flying straight to Cork, actually." Of course – it was Siobhan.

"No problem. Have fun, and I'll see you in a couple of weeks if I'm still around."

"I hope you will be," Siobhan said, then bent and kissed Joe on the cheek before wheeling her bicycle away up the path. Elaine pressed herself against a tree while Joe turned round and returned the way that she and Dorothy had come. Elaine counted to sixty three times, then led Dorothy back down the same path.

+++

Joe was waiting at the seating area when Elaine arrived a bit before eight o'clock. He had parked his wheelchair and manoeuvred himself onto one of the benches.

"Hi, all well? Come and sit here with me." The Irish accent had been replaced by his usual Home Counties one. "With a bit of luck, we won't be disturbed. And it's a nice clear evening, so the lightshow should be good. Would you like a roll up?"

Elaine nodded and Joe produced a pre-rolled one from his top pocket, lit it for her, and handed it over.

"And here's the surprise." Joe put his hand inside the flying jacket and produced a black bottle. "Sherry. Sweet, unfortunately, but a good brand. Apparently some greedy buggers polished off the dry."

Joe cocked his head and made a wry face at Elaine.

"Oh, damn," she said. "Guilty as charged. Did you bring glasses? Or shall I pop back to my unit and get some?"

"No, it's getting dark. You don't want to draw attention to yourself by blundering about half-blindly while carrying a couple of tumblers."

Joe removed the screw top, wiped the neck of the bottle on his T-shirt and handed the bottle to Elaine. She took a large swig and passed it back.

"So you saw me at the party yesterday?" she asked.

"Yes, with those large glass walls, the dining hall is like a fish tank in a municipal aquarium. You may run from me, Elaine, but you can't hide. And this afternoon's attempt at hiding was particularly risible."

Elaine could feel herself blushing and hoped this wasn't

visible in the twilight. "Shit. So what's with you and Siobhan, then?"

"The dear girl feels sorry for a fellow countryman who was paralysed in a construction accident, and left to fend for himself on the streets of London by the cold and callous English." The Irish accent was back.

"That's not true, though, is it? You don't sound Irish normally."

"No, I'm of Italian extraction actually, but I did spend three years living on the streets of London. I thought I'd told you that before."

"So basically you've conned Siobhan into pilfering booze from the dining hall. Isn't that a bit mean?"

Joe passed the bottle back and Elaine took another swig.

"Well, you seem to be happy enough to drink it, so don't get on your high horse," he said.

"You're right. I'm sorry," Elaine said. She was enjoying the sherry, even if it was sweet. "But isn't there a risk that she'll lose her job if she's caught?"

"I doubt it. Apparently clients pay for a set number of bottles. Any unopened ones are stored after a party, but the partially drunk ones get poured down the sink. They've been paid for, so nobody cares. If you think about it, I perform a kind of informal garbage disposal service for them."

"Yeah, in that case, I'm cool with it. Here's to garbage disposal!" Elaine took a third gulp and passed the bottle back. "So is the tobacco from Siobhan, too?"

"You're very nosy, Elaine. But no, that's Lyndsay. Another of my young sympathisers."

"Where does she work?"

"Lyndsay is a young man with a fondness for fancy shirts. He works in the commissary. Haven't you been there?"

"Yes, I have actually, but he didn't have what I wanted," Elaine said.

"That's probably because you don't have what he wants. He has a weakness for silver foxes," said Joe, running the fingers of one hand theatrically through his hair, then giving Elaine an exaggerated wink, "especially wounded war veterans."

"War veteran? Which war?"

"The Iraq one. He's too young to have heard of any other ones."

"And surely you're too old to have served in it," Elaine said.

"Certainly not. I'm only fifty-three now, and anyway I was in the SAS – that means five more years of service."

"Huh! I don't believe a word of it."

"You don't need to," Joe said. "The point is that he does, and consequently packets of tobacco conveniently fall off the counter into my pocket."

"You're a rogue."

"I don't deny it."

"So what's the truth?"

"A very good question, and one debated by many philosophers. Personally I find the views of Bertrand Russell on the matter quite enlightening. Are you familiar with them?"

"Come on, Joe, you know what I mean."

"Another time. Look at the sky. Can you see that?"

The horizon was striated into bands of vibrant colour – a deep blue, a dusky rose pink and an intense pure yellow.

"Wow. It's magnificent."

"It is. Tell me, Elaine, when was the last time you watched the sunset while getting drunk with a man who sports a full head of hair?"

Elaine laughed. "A long time ago, at least where the hair's concerned."

"Then enjoy it while it lasts."

Joe passed the bottle to Elaine with one hand and took her free hand in his other one and cradled it on his thigh. His grip was firm and warm and comforting.

They sat in silence until the gold and pink had gone and the sky had turned to dark blue and purple.

"Time to go," Joe said. "I don't want to miss my curfew. Have we finished the bottle?"

Elaine shook it. "Not quite, but I don't want any more. I've had more than enough."

"Then I'll take the rest back to my housemate, Pete. Will you see all right to get back to your unit?"

"I'll manage. I've done the route often enough. Thank you, Joe, I had fun."

Joe lifted her hand and touched it to his lips while staring intently into her eyes.

"My pleasure, Elaine. I did too."

Joe released her hand and reached out to drag the

wheelchair towards himself. "You go ahead. It'll take me a while to get myself back into this thing."

"OK, then. Good night."

"Good night, Elaine. See you around."

Chapter 9

Monday 9 April

Elaine woke with a dry mouth and a thumping head. She had fallen into bed almost immediately after returning to the unit the night before but had woken up suddenly in the small hours. On her way to the kitchen for a glass of water, the lights in the unit had gone out suddenly. They hadn't come back on again, but a bright full moon filtering through her curtains had kept her awake for hours thereafter. Images and snatches of conversation from the last few days had flitted through her mind, making sleep even more elusive.

… Ernie's yellow sideburns and skeletal hands … *I'm going out in style, doll* … Nicola's impeccably conventional navy suit … *that gives you an adjusted waiting period of thirty days* … Siobhan's pretty, blushing face … *You look far too young to be exiting* … Dorothy's thick wire-rimmed glasses … *the doctor said I was vulnerable and would be safer here* … the twink from the commissary doing up his flies … *He has a weakness for silver foxes* … Hamish avoiding eye contact … *Mums are special. My Mum had Parkinson's* … Dorothy again … *What if they put Binkie and Boxer down* … Miss Latimer sweetly asleep in her wing chair … *The old bat is totally gaga, she thinks she's in a posh care home* … Olivia and Rose holding hands … *We can't eat much as it would interfere with the pills* … Joe laughing at her swearing … Joe's combative flirting style… Joe's theatrical kissing of her hand… *See you around … See you around …*

She had finally got back to sleep when she heard birds starting to twitter outside.

Elaine reached across to the desk to check the time on her

Nexus. The screen was blank and it didn't respond to swiping or button pressing. Either Hamish's clean-up hadn't worked, or she'd forgotten to charge it again. No, it was plugged in at the wall, but it didn't seem to be charging. She hoped it hadn't finally given up the ghost.

Elaine decided to ask one of her housemates if she was too late for breakfast. Dorothy wasn't in her room, so Elaine tried Miss Latimer instead. The old lady's bed was covered with a medley of cardboard folders, biscuit tins, handbags and carrier bags with papers spilling out of them. The old lady was bent almost double over the bed, moving objects from one position to another and back again.

"Hello, Elaine, I'm so glad you're here! I can't find my chequebook!"

Elaine smiled, happy that Miss Latimer had remembered her name. "Well, can you recall when you last used it?"

"I think it was yesterday. Did we see each other yesterday?"

"Yes, we played Scrabble in the afternoon," Elaine said.

"Had I had my hair done?"

"Yes, you said Betty had taken you to the hairdresser, and it looked like it had just been set."

"Good, then I would have given her a cheque yesterday. Could you put the light on, please, dear? That might help."

Elaine flicked the switch, but nothing happened.

"That's strange. The power went off in the middle of the night and it's still not back on. Do you happen to know what time it is, Miss Latimer?"

The old lady checked her watch. "Half past ten."

Breakfast was out of the question in that case, so Elaine persuaded Miss Latimer to sit down while they sorted through the things on the bed. After twenty minutes of fruitless effort, Elaine had an inspiration.

"Perhaps it's in the Scrabble box, Miss Latimer?"

"I very much doubt it. I pride myself on my organisation."

Elaine lifted the Scrabble board out of the box and found a chequebook nestling beneath it. "Is this the one?" she asked.

"Oh, dash, now I've mislaid my glasses! Have a look, dear. Who was the last cheque made out to?"

"It says *J. Randall, hairdo.*"

"Good, that's the one. So if I can just find my pen and glasses, I can pay my bill. I always pay on the tenth of the month. It is the tenth today, isn't it?"

"Hold on. I've rather lost track of the dates," said Elaine. She looked at her ID card and did a calculation on her fingers. "No, tomorrow, is the tenth actually."

"That's fine. I'll have it ready for the morning girl when she comes in with my breakfast tomorrow," Miss Latimer said.

"Who exactly do you want to pay?" asked Elaine.

"The manager, of course. Oh dear, her name escapes me. It's on the cheque stubs."

Elaine looked at the second last stub – it read *N. Pemberton, March fees, £3,000.*

"Nicola Pemberton," Elaine said, frowning.

"That's right. Tell me, dear. I know this is a bit indiscreet but, ehm … don't you find the home a bit on the pricey side?"

"Yes, rather," said Elaine, shocked that the Facility Administrator was charging Miss Latimer for her stay.

"I thought so too, but Betty assures me it is good value. Apparently the going rate for residential care is £1,000 a week, but Betty got a discount for me from the manager. They're cousins on her father's side, you see."

"I see." Elaine flipped through a few more cheque stubs to make sure her sight wasn't paying tricks on her. Sure enough, Miss Latimer was making payments of £3,000 a month to Nicola Pemberton.

"And while I'm being frank," Miss Latimer continued, patting her hair absent-mindedly, "I must say that I don't find the standards are really up to scratch either. Still, needs must. I don't want to use up all my savings on myself before I die. Betty's been very kind to me, and she will get what's left over. She's divorced, I'm afraid, so things haven't been easy for her."

Elaine helped Miss Latimer clear the bed and locate her pen and glasses, then headed for the central building, once more burning inside with outrage.

Hamish was in the media room and was coding again.

"Hi, Elaine. How are you? I didn't see you around at all yesterday."

"Yes, it was kind of a busy day. So, I see there's power in here, but not in my unit. What about yours?"

"There was none in mine either when I left. I don't know what's going on. There was some kind of incident last night and it seems like the power's been off since then in the older blocks."

"What do you mean by an incident?" Elaine said.

"Didn't you hear the siren? No? Well, first a siren went off, then a few seconds later the power failed. I reckon something that's on the old system shorted out, maybe a deer wandered into an electric fence or something. The newer buildings, like this one and the admin block, wouldn't have been affected cos they're on the modern power supply."

"Yes, that sounds logical. So where's your block, Hamish? Mine's down to the south-west side of here."

"I'm in an all-male block up the ridge, overlooking the river."

"Wow, I didn't know there was a river near here," Elaine said. "Can you see it from your unit?"

"No, cos my room's on the south side. But you can from the back of the block."

"Can you take me to see it?"

"I suppose so. I was rather hoping you'd let me use a bit of your internet time via the tablet, though."

"Sure, but I don't have it on me. How about after lunch, assuming the power's back on? It ran out of charge during the night."

Hamish and Elaine left the central building and headed up a path that went north, walking in silence. Elaine considered telling him about Miss Latimer's niece, her connection with the Facility Administrator and the scam they appeared to be running at the old lady's expense, but decided against it. Hamish seemed harmless enough, but he wasn't exactly forthcoming with her.

Their path intersected with the one she and Dorothy had been on when she had overheard Siobhan and Joe. Hamish turned right and led her further along that path. It climbed steadily, bringing them to the front of a three-storeyed building.

"Is this your block?" Elaine panted, stopping to stretch her aching hip. Hamish nodded and left the path and stepped onto the grass. He waited until Elaine got her breath back and then they walked round to the back of the block.

A stunning view awaited them. Looking down and slightly to the left, Elaine could see a single-arched stone footbridge spanning a river that sparkled greeny-blue in the sunshine. On the other side of the bridge there was a wood, and Elaine thought she could make out a small village beyond that.

"Oh, it's beautiful. I had no idea we were so close to water," Elaine said. Suddenly, her eyes filled with tears and her nose started to prickle. She grabbed a tissue from her pocket and blew her nose.

"Are you OK?" Hamish asked.

"Yes, sure. I'm fine. It's just I used to go wild water swimming and seeing the river made me remember how much I loved it."

"That's the Dour," Hamish said. "The sea's only about half a mile downstream." He pointed off to his right as he spoke.

"The what?"

"The Dour. We're in Inverdour. In what used to be Riverside Halls of Residence, Inverdour University, to be precise."

"Holy shit, Hamish! How do you know that?" Elaine's surprise banished the grief for her past, at least for now.

"Because I lived here for a while when I was a student."

Elaine sat down abruptly on the grass and patted the space

beside her. "Sit down, Hamish, and explain all this from the beginning. It's a lot to take in."

"OK. So, like I said, I lived in these halls twenty years ago when I was an undergraduate. I wasn't sure when I first came in, because a lot has been rebuilt since then. The central building, the admin block, the medical building and the blocks for the terminal patients must be pretty new, probably built since the Exit Facility took over the whole complex. I think this block and the ones at your end must have been rebuilt since I left, but while it was still a hall of residence."

"That makes sense. It's funny, but when I arrived I actually thought it reminded me of a hall of residence. And those awful capsule bathrooms look like something added later. They had those at Alexandra's Uni too. It was a right con – they charged parents an extra fifty quid a week by claiming the bedrooms each had an ensuite bathroom."

Elaine noticed Hamish was absent-mindedly pulling blades of grass out of the turf and wasn't really listening to her comments.

"What clinched it for me," he said, "was a line of blocks over that way, not far from yours." He pointed to show Elaine where he meant. "I recognised them from my days here."

"I know the blocks you mean. They are near mine." Elaine thought she shouldn't open the topic of the Indigents at present. "But where do the students stay now?"

Hamish looked completely blank.

"The Inverdour students, Hamish. Where have they gone if this was their hall of residence?"

"Don't you watch the news, Elaine?"

"No, I've never owned at TV. The first time I watched one in years was in the media room the other day."

"Wow. But you must have followed the news online, or in newspapers."

"Only intermittently; latterly I found it all too depressing."

"Right Well, think back to the autumn of 2020. Students arrived at universities all over the country for the first term of university to find their classes were being delivered online and they were cooped up in halls for weeks with coronavirus running rampant among them. Do you remember that?" Hamish asked, sounding like a man trying to explain the ten times table to a very small child.

"Of course I do, Hamish.   Fortunately that was one catastrophe that Alexandra actually avoided."

"Good. So after that parents weren't very keen to fork out for their kids to be cooped up in halls only to be educated online, which could have been done just as easily at home. It only took a couple of years for on-campus education at all the newer and less prestigious universities to be replaced by distance learning. And that left those universities sitting on loads of empty real estate that was earning them no income. Are you with me so far?"

Elaine nodded.

"Then the laws on assisted suicide changed," Hamish continued. "Some bright spark, I don't know who, hit on the idea of buying up university properties and converting them into exit facilities. That last bit is hush-hush, of course. Nobody on the outside knows how many exit facilities there are, or where they are located."

"Wow, I had no idea about most of that," Elaine said, thinking she probably should have paid more attention to the world around her since Alexandra had left. She might not be sitting here in an exit facility if she had done so, or if the world had paid more attention to her.

They sat in silence while Elaine pondered what Hamish had told her. "How long have you known where we are, Hamish?"

"I've only been absolutely certain for a couple of days. Since you let me send that email from your account."

"Has knowing where you are affected how you feel about your Exit decision?"

"I don't think so. Not really."

"So why were you so excited when you got a reply to that email?"

This time Hamish hesitated before replying. "Ehm, well, you know, it's always nice when a hunch is proved right."

Elaine said nothing.

"Why?" Hamish asked. "Do you feel different now that you know?"

"Utterly and totally. I was in limbo before. Now I feel connected to the outside world again. I need some time to process this, Hamish."

"I'm sorry, perhaps I shouldn't have told you."

"It's not your fault, I pressed you to tell me." Elaine rubbed the space between her eyebrows with the tips of two fingers. "Look, I've got a headache coming on and I'm starving because I missed breakfast. Shall we go and have lunch?"

Chapter 10

Tuesday 10 April

Elaine's copy of Manet's *The Execution of Maximilian* was almost finished. The previous afternoon, after using up her internet allocation, Elaine had slept off the last of her hangover. Then, inspired by Dorothy's tailor's chalks and the electricity being restored, Elaine had worked till late at night to complete her drawing, adding colour to the background and using the white chalk to highlight Maximilian's shirt and the belts of the soldiers in the firing squad.

She moved back to admire her handiwork, noticing as she climbed off the bed that one of the urchins peeping over the wall looked uncannily like a prepubescent Alexandra. The drawing wasn't bad, but she wondered now if the emperor perhaps had yellow trousers in the original? Or was she confusing it with the Goya painting that had influenced Manet's? She'd check both paintings out online after breakfast, assuming she hadn't missed it again.

Elaine showered and dressed quickly and hurried over to the central building. Hamish was coming out as she reached the double doors to the dining hall.

"Hi, Hamish. Am I too late for breakfast?"

"No, you'll just make it."

"Good, I'm dying for a coffee. Are you going to the computer room?"

"No, I'm having a walk first, but I'll see you there later."

Joe was in the outdoor seating area when Elaine left the dining hall and made the circuit round the building.

"Hi, you're OK then?" he greeted her.

"Yes, I'm fine. Why wouldn't I be?"

"Just wondering. Something happened the night before last, and we were on lockdown for twenty-four hours. Normally I get more freedom than the other Indigents, but I wasn't allowed to leave my unit yesterday," Joe said.

"Yes, I was thinking about that. How come you're allowed to go wherever you like?"

"Because of the chair I reckon. I can't move very fast and they think I'm harmless because I'm disabled. My tag allows me to go pretty much anywhere in the grounds, but the others are on a much shorter radius."

Joe gestured for Elaine to sit down on the bench nearest to his chair, and lowered his voice. "So, did you hear anything about what happened?"

"Hamish reckons a deer wandered into a fence and triggered an alarm."

"That's possible, I suppose, but word has it in my section that someone tried to break out."

"One of the Indigents?" asked Elaine.

"Nope, we were all accounted for at roll call."

"Strange. I'll tell you who might be missing, though. My housemate Dorothy. I haven't seen her for a couple of days. I doubt she'd have tried to break out, though. She sees even worse than I do."

"She's probably been transferred to the medical block for

some reason; she looked a bit unhinged when I saw you two patrolling the grounds," Joe said. "So, tell me, who's Hamish? Is he the guy I've seen you with in the dining hall? The pallid one with baggy grey jumpers and a bald patch?"

"I hadn't noticed the bald patch."

"Well now I've alerted you to it, I'm sure you'll never feel the same about him again," said Joe.

Elaine laughed. "I don't think a bald patch will make much difference to my friendship with Hamish."

"Seriously, though, Elaine. I think you should be careful around him. He's been spending a lot of time walking the grounds around the back of our blocks."

"Well, the weather's been quite nice the last few days."

"Or maybe I should say pacing, rather than walking. He goes up and down in lines, counting and looking at the ground."

"Really?" Elaine could sympathise. "I also count when I'm nervous"

"I don't know, but I don't trust him. Just be careful. So, can we meet later? Get to know each other better?"

"Sure, sounds fun. Same time, same place?"

"I think my curfew may be earlier because of the incident; the staff seem to be pretty jittery. How about this afternoon instead? Or have you got other plans? The cinema with Hamish perhaps? Or tea and scones with another admirer I haven't met yet?"

Elaine gave him a baleful look, then laughed. "OK."

"Fine. Remember that tree you tried to hide behind the other day? There, at three o'clock."

+++

Elaine was studying online reproductions of Goya's *The Third of May 1808* and planning a companion piece to her existing wall-painting when Hamish entered the media room.

"Interesting painting," he said, glancing over her shoulder. "But the subject matter's a bit grisly. Why are you looking at it?"

"I'm going to make a copy of it."

"Oh, are you an artist? A well-known one?"

"Yes, to the first, no to the second."

Elaine turned back to the screen, memorising the details of the painting. She loved the drama of this work and the contrast it made to the stiller, flatter figures in Manet's execution scene. Goya's victim was irate, arms in the air, protesting his imminent death, while Manet's emperor was flinching elegantly from the approaching bullets. And of course, it was Goya's resistance fighter who was wearing yellow trousers, not Manet's emperor.

"It's not really my business," Hamish said suddenly, "but you do know it's not good to get so close to a computer screen, don't you?"

"Of course, but I can't see any details otherwise."

"So you must be very short-sighted, but you don't wear glasses?"

"Glasses don't help my condition," Elaine said. "Things look corrugated and there are sort of shimmering holes in parts of the centre."

114

"My Mum had something like that," Hamish said, "for a couple of years before she died." He pulled a tissue from his pocket and blew his nose.

"Yes, that's the age-related version of macular disease. It's very common. What I have is rare and starts when you're young. It didn't bother me that much thirty years ago, but it's a degenerative condition and it's made life much tougher recently. I used to do office work to supplement my income, but I had to give that up. Nobody wants a half-blind admin assistant."

"I'm sorry. But painting or drawing. How do you manage that?"

"My work is impressionistic rather than realistic. Things pop if you stand far back enough, just don't call me out on the details."

"I'd like to see it. Bring your drawing over to show me when it's done," Hamish said. "And if you want me to download the picture to your tablet for reference, I can do that for you."

Skirting the issue of showing him the painting, Elaine said: "Thanks, Hamish, that would be useful. But for now I'm off to do some more work on it while I'm feeling inspired."

Elaine was halfway out the door when Hamish called after her.

"Oh, one other thing before you go. Do you know a man in a wheelchair with longish white hair?"

"Yes, I do," said Elaine. "His name is Joe. Why?"

"Just curious. I presume he's a Terminal since he's in a chair, but he never has a nurse or a helper to push him."

Elaine said nothing.

115

"And he doesn't live in the Terminals' block. He's in those very old buildings to the west, the ones that were here when I was a student."

"Yes, I had gathered that."

"Anyway, I happened to be walking past the back of those blocks one day, and I saw him leaning out of a window on the ground floor and smoking. I thought that was a bit odd."

"Why?" Elaine raised her eyebrows.

"Well, for a start the windows in my unit don't open more than ten centimetres. And all of his upper body was visible above the window ledge. He was standing up, definitely."

"Really? Perhaps he can stand if he's supporting himself on something. Anyway, the windows are probably different in those old blocks. Lower down and able to open further. It's hardly sinister," Elaine said.

"I don't know, I'm just saying there's something not quite right about him, or the blocks over there. I think you should be careful around him."

"Thanks for the warning, Hamish. I'll catch you later."

+++

Joe was already there when Elaine reached their meeting point in the afternoon.

"Are we staying here?" she asked.

"No, there's a nice spot with a bench in the kitchen gardens. I haven't seen anyone there at this time of day, so we should be private enough."

Joe led the way to a small potting shed which had a south-facing bench outside it. The planks of the bench were gently warm from the sun.

"You know your way round pretty well," Elaine said. "I've only just started moving around the place a bit more."

"I've explored most of the Facility, apart from the medical block and the units for the Terminals. They're fenced off and there are more guards there. And there's another accommodation section, in the north-east. I can't get there because it's uphill, but I think it's for male Vs."

"Yes, that's right. Hamish took me up there yesterday."

"Really? I didn't realise you two were so intimate." Joe raised an eyebrow quizzically.

"Stop teasing me about Hamish!" Elaine said. "It's my tablet he's interested in, not me!"

"Ah, the great Scottish love of sugar! You even brought tablet to an exit facility. I suppose that's one way to sweeten the pill."

"Huh? Oh, I get it. No, it's an old Nexus 7 I'm talking about, not confectionery. He's a computer geek. And just for the record, I wasn't in his room. He was showing me the river."

"River, what river?" Joe asked leaning forward in his chair.

Elaine hesitated before answering, wondering how much she should tell Joe, and then gave him a brief summary of what Hamish had told her the day before.

"Interesting. Very interesting. Do you think he's trying to find a way to get out now that he's worked out where he is?" Joe asked. "That might explain the pacing and counting."

"Could be. It sounds like he's up to something, but I don't know what."

"Would you leave if you could, Elaine?" For once the undertone of mockery was missing from Joe's voice.

Elaine sighed heavily before answering. "Well, the enforced wait has certainly made me think about my decision, and seeing the river yesterday reminded me the world is sometimes beautiful. But there'd be no point in going back. Materially speaking, nothing has changed."

Joe reached over and patted her hand briefly. "How come you're so down on your uppers, Elaine?"

"It's a combination of things. I never managed to do more than scrape an income from art. I married a man who was allergic to work, so that was no help. Things improved, financially speaking, after Mum died; she was divorced from my Dad so she left everything to me. I invested in a small flat here in Britain – about the only sensible financial decision of my entire life – and returned to Cyprus, where Alexandra and I were living. I put the rest of the money from Mum in the Laiki bank in Cyprus and …"

"Oh, shit!" Joe interrupted. "And lost the lot in 2013, I guess."

"Yes, the government impounded money from private investors to pay for the bailout. I had just over 100,000 Euros deposited with the Laiki bank. Ten thousand less and I'd have been OK as they didn't take money from smaller investors. But how the hell do you know about what happened? Most Brits I've ever spoken to about it look at me like I'm making it all up or something."

"Simple. I used to work in the City," Joe said.

"Oh, I hadn't expected that! So between high finance, the construction business and the SAS you had your work cut out."

"Come on, Elaine, I wouldn't lie to you. Anyway, finish your story before I tell you mine."

"But you will tell me it this time?"

"I promise." Joe crossed his heart and winked at her.

"Well, the rest is less dramatic. Like many people, I got sandwiched between the needs of two generations. As an EU student in Scotland, Alexandra's tuition fees were paid, but she didn't qualify for a student loan, so I rented out my flat to help pay her living costs. Then Dad got ill. I moved in with him and looked after him, which cut my costs but meant I didn't have time to work. When he got too ill for me to manage he went into a care home, and his house was sold to pay the fees. I had to move into my own flat so lost that income. When I finally reached pension age, it turned out I only qualified for a minuscule one as I had spent too much time living abroad. So here I am."

Too late, Elaine realised she'd just given away her real age.

"Poor Elaine, a catalogue of bad luck." It was hard to tell from his tone of voice whether Joe was being sympathetic or sarcastic.

"And some poor choices," Elaine said. Perhaps he'd missed the inference about her age.

"What about the workshy husband?" Joe asked.

"He died of liver failure. Your turn now, tell all."

"We're forgetting something." Joe reached into his pocket and pulled out a pack of Gold   Leaf and some rolling papers. "Do you know how to do it?"

"I used to. I'll give it a try."

Joe passed the tobacco to Elaine. It was a brand new packet. He must have paid a visit to Lyndsay that morning.

"So, yes, I worked in the City. I had a good salary, a nice car, a flat in Canary Wharf and a very high maintenance girlfriend. Too high maintenance even for the money I was making. I should have broken it off when I realised she expected regular gifts of jewellery and city breaks in luxury hotels, but I was besotted. It was the first time in my life that I had felt that way. So I started diverting money from some of the funds I was managing to an account of my own. I thought I'd covered my tracks well, but I was caught a few months later."

"Wow! Did you go to jail?"

"No, I was lucky. The firm didn't want to make it known that an employee of theirs had been embezzling, as it would destroy investors' confidence in them. I was fired and ordered to pay back all the money I'd taken in exchange for non-prosecution. So that was the end of the flat in Canary Wharf."

"And the girlfriend?"

"No, surprisingly not. Not then. Maybe it was my natural charm and good looks she liked, not just the presents and weekend breaks. Then I had the accident. I drove down to Kent to see an old friend, got pissed as a fart and decided to drive back to London. I crashed into a tree. That was the legs done for and the car gone."

"I'm sorry. You've had bad luck too. Worse than mine."

"And made poor choices. Worse than yours. Good God, Elaine, do you call that a roll-up? It's enormous!"

"It is a bit fat, I guess. I've only ever rolled joints before, you see."

"Really? You're a dark horse."

"Well, I did grow up in the 70s, Joe. Everyone smoked dope then…" Elaine trailed off, realising she'd given away her real age yet again.

"Here pass the stuff over, I'll redo this one and make one for you. We'll get through the whole packet in an afternoon if I leave it to you."

"So what about your girlfriend? She didn't chuck you out, I hope?"

"Not until she came home early from work one day and caught me shagging her friend in the spare bedroom."

"Oh, no! How could you, Joe, after she'd stood by you?"

"Vanity, boredom, I don't really know. In my defence, the friend seduced me, but it was a poor choice to say yes. The next day Samantha took me on the Underground to the opposite side of London and abandoned me on the platform with no ticket and no money. And thus began my career as a beggar."

Elaine reached over and patted Joe's hand briefly. She could think of nothing to say. Aspects of Joe's story seemed too baroque to be credible, but she couldn't pinpoint which were true and which fake.

"Well, here I am, still alive, sitting in the sunshine and smoking and chatting. It could be worse," Joe said, filling the awkward silence. "And I sleep in a bed, eat twice a day, and am able to have a shower. All those things are a comfort when you haven't had them for a while."

Elaine was torn between pity and disbelief. She decided a change of subject might ease the awkwardness. "I've been wondering. Why do I never see all the Is coming over for lunch after the Vs have eaten?"

"We're not allowed in any part of the central building. They bring the food over to us on trolleys."

"I never see those either."

"They use tunnels, Siobhan tells me. Apparently there's a network of them linking all the main buildings and some of the blocks."

"Clever. Discreet and not weather dependent," Elaine said. "What about the other Indigents? Are they people you knew from your days on the streets?"

"No, I don't know where the other rough sleepers I knew were taken. Vans went round London before the Coronation, sweeping us up and carting us off as if we were stray dogs. Nobody in government gave a damn about homeless people before that, but when it came to visiting foreign dignitaries seeing beggars on the streets, they certainly acted fast enough."

The sun was still shining, but Elaine shivered suddenly.

"Is there anything I could do? Get word out to a human rights organisation, or something? I've got internet access."

"No, Elaine, keep your head down and your nose clean. Your word against theirs won't make any difference at all. Have you found your friend, by the way?"

"Who? Oh, God, yes, Dorothy. I forgot to check after lunch." Elaine leapt to her feet. "That's awful of me. Thanks for reminding me, Joe, I should go and look for her now. And thanks for the smoke and the chat. I'll see you around."

Chapter 11

Wednesday 11 April

Elaine arrived early outside the Facility Administrator's office, but Nicola was there even earlier. Her office door was slightly ajar and she could be heard from the corridor.

"No, it's out of the question." Nicola said. "We are at capacity."

There was a pause before she spoke again.

"The problem is not beds. I have plenty of free beds. It's the Closure Procedure and Post-Closure Processing that are bottlenecks. I need at least another five medical orderlies. The last intake of Terminals was already more than we can handle with Due Compassion, not to mention the other rag-bag lot you sent me. "

Nicola paused again. Elaine couldn't hear anyone else speaking, so presumably the Facility Administrator was on the phone.

"Another accident? That's most unfortunate," Nicola said.

Elaine was gratified that someone else was on the receiving end of the icy sarcasm that Nicola usually directed at her.

"Yes, I appreciate that you're in a difficult situation, but …"

The next pause was longer. When she spoke again, Nicola sounded less tetchy.

"Yes, absolutely. If you can allocate resources for the

immediate completion of the second on-site Post-Closure Incinerator, and assign me the orderlies I need, then I ..."

A door behind Elaine opened and someone yanked her elbow. Elaine turned round to see Ashley baring her teeth at her.

"What are you doing there?" Ashley hissed.

"I want to speak to the Facility Administrator. I need to report a missing person."

"Come in here," Ashley said, pulling Elaine towards the door she had emerged from. "I'll deal with whatever your problem is." She propelled Elaine into an office that was similar in design to the Facility Administrator's one, but about half the size. "I've been promoted. You can tell me anything you would tell the Administrator. She's a very busy woman, so she can't deal with all the details."

"Well, it's hardly a detail," Elaine said. "Someone has gone missing from my unit."

"Name?"

"Mine?"

"No, of course not. I can read yours on your badge. The missing person's name."

"Dorothy. She's classified VM. I don't know her surname."

"Are you her next of kin?"

"No, of course not. I'd know her surname if I was a relative. We're in the same unit. Anyway, you know who I am. You registered me when I came in."

"We do a lot of intakes; I can't remember you all. Pass me your badge."

Ashley scanned Elaine's ID badge over her console. "Ah, OK, got her. Unit 1, Block 5, South-West Section. Dorothy Brown, schizophrenic, due to Exit in four days."

"Yes, though I don't think she's actually schizophrenic. But I'm really worried because she's severely visually impaired. She could be anywhere."

"OK, thanks for informing me. I'll look into it." Ashley rested one hand on top of the other on her desk and sat up straight.

"Is that it?" Elaine asked.

"What do you mean 'Is that it?'"

"Don't you want details of when I last saw her?"

"I told you, I'll look into it."

"When you find out what's happened to her, will you let me know, please?

"I can only release that kind of information to her next of kin."

"She hasn't got any next of kin."

Ashley looked at the screen again. "Fine, her lawyer will be informed."

"I don't think her lawyer gives a shit. I'm the one who's worried."

"Stop getting het up. I have to follow procedures." Ashley stood up and went over to a coffee machine in the corner of the room. She poured coffee into a polystyrene cup, opened a jar and added a large spoonful of white sugar.

"Milk?" she asked.

"Is that for me?" Elaine said in surprise. "No, I don't take milk, or sugar actually."

"Too late, I'm afraid," said Ashley, attempting a smile. "I've put some in already. Here, have this anyway. You seem a bit agitated so I'm sure it'll do you good."

Elaine contemplated throwing the contents of the cup in the woman's face, then thought better of it. Fighting the system had got her nowhere so far. Besides, she'd been severely caffeine deprived since Daphne's leftover Nescafé had run out a couple of days ago.

The sun was shining brightly as she left the admin building. It wasn't particularly hot – she wouldn't have expected that this far north in April – but it was pleasantly warm. Elaine decided to walk up to the kitchen garden area and enjoy the sunshine while sitting on the bench where she and Joe had been yesterday afternoon.

She headed away from the admin block with the sun at her back until she came to a fork in the path. Presumably she should take the right fork to reach where she'd been yesterday, but then she and Joe had approached from the other direction and she hadn't really been paying attention.

"That's a bad habit, Elaine," she said to herself aloud. "People who don't see well should always pay attention to where they are going."

She contemplated the two paths, which were now shimmering and dancing in the sunlight.

"One fork makes you taller and the other fork makes you smaller." She was speaking aloud again.

"Smaller, taller. Taller, smaller." Elaine noticed her arms were making fluid movements, gesturing at each fork in turn.

"Smaller, taller. Oh, what the fork am I doing?" Elaine laughed uproariously at her own pun.

A huge butterfly flitted past her and took the left fork in the path. Elaine followed the butterfly, skipping a little to try and catch up with it. Everything was beautiful, the colours were beautiful, the sunshine on her skin was beautiful, life was beautiful. Elaine removed her jacket and threw it over a low hedge. She felt free and light, the sun was kissing her arms now. Beautiful. The colours of the plants and trees were vibrant, their outlines blurred into the background. She was walking through a pointillist painting, at one with nature, at one with her surroundings. She was the painting and the painting was her.

A section of the painting detached itself from the background and moved towards her – a bush, a burning bush, a bush burning with a silver flame at the top. The bush spoke.

"What the flaming fuck are you doing, Elaine? Why are you waving your arms about?"

"I'm dancing to nature, the beauty of nature. And you, you are flaming, you're a burning bush, flaming with a silver fire." The pointillist effect was stronger now, the dots were dancing in front of her eyes.

"Are you drunk? At this time in the morning?"

"I have drunk of truth and beauty. I have drunk of light and fire. They are beautiful, life is beautiful."

"… hospital block ... block … block … follow me … me … path … path … path." Now the bush was echoing.

"I have followed the path already. I am one with the path and the path is with me."

"OK … kay … stay … stay … shall return … return … soon

… soon … oon," the bush echoed, then faded into the background. The coloured dots were even brighter, the sun was even warmer. Beautiful, beautiful, beautiful.

+++

Elaine was lying on something hard and lumpy. A ring of pain surrounded her head like swimming goggles that were on too tight. She opened one eye and shut it hastily. Her vision was blurred and coloured dots were dancing about in it. Shit, the last thing she needed.

"Did you see her eyelid flicker? Maybe she's coming round?" a male voice said.

"I didn't see anything," another man said. "Look, it's been over an hour. I don't think your cure's working. We should get medical help."

"I told you I don't trust them. Let's try waking her up."

A hand was placed on her forehead. "At least she's not burning up any more."

"Huh?" Elaine said. "What's up?" She kept her eyes shut.

"Thank fuck," Joe said. "Can you manage to drink something, Elaine? But don't sit up, I've got a spoon here."

"What is it?"

"Hamish's recipe. He swears by it."

Elaine raised her head slightly and opened her mouth. A sugary liquid was poured into it.

She swallowed and asked again. "What is it?"

"Irn Bru with homoeopathic phosphorus in it," Hamish said. "I find it works for most psychotropic drugs. Fresh orange juice is good too, but the commissary didn't have any."

"What? Are you talking about hallucinogens?"

"Talk later," Joe said. "Have some more medicine now."

Elaine sipped three more spoonfuls, then opened her eyes. She was in the media room, lying on the seats in front of the TV screen. "It's too bright. I can't see."

Joe wheeled himself in the direction of the door and put the lights off.

"Don't worry, I think the visual disturbance will wear off in an hour or so," Hamish said. "I've seen this kind of thing happen before. I had friends who used to do MDMA. I didn't like it much, so I was the one who stayed straight and looked after them."

"More Hamish juice coming up," Joe said.

Elaine had another spoonful. The pain in her head had abated slightly, but she shut her eyes again. "OK, tell me what happened," she said.

"I saw you meandering about in the kitchen gardens, waving your arms in the air," Joe said. "I came to see what you were up to and thought you were drunk at first. But you were talking utter rubbish, so … "

"I was being lyrical. Everything was beautiful."

"Oh you remember that, do you?"

"I remember seeing a beautiful butterfly, and dancing in the sun, and feeling at peace with the world, that's all."

"Well, I got really worried when I realised you couldn't see well enough to follow me to the medical block," Joe said, "so I went off to get help."

"And he bumped into me," said Hamish. "I'd spotted you leaving the admin block earlier and wondered what you'd been doing there. Joe said you had probably been making a fuss about the woman from your unit that you were worried about. When he described the way you were acting, we put two and two together and guessed someone had spiked you with something."

"MDMA, you think?" Elaine asked.

"I don't know;" Hamish replied, "a mild hallucinogen perhaps, and maybe some kind of muscle relaxant or sedative. It certainly affected your legs as well as your brain and your vision. By the time Joe got back with his friend from the commissary bringing Irn Bru and bottled water, you were lying against a hedge like a rag doll. It was all we could do to get you to drink some water. Then the commissary boy and I half-carried, half-dragged you here."

"Oh God, how embarrassing!" Elaine groaned. The image of a rag doll was vivid but undignified; she didn't want to be seen that way. A minute or so passed in silence, then Elaine realised some gratitude might be in order. "Thank you both for saving me. I might have died of dehydration or something if you hadn't found me. Do you think that was the intention?"

"To kill you? It seems a bit messy, and the Lagerkommandant likes to do things according to procedure. You're not due to go for another twenty-two days," said Joe, looking at Elaine's ID card, which was still hanging round her neck.

"It wasn't her. It was the one called Ashley. I was asking her about what happened to Dorothy. She insisted on giving me a coffee, and putting sugar in it without my asking for it. It probably wasn't sugar then, was it?"

"I expect she just wanted to stop you asking too many questions," Hamish said.

"I should go," Joe said. "I'm not meant to be in here. How are you feeling now?"

Elaine opened her eyes. "Better, I think. A bit floppy and I'm seeing coloured dots still. I really hope that passes."

"I can't believe she gave you, of all people, something that affects the vision. What a bitch!" Joe patted Elaine lightly on the leg. "Anyway, I'm off. See you guys around."

"Thank you again, Joe. Bye." Elaine swung her legs off the seats and sat up slowly. "And I owe thanks to you, Hamish. You knew what to do to save me."

"Ah, that's OK. It was a joint effort. Do you feel well enough to move now?"

"I hope so. I should go and lie down in my unit, I think."

"That's probably the best. I'll walk you over there to make sure you're OK." Hamish helped Elaine to her feet and offered his elbow to lean on. "Here you carry the concoction and I'll bring the water bottle. You'll still need to keep drinking both of those."

Chapter 12

Thursday 12 April

Elaine woke up the next morning feeling refreshed after sixteen hours of almost continuous sleep. Her eyesight was back to normal, or as normal as it ever was, and all traces of a headache had gone. Remembering what had been the catalyst for the previous day's events, she checked Dorothy's room again, but she wasn't in it, and the bed had clearly not been slept in.

Elaine couldn't find her jacket, either in her room or in the communal kitchen, so she walked briskly over to the central building with her arms wrapped round herself to keep warm. The weather had been nice lately, but it was still chilly first thing in the morning.

Hamish was in the dining hall. Elaine sat down opposite him and noticed that his normally sallow face looked rather pinker and healthier. Maybe the sunshine and all the walking Joe alleged he was doing were improving his circulation.

"How are you feeling, Elaine?"

"Back to normal. Thanks again."

"Your vision too?"

"Yes, thank God. The dancing dots have gone."

"I'm glad. Oh, Joe gave me this. He said he found it in one of the kitchen gardens." Hamish lifted Elaine's jacket off a chair beside him and gave it to her. "And he wants to meet you in the afternoon at a potting shed. He said you'd know what he meant."

"Great, thanks. Yes, I know the place. Shall we go to the media room once we've eaten? I want to see if my daughter's been in touch."

There was an email from Alexandra.

Dear Mum,

What's going on? I wanted some advice, so I tried to Skype you two days running, but you were never online. Has the tablet finally died? Last night I called the flat, but all I got was a continuous tone, like the line had been cut off. What the hell is happening? I am really worried. Please get in touch.

Anyway, I wanted to discuss the Rome thing. I went to a travel agent to book the stopover and they told me that Brits need a visa to get into Italy these days, which I'd forgotten, of course. It's not cheap, and Rome is going to be much more expensive than Goa. So I think I should just come straight home. I could get a direct flight to London in the middle of next week, but I would need to book it soon.

Please get back to me fast; I am getting really anxious about you.

Love you lots,

A xxxxx

Elaine put her head in her hands. "Oh, shit! No, no, no!"

"What's wrong?" Hamish asked.

"My daughter is planning to come back early from her holiday in Goa. Before my Exit Date."

"Surely that's good. Don't you want to see her one more time?" Hamish asked.

"No, the idea was to Exit before she returns. She doesn't know I'm here."

Hamish scratched his beard before replying. "Oh, I see." Clearly he didn't, but he was too polite to pry.

"Look, I'll explain in a minute, but I really have to come up with an answer to this fast." Elaine typed as rapidly as the gaps in her vision allowed.

> Dear Alexandra,
>
> All is well with me. You were right about the tablet – it's given up the ghost. As for the router and landline, I'm afraid I couldn't afford the last bill, so everything was cut off. I've been writing to you from the internet café round the corner since then. You're right to be upset – I was trying not to worry you on top of the stress of losing your job and being kicked out of Hong Kong. But it seems I've done the opposite. I'm really sorry to have upset you.
>
> I think it's wise to skip the side trip to Italy if it's going to be that expensive. Why don't you just stay on in Goa until the end of the month since you're enjoying it there? In fact, you'll probably use up less of your savings there than you will once you're back home, so that would even help the family finances!
>
> Enjoy the sunshine and don't worry about me; everything will resolve itself one way or another.
>
> All my love,
>
> Mum xx

Elaine wasn't sure the second paragraph was very convincing, but speed was essential. She hated lying to Alexandra, but it had to be done. Knowing how impulsive her daughter could be, would she blow her remaining savings on a full-price ticket in order to get home fast?

"I'm done for now, Hamish. Do you want to use some of my internet time?"

"Thanks. That would be good if you don't need it. Ehm … have you put your daughter off?"

"I hope so. See, it's like this, Hamish. I have no savings left and next to no income. Alexandra has just lost her job. It could take her months to find another one, so we'd have to sell my flat and live off the proceeds.   My sight is deteriorating, slowly, but inexorably. If I accidentally fall down the stairs one day or walk in front of a car, there will be nothing left to sell to pay for my care. I am shortcutting that process so that she can at least have a place to live."

Hamish sniffed loudly. "Well, I see your point in a way," he said, "but won't she miss you terribly?"

"I'm sure she will," said Elaine, "but she's young and deserves a future. I can't see how else to assure one for her."

"I didn't get a choice in the matter either," Hamish said.

"What do you mean?"

"Well, I told you my Mum had Parkinson's. She was still quite young when she was diagnosed and the medication they gave her helped a lot with the illness. The problem was it had some rather nasty side effects. Mum had always enjoyed going to the bingo once every couple of weeks with her friends, but on the pills she developed a full-scale gambling addiction. She began playing bingo on a daily basis. After that she started going to casinos to play roulette and blackjack as well. She lived alone and I was working in another city at the time, so there was nobody to notice what was going on. By the time I realised, she had re-mortgaged her house in order to raise more money for gambling."

"Oh, no, that's awful." Elaine resisted the urge to rush round the table and give Hamish a comforting hug.

"When I found out, they changed her medication and she went into a home. I sold her house, but there wasn't much money left over after paying back the bank. I got in a spot of bother trying to raise extra money to help her." Hamish looked down at his desk as he spoke, then shrugged. "As it happens, she went downhill fast after entering the home. Then she died in the first wave of the pandemic." Hamish sniffed loudly again and wiped his eyes with the back of his hands.

Elaine searched in her jacket pockets, found a tissue that was crumpled but clean, and handed it to Hamish. "I'm very sorry to hear that, Hamish. You were obviously very fond of her."

"She was a wonderful mother. My dad died when I was twelve and she raised me on her own. Still, it could have been worse, I suppose. Some patients on the same drugs developed a different kind of impulsive behaviour."

"What was that?"

"They became sex addicts," Hamish said, avoiding Elaine's eyes.

"Are you kidding?" Elaine said, struggling to control a highly inappropriate urge to laugh.

"Certainly not! Anyway, that's why I had no say in the matter. I'm flat broke now, just like you."

Elaine thought about giving Hamish a hug to cheer him up,

but decided it would only embarrass him.

"I'm sorry you've had such a hard time, Hamish. Look, there's nothing more I need to do on the computer today so you can use the rest of my time if you like. I'll get my ID card back from you at lunch. Shall we meet outside the dining hall at one p.m.?"

It felt like giving sweeties to a five-year-old with a scraped knee, but it was the best she could think of in the circumstances.

+++

Elaine found the potting shed without difficulty this time but Joe wasn't there when she arrived. She occupied herself by examining the shed more closely. The door was padlocked and the two small glass windows were dusty and dirty. Elaine breathed on one of the window panes and rubbed it with a tissue, then bent and applied her nose to the glass. She thought she could see what might be a garden fork and a spade leaning against the back wall inside the shed.

"Nice view," a voice behind her said.

Elaine turned round to see Joe close behind her, grinning broadly. "Not really," she said. "There's nothing much in there other than … Oh, nice view for you, you mean." Elaine felt herself blushing. "Shame on you, Joe. A gentleman would have coughed to let me know he was here, or something."

"Possibly. But I have never claimed to be a gentleman. What were you up to, anyway, peering in there?"

"Hamish was interested that we were meeting at a potting shed, and asked me to look out for any tools you could dig with."

"Really? It sounds like your grey Lothario is up to no good.

138

I did warn you."

"I thought you'd got over your objections to him since you both rescued me."

"He seems OK where you're concerned at least," Joe said. "Anyway, how are you today? You look much better."

"Yes, no lasting ill effects it seems. You no longer look like a flaming bush."

"That's a relief. I am restored to my persona of a rakishly good-looking cad."

"Well that's one way to put it." Elaine gave him an old-fashioned look. "Thanks again for rescuing me, and thank what's-his-name from the commissary too when you see him next. He must have taken a risk getting involved in helping me. Talking of whom, have you got a smoke?"

Joe handed her the tobacco packet. "Try rolling one again. You need the practice."

Elaine sat on the bench and managed a passable roll-up.

"So," Joe said, leaning over to give Elaine a light. "Do you reckon Hamish is trying to dig his way out?"

"I doubt it. We were talking in the media room this morning. It turns out he's got nothing to go back out for, so that wouldn't make sense."

"OK, so if he's not about to start tunnelling, what is he up to? The way I see it, there are only two other reasons people dig. Either to put something in the ground or to remove something from it, right?"

Elaine thought about it. "Yes, I suppose so. But I don't see where you're going with this, Joe. Are you implying that

Hamish wants to bury something?"

"Sure, he probably murdered your pal Dorothy and is trying to get rid of the body. Oh, come on, Elaine! There's no need to look so outraged. It was a joke. As I told you a couple of days ago, I often see him pacing about behind our block and counting his steps. Now he's trying to get tools for digging. Doesn't that seem more like he wants to excavate something than to bury something?"

"Yes, you're right, that seems more logical. But what?"

"What do you think?" Joe asked. "You know him better than I do."

"Maybe something he left here when he moved out. He stayed here for a while when he was a student, and he told me that was over twenty years ago, so whatever it is would have to be pretty durable to have lasted that long in the ground. Metal, maybe? Coins?"

"Could be, I suppose," Joe said. "Money would certainly be useful to him now. He couldn't even raise the price of an Irn Bru from the commissary yesterday. But what student would bury money in the grounds of their hall of residence? They'd be too busy spending it."

"True," Elaine said, remembering her own student days. "Shall I just ask him, then?""

"Wait a bit," Joe replied. "I want to show you some proof first." I think it'll convince you."

"Good, if you've got proof, show me it."

"It's not here," Joe said. "You know that little patch of mature trees between your block and mine? Good, so do you think you can get there on your own without turning into a butterfly on the way? It's straight ahead down that path. I'll catch you up there in ten minutes or so. Hide behind a tree and I'll be sure to find you."

As Elaine walked along the path, the sun came out and she had a brief reprise of the peace and connectedness she'd experienced before Ashley's Mickey Finn had felled her. She hummed to herself quietly as she walked. It was a while before she identified what it was she was humming – Bob Marley's *Three Little Birds*. It was highly unlikely that 'every little thing was gonna be all right', but what the hell? The sun was shining and Joe made her laugh. Better still, he erased the feeling of being invisible that had haunted her for the last ten years.

Joe caught up with her not long after she'd reached the little cluster of trees. "I didn't see any staff on the way down. What about you?"

Elaine shook her head. "Me neither. Actually, I think they've got a staffing problem at the moment. I overheard the Facility Administrator talking about it on the phone yesterday, before Ashley whisked me away. She was getting pretty shirty with someone"

"So the Lagerkommandant was stressed, was she? That's good to know. OK, come with me." Joe wheeled himself towards the line of blocks where he stayed, then turned to follow a route over a lawn parallel to the blocks, but behind them. "It's lucky it hasn't rained for a while – the ground is hard and it makes it easier to wheel the chair." He paused in line with a window. "That's my room there, second from the end. OK, I need you to count your steps now. And take strides that are a little bit longer than your normal ones. Yes, that's good. Thirty like that should do it … OK, good. Now turn, we're going to go at right angles now, towards the west. Let's try fifty steps in this direction. No, don't get too enthusiastic, Elaine. I don't want you getting ahead of me."

Elaine stopped abruptly and glared at him. "Don't be so bloody controlling, Joe."

"There's an electric fence over there, but you probably can't see it from here. We don't want you striding on ahead and walking into it by accident."

"Why? Would it short out, like the other night?" Elaine asked, starting to walk again, but more slowly.

"Who knows? It could just be a pulse fence that gives a gentle shock, or it could be a lethal one. Not something to find out by trial and error."

"God, no! But how do you know it's electrified if you haven't touched it?" Elaine was walking still, looking at her feet as she did so.

"There's a warning sign on it, but it could be fake, of course. I expect you can't see that either, though."

"Nope," Elaine said. "Not unless you show me exactly where to look. Are you still counting?"

"Bugger, I lost count during your Q and A session."

"Lucky I didn't then, eh?" Elaine said, and stopped four paces later. "That's fifty from when we turned. What now?"

Joe looked around him, his gaze sweeping the grass. "Hey, well done! We fell a bit short on the first leg, but there it is." He wheeled his chair about five metres further and pointed at the ground. Elaine followed. Their ends shallowly embedded in the dry earth, a plastic knife and fork from the canteen stood crossed over each other like crossbones on a pirate flag.

"X marks the spot!" Elaine laughed.

"Yes, a little puerile, but that is Hamish's mark. Do you

believe me now?"

"I didn't entirely disbelieve you before, but with your track record …," Elaine said. "OK, I'll quiz him about it tonight at dinner and I'll update you tomorrow whenever our paths cross. See you around, Joe." Elaine winked and headed towards her unit.

Chapter 13

Friday 13 April

Elaine got up early, intending to find Joe as soon as possible and pass on what Hamish had told her the previous evening. As she was pulling on her jeans, she heard the sound of vacuuming from the floor above and realised she'd need to stick around and prevent the cleaner from entering her room. She paced about her room impatiently, too excited to begin work on the Goya copy she planned as a partner to her Manet drawing.

Finally, the door of her unit banged and footsteps went briskly up the corridor. Elaine sauntered towards the kitchen and intercepted the cleaner.

"Oh hello, you're early this week," Elaine said.

"Hello, there. Yes, I'm on an earlier shift today. Look, since you're here, would you mind helping me with the old lady again? You know, explain why I'm moving her and the chair to the other room. I can't face her getting irritable with me."

"Of course, no problem. And I can vacuum my own room again this week."

"There's no need, really. My shift's only just started so I'm not tired yet."

"Honestly, I'm happy to. To tell you the truth, I'm so bored in here I'm glad to have something to do!"

"Really?" the cleaner said. "Well, if you put it that way why not? If I was ending it all I'd put my feet up and do nothing, but we're all different, I suppose."

By the time the cleaner had finished the other rooms and handed the vacuum over, Elaine had missed breakfast. The dining hall was locked, Joe was not at the seating area, and Hamish was not in the media room. She logged on and checked her email.

Hi Mum,

You can't imagine how relieved I was to hear from you! I'm really sorry the phone and the internet were cut off, but you really should have told me sooner. I wouldn't have panicked if I'd realised you were relying on the internet café to keep in touch with me.

Anyway, I thought about what you said about living costs, and have booked to fly back on the 1st of May. It's a London flight, and gets in quite late, so I'll spend the night at Maria's flat in Islington, then get a train north the following day.

The Australian girls have left for Rome now, so I'm moving into a dormitory – it's cheaper and I expect I'll meet lots of other people that way.

Try and get round to the internet place every couple of days, or I'll start to worry again!

Love,

Alexandra

Alexandra sounded polite but chilly; it seemed she'd bought the lie about the unpaid phone bill, but was hurt about being told to extend her visit. Elaine would need a good reply to this message but she needed time to think of one.

She used the computer's calendar to calculate the days. Her ID card showed 020, which meant she would Exit in twenty days, on the third of May. How ironic – the date commemorated by the Goya painting. Or did it mean she had twenty days left to wait, and would Exit on the day after that? She'd have to check with the admin office. Either way, it was still too late to have the deed done before Alexandra got home. Elaine put her head in her hands and sighed.

Somebody knocked on the open door of the media room. Elaine looked up and saw a figure standing in the doorway.

"Excuse me. Are you Elaine, by any chance?" the stranger said.

Elaine nodded, and the figure advanced towards Elaine. It turned out to be a thin, slightly stooped man in a dark suit. "My housemate asked me to give you a message. His name's Hamish."

"Thank you. What's up?"

"He's indisposed. It's a food allergy apparently – nuts in the curry last night," the man said.

"Oh, no, poor thing! Is it serious? Shall I come and see him?"

"No, I don't think so. Apparently he's got his own medicines. He told me you shouldn't worry and he'll be back on his feet tomorrow."

"I see. Well, thanks for letting me know."

The man was leaving, but stopped again in the doorway.

"Oh, and he asked you to watch the X-factor and tell him about the episode tomorrow."

"The X-Factor?"

"Yes, I believe it's a TV programme." The man turned and left.

Elaine Googled "X-Factor" and discovered it was some kind of music reality show. It didn't look like Hamish's kind of thing and they had certainly never watched it together. She needed to talk to Joe more than ever now. Elaine logged off and went to look for him.

+++

It was nearly three p.m. before she found Joe at the potting shed. "Where have you been all day? I've been looking for you. I even thought of coming and tapping on your window, but there were a lot of guards milling about your section this morning."

"Yes, there was a fight in the women's block apparently. The victim has been carted off to the hospital block with a busted face, and the perpetrator has been taken we know not where," Joe said.

"Wow! That's not good. What was the fight about?"

"I'm not sure. Some say it was about a man; others say it was over the last sausage on the breakfast trolley."

"Wow, it all comes down to sausages, sooner or later," said Elaine, laughing. "Well, the attacker may not be the only person who's disappeared. Hamish seems to be missing too."

Joe grinned. "Excellent news! We can split his loot between us. Did you find out last night what it is?"

"Yep, hash, or maybe weed."

"What, you're telling me he buried hash in the lawn twenty years ago and he thinks it'll be worth digging up and smoking now? He's mental."

"Not that long ago, in fact. Only five years. And it wasn't he who hid it."

"OK, tell all."

"Right, some of this is me reading between the lines. Hamish is a bit cagey about some aspects of his past." Joe was drumming his fingers on one knee impatiently, so Elaine got on with her story. "Anyway, it seems he had a computer buddy who studied at Inverdour and was living in the halls here. Both of them were short of money so they cooked up a scam. They hacked into the University's computer and sold fake degrees or upped people's grades, as I understand it. Hamish's share went to pay the care home bills for his Mum, who had gambled her savings away. Everything went well for about a year, but then they were traced. Hamish was arrested first, but he got a message to his mate in time for him to get rid of some evidence and the stash of dope he had in his room. He's the one who buried the stuff here."

"Wow! Were they sent down?"

"I think Hamish may have spent a few months in jail. I don't know about the other guy."

"And what about this alleged accomplice?" Joe asked. "Why didn't he come back and retrieve his stash?"

"Apparently he tried to, but the University had closed by then, and extensive construction work was going on, presumably to convert it to an exit facility. He couldn't get in to the site."

Joe didn't seem convinced. He combed his fingers through his hair absent-mindedly a few times before he spoke. "So you're saying that Hamish has deliberately checked himself into a suicide camp in order to smoke some five year-old dope? If that's the case, he's completely deranged."

"No, that's not possible," Elaine said, "you're not told which facility you're going to when you sign the papers. He came in because he's broke, like me, and you too, of course. He only figured out where he was after he'd got here. Then when I showed up, he was able to email his friend and get the coordinates to look for the stash."

"Why didn't he just email his friend directly?"

"He doesn't have internet privileges, because of the hacking offence."

"I see. At last a bit of the story that sounds plausible."

Elaine was disappointed. She'd thought Joe would be as excited about the prospect of smoking some weed as she was. "Well, it all seemed to make sense when Hamish told me it last night."

"And now the great man himself has disappeared, you say?"

Elaine explained the visitation she'd had in the media room that morning, but Joe wasn't impressed with that story either. "Right, so Hamish hasn't disappeared at all. He's merely confined to his room with Botox lips or a nasty dose of the shits. Your imagination is running riot, Elaine."

"Hamish never said anything to me about having food allergies."

"Why should he? But when you were out of it the other day he told me that he carries various remedies with him for his allergies. That's where the phosphorus he put in your concoction came from."

"OK, then what do you make of the nonsense about watching the X-Factor?"

"Think, Elaine. Imagine you're an aging computer nerd and weed fiend and you have the soul of a seven year old who likes secret codes and pirate stories."

"Of course. X marks the spot. He sent a message for me to watch the X-factor, so he wants us … me … to keep an eye on the stash."

"Exactly. But I think I'm better placed to do that, seeing as it's visible from my window," Joe said. "It's lucky the guards confined their presence to the front of the blocks this morning. But I think we should get rid of that bloody stupid marker before someone else does spot it. I'm pretty sure I could find the place again without the markers. If only I had some kind of tool to dig it out with."

"Well, yeah, that's obvious, Joe. That's what's prevented Hamish from digging it up so far. But there's nothing portable and metal in the place, not even a butter knife. Plastic plates, plastic cutlery, furniture bolted to the floors and walls. I wonder why?"

"Presumably to prevent serious attacks on the staff? Or maybe to stop people topping themselves in a nasty, messy fashion before the staff get round to offing them cleanly?"

"Well, thanks, Joe. I can always count on you for a spot of black humour."

They sat in silence for a while, Elaine fiddling with one of the buttons on her jacket. "Have you finished the tobacco?" she asked finally.

"No, I have not quite finished my tobacco. I've got just about enough to see me through to tomorrow."

"Right. Sorry, forget I asked. Listen, I was thinking – there are ping pong bats in the games room," Elaine said. "Do you think you could dig with them?"

"Only if the ground was wet and very soft, but it's really hard and dry now. You saw that yesterday. Leave it to me. I'll run the chair over the plastic cutlery a couple of times. That should crush it but will still mark the place. If anyone else sees it, they'll probably just assume it's litter."

The plan didn't sound great to Elaine, but she couldn't think of anything better at present. Joe and she sat in silence while he rolled a cigarette. Elaine suddenly felt deflated and anxious.

"I think I'll head back to my unit now."

"So soon? That's a pity," Joe said, taking a long drag, visibly relaxing as he exhaled.

"I'm in a funny mood. I was excited to tell you about the hash this morning, but then things went all wrong. Hanging about to keep the cleaner out, that weird man who said he was Hamish's housemate, the email from Alexandra, the fight in your block, you not believing Hamish's story. Then there's the business with Miss Latimer being defrauded, and Dorothy is still missing. Plus I still haven't got any bloody coffee and I seem to have acquired a nicotine addiction." Elaine could hear her voice rising and felt she was acting like a petulant child.

"I don't know about half of those things." Joe spoke mildly. "Do you want to talk to me about them?"

"I will, but not now. No. I want them to not be happening. I want a coffee and a cigarette and to move towards my Exit in swift, ignorant bliss. My head is spinning. Some drawing will calm me down."

Elaine got to her feet and looked at Joe. She was surprised to see that he looked genuinely disappointed. On an impulse, she bent over, took his face between her hands and kissed him full on the lips. It lasted no more than two seconds and he didn't respond. Elaine pulled away, shocked by her own impetuosity.

Joe stared at her, one eyebrow raised. "Mixed messages, my dear Elaine. What's going on?"

"Mixed feelings, Joe, I guess that's the problem. I'll see you tomorrow, OK? In the morning?"

"I'll try."

Chapter 14

Saturday 14 April

Elaine found Hamish in the dining hall the next morning with a plate heaped with scrambled egg, bacon and sausage in front of him.

"Hi Hamish! Are you feeling better?"

"Much better, thanks. I won't be trying Exit Facility curry again in a while, though."

"Yes, nut allergy, your housemate said. Is it severe?"

"No, it wasn't anaphylaxis. Just a bit of a rash and an upset stomach. I'm pretty used to it."

"Well go easy on the bacon and sausages; they're quite fatty." Elaine said. She glanced round the dining hall to see if the stranger from yesterday was in there, but couldn't see him. She dropped her voice anyway. "So who was the guy in the suit? I thought he might be staff at first, and didn't really trust him. And why did you send him?"

"Firstly, I didn't want you to worry and assume I'd gone missing, like Dorothy. I thought you might go to the admin staff and get in trouble again." Hamish lowered his voice too. "Secondly, because of you-know-what. You did get the X-factor reference, didn't you?"

"Of course, I got it instantly," Elaine said. Hamish looked somewhat disappointed so she covered her lie with a compliment. "But it was a clever clue. And, as far as I know, the stash is still safe. Joe's keeping an eye on it. So who's the guy?"

"That's Roland. He joined my unit a couple of days ago. He seems OK, as far as ex-civil servants go."

"A bit po-faced, perhaps?" Elaine suggested.

"I think he's depressed," Hamish said. "He wasn't expecting a delay, and you know how that affects you. I was down too, until I got to know you."

"Oh, thanks, Hamish. That's really sweet." Elaine leant across the table and patted the back of his hand. Hamish turned pink, rapidly forked more sausage into his mouth, and then choked on it. Elaine jumped to her feet and thumped him between the shoulder blades. Hamish took a sip of a water and neatly placed his cutlery on his plate.

"Defeated?" asked Elaine. Hamish nodded. "Come on, let's get some fresh air."

Elaine and Hamish walked round the central building to the seating area. To Elaine's embarrassment, Joe was there, parked beside a bench. He nodded at Elaine, who sat down at the farther end of the bench, trying to appear nonchalant and leaving Hamish to occupy the middle position. Elaine closed her eyes and half-listened as the two men spoke in quiet voices.

"There's a loose extractor fan grille in my kitchen that might do for digging," Hamish said. "But I'm not sure it would be rigid enough. It all depends on the condition of the ground."

"That's what I told Elaine," Joe replied. "What we need is something solid and metal. Or a lot of rain."

"Don't jinx the weather, guys," Elaine said, opening her eyes. "I like the sunshine."

"Yes, but ..." A spasm crossed Hamish's face and he clutched at his abdomen. "Oh, dear, I think, ehm, maybe you were right about the food, Elaine. I'll catch you later."

Hamish got up and walked away with a short, rapid, splay-legged gait. Elaine turned to Joe and found him laughing so hard that his chair was rocking backwards and forwards on the paving slabs.

"Have you no pity?" she said, trying to look stern, but the corners of her mouth crept up despite herself.

"None at all," said Joe. "Or maybe I do, for some people. Close your eyes and hold out your hands." Elaine shuffled along the bench, shut her eyes and cupped her hands, feeling mildly apprehensive. Once she opened her eyes again she found she was holding a roll-up and a stick-shaped sachet of Nescafé .

"Wow! Thank you, Joe. Just what I wanted!" Elaine grinned broadly.

"See, I took pity on a poor helpless addict. There's more where those came from ... if you behave yourself." Joe pulled a lighter out of his pocket, but lit it rather than handing it to Elaine, forcing her to lean in close to him to light the roll-up. As she did so he spoke in her ear. "Oh, and you don't need to give me a thank-you kiss. We're in public."

Elaine decided to let the comment pass and tucked the coffee sachet safely in her pocket.

Joe broke the silence first. "So what are we going to play at today, seeing as how we can't get our hands on Hamish's loot?"

"Actually, I have an invitation for you, if you're interested. I was telling Miss Latimer about you and she said I should ask you round for tea with her."

"Is that the charming but demented old bat who lives in your unit?" Joe said. "I know you're fond of her, but why would I want to meet her?"

"I can think of one reason. In addition to tea, she has a very fine bottle of twelve-year old Glenfiddich in her room and she's not averse to sharing it."

"Ah, now you're talking! When are we to visit this admirable old lady?"

"Any time this afternoon, but there is a small price to be paid," said Elaine. "Scrabble. Do you know how to play it?"

"Yes, but I hate it! Wouldn't she be up for a game of poker instead?"

"I doubt it. Just keep your mind on the whisky, then" Elaine said. "And there may be a bit of a logistics problem. She can't reach the desk from her chair, and there's no other furniture, so I perch on the bed and we pass the board between us. If one of us shakes or sneezes, that's the game over. With three of us in there, we could really do with something to put the board on."

"Well, I think I may have just the thing," Joe said. "Can you come round to my window before the tea party and help me carry it?"

+++

Elaine tapped on Joe's window. Almost immediately, it swivelled open and a white plastic bathroom stool was thrust out of the opening. Elaine grabbed it. "See you at the corner of the building" Joe said.

"How did you get this?" Elaine asked when Joe appeared.

"It's probably the only movable piece of furniture in the whole facility."

"My health and hygiene assistant, insists I need this in order to shower safely. I don't actually use it, but at least it's come in handy now."

It worked out perfectly. The bathroom stool supported the Scrabble board, Elaine sat on the bed and Joe's wheelchair just fitted in the remaining space between the bed and the desk. After Assam tea and fruitcake, Miss Latimer served generous portions of Glenfiddich. She and Joe swopped memories of her dear departed fiancé Freddie while Elaine struggled to make words composed entirely of vowels and the letter Q.

Elaine and Joe were on their third whisky when Miss Latimer added C, A, M, E and A to a dangling R. "Two tiles left, and none in the bag," she trilled.

Elaine surveyed her profusion of Es and Os and the recalcitrant Q. "Pass" she said, taking a large swig of her whisky.

"Gotcha!" Joe laid the letters F, U, and K to frame Miss Latimer's C. "And I get a triple word score on that one."

"Joe!" Elaine used her most disapproving tone, cocking her head in Miss Latimer's direction.

"Don't worry," he said, "our lovely hostess has fallen asleep."

Elaine turned to check and saw Miss Latimer in a familiar pose, her head nestled against the wing of her chair, pearls rising and falling slowly on her mint green jumper.

"So she has. Honestly, Joe, how could you come up with all that crap about knowing Freddie and serving in the commandos with him in Korea? It's horrible to be so deceitful."

"Why is it horrible? I told her what she wanted to hear – that Freddie was a good chap, and everyone adored him. I validated her memories and made her happy. Is that such a bad thing to do?"

Elaine shrugged. "I suppose not."

"I mean there are some people who tell different sorts of lies, lies of omission rather than commission. About their age perhaps?"

"My lips are sealed."

"Exactly. Or who tell out-and-out whoppers to their daughters."

"Let's not go there tonight, Joe. We've had a good day."

"True. One for the road? It seems to be getting dark already."

"Why don't we share one? I feel rather tipsy already."

"Fair enough. That cake was good," Joe said, picking a couple of raisins and half of a maraschino cherry off the edge of the silver cake slice and popping them in his mouth. He stopped suddenly and stared at the cake slice. The blade of it was at least five inches long and was made of thick solid silver. He glanced at Elaine. She too was transfixed by this old-fashioned item of cutlery. "Are you thinking what I'm thinking, Elaine?" he asked.

It was starting to rain as they left Elaine's unit. "Why don't you carry the stool on your lap, and I'll push your chair?" she said. "Just this once. We'll get to your block faster."

"No, you can use the stool as an umbrella, and I'll wheel myself."

"It's full of perforations! It's not going to offer much protection from the rain!"

"Tough luck," said Joe. He set off surprisingly rapidly up the path, weaving about in a zig-zag pattern.

"Are you pissed, Joe?" Elaine said, lengthening her stride to keep up with him and meandering onto the wet grass verge as she did so. Your steering's a bit wonky."

"Not as wonky as your walking. You can't even stay on the path!"

"That's because I've got a bathroom stool on my head. It obscures the vision."

"Ah, and there was me thinking you were off to do a spot more tree-hugging or communing with nature."

By the time they reached Joe's block, Elaine's fringe was dripping down her nose and the rain had soaked through her jacket and T-shirt. "Right, I'll go round to the window with this."

"No, it's OK, bring it in. You can wait in my room till the rain goes off. Just don't make a noise. Three of the other rooms in my unit are occupied."

Joe's room was even smaller than Elaine's, but still had a capsule bathroom crammed in the corner of it.

"You're soaked," he said. "Why don't you dry your hair as best you can – there's a towel in the bathroom. And you can borrow this." He stuck a hand in his desk drawer and pulled out a crumpled T-shirt.

"What about you?"

"Only my hair and the thighs of my jeans are wet. Unlike

you, I had the foresight to invest in a flying jacket before taking to the streets."

Elaine took the proffered T-shirt and went into the bathroom to change and towel her hair. When she came out, the wheelchair was parked beside the desk, and Joe was reclining on the bed, naked from the waist up and with a blanket draped over his lower half.

"Hey, you look rather cute with wet hair standing on end. Why don't you take your jeans off as well, come over here, and sit on top of me."

"But I wasn't, I thought you, ehm …"

"Don't be coy with me, Elaine. Like you said, we've had a good day."

"True. OK, then, I'll put the light off."

"Go ahead, if it makes you feel more comfortable."

+++

Elaine collapsed onto Joe's chest, her heart racing. "God, that was amazing. Wow."

"I'm Joe, actually, not God, but thanks anyway. You were pretty good too."

"Pretty good – is that all?"

"Don't fish for compliments. Let's just say I wouldn't say no to a return match. In the meantime, if you could remove your nose from my armpit and roll off me, I might be able to get my breath back."

"Sorry, I'm a bit of a heavyweight these days," Elaine said, rolling into the narrow gap between Joe and the wall.

"Not in the slightest. You're in good shape for ..."

"... for my age?"

"No, I was going to say for a suicidal caffeine addict, actually." Joe turned and kissed Elaine lightly on her forehead. "Now, how about a smoke?" Joe swung his legs off the bed, stood up and leaned over to take the tobacco pouch off the desk. Elaine gasped. Joe froze for a second, then sat down again and put his face in his hands.

"Shit, fuck, I don't believe it. I've blown it."

"You most assuredly have. Start explaining."

Joe stood up again, grabbed the tobacco, sat on the edge of the bed and began rolling a cigarette. "It's all true, apart from the accident," he said.

Elaine snorted. "Yeah, sure."

"It is, honestly. I lost my job and my flat. I sold the car, I didn't crash it. Samantha chucked me out for shagging her friend, that's true too."

"But she didn't abandon you on a tube platform?"

"No, I came home from the pub one day to find my stuff on the pavement and the locks changed. And I ended up living on the streets." Joe shrugged. "I guess I deserved it."

"So, why the wheelchair?"

"I got friendly with a guy called Andy who'd lost his legs when he stood on a landmine in Afghanistan. The chair was his. We used to beg together and he usually did better than me – the wheelchair elicited sympathy."

"Or people clocked you for a lying, deceitful chancer," Elaine said.

"Whatever. When we failed to raise enough money for a night in a shelter we used to sleep in a graveyard. One particularly bitter night in December, Andy failed to make it. I found him dead in his sleeping bag when I woke up." Joe began rolling another cigarette, keeping his eyes averted from Elaine. "Being, as you so charmingly put it, a lying, deceitful chancer, I took the wheelchair, hoping it would lead to better earnings for me too. I was still using it when we were rounded up. Shall we smoke now?"

"Yeah, OK. But where? Don't you have a smoke alarm in the room?"

"A housemate disabled it for me. But I stick my head out of the window to be on the safe side. The same housemate dealt with the window locks. He used to be a good locksmith, but he wasn't quite so lucky when it came to safe-breaking, I'm told."

Elaine wrapped the blanket round herself sarong-style. Joe tilted the window to a horizontal position and they leaned side by side on the window ledge exhaling clouds of smoke out over the lawn. It had stopped raining and a three-quarter moon had risen above the trees. Elaine suddenly started shaking. Joe put an arm round her and pulled her closer to him. "Are you cold? Or In shock? Shit, you're not crying, I hope."

"I'm actually trying not to laugh out loud and wake your housemates. Life is absurd."

"Given the noise you made earlier, they're probably wide awake already. But you know what I like about you, Elaine? You spend a lot of time getting het up about things, but you always see the funny side in the end."

They stubbed their roll-ups out in a small pool of water on

the window ledge and shut the window. "Am I forgiven?" Joe said.

"Not yet. I need time to process deceit of this magnitude."

"No more shagging then?"

"I didn't say that. I've only got eighteen days left in which to make up for lost time."

"Very pragmatic. Put your moral objections on the back burner and focus on the pleasure principle. Which reminds me – these are for you." Joe reached into the desk drawer and offered Elaine two Nescafé sticks.

"Ah, bribery," Elaine said. "Thank you. And don't worry, I won't tell."

"Good, because if you do, at worst I'll be carted off to an unknown destination. At best, I'll be instantly confined to this block, along with my housemates. My meagre chance of survival depends on being able to get out and about and butter up the sympathetic members of staff."

"Yes, I get it," Elaine said. "I think I should go back to my unit now. I wouldn't want to be caught slumbering in your arms when your delightful health and hygiene assistant appears in the morning." She retrieved her jeans and knickers from the floor and put them on under cover of the sheet, then collected her damp T-shirt from the bathroom and wriggled back into it.

Joe got off the bed and hugged Elaine. The top of her head barely reached his chin. "I'm sorry I can't take you back to your unit, but it's past curfew. It's not that dark so you should see OK. Just stick to the path, all right?"

"I'll be fine, Joe. Don't fuss."

"Good, I just don't want you doing a Dorothy and disappearing in the middle of the night. I'd miss you."

Chapter 15

Sunday 15 April

Elaine woke to a beautiful sunny morning. Her Nexus told her it was a Sunday, and her ID card was now showing 018. It was hard to believe she'd been in the facility for nearly two weeks and that, even so, she wasn't even halfway through her wait. A twinge of pain shot through her right hip as she stepped up and into the cubicle bathroom. Obviously there was a price to be paid for indulging in vigorous sex at her age.

After washing and dressing, Elaine checked Dorothy's and Miss Latimer's rooms. Both were empty. If Dorothy had not disappeared, today would have been her Exit day anyway. Miss Latimer presumably was having another outing with her niece. The cake slice still lay where they had left it after the Scrabble game. Elaine picked it up, washed it in her bathroom sink and then hid it, along with the tailor's chalks, under her mattress.

She found Hamish in the dining hall, toying with a bowl of porridge.

"Hamish! I hope you're a bit better now. I've got exciting news for you, plus it rained last night, so the ground should be softer."

Hamish glanced over his shoulder. Nobody was near them but he spoke softly anyway. "Did you find a suitable tool? Something from that potting shed you mentioned?"

"Yes and no. The potting shed was locked, but I happened

upon something else that might do the trick. It's a sturdy metal cake slice. I'll tell you the details later. I'll get some breakfast."

"OK. Oh, you'd better pile your plate. There's a notice on the wall but you may not be able to read it. It says we're getting a self-service buffet lunch today. Apparently it's Easter Sunday, so a lot of staff are off."

"The stingy buggers," Elaine said. "They get a holiday, and we get limp sandwiches for lunch!"

"True, but it could be better for us, Elaine. Not so many guards about."

Elaine had planned to look for Joe immediately after breakfast, but remembered as she was eating that she had still not answered Alexandra's latest email. She spent half an hour in the media room composing another disingenuous message to her daughter and feeling guilty and sad about what she was doing. Still not entirely pleased with her final effort, she hit "Send" anyway, and headed outdoors to clear her head. Hamish followed her.

They walked up to the potting shed together, the smell of drying earth in their noses and the sunshine gentle on their faces.

"Good morning, Hamish," Joe said. "Hope you've got over the upset stomach. And Elaine, good morning. You're looking well, though I think I detect a slight limp – I do hope you haven't been overdoing things." He turned his head towards Elaine and winked exaggeratedly.

"Certainly not. I'm sure the extra exercise I get in this place is doing me a power of good," Elaine said, aware that she was blushing slightly and hoping it would be interpreted as the effect of the sunshine.

"So, where is this cake slice you've found, Elaine?" asked Hamish.

"In my room. I couldn't bring it with me because of the metal detector in the dining hall."

"Right, of course. So can I come round to your room now and collect it?" Hamish said. "I'll try digging around dusk. That should be the safest time."

"No," said Joe. "We're all in this together. It's your friend's stash, but I've been watching over the spot and Elaine found the digging tool. Besides, it's shaping up to be a warm day. The ground could have dried out again by the evening. I say we go and get the stuff now."

Hamish shook his head. "It's going to be pretty obvious that we're up to something. I still think it's better to try when it's getting dark."

"Maybe not," Elaine said. "Listen, didn't you say it's a self-service sandwich type lunch today? Hamish, at lunchtime you can take my ID card and scan it for me at the dining hall, then pick up enough food for the three of us. I'll bring the cake slice and some mugs and water from my kitchen. The three of us can meet up by the markers as if we were just having a picnic in the sunshine. Then …"

"Wonderful idea, Elaine," Joe said. "And I'll bring the champagne and some strawberries and cream."

"Ha, ha, very funny, Joe."

"Actually, it might not be such a bad idea" Hamish said. "When do the people in your blocks go to the dining hall, Joe?"

"We don't. The food is brought to us."

"Oh, I see. And when is that?"

"Whenever the Ts and Vs have been fed and the staff have loaded up the trolleys for us. A bell rings to let us know."

Hamish stroked his beard and then said, "That could work. We eat first, then dig after the bell goes off without fear of attracting attention from people whose rooms overlook that stretch of grass. We'd have to be fast, but let's go for it."

"See, I told you it was a good plan," Elaine said.

+++

The blade of the cake slice slid cleanly and easily into the still slightly damp earth. The third time Hamish inserted it, the tip hit something and stopped with half an inch of blade still above the surface of the grass.

"Yes!" he said, his face pink with excitement. "Got it!"

"Cut it out neatly if you can," said Joe. "We'll need to fill the hole back in after."

Hamish poked the blade into the grass several more times, then cut out a neat rectangle of turf, revealing a Tupperware box sealed with silver duct tape. He prised this out of the ground carefully and replaced the turf.

"Nicely done, Hamish," Elaine said. "Gosh, your friend used a lot of duct tape. How will we get through that?"

"I think the cake slice will manage that too," Joe said. "Stick the end under the tape and ease it off. It's a nice solid piece, that."

"The Tupperware box?"

"Don't be daft, Elaine. I mean the cake slice. It's Danish, Georg Jensen, circa 1950. Quality design."

"How on earth do you know that? "Elaine asked.

"My parents had one. I spent my childhood being dragged round design studios while my parents drooled over Scandinavian and Italian classics."

"Really? That childhood neglect probably accounts for your narcissism nowadays, then."

"Actually, if you had completed your Basic Psychology class, I think you'd find …"

"Stop bickering, you two," Hamish interrupted, "and look at this."

Hamish eased the duct tape off, removed the lid of the box and revealed a clear plastic bag wrapped inside layers of tin foil, and stuffed with what certainly looked like weed. Beside the plastic bag was nestled a metal object that resembled a black cigarette packet with four or five black cigarettes protruding from one end of it.

"Wow, that'll keep us going for a while. I hope it's not gone off," said Elaine.

"Now, that's an interesting object," Joe said.

"The black metal thing? Clearly it's an ironic postmodern cigarette lighter masquerading as a packet of fags. No doubt a classic, and Joe's parents had one prominently displayed on their 1960s Italian glass and chrome coffee table," Elaine said, pleased with her own sarcasm.

"Nope, a long way out," Joe said. "If I'm not mistaken, that's a GPS jammer, circa 2014. I kept one very similar to that in my Lexus for avoiding speed traps."

Hamish shot a surprised look at Joe at the mention of owning a Lexus, but didn't question him on the matter. "Yes,

I think you may be right, Joe. My friend Mark didn't mention it, but it's exactly the kind of device he'd have had. ."

"What does it do?" Elaine asked.

"It blocks GPS signals so that your location can't be traced from your mobile phone, or satnav or …"

"… your electronic tag," said Joe, tapping two fingers above his left ankle.

"Exactly," said Hamish. "But don't get too excited. The battery may have died or corroded in the time it's been buried."

"Can we get on with trying the weed?" Elaine said. "That would be more fun."

Joe scanned the windows of the blocks that overlooked the lawn where they were sitting.

"I think lunch must be over for the 'Is'. We've got a bit of an audience now."

"Where should we go then? That little patch of trees over there? Or back to the potting shed, perhaps?" Elaine suggested.

"Let's go for the shed," Hamish said. "There probably won't be any staff doing gardening on Easter Sunday afternoon. Go ahead you two, I just need to pop behind one of those trees over there. I'll catch you up."

By the time Hamish reached the shed, Joe had already rolled a joint. "Here, Hamish, you can light it. It's your mate's stash after all."

Hamish inhaled cautiously, held his breath and then blew out. He shook his head. "Too old, I think. Was it damp?"

"Nope, perfectly dry."

Elaine tried next, then Joe. They all looked at each other, anticipation tinged with incipient disappointment. It was Hamish's turn again. "Oh well," he said as he exhaled. "At least the quest kept me occupied for a while. It took my mind off you-know-what."

"I guess so," Joe said. "But apart from smoking it ourselves, it could have been a handy medium of exchange."

"What do you mean?" Hamish asked.

"I have a couple of friends among the staff. I might have been able to exchange some of this for other stuff we might need."

"Like that chap from the commissary who helped when Elaine was roofied?" asked Hamish.

"I don't reveal my sources."

"Hamish, don't Bogart!" Elaine said. "Come on, pass the joint. It's my turn."

"Really?" Hamish said, sounding a bit dreamy. "Oh, sorry. You know, I think maybe it's not totally past it. Unlike me." Hamish began to giggle.

"I don't feel anything," Elaine said, exhaling and passing the joint on to Joe.

"No? You're grinning like a Cheshire cat," Joe said.

"So are you."

"Yes, but that's only because you and Hamish look so ridiculous."

Elaine shut her eyes and turned her face up towards the sun, aware that the corners of her mouth were rising. "Well, maybe there's just the tiniest effect," she said.

A couple of joints later, Elaine invented a game in which each person had to hum a song relevant to their current situation and the others would guess the band and supply the lyrics. She kicked off with *Candle in the Wind*. This was voted cheesy and not particularly relevant by both Hamish and Joe, but they all sang as much of it as they could remember n anyway.

Joe followed with *I Just Died in Your Arms Tonight*, which neither Elaine nor Hamish recognised. Once Joe had revealed the words and sung them somewhat tunelessly, Hamish hotly contested its relevance while Joe smirked and Elaine developed a sudden keen interest in a nearby rose bush.

Hamish turned out to have a good ear and a fine tenor singing voice along with a bizarrely wide knowledge of songs that were popular a decade or so before he was born.

"I remember that one," Elaine said as Hamish hummed a jaunty tune. "It's about somebody who's going to be hanged tomorrow, I think."

"That's right," Hamish said. "It's *Tom Dooley* as sung by a band called the Kingston Trio. There's a strange mismatch between the topic and the tune."

"Just what I was thinking," Elaine said. I remember somebody working on our house when I was really small, a joiner, or a plumber, maybe. He used to whistle the tune as he worked and I always thought it was a jolly song. It was ages later that I discovered it was about a hanging. How do you know it?"

"My Mum used to sing hits from the fifties and early sixties when she was doing the ironing. I know songs from those eras better than ones from my own."

"OK, my turn again," Elaine said. "This one's easy, but I think it's relevant."

"*Hotel California* by the Eagles," Joe said almost instantly. "But I contest the relevance. You may be a prisoner of your own device, but I am not. Plus, unlike the character in the song, we will leave, albeit feet first. Anyway, my turn. I've got a good one and I like the message better." Joe hummed the Animals' *We Gotta get Out of This Place*. Hamish and Elaine both got it rapidly and approved his choice.

"Hamish, your turn now," Elaine said. "Why don't you give us another one from your Mum's repertoire of golden oldies?"

Hamish thought for a while, then began humming *Twenty-five Minutes To Go*. Elaine and Joe looked perplexed and shook their heads.

"Really? You don't know it? It's about a hanging again, and the lyrics are pretty chilling. Shall I sing it?"

"Yes, why not? Go for it," Elaine said.

Hamish had been right about the lyrics; the song tracked the course of a countdown to an execution and the condemned man's thoughts as the minutes passed by. Elaine regretted asking to hear it, but she didn't want Hamish to think his singing was bad, so she shut her eyes and tried to conjure up happy memories to offset the images in the song.

The song had reached five minutes before the execution and the prisoner's head was in the noose when a siren suddenly blared, followed by a clamour of excited voices coming from the direction of the Indigents' blocks.

"What the hell's that?" Elaine said. "Do you think someone saw us digging?"

"I doubt it. It would be the Kommandant's style to confront you with that piece of wrongdoing tomorrow, not to set off a siren. It's something far more serious. I'd better go. There'll be a roll call for us." Joe wheeled himself away rapidly.

The siren stopped but the shouting continued, followed by the sound of someone speaking through a megaphone. "Return to your rooms. Return to your rooms now."

"Oh shit! Us too I suppose?" Elaine said.

"Well, I'm not risking being found here, especially with a box of weed and a GPS jammer." Hamish gathered the stuff together and made to leave.

"Have you got somewhere safe to hide it?" Elaine asked.

"I've got an idea. I hope it's safe enough," Hamish said. "Look, you'd better go back to your unit too. And return the cake slice. It's probably safest where it was with the old lady. I'll see you at dinner time in the dining hall, probably."

Elaine walked back to her block, passing the line of units allocated to the Indigents. The blocks were deserted at the front, but as she passed Joe's unit, she glanced towards the lawn behind it. In the distance she thought she could make out a black figure with two orange-clad ones beside it. The guards were gesticulating at each other but the black figure was motionless, slumped but semi-upright, arms outstretched like a crucified Christ without a cross. Elaine hurried on to her block, the euphoria induced by the afternoon sunshine, songs and smoking now totally evaporated and replaced by a feeling of dread.

Miss Latimer was back, but was asleep in her wing chair. Elaine washed and wiped the cake slice and replaced it on the old lady's silver salver. She went back to her own room, put on a jumper and got into her bed and wrapped the thin blanket around herself. She chose a folder of photos from Alexandra's pre-school days and set her tablet to 'slideshow', then cried herself into an uneasy sleep.

Two hours later Elaine pushed on the doors to the vestibule leading to the dining hall, but they were locked. There was a hand-lettered notice in the adjoining pane of glass. Elaine examined the notice sideways on and finally made out some of the words. '…. staff holidays … unforeseen circumstances … unable to serve dinner … –ning'.

Elaine returned to her block. With a bit of luck, perhaps Miss Latimer would have woken up and be in a mood to offer some fruitcake and whisky, along with a game of Scrabble.

Chapter 16

Monday 16 April

The dining hall was unusually busy when Elaine arrived and there was a queue at the counter. A woman she had never seen before asked for everything on the menu and then helped herself to six slices of toast. Hamish slipped into the queue behind Elaine. "Morning Elaine, are you OK?"

"Yes, thanks, Hamish. And you?"

"Yes, no complications, if you know what I mean."

They made their way to a table near the windows and sat down side by side, the more easily to converse privately. "Have you heard anything about yesterday's event?" Elaine asked. "There's no one left in my unit except Miss Latimer, so I haven't had a chance to get any news."

"People in my block are saying that someone tried to break out, but they're confused why anyone would want to do so. They don't know about the existence of the Is, of course."

"I see. And was he or she successful?"

"Er, no." Hamish hesitated. "I believe the poor person got electrocuted on the fence near where we were eating yesterday." Elaine gasped.

"Oh shit. So it is a lethal fence. Joe thought it might be but he wasn't sure."

"We need to speak to him," Hamish said. "He'll know more."

"Yes, but he'll probably be on lockdown again, like after when Dorothy disappeared."

A lugubrious voice behind them interrupted their conversation. "Do you mind if I join you?"

Elaine turned and saw the tall, stooped man who was Hamish's housemate. Hamish gestured for the man to sit down opposite them. "Elaine, I think you've met Roland before, haven't you? Roland, this is Elaine."

"Terrible business about the poor fellow who got fried on the fence, isn't it?" Roland said.

Elaine gagged suddenly, an image of the black-clad figure she'd seen slumped in mid-air yesterday flooding her mind. She spat the piece of bacon she'd been chewing into her napkin and pushed her plate away. "I think a fried breakfast is more than I want today," she said. "I'm going to get some toast and cereal instead."

Hamish and Roland were still discussing the event when she returned.

"… unless it was a suicide attempt. You know Auschwitz prisoners used to hurl themselves onto the electric fences when they couldn't bear the conditions in the camp any longer."

"Yes, I've read that too," Hamish said.

"But why do that when you are in line for a humane and painless Exit in the near future?" Roland continued. "Whether it was a breakout attempt or a suicide, it makes no sense."

"Do you think we could discuss something else?" Elaine said. "This is all rather distressing."

"I do beg your pardon," Roland said. "Most thoughtless of

me. Actually, I have to go now anyway. I have an appointment in the VR room. I tried bungee jumping from the Victoria Falls Bridge yesterday, but I can't say I really enjoyed it. Today I'm going ice-floe hopping with polar bears in the Arctic. I think that'll be much more entertaining."

"That man's a jerk," Elaine said, glaring at Roland's departing back. "I bet he used to be a climate change sceptic. And how come he gets to use the VR room as soon as he arrives here?"

"Probably some special privilege due to his old civil service connections," Hamish said. "Anyway, he was quite interesting about the fences. It seems he used to have something to do with site security for MoD installations, and he's astonished that they haven't put covert fences all round this facility. He reckons …"

"Could we just stay off the subject of fences for today, please, Hamish?"

"I'm sorry, Elaine, but I can't. I have to show you something. Let's go to the seating area when we're finished with breakfast."

Hamish and Elaine sat together on one of the benches and Hamish looked round to check that nobody was observing them. "Remember I went behind a tree to answer a call of nature yesterday? Well, I found these on the ground in that little thicket when I was there. I didn't show you them yesterday because we were all feeling happy and I didn't want to spoil the atmosphere." Hamish reached into his pocket, pulled out a pair of glasses and handed them to Elaine. The frame, slightly bent, was made of wire and the round lenses were so thick they looked like the bottoms of bottles. "Do these look like Dorothy's?"

Elaine turned them over in her hands. "Oh God, I'm pretty sure these are hers, Hamish. I wonder how they ended up in that little wood."

"Well, if I remember correctly," Hamish said, "the night she went missing there was a very bright full moon. With her sight, she might have thought it was daylight and decided to go out for a walk. Maybe she bumped into a tree, knocked off her glasses and ..."

"... and blundered into the electric fence by mistake?" Elaine said. "Oh no, that's a horrible possibility." She thought back to the events of that night. She'd got drunk with Joe and watched the sunset, and gone to bed early. Then she'd woken up in the middle of the night and the power had gone off. And, yes, there had been a really bright moon, so bright that the light had kept her awake for several hours afterwards. Hamish's theory was plausible. But if that was the case, then it was all her fault.

"This is awful, Hamish! I'm to blame. If I hadn't taken her out for a walk the previous day, this wouldn't have happened."

Elaine was distractedly winding the glasses round in her hands, causing the wire frame to bend even more. Hamish reached over and took them back from her. "What are you talking about, Elaine?"

"Dorothy had never been for a walk in the grounds until I took her; she thought it was forbidden. So if I hadn't put the idea in her head, she wouldn't have gone wandering in the middle of the night and ended up electrocuting herself. This is terrible. I as good as murdered her." Elaine's chest was heaving and she could feel a panic attack coming on.

"Breathe, Elaine. Try and think logically. Of course you

didn't murder her. You didn't drag the poor woman from her bed and throw her against an electric fence."

"I might as well have done. Dorothy would have stayed indoors if I hadn't put the idea of the outside world into her head."

"Look, it's only a theory. It might not have happened like that at all. She might have felt unwell and gone looking for help and lost her way or something. We don't know that she walked into the fence; it could have been a deer like I said before. Oh, Elaine, please calm down. Breathe…. Here, try these. Put them under your tongue and let them dissolve." Hamish extracted two little white pills from a small brown bottle in his jacket pocket, and offered them to Elaine. "Aconite. It's a homoeopathic remedy for shock and panic."

An orange-clad figure was striding across the grass towards the paved seating area. "What's going on here?" he shouted. Elaine recognised Brendan's voice and the familiar movement of his right hand towards his Taser pocket.

"Everything's fine," Hamish said. "The lady here is just feeling a little emotional. There have been rumours about strange events yesterday. Perhaps you could set her mind at ease about what went on?"

"Nope. It's more than my job's worth to talk to clients about incidents. It was just a small security blip. Oh, it's you, Elaine. Are you alright?"

"I'm fine, thank you, Brendan."

"Don't need a visit to the hospital block?"

"No, I'm absolutely fine, thanks, I assure you."

"You handled that well, Hamish," Elaine said after Brendan had departed. "And you're a dab hand with the home remedies, too. I feel a bit calmer. Still guilty as hell, but calmer."

"Please don't start beating yourself up again," said Hamish. "Whatever happened, Dorothy would have found Closure by now anyway, wouldn't she?"

"We don't need the velvet gloves, Hamish. You're right, poor Dorothy would have died by now come what may. That's it. She's fucking dead and she would be no matter what happened or didn't happen that night. Fuck it all. Let's go to the media room."

+++

"Any word from Alexandra?" Hamish asked, interrupting Elaine's twelfth game of Spider Solitaire that afternoon. As Elaine had expected, there had been no sign of Joe all day and time had dragged by slowly.

"No, I think she's angry with me, so she'll punish me by staying out of contact for a while."

"May I ask why?"

"Well, I've been trying to put off her return to the UK so that she doesn't get here before I Exit. She doesn't know that, so she'll think I'm not in a hurry to see her even though we haven't seen each other for over three years. So she's probably feeling hurt."

"I still don't understand."

"Oh, come off it, Hamish. You're the Mummy's boy – surely you would have felt upset if your mother appeared not to want to see you."

"That was an unnecessary jibe." Hamish's voice sounded small and choked.

A wave of guilt washed over Elaine for the second time that day. "You're right. I'm sorry, Hamish. I meant you were a devoted son, but that was a stupid way to put it. I apologise. You're always kind and thoughtful with me, and I'm just a snappy old cow."

Hamish sniffed loudly. "OK, apology accepted. You're under stress. But what I meant was, what does either of you gain by your not seeing Alexandra before you go? She'll be horribly confused and upset when she gets home and you aren't there. Won't she go looking for you?"

"I've left her a very long letter explaining everything but, you're right, I don't want her to come looking for me and try to stop my Exit."

Hamish cleared his throat, made as if to speak, then stopped. Elaine looked at him questioningly, and he started again. "Ehm, didn't you read the small print when you signed the agreement, Elaine?"

"With my eyesight?"

"As a partially-sighted person you should have been given a state-paid lawyer to talk you through the agreement in detail."

"You seem to know a lot about this, Hamish."

"Well, I researched it all thoroughly before I came in. It's not a decision to be taken lightly."

"So what did I miss?"

"There is no opt-out clause," Hamish said. "Once you've signed, you can't change your mind, so your daughter wouldn't be able to alter your fate in any way at this stage."

Elaine considered this unexpected piece of information.

"Even if she or I happened to win a fortune on the lottery in the meantime?"

"That's correct. In theory, for Voluntaries, there should be a maximum of seventy-two hours between Intake to the Facility and Closure, so little time for second thoughts. It's this bloody delay that makes the lack of an opt-out clause so awful."

Both Hamish and Elaine sat in silence for a while, lost in their own thoughts. Elaine spoke first. "Talking of the delay, I wonder why there are so many Ts coming in and clogging up the system at the moment? I overheard the Facility Administrator saying something about an accident. Actually, another accident is what she said."

"Roland's got a take on that."

"You're getting very chummy with Roland."

"He likes the sound of his own voice. And some of the things he says are quite interesting. He seems to feel he's no longer bound by the Official Secrets Act now that his only companions are slated for imminent Exit."

"I see."

"So, you know they began decommissioning the old nuclear subs some months ago." Elaine shook her head. "Oh, I forgot you don't follow the news. Well, apparently there was a huge radiation leak and hundreds of people in the vicinity were poisoned. The accident wasn't reported in the news, but the health effects are showing up now. Hence the spike in terminal cases." Hamish glanced at Elaine, "Oh no, you look distressed again, Elaine. I shouldn't have told you that. Or about the lack of an opt-out clause. I'm sorry."

"It's OK. It's all just a bit of a bombshell. I think I'll go for a long walk and then maybe do some drawing."

"Well, stay away from the boundaries and keep to paths. There may be other kinds of fences and security systems that you won't be able to see. By the way, could you bring your tablet tomorrow morning? There's some stuff I'd like to research. And don't worry, we'll have some more weed and songs before we go. We just need to wait until the staff have calmed down a bit."

"Thanks, Hamish. I'm sure we will."

Elaine walked twice round all the paths she knew, circling in an anti-clockwise direction. The north and south ends of the Indigents' blocks were cordoned off with black and yellow striped barrier tape, and there were guards outside all the entrances. On her second circuit, she was stopped and her ID checked by a guard she didn't know, and she was told to return to her own block. No chance of even exchanging a couple of words with Joe, or setting up a meeting for the next day, then.

She pushed open the door of her own unit and found Miss Latimer in the corridor, knocking on Dorothy's door. "Oh, hello, dear, there you are! Where is everybody today? I can't find Daphne, or Gladys, or the lady who stays in this room."

"I'm afraid they've all gone," Elaine explained. "There's only you and me here now."

"Gone out? Where to?"

"No, gone, as in passed away."

"Oh, dear, that's sad. So who will come to my party?" Miss Latimer asked. "You see, it's my birthday today. I'd forgotten all about it, but Betty dropped in with sherry and a cake for me. She couldn't stay because she's working, so I thought I'd invite you and the other ladies."

"Happy birthday, Miss Latimer. Don't worry, I'm sure you and I can have a nice time together," Elaine said. "Shall I put the kettle on for some tea?"

"Good idea. Oh, I know, what about your beau? That nice young man who was in Freddie's regiment. Why don't you invite him?"

"Joe? Oh, I'm afraid he's away on business."

"That's a pity; he was very charming the other day. Well, I'm sure we'll manage. Off you go and make the tea, then, dear."

Elaine sipped Assam tea and expensive dry sherry, ate four chunks of Black Forest gateau and expressed regular appreciation of the florid card from Betty that read '91 today! Happy Birthday, Auntie Vee, with love from your little Betty'. She dredged her memory for jokes and puns that were innocent enough to tell to Miss Latimer and prompted the old lady to reminisce about her school days, her teacher training college and the cruises she'd taken to Norway after her retirement.

Around seven thirty p.m., Miss Latimer, pink-cheeked, animated and slightly tipsy, suddenly fell asleep mid-sentence. Elaine cleared up the plates and glasses and washed them in the kitchen, wondering to herself at which point in her life she had fallen down a rabbit hole and failed to notice the fact. Wired on sherry and sugar, she decided to skip dinner and went to her room to complete work on her copy of Goya's *The Third of May*.

Chapter 17

Tuesday 17 April

Elaine woke up suddenly, thinking she'd heard a sound from outside, but whatever it had been was now drowned out by the tune of *Twenty-Five Minutes To Go* repeating like a broken record in her head. Then she caught the external sound again – someone was tapping on her window. She twitched the curtain back and saw a hand reaching up past a familiar silver head of hair. She pushed the window open to its full extent of two inches.

"At last! Come round to the front door and let me in, Elaine."

She threw a jumper on over her pyjamas and did as instructed.

"Holy shit, Elaine, you're hard to wake up! It's nearly eleven. They lifted the lockdown after breakfast, so I went to look for you. Hamish said he hadn't seen you this morning and you hadn't been at dinner last night."

Elaine held the door to her room open and Joe rolled the chair inside. He parked it against the door, got out of it and hugged Elaine. "You're OK, then? What happened?" Joe asked.

"Nothing. I just had this massive sugar high after an impromptu birthday party for Miss Latimer, so I completed the *Third of May*, by which time it was quite late. Then I had an equally big sugar slump, and a slight hangover, and I zonked out."

Joe looked round the room, taking in the drawings on the

walls. "I know that picture," he said, indicating Elaine's version of Manet's *The Execution of Maximilian*. "I sometimes went into the National Gallery at lunchtime to look at it. How come there's a copy of it on your wall? Did you qualify for a luxury room?"

"No, I drew it. And the other one. That's a copy of the Goya painting that inspired the Manet one."

Joe examined both of Elaine's drawings more closely. "They're very good, I must admit. But are you out of your mind, drawing on the walls?"

"On the contrary, it's keeping me sane."

"Haven't the staff complained?"

"I keep the cleaner out of my room, so no one will find out."

Joe sat down on Elaine's bed. He looked at her intently, raising both eyebrows and shaking his head. "You are astonishingly lacking in any sense of self-preservation, Elaine. The Facility Administrator will find out sooner or later, and you'll be crucified for it. They took all the Is' rooms apart looking for anything illegal after Sunday's event. The Vs will be next."

Elaine seized the opening he had offered. "So was it an attempted breakout? Who was it?"

"Some guy from Birmingham I barely knew. Apparently he thought it was a pulse fence and if he moved fast enough he could get over it and away with only a minor shock. Turned out it's a lethal one. Poor, deluded bugger."

"God, that's horrible. Poor man. Definitely not a suicide attempt, then."

Joe exhaled loudly. "No, Elaine. We leave that nonsense to

the Vs. We Indigents are doing the best we can to survive in hideous circumstances."

Elaine sat down on the bed beside him. "Sorry, Joe. It was just a theory."

"Hamish, you and I were seen on the lawn together," Joe continued, "and some people told the guards. In fact, that gave me an alibi for some of the time leading up to the escape attempt, but I've been worried that you and Hamish might have got into trouble. Has anything been said to you?"

"Not so far. What about the hole in the lawn? Were you asked about that?"

"Fortunately not. They cordoned off the whole lawn at the back, but all the searching was focussed on the units, as far as I know."

"Thank goodness. I can't think of a plausible excuse for that. What are you doing, Joe?"

Joe had got off the bed and was standing on his right leg, with his hands on his waist, while raising and lowering his left leg out to the side. "Leg exercises, darling, what's it look like? These are lateral leg lifts. When I'm alone, I also do squats and lunges to pass the time and prevent my leg muscles from atrophying by sitting in the chair all day. I'm hoping I'll need strong legs for getting the hell out of here sometime soon."

"Mmmm," said Elaine, pushing thoughts of Joe's potential escape to the back of her mind and giving him the once-over. "Well, it seems to be working. You're in good shape for … "

"… for a lying, deceitful chancer?"

"Indeed." Elaine laughed. "And talking of exercise, do you think it would be safe for you to stay here a bit longer?"

"Possibly not, but I'll risk it." Joe glanced at Elaine's ID card, which was lying on her desk. "You've only got sixteen days to go."

"Exactly," Elaine said, pulling her jumper and pyjama top off. "So let's not waste time."

+++

Intermittent drops of rain were sliding down the glass walls of the central building as Hamish and Elaine left the dining hall after lunch. She collected her jacket from a hook in the vestibule, checked that the Nexus was still safely in the pocket and slung the jacket round her shoulders. As they left the building and circled anti-clockwise towards the door for the media room, the sky darkened and black clouds moved in from the east.

"I saw Joe earlier," Elaine said. "He asked if you could bring the GPS jammer for him to try out, and maybe a bit of the weed. He thinks he may be able to exchange that for a new battery if it's needed."

"Why would he do that? He seems to have a pretty wide range of movement enabled on his tag."

"He reckons there'll be a security clampdown after Sunday's accident, so he wants to be prepared to block anything that might curtail his movement."

A flash of sheet lightning lit up the eastern horizon, shortly followed by a peal of thunder and a downpour of rain. "Run for it, or we'll get soaked!" Hamish said. They entered the media room damp and breathless. It was empty as usual. "What a pity the nice, sunny weather has gone," Elaine said.

"Yes, but some heavy rain might help to cover up any evidence of the hole in the grass. I've been worrying about that."

"Me too. But Joe says he and the other Indigents were searched and questioned thoroughly but that wasn't mentioned." Elaine hung her wet jacket over the back of a chair and gave the tablet to Hamish. "Let me just see if there are any messages from Alexandra, then you can have this and use my internet time." Elaine logged into her email account, but there was still nothing back from her daughter. She fired off a quick message:

> Hi darling,
>
> I hope you are still enjoying Goa. No big changes here.
>
> I miss you a lot and am really looking forward to seeing you on the 2nd of May when you get back.
>
> Drop me a line when you have time.
>
> Lots of love,
>
> Mum xxxxx

"All yours, Hamish."

"Thanks. What are you going to do? You must be bored with playing Spider Solitaire."

"A bit, yes, but it passes the time. I'll play until the rain goes off. Then maybe have a walk."

It rained steadily and heavily throughout the afternoon. Around four o'clock Elaine's vision was blurring from staring at cards on a computer screen. She stood up and began to pace around the media room. "I feel like I'm trapped in here. Inside a trap within a trap. Could you look up what's on the television for me, Hamish?"

"Sure. I'll see what I can find, but they haven't got many channels in here, I'm afraid. What sort of thing do you like?"

"I don't know; I've never had a TV. But that programme on art you found for me the other day was OK."

Hamish searched while Elaine strode around the room to stretch her legs. At least her hip wasn't hurting today, that was good.

"I can't find anything about art on at the moment," Hamish said, "but you could see the next episode of the programme you liked on catch up. That means you'll have to watch on your monitor, not on the big TV screen. Will that do?"

"That's fine. Many thanks, Hamish."

The programme opened with a review of a contemporary art fair in Brussels, then moved on to news from recent art auctions. A Georgia O'Keefe painting had been sold in New York to a private collector for 47 million dollars, breaking that artist's previous record. Two paintings by a little-known Cypriot artist had fetched surprisingly high prices at a recent auction in London. Elaine had been close to nodding off, but sat up at the mention of Cyprus.

"The paintings, which came from a private collection," the presenter said, "had been listed by the auctioneers Fordyce & Wiley with an estimate of £4,000 to £4,500 each." The screen showed a shot of the frontage of the auction house. "However, the paintings, entitled *Oleanders 3* and *Oleanders 5*, finally fetched over four times the top estimate, selling for the combined sum of £36,500 to an anonymous telephone bidder."

Elaine's heart started racing. *This had to be a coincidence, surely?*

The screen now showed a man in his early thirties, with a subtitle printed below him. Elaine read his first name, Dominic, but was too slow to get his surname or job title. Two large, vibrant pictures could be seen in the middle distance behind him. Elaine peered even more closely at the screen. They were her paintings.

"We are utterly delighted with this sale," the young man was saying. "The final price is not particularly high in absolute terms, of course. In percentage terms, however, this is the biggest positive price shock the art market has seen in the last year and bodes well for future interest in the work of Emmanouel Timotheou."

"Emmanouel Timotheou, my arse!" Elaine shouted, "I painted them!"

"What's up, Elaine?"

"Come and see this, Hamish. It's plagiarism, or outright theft. They're talking about some paintings that have been sold for £36,500, Hamish. They're saying they're by Emmanouel Timotheou but they're not! They're mine! I painted them! Those paintings are mine."

Hamish dashed round to Elaine's side of the computer table and looked over her shoulder. The presenter had invited Dominic to talk more about the artist.

"Timotheou, who died two years ago, was not widely known outside his own country other than among a small coterie of international fans who admire his vibrant palette and bold, impressionistic style. This painting, *Oleanders 3*, shows the blooms of the shrub in extreme close-up, with a hill village visible in the far distance between the foliage in the upper right quadrant." The camera panned over the flaming pink and purple blossoms and then zoomed in on the detail of the village. "Its partner has a similar foreground but a small harbour can be seen in the background, this time in the bottom left quadrant. The artist's initials, ET, can be seen here in the bottom right hand corner."

"Hamish, can you pause this, or wind it back or something?" A cocktail of emotions – shock, excitement, outrage – made it hard for her to get the words out.

"Of course. Do you want to see it all from the beginning again?"

"No, just from the start of this bit in the auction house, if you can locate that. I want you to see this, Hamish, it's a bloody outrage. I am ET, I painted those pictures that have just sold for over thirty-six grand. This is un-bloody-believable." She ran her shaking fingers through her hair, making it stand on end.

Elaine got Hamish to pause after the original estimate was mentioned. "Did you hear that? £4,000 to £4,500 each. Even that's incredible. I sold those paintings to a Russian through a small gallery in Paphos in 2008. I tried to get him to take the full series, but he only wanted those two. He offered me 400 Euros for each of them, and I was so short of cash I accepted."

They paused again on the close-up of the initials on *Oleanders 5*. "See that, Hamish? 'ET' stands for Elaine Treasoner. Come to think of it, he might well have signed 'TE'. Lots of people put their surname first in Greek."

"And why would he name the paintings in English if he's Cypriot?" Hamish scratched his beard. "That doesn't make sense. They don't seem to have done their research very well."

"Well, he probably spoke English. Most Cypriots do. But as far as I know all his paintings were titled in Greek. And there are other clues in my paintings that Dominic Whatsit hasn't noticed."

"You haven't got much internet time left," Hamish said. "I don't want the time to run out before the programme ends." He pressed play again.

"Surely the numbering of the titles implies that these are not in fact a pair, but part of a series of paintings?" the presenter asked.

"Absolutely. Unless of course this is some kind of subtle joke on the artist's part, but his other works have very logical titles. For example, this is his best-known work, *Agora*, from 1986." The camera zoomed in on the young man holding a large art book which was opened to display a reproduction of Timotheou's pink and purple-dominated painting of a marketplace.

"He produced another version of this painting three years later, with a different palette but painted from the same viewpoint, and called it *Agora 2*. So I think we can safely assume that the two *Oleander* paintings we have just sold come from a series of at least five." The young auctioneer smiled into the camera.

"Well, it will be interesting to see if the others from the series come onto the market following the unexpected success of these two paintings," the presenter said.

"Indeed it will," Dominic replied "And I very much hope that we at Fordyce & Wiley will have the honour of hosting the sale in that case."

The credits began to roll over Dominic's satisfied smile, and Hamish closed the browser. "How are you feeling, Elaine? You look pretty angry."

"Angry? I am totally livid! I think Dominic Whatsit did some very sloppy research before the paintings went up for sale, but the little prick has earned a nice commission for his auction house, and a lot of money for whoever the seller was."

"I can understand that. I'd be furious if somebody had ripped off one of my programs and taken the credit for it. Were these paintings particularly special to you?" Hamish asked.

"Well, yes. What that smartarse failed to notice is that the section of blooms in the absolute centre of each painting is completely blurred, or is 'highly impressionistic', as he would no doubt have put it had he noticed. That's important because it's an allusion to the fact that oleanders are poisonous, and can cause blurred vision or dark spots in the vision if ingested. It's also because of my eye condition. It's a degenerative illness, but my eyesight doesn't decline in a gradual, ongoing way. I can have years of no change, then a sudden crisis and severe loss of acuity, usually in one eye at a time. That had happened in 2007, and I was depressed about the change. *Oleanders 1* doesn't have anything in the background, it's just the blooms and greenery and a shimmering blur in the centre, reflecting how I saw. Then I came to terms with the situation a bit, and focussed on what I could see with my peripheral vision. This is represented by the different backgrounds in paintings 2 to 5 – they lead the eye in a clockwise direction, with a different scene in each quadrant for each painting."

"That's amazing," Hamish said. "What a great idea. They must have looked incredible as a sequence. Even on an individual basis they are beautiful. You're very talented. Where are the other paintings in the series?"

"In the attic in my flat. Along with about twenty other paintings I never sold."

Hamish whistled. "Wow. So on a quick calculation, based on

an average of around £18,000 per painting, you could be sitting on about £400,000 worth of art."

"Fuck, that's a lot of money." Elaine flopped back in her chair, suddenly inundated with images of what she could do with that amount of cash. Then reality intervened again. "But I'm not Emmanouel Timotheou."

"No, you're not. But the paintings didn't fetch that price because they were by him – the presenter and the so-called expert as good as said he was a nobody, virtually unknown outside Cyprus. They fetched that price because they're beautiful paintings."

"You reckon?"

"Of course. So what are you going to do about it?"

Elaine shrugged. "I have no idea. It's all a shock."

Hamish turned in his seat so that he was looking Elaine right in the face, and spoke with a directness and enthusiasm she hadn't heard from him before. "Then I'll tell you. You've got to come clean to Alexandra. Tell her you need to see her urgently to explain something in person. Mention this art auction and the misattribution and let her know that she could earn a small fortune if she plays her cards right. You've achieved what you wanted, Elaine. You've assured a future for your daughter."

"I suppose so." Elaine felt strangely flat and drained of energy. "She needs to know that the paintings could be valuable. I'll do it now." Elaine returned to her monitor, which had gone to sleep. She activated it, but she was no longer online. "Oh, my internet access has ran out. Never mind. I'll do it first thing in the morning. That'll give me time to think of the best wording too."

"Fair enough," Hamish said. "I'll check the weather." He left the media room and returned seconds later. "The rain seems to have eased off a bit at last. Shall we dash round to the dining hall and have an early dinner?"

"Thanks, but I think I'll skip it today. This is a lot to process." Elaine returned to her unit, cold and damp, and looking forward to a hot shower. She entered her room and saw a note on her desk, held in place with a coffee mug from the kitchen. It was on official Exit Facility notepaper, but handwritten in large letters:

Report to the Facility Administrator's office
tomorrow (18 April) at 9.00a.m.

Chapter 18

Wednesday 18 April

Elaine slept fitfully, waking between dreams of digging up a lawn in search of her series of *Oleander* paintings, then of Alexandra drilling a hole in Elaine's cranium with a dentist's drill and shaking her mother's head over the bathtub until her brains fell out. She woke around five, tossed and turned for ages and then finally drifted back into another intermittent sleep.

She was up, washed and dressed by eight thirty and dashed over to the dining hall for a quick coffee boost before her appointment with the Facility Administrator.

Nicola Pemberton opened her office door on the dot of nine o'clock. "Come in, Elaine. Do take a seat. We haven't spoken for a while. How are you enjoying your stay?"

Elaine had been expecting a full frontal attack, and was floored by the unexpected affability. "Ehm, not bad," she said. "Well, the wait is a bit tedious, but I have no complaints at present."

"I'm glad to hear it," Nicola said. "I, however, am less than pleased." She swung her large screen round to face Elaine. It showed photographs of the two drawings Elaine had made on the walls of her room. "Can you explain these?"

"Certainly," Elaine said. "The one on the left is a copy of a work by the French painter Edouard Manet. It depicts …"

"I am aware of what it is. What I want to know is why. Why are there drawings on the walls of your room? How dare you deface state property in this manner? Your behaviour constitutes downright vandalism."

A surge of rage forced all Joe's and Hamish's words of caution out of Elaine's mind. "How dare the state con me and countless other people into believing they will receive a swift and compassionate death, and then subject them to a thirty-day delay? That behaviour constitutes downright mental torture. How do you expect people to pass their time while under a death sentence?"

Nicola pressed a button on her keyboard and spoke. "Send Janice in now, please." The door opened and a woman wearing a blue uniform entered. As she got closer, Elaine recognised her as the cleaner who was assigned to her block.

"Tell me, Janice," Nicola said, indicating the screen, "have you seen these drawings before?"

"No, Miss Pemberton," the cleaner replied, barely able to look up from her shoes.

"Is that so? Why not, I wonder? We found them in the course of an inspection visit by the Ministry yesterday afternoon. They are on the walls of Room 5, Unit 1, Block 3, South-West Section. I hardly think they appeared overnight." Nicola paused, keeping her gaze fixed on Janice. The cleaner did not reply. "You are the cleaner for Room 5, Unit 1, Block 3, are you not?"

Janice shifted from foot to foot, cleared her throat, stammered and finally nodded her head.

"I have cleaned my own room since I got here," Elaine confessed. "I quite like cleaning, and I was bored. So I told Janice she didn't need to do my room."

"It is none of your business to interfere with the running of this facility," Nicola said. "We employ cleaners whose job is to clean the rooms assigned to them. Janice, you are dismissed. You may collect your P45 from the administration office in thirty minutes. Leave the room, please."

"That's not fair," Elaine said, as Janice dashed out of the room. "It's my fault, not hers."

"She had a job to do, and she failed to do it. Now, I have had a quote for redecorating the room. The money will be automatically deducted from your bank account within the next three days."

"I doubt it, "Elaine said. "I had £17.29 left in my bank account when I checked in here. I don't think that will cover the cost of repainting the bedroom."

"My goodness, is that all?" said Nicola, surveying her computer screen. "Yes, it appears you're right. In that case, protocol 57B will apply. The bill will be passed on to your next of kin along with your ashes. He or she will be given thirty days from that date to settle it, along with any other outstanding expenses your Exit may incur."

"Hold on," Elaine said. "Is it normal to pass the ashes to the next of kin? I don't recall anything about this when I filled in the form."

Nicola consulted the data on her screen again. "You have initialled the box giving your consent for cremation and for delivery of your remains to Alexandra Treasoner-Andreou. Your daughter, I presume." She swung the screen back round again and Elaine stood up so that she could look at it more closely. It displayed a copy of her consent form and showed that Elaine had indeed initialled that box, though she had no memory of doing so.

"While we're on the subject, there are a couple of points I'd like to clarify about my Exit," Elaine said. "The number on my ID card. Does that refer to the days I still have to wait, or the day on which I will Exit?"

"The waiting days. So you are currently on E minus 15, which means your Exit Date is scheduled on the sixteenth day, which is … let me check … the third of May."

Exactly as she had suspected, the very date commemorated in the Goya execution painting. And the day after Alexandra would arrive back at their flat and find the letter Elaine had left for her. "I don't suppose there's any way of bringing that forward a bit, is there?" she asked.

"I'm afraid not. I explained to you two weeks ago that I am under pressure due to the need to deal with a very large number of Terminal clients who are currently undergoing suffering and distress. Recent events have made that situation even more acute."

"In that case, would it help if I rescinded my agreement?" Elaine said. "The lengthy wait has caused me to reconsider my decision. Perhaps one less person to process would ease your burden a little?"

Elaine was still standing by the screen and thus was close enough to see Nicola's eyebrows shoot upwards briefly before the Administrator regained her usual icy mien.

"My goodness, Elaine. How mercurial you are. One minute you want to bring your Closure Date forward and the next to cancel it entirely. I'm afraid cancellation is not an option. Imagine the unnecessary administrative load and expense to the state if everyone who checked in decided they didn't want to go through with their Exit. What's more, you agreed to this when you signed."

Nicola scrolled down to show a section that read *I hereby*

confirm that I have read and fully understood the terms of the Voluntary Closure Agreement. Elaine's signature was scrawled below it. "And, the clause that refers to the lack of opt-out is here, clause 8.2." She scrolled back up again.

"Could you magnify it a bit further, please?" Elaine read through the clause; as Nicola said, there was no opt-out available. "Thank you, that's very clear now," Elaine said, making for the door.

"Not so fast," Nicola said. "There are a couple of other points I wish to raise with you. You may sit down. Thank you. How good are your IT skills, Elaine?"

"Pretty basic, I'd say." Elaine replied, puzzled at the change of topic.

"That's interesting, because yesterday's inspection also included a review of our computer security. It revealed that somebody has been using a device to send and receive encrypted emails and hide their browsing history. The activity has taken place only at times when your internet access from the media room was enabled. I assumed that perhaps your multiple talents encompassed advanced IT skills as well as art, ophthalmology and psychology."

"Sadly not," Elaine said.

"In that case, who has been doing so?" Nicola asked.

"I'm afraid I can't help you there," Elaine said. "I may have been careless about logging out sometimes. I guess somebody could have used my time for their own purposes."

"Perhaps someone who has already spent time in jail for computer offences?" Nicola suggested.

Elaine rearranged her features into what she hoped passed for incomprehension. "I don't know anyone in that category."

"I see," Nicola said. "I must also warn you about a Terminal patient called Joe whom you have been seen consorting with. He appears to be charming, but I assure you he is severely deluded and is fond of spreading conspiracy theories. In addition to creeping physical paralysis, his mental condition is deteriorating, resulting in a severe persecution complex."

Two weeks earlier, Elaine would have argued with Nicola, presenting evidence as to why the Facility Administrator was lying. Now she sat in silence, considering her options. She could hint that she knew that Nicola was taking money to house Miss Latimer, but that was really the only card she held, and it was hard to see what she could do with it. She decided silence was the better part of valour in this situation.

"So, I think we understand each other," Nicola continued. "Our next meeting will be your Exit Interview, in a week to ten days from now. At that meeting we shall discuss the arrangements you wish to make for religious or civil ceremonies before your Exit, and your choice of Closure Method. Let me just remind you now that some ways are less pleasant than others. What's more, some methods are much cheaper than others, and the state doesn't need to spend extra money on busybodies and troublemakers."

"Is that it?" Elaine asked, getting to her feet.

"Yes," Nicola said. "Just keep your hands off the colouring chalks, and bear in mind that this is a facility that serves to end the suffering of physically and mentally ill patients, not a dating agency for superannuated cougars. You may go now."

Elaine ran from the administration block to the central building, hoping to catch the tail end of the breakfast service. Having skipped dinner the previous night, she was absolutely ravenous. She burst through the double doors into the vestibule and scanned her ID card, but the door into the dining hall remained shut. Fuming, she pounded her fists on the door. A white-clad figure moved towards her on the other side of the glass. As the figure approached, Elaine recognised her. Siobhan opened the door, a smile on her face. "Hello there, Elaine! I'm glad you're still here. What happened – did you sleep in and miss breakfast?"

"Siobhan, welcome back. No, I had an interview with the Facility Administrator, and have only just got out. I could really use a coffee, and something to eat if there's anything left."

"Well, we're just loading up the trolleys for the Ind– I mean, for the bins, the recycling bins. But I'll see if I can grab something portable for you before it all goes."

Siobhan reappeared a couple of minutes later with a croissant and coffee in a polystyrene cup. "Is that OK for you?"

"It's wonderful, thank you. You're an angel, Siobhan. I hope you had a good holiday."

Elaine walked round to the media room, still fuming about the Facility Administrator's treatment of her. Hamish seemed relieved to see her. "All well? You missed breakfast again." He beckoned to Elaine to follow him and they sat down in the TV armchairs furthest from the door.

"Nicola's onto us, Hamish. She all but said she knows you're using my internet access. She warned me off Joe, too, basically calling him a lunatic. And they've been in my room and are now billing me for vandalism. I had done a couple of drawings on my wall."

"Our block was inspected too," Hamish said, "but luckily they didn't find anything. My hiding place for you-know-what wasn't discovered."

"That's good, but they must know something is going on with the internet. I suggest we send that email about selling my paintings to Alexandra now, and do it via your method, so if anyone's looking they can't read it." Elaine slipped her lanyard over her head, went over to a monitor and swiped her ID to turn it on. She tried to load her favourite browser. A notice appeared on the screen in fat, black letters: *Internet access denied*.

Elaine's stomach lurched. "Hamish, come and have a look at this," she said. "Is there something you can do?"

Hamish took one look at her screen and his face fell. "Nothing at all. It's too late. She's blocked you."

Elaine leapt to her feet and paced round the room. "That sanctimonious bitch! I'd like to punch her perfect teeth right down her lying, priggish, hypocritical throat. Now, of all times. Why do my paintings earn proper money, fucking now, when I'm about to bloody die? Why not when I was young and desperate and bringing up a child virtually alone? I'll bet Miss Nickel-Arse Pemberton never had a setback in her life. She'll have been too busy brown-nosing the Minister for this or that and climbing her precious hidebound, rule-ridden career ladder. And now she has the gall to block my internet access. Now, when I need to write to Alexandra and tell her that all my efforts weren't for nothing after all." Elaine kicked the back of one of the TV chairs. "I'm not having it. I'm going back over there and I am going to fucking throttle her!"

Hamish ran to the door and barred Elaine's way. "Elaine, no. That won't help."

"I don't care. If I have to go, I'm taking her with me."

Elaine gave Hamish a shove, but he wouldn't move. "Calm down, Elaine. Please, sit down, stop this. You'll give yourself a stroke. Besides ..." Hamish made an exaggerated 'keep quiet' gesture and pointed at a white column near the door that Elaine had never seen before. On the top of it there was a small screen and a panel with four large buttons on it.

"What's that?" Elaine moved closer to the device. The screen read: 'Please rate your experience in the media room today'. The buttons, ranged from left to right, were green, yellow, orange and red and had emojis on them.

"Feedback machine. They've put one in the dining hall too," Hamish said loudly, then leant towards Elaine and spoke softly in her ear. "Possibly housing CCTV or recording equipment."

"Feedback? Fuck, yes, I've got feedback!" Elaine thumped repeatedly on the scowling red button.

"OK, don't break it or that will go on your bill as well."

The full fire of Elaine's rage was abating and Hamish's words made sense. The veins on Elaine's temples were throbbing and she could feel her heart pounding far too fast. She walked over to the semi-circle of chairs in front of the TV and lay down along them, waiting for her breathing to settle and her heart rate to return to normal. Hamish sat down beside her feet.

"Sorry, Hamish," she said. "I'm not angry with you. Did I frighten you?"

"A bit. But it's understandable in the circumstances. I feel pretty angry too. I'm just not as vocal as you when it comes to expressing it."

A couple of minutes passed in silence, then Elaine sat up. She ran her fingers through her hair a couple of times, making it stand on end.

"Are you feeling calmer now?" Hamish asked.

"I'm still furious, but in a different way. Now I'm angry but focussed. And I've come to a decision" Elaine glanced over at the feedback machine by the door, then quietly hummed the Animals' song *We've Got to Get Out of this Place.* She raised her eyebrows and looked at Hamish intently to see if he had understood her hidden message. Hamish looked at her questioningly for a second or two, then smiled and nodded his understanding.

"I'm going for a walk to clear my head," Elaine said. "I'll see you later, Hamish."

+++

When Elaine arrived at the potting shed in the evening, Hamish and Joe were already there deep in hushed discussion. It soon became apparent that Hamish had floated the idea of an escape attempt to Joe before she arrived. "This isn't fair," she said. "It was my idea, so you shouldn't be making plans behind my back."

"Nobody's making any plans yet," Hamish said in a soothing tone. "We were talking about fact-finding. Things like staff routines, perimeter fences and security systems, weak points, and so on. Those all need to be researched first. And we both feel that sort of thing would be better left to us." He looked at Joe, who nodded to confirm his support. Elaine scowled at both of them. Hamish gulped and cleared his throat before continuing. "You see, you're the one who's been specifically warned to keep out of trouble, so they'll probably be watching you more than us."

"I'm not sure about that," Elaine said. "Pemberton has both of you marked down as troublemakers. It wouldn't be because I'm a woman that you want to keep me in the background until we're ready to explain your nice, logical, masculine escape strategy to me, would it?"

"I told you she wouldn't buy it," Joe said to Hamish. "Look, Elaine, to be brutally frank, there is also the fact that you can't see anything properly until your nose is practically resting against it," Joe said. "That makes it rather hard to investigate fences or other perimeter systems unobtrusively."

"I'm not quite that blind, but I guess that is a valid point. So what am I supposed to do while the pair of you are observing and researching?"

"Keep out of trouble, like Nickel-Arse told you to do," Joe said. "I love your new name for her, by the way."

"You could keep Roland off my back," Hamish suggested. "I might be able to hot spot via his internet account if you could keep his attention off me. He rarely misses an opportunity to corner me and talk at me. Some of it's interesting and might even be useful, but it gets a bit wearing."

"Maybe he's gay and he fancies you?" Elaine said. "In which case, I'm going to be a poor substitute."

"I think he's just lonely and overcome with guilt. He told me his wife and dog were shot dead by a burglar during a break-in at his house in Surrey. He wasn't there because he had an early meeting in London the following morning so he was staying in town that night."

"Ah, I get it. The early morning meeting is a classic excuse. He was probably spending the night with his mistress, or shagging a fancy whore in a hotel," Joe said. "Why else would he feel guilty rather than angry or heartbroken about what happened?"

"I don't know about that," Hamish said, "anyone normal

would feel guilty about being absent in those circumstances. It's the reason he checked in here. Funnily enough, he seems more distressed about the dog than the wife. He's left all his money to his local dog's home in their memory."

"You're kidding. How much?" Elaine asked.

"About a million, I believe. They didn't have any kids, you see," Hamish said.

Joe groaned. "God, all that dosh literally gone to the dogs. It would make you weep."

"Well, abandoned dogs have needs too, Joe," Hamish said.

"Yes, of course they do," Joe said. "They really need a million so that they can go to Vegas for their holidays and drink champagne …"

"… and watch lady dogs dance on the bar top to Rihanna's *Bitch Better Have My Money*," Elaine said, winking at Joe.

"I don't think I know that song," Hamish said.

"You're not missing much. I only know it because Alexandra used to like it."

"OK, so it looks like dogs are his soft spot," Joe said. "Elaine, can you reinvent yourself as an ardent dog lover? Show him some photos of your former pets, maybe."

"I don't have any."

"Then download some."

"We don't have internet access any more," Hamish and Elaine said in unison.

"Fuck! Look, I think we all need to think this through a lot more. Shall we reconvene tomorrow?" Joe said.

"Good idea," Elaine said. After all, I've been told I mustn't spend too much time consorting with undesirables."

Chapter 19

Thursday 19 April

D o you trust Hamish?" Joe asked Elaine, as they lay in her narrow bed. He had arrived at her window early in the morning, immediately after his curfew had been lifted, and they had tugged each other's clothes off urgently.

"Why not?" Elaine replied. "Everything he's said has checked out so far. Don't you?"

"I'm surprised how rapidly he accepted the idea of an escape attempt. It makes sense for you – you've just discovered you've actually got money, at least potentially, and your communications with your daughter have been cut off. It makes sense for me, as I have nothing to lose and I never wanted to come here in the first place. But what's changed for him? He will still have lost his beloved mother, and will still be penniless if he gets out."

"I know. I offered to help him financially if my paintings sell, in return for help with getting out. That goes for you too, of course."

"That's very generous. I hope you don't come to regret that offer."

"Are you going to confront him about his motives?" Elaine asked.

"Certainly not," Joe replied. "Not my style. I gather information and wait and watch. I only act when the moment is ripe. You're the one who rushes in like a blind bull in a china shop, tackling everyone head on."

"Not always. I actually kept cool yesterday when the Facility Administrator was threatening me, and didn't let on what I know about her. "

Joe looked baffled and Elaine then remembered that she had not yet told Joe about Miss Latimer's cheque book and the link between Betty and the Administrator. She explained what she knew and watched Joe's frown intensify.

"You were quite right to keep quiet about what you know," Joes said. "You'll have much more leverage with that information when you're out than you would now."

"Thanks. Do you have any tobacco, Joe?" Elaine asked.

"No, I'm out, but I'll try to see Lyndsay later today. The jammer didn't work, so I've taken the old battery out. I'm hoping he'll be able to replace that."

"In exchange for … ?"

"Some weed, of course."

Elaine was silent for a while, thinking of the least intrusive way to find out more about Joe's relationship with the young man in the commissary. "Does Lyndsay know that you're not really disabled, Joe?" she asked.

"Nobody knows except you. I'll have to tell Hamish at some point soon, but so far it's only you."

"I see. So whatever you and Lyndsay do together is …"

"Absolutely none of your business, Elaine. Come on, don't look at me like that. Look, I don't have tobacco, but I do have two more of these," Joe leaned over to the desk and felt in a pocket of the jeans he had thrown there. He produced two crumpled sticks of Nescafé. "I can make it. There won't be anyone around now, will there?"

"I doubt it," Elaine said. "Miss Latimer's morning helper comes in around ten, and there's nobody else in my unit now. The kitchen's down at the end of the corridor, to the left."

Joe put on his jeans and T-shirt and left the room. Seconds later, Elaine heard him talking to someone. She pulled the door open slightly and put her ear to the gap.

"Miss Latimer, what a pleasure to see you again."

"Who are you? Are you a new helper?"

"Not exactly, but I'd be happy to help you with that teapot. It looks rather heavy."

"Thank you. I'm sure I've met you before. I know, you're Elaine's beau, aren't you?"

"Yes, Miss Latimer, I am indeed," Joe said.

Elaine felt absurdly pleased that Joe had accepted this role in Miss Latimer's version of reality, then bit one thumb hard to stop herself from behaving like a lovesick teenager.

"Weren't you away somewhere?" Miss Latimer asked. Joe's reply was drowned out by the noise of the kettle coming to the boil. Miss Latimer spoke again. She sounded happy and girlish, flirtatious almost. "I know where you've been. I've guessed it. It was Lourdes, wasn't it?" Joe spluttered and then made the sound into a cough. "I'm strictly Presbyterian, of course," Miss Latimer continued, "but I'm not prejudiced, you know, not in the slightest."

"I don't quite follow you, Miss Latimer," Joe said.

"I had a school friend called Janet who was a Catholic.

Janet's Granny had the most dreadful psoriasis until she went to Lourdes, then she was never troubled with it again. And you were in a wheelchair last time I saw you, and now you're walking. Ergo, you have been to Lourdes."

"How clever of you to guess it, Miss Latimer. Yes, blessed be Mary, Mother of God. Thanks to her I am cured. It is a true miracle," Joe said, lapsing slightly into the Irish accent he used with Siobhan. "Your tea is ready now. Let me help you back to your room. I'll carry the teapot. Careful with the Zimmer frame going round the corner now."

Joe returned to Elaine's room soon afterwards, carrying two cups of coffee. He was laughing so much that he slopped coffee onto the desk as he laid the cups down. "Did you hear that?"

"Yes, I confess I was eavesdropping. I'd have thought that with your Italian background, you could have come up with a bit more in the way of religious benedictions."

"She caught me off guard. I thought she was completely gaga, but on this occasion she was entirely on the ball. "

"It's funny how her dementia works. She'll be a hundred per cent rational one minute, and five minutes later she'll have forgotten who you are," Elaine said.

"Well, I just hope she's forgotten about me and my miraculous cure by now," Joe said. "We don't want her telling anyone about a crippled inmate who can suddenly walk. In fact, I'd better get going in case her carer comes early today." He gulped his coffee, pulled on his socks, boots and flying jacket and eased himself back into the wheelchair. "Damn. Another twelve hours of self-inflicted torture in this contraption to look forward to."

"It's not for much longer, hopefully. Be patient. I'll catch you later, Joe."

+++

Elaine and Hamish were sitting at the table farthest from the new feedback machine in the dining hall. He addressed Elaine in an undertone, masking his mouth with a napkin as he spoke. "You've got the tablet, right?" Elaine nodded. "Good. Then, you go ahead to the media room and give me it when I get there. Roland said he wants to use the computer today, so if he shows up, wait till he goes online and then dissect him. OK?"

"Dissect him? What the hell are you on about Hamish? Remove the napkin, nobody's within earshot."

Hamish wiped his mouth, put the napkin on the table and then directed his next remark at his bowl of tinned fruit and ice cream. "Distract, Elaine, not dissect. We need him to go online and then get distracted so that he forgets to log off when he leaves. Can you manage that? I'll try and suss out his password so I can tether and use the tablet once he's gone."

Elaine loaded her used dishes onto her tray, returned it to the conveyor belt, and left the dining hall after punching all four buttons on the feedback machine. She had no idea how she'd fulfil Hamish's task, but decided just to wing it if the opportunity arose. When she reached the media room, she logged on at her usual monitor and tried to load a browser but once again got the *Internet access denied* notice. "Bugger you, Nickel-Arse," she said, then settled to playing Spider Solitaire until Hamish arrived.

Hamish entered the media room, removed his jacket and hung it over the feedback device, obscuring the screen, then beckoned to Elaine to join him beside it. As she approached, he put his finger over his lips. Elaine gave him the tablet. He lifted his jumper, stuffed the tablet in the top of his jeans and retrieved his jacket from the device.

They walked over to the computer table together and spoke quietly with their backs to the door. "There's a message in my Outbox for Alexandra," Elaine said. "If you manage to piggyback off Roland, please send that off before you do any of the other stuff you need to do." Hamish nodded and moved over to the TV seats.

Elaine was on her sixth game of Spider Solitaire and Hamish was watching television when Roland appeared. "Good afternoon, Hamish," he said, "I missed you at lunch today." Roland walked over to the computer monitors and chose the one diagonally opposite Elaine's. He nodded briefly to her in acknowledgement of her presence. "Anything interesting on TV, Hamish?" he called. "Have I missed the news?"

"Yes, just," said Hamish. "But there wasn't much of interest."

"Well, I can catch up online for a bit," Roland said, scanning his ID card. "I've got a VR appointment in half an hour. Must say, it's quite addictive after a while."

"Chance would be a fine thing," Elaine said under her breath. "Some of us haven't even had our first go at it yet."

"I beg your pardon?" Roland replied.

"Nothing," Elaine said. "I'm just annoyed because my internet access has run out again. I'm such a twerp! I keep forgetting to log out and then it runs out before I've finished what I want to do."

Elaine saw Hamish removing his jacket and hanging it round his shoulders, presumably to conceal her Nexus from both Roland and the CCTV camera that might be hidden in the feedback device.

"Oh, easily done, I expect," Roland said. "Was it something important you wanted to do?"

"Well, yes," Elaine said. "It's my niece's twelfth birthday next week, and I wanted to do something special for her."

Elaine summoned every memory of every birthday Alexandra's father had forgotten about, and conjured up a tear. "She thinks I'm in hospital and she doesn't know I'm going to die soon. And she just loves dogs, so I thought I'd send her a puppy for her birthday. Then she can remember me forever." The memory of the puppy Alexandra had adored and that had been shot by a neighbour after it got into their chicken coop was sufficient to reduce Elaine to a bout of entirely plausible weeping.

"I'm sorry, it will all be OK. Please don't cry," said Roland, sounding panicked.

"And now I can't access my internet to choose a little dog for her," Elaine wailed.

"Don't worry," Roland said. "You can use mine. And I'd be happy to help you choose. I'm quite a dog fan myself, you know. Bring your chair round here."

"Really? That's very kind of you. But I can't bring my chair. They're all fixed to the floor."

"Is that so? My goodness, you're right. Well, never mind. You can take my seat in front of the monitor, and I'll sit where Hamish usually sits."

Roland spent the next half hour or so lecturing Elaine on the merits of various breeds that he showed her online. Elaine dithered and backtracked and changed her mind and asked Roland to repeat information until he became noticeably impatient and the half hour wait to his VR appointment was nearly up. "Perhaps you should discuss it with your sister before you make the final choice," Roland said. "Once you've decided, I can give you the addresses of some very reputable breeders."

"Oh, dear, I didn't explain myself well," Elaine said. "I haven't got much money left, so I was thinking in terms of a rescue dog."

"Well, good thinking." Roland perked up. "There are lots of dogs in need of a good home. In fact, I have endowed a dogs' home myself. Look, I have to go to my VR session now, but I'd be happy to help you pick out a rescue dog online tomorrow if you like."

"Oh, yes, please. You're so knowledgeable, and I wouldn't want to make the wrong choice for my niece." Elaine smiled sweetly.

"Indeed. Well, my pleasure. I have to go now. Hamish, I'll see you later." Roland rose to his feet hastily, and headed for the door.

Hamish waited until he was sure Roland had definitely gone, then joined Elaine and spoke quietly. "You were great, Elaine, really convincing and you kept him totally focussed away from anything I was doing on the tablet. And you've set it up so we can do it again tomorrow. Absolutely brilliant!"

Elaine grinned. "Thanks. So, have you got into his account and did you send the message to Alexandra?"

"I managed to get online via his Exit Facility account, but you're logged out of your email app on the tablet so I can't get in. Can you give me your password?" Hamish asked.

Elaine spelled her password as Hamish typed it in on the

tablet. "That's weird" said Hamish, brows furrowed. "It's saying the password is wrong. Spell it out again, slowly this time." Elaine repeated the password. Hamish looked up at her, concern flooding his face. "I'm really sorry, Elaine, but I can't log in. Are you sure the password you gave me is the right one?"

"Yes, I'm sure. I use the same password for everything."

"That's not very wise, Elaine. If you're sure the password is correct then it looks like someone may have hacked your account and changed your password. It's impossible to get in."

"Shit, so what do I do now? I really need to contact Alexandra."

"Don't give up hope, I'll think of something" Hamish said. "In the meantime I'd better go on with the research. Roland may remember his account is still active when he gets out of the VR session and come back to log off."

Elaine was angry that she had pulled out all the stops to bamboozle Roland, but Hamish had failed to get her message to Alexandra. And now it looked like Nicola had hacked her email account. Rather than fume or sulk in the media room, she decided to return to her unit and see if Miss Latimer could provide a soothing glass of whisky and some inconsequential memories from decades ago.

As she neared her block Elaine made out what looked like an ambulance parked at the end of the path, and a gurney being wheeled towards the building by two orange-clad figures. Her pulse, already quickened by anger, began to race. Praying it was someone from the unit above hers who was ill or injured, Elaine ran towards her block.

She burst through the main door and the door into her unit and found two guards in the corridor loading a tiny recumbent figure onto the gurney. "What happened to Miss Latimer? Is she ill?" Elaine shouted.

The nearest guard turned towards her. It was Brendan. "Nope, popped off her perch," he said cheerfully.

"No!" cried Elaine, and moved to the head of the gurney. She pulled back the white sheet covering Miss Latimer's face and found the old lady with closed eyes and a beatific smile, her pearls in place on her powder blue cashmere jumper, but no longer moving gently up and down.

All the tears Elaine had only half-cried since she arrived in the facility, all the emotions she had suppressed or denied for the last three weeks, welled up and spilled over. She threw her arms round Miss Latimer's body and laid her head on the pillow beside the old lady's and sobbed uncontrollably.

"Is she the next of kin?" the other guard asked Brendan.

"No," Brendan said. "She's a complete randomer. The next of kin is the fat one who's clearing out the old bird's room. Hey, come on Elaine, pull yourself together. Get up!"

The door of Miss Latimer's room opened and someone came out. Elaine recognised Betty from her mauve velvet-clad legs. "What are you doing? Please remove yourself from on top of my aunt. This is most undignified."

Elaine stood up and looked at Betty. Her face was impassive and bore not the slightest sign of grief. "I am mourning, Betty. I was very fond of your aunt. She was a sweet, wonderful, kind, clever woman. And a good friend to me. I am sorry for your loss, and mine."

Betty's bovine expression now bore traces of irritation. "Thank you, Elaine. I know she was fond of you, too. But she was ninety-one, you know, so it was to be expected one of these days. Now, if you could just stand back, please …"

"What happened? She was fine this morning."

"We don't know for sure," Betty said. "The girl who serves her lunch found Auntie Vee asleep in her chair, so she left the lunch tray for her. When she came back to collect it, the food was untouched and Auntie hadn't moved. The helper checked her pulse and realised she was dead. She seems to have gone peacefully, in her sleep."

"Will there be an autopsy?" Elaine asked.

"Why? It was clearly natural causes." Betty leant over the gurney and pulled the sheet up over Miss Latimer's face once more. "You may take her away now," she said to the guards.

As the guards wheeled the gurney out of the door, Elaine leaned against the wall of the corridor and slid down it to a sitting position on the floor and began crying again. Betty tut-tutted with exasperation then, perhaps feeling that she was coming across as too cold-hearted, went back into Miss Latimer's room and emerged carrying the Scrabble box.

"This has obviously been a shock for you. Auntie Vee told me you played Scrabble together, so perhaps you'd like this as a memento," she presented the box to Elaine.

"Thank you," Elaine said and clutched the Scrabble box to her chest. "Look, I know it's a bit early and these things take time to arrange, but could I possibly come to the funeral? I'd like to say goodbye to your aunt properly."

Betty hesitated before answering. "Well, seeing as you're in this fac– ehm, I mean … home, it might be a bit difficult to arrange, if you know what I mean."

"There is a chapel here," Elaine said.

"Oh, I don't think that would do at all. Her friends might wonder …" Betty tailed off and shifted awkwardly from foot to foot. Elaine stared her in the face. "As you say, it's early to be thinking about this, and I wasn't to know that auntie would pass today," Betty continued. "But I'll see what I can do once the arrangements have been made."

"Thank you," Elaine said, "I'd appreciate that. Can I help you now in any way?"

"No, it's all under control," Betty said, sounding almost cheerful.

Elaine went into her own room and lay down on her bed cradling the Scrabble box and cried some more. When her tears had run out, she threw cold water from the bathroom tap on her puffy face, then unpacked the Scrabble box. The scorecards from her last game with Miss Latimer lay on top of the board – as usual Miss Latimer had won. Underneath the board, alongside the bag of tiles, she found an old but handsome Parker pen, and the chequebook Miss Latimer had used to pay for what she thought were her care home bills.

Chapter 20

Friday 20 April

Elaine woke from a dream in which Alexandra was walking into a lake. She had walked in silently and resolutely, unaware or uncaring as the level of the water reached her neck and then rose over her head. Elaine had watched helplessly from the shore, longing to run in and rescue her daughter, but her legs were encased in blocks of concrete. She had screamed for help, but no sound had issued from her mouth.

It was five a.m., her worst hour of the morning for anxieties and fears. The unit felt spooky and empty without the presence of Miss Latimer in the room opposite. She tossed and turned for an hour or more, with nothing to distract her but the sound of intermittent coughing from the unit above hers.

Images of Alexandra and of the unsent email came into her head. *She really must find a way to send that email. … Alexandra would never think of selling her old paintings … Would she even remember they were in the attic? …* Hamish's face popped into her mind. She noticed with her inner eye what she had not consciously been aware of in person – his beard was longer and stragglier than it had been when they first met. *… Could they trust Hamish? … Hadn't he been researching something before she'd raised the idea of escaping? … Yes, he'd asked for her tablet the day they spoke about the lack of an opt-out clause.* Next Roland's lugubrious face popped into her head. *Were he and as Hamish in cahoots in some way? … Had they changed their minds about exiting and would shop Joe and Elaine in return for their own freedom? …*

Elaine got out of bed and went down to the kitchen for a glass of cold water. Her throat was dry and her head needed clearing. But on the way back down the corridor, she was reminded of her similar excursion to the kitchen on the night when Dorothy had disappeared. Her churning thoughts now filled with guilt for Dorothy's disappearance, and for all the lies she had told to Alexandra, and for poor Janice losing her job. *Christ, what a fucking hash she'd made of everything!*

Trying to push self-doubt to the back of her mind, Elaine went into her bathroom to pee. As she stepped up into the tiny bathroom, she noticed a twinge in her right hip again. *If Joe was doing leg exercises to be fit for running, she should probably be doing something too. Some Pilates, maybe.*

An hour later Elaine lay on the floor, her leg muscles twitching with the effort she had put in. She was pleased with herself. It had been years since she'd done these exercises, but her body had remembered the movements her brain had forgotten. She showered and washed her hair, put on a clean T-shirt and applied some mascara to keep her spirits up.

As she was heading for the central building she met Joe wheeling himself in the opposite direction. "Hi, Elaine," he said. "You're up early today. And you're looking rather Goth, I must say – pallid skin, hair standing on end, shadows under the eyes. Or did your hand slip when you were putting the mascara on?"

"Cheeky bugger," Elaine said. "If you were hoping for a morning shag, you're going the wrong way about it. Anyway, it's cleaning day today for my unit, so it's probably not a good idea to come in. Where can we go and talk at this time of day?"

"How about the little copse where Hamish found Dorothy's glasses?"

They reached the shade of the trees and Elaine sat on the ground, leaning back against a tree while Joe rolled two cigarettes. "I've got awful news," Elaine said. "Miss Latimer died yesterday afternoon."

"You're joking! I was chatting to her just yesterday morning. She seemed fine then."

"I know. But she was ninety-one, so I suppose it's not surprising. She seems to have passed away peacefully in her sleep."

"That's the best way to go, but you'll miss her, won't you?" Joe reached out and touched Elaine on the cheek, then handed her a lit roll-up. "I'm sorry, Elaine, I really am."

The two of them sat and smoked in companionable silence.

"Have you seen Hamish?" Elaine asked. "I did a good job of distracting Roland and Hamish got some of your research done, but he didn't send my message to Alexandra. I'm starting to get a bit paranoid about him. Aren't you?"

"I'm still waiting and watching, like I told you. But some things have changed since yesterday. I have good news and bad."

"OK, I'll have the good news first," Elaine said.

"Well, you're smoking part one of the good news already, Elaine. Part two is that I saw the Lagerkommandant leaving yesterday evening. She got into a limousine with Ministry plates, carrying a large black briefcase and a small navy-blue trolley bag."

"Oh, wow. Do you think she's been fired over the security problems?"

"Who knows? She looked as snooty and confident as usual.

I think it's more likely she's off to high-level meetings with the Ministry. Either way, we may be under less scrutiny without her on the premises."

"That's a relief," Elaine said. "And what's the bad news?"

"I've finally been sorted."

Elaine laughed. "After all this time? OK, let me guess – you've been put in Slytherin. Entirely suitable for a devious, self-serving individual such as yourself."

Joe reached across and delivered a gentle cuff to Elaine's ear. "Certainly not. I've always identified as a Ravenclaw, Elaine. I am witty and highly intelligent."

"Dream on," Elaine said. "Seriously, though. What's up?"

Joe, slipped his lanyard over his head and handed it to Elaine. She turned the attached ID card towards her and brought it into her field of vision. "Six! Am I reading this right, Joe? You're Exiting in six days?" Joe nodded silently. "How did this happen?" Elaine asked, her heart beginning to race. "Did you have an Exit Interview?"

"No. Overnight, all the Indigents' ID cards suddenly registered numbers. My block are mainly 6s and 7s. Most of the people in the units at the north of the line of blocks have 1s or 2s."

"Most of the people in those units, you say. What about the others at the north end?" Elaine asked.

"They've disappeared since yesterday's morning roll call."

"Shit!" Elaine stubbed out her roll up, grinding the butt into the damp moss at the foot of the tree. "Do you think they've been given a mass Exit?"

"Who knows? I suppose they could have been set free, but it seems unlikely when the rest of us Inidgents have been assigned Exit Dates. Whatever's going on, I think we have to put faith in Hamish. He seems to get hot under the collar about human rights abuses, and this falls into that category if ever anything did."

"I agree," Elaine said and got to her feet. "I'll go and look for him now."

+++

Hamish was leaving the dining hall as Elaine arrived, so she postponed her breakfast and they went outside to talk at the seating area. She updated him on Joe's news, which seemed to surprise him less than it had her. "All the more need to get our research done fast, then," he said. "Can you distract Roland again? He's been following me like my shadow."

"OK. I forgot to bring the tablet today, but I can go back for it. Are you going to piggyback on his internet again? In which case, will you please get me back into my email account so I can send my message to Alexandra?"

"Not this morning. What I need is a couple of hours without Roland breathing down my neck. I'll try and get into your email later, Elaine, I promise."

"Just don't forget about it, OK? I'm getting frantic about her, and she'll be worried about my ongoing silence. So what do you want me to do with Roland?"

"Continue the saga about the puppy for your niece as long as you can," Hamish said. "That was great. And then anything else you can think of. Get him to show you the VR room, or go to the commissary together, or something. But keep off the subject of fences. I think I've pumped him enough about those."

Elaine ran Roland to ground in the dining hall shortly before the breakfast service was due to finish. She managed to provoke him into a twenty-minute monologue on the relative merits of poached eggs and fried eggs. Siobhan finally ousted them from the dining hall, and they went round to the media room, purportedly in search of Hamish. He wasn't there.

"Oh, I remember now," Elaine said, having rehearsed a plausible excuse in advance. "Hamish told me he had to have a medical check in the hospital block this morning. So shall we have a look at rescue dogs until he shows up?"

Roland was delighted to help until he discovered that Elaine had once more forgotten to log out of her account overnight and thus had no internet access. As a result, Roland had to use his own account and lean over her shoulder while assessing the merits of various stray puppies that he himself was sponsoring. His patience appeared to be wearing a little thin after Elaine evaluated and rejected the fifteenth dog in a row.

"Oh, what about this one, Roland? Isn't she cute? I can't read that bit there, it's written in grey on white. I do wonder why people make websites with grey text on a white background, they're so illegible. Could you read it to me, Roland?"

"West Highland Terrier," Roland said. He was starting to sound a little weary.

"Oh, isn't that what they used to call a Scottie dog?"

Roland nodded.

"Oh, she's so sweet, don't you think? I'm sure Annie would love her. On the other hand, now I come to think of it, Annie does have a lot of allergies. Do you think she'd be allergic to a dog with a lot of hair, Roland?"

Roland straightened up and stretched his long arms, which

cracked as he did so. "Frankly, I have no idea. Look, Elaine, I think you need to do a bit more research on your own before you make a decision. I've got a bit of a headache, so I'm going to take a walk in the grounds. Feel free to use my internet account to keep checking out the choices."

"Oh, that's very kind of you, Roland. I do hope I haven't tired you out. It's so hard to make such a big decision, as I'm sure you'll understand. Look, before you go, I've got an idea. Like you suggested, I should discuss it with my sister. After all, the dog is for Annie, but her mum – that's my sister, you know – will probably end up spending a lot of time with it too. Could I possibly email her from your account?"

"Yes, fine then. But, please do not look any of my correspondence."

"Of course not, I wouldn't dream of it. Thank you so much, Roland. Could you log into your email account for me?"

"Yes, no problem," said Roland, rubbing his temples. "There you go. And please don't forget to log out of the email when you're done."

"Of course. Thank you very much. I do appreciate it," Elaine said, but Roland was already halfway out the door.

Elaine wondered quite how covert she should be, given that Exit Facility staff were probably now monitoring all incoming and outgoing emails. After three hurried drafts, she settled on a message that she hoped would sound innocuous to third parties while still conveying information and caution to Alexandra.

Darling,

Things are a bit difficult here – my hip has

been giving me a LOT of bother, and I may not be able to get to the internet café to contact you again before your return. A new neighbour let me send this from his account, but I won't bother him again, as you'll be back very soon.

In case I forget this in the excitement of seeing you again, your friend Oleandra dropped in to see me, looking pretty as a picture as usual. She's completed her PhD and was on her way to take up a job at an auctioneer's in London. She asked me to look after some of her stuff until she finds a flat there, so I stored it in our usual place. She says you should look her up when you're back – apparently she owes you money and can afford to pay you back now she's found a job. It sounds like that's worth following up!

Anyway, really looking forward to seeing you soon, as is your old teddy Mina-Pandisis!

Lots of love,

Mum xxx

Elaine re-read her email, hoping it would make sense to her daughter if she failed to get out of the facility alive. Perhaps it was too cryptic, but she was pleased with the hint in 'pretty as a picture' and she knew that only Alexandra would realise that the fictitious teddy bear's name meant "do not reply" in Greek.

Elaine sent the message, waited for confirmation that it had gone, then deleted it from the sent folder and the bin and logged out of Roland's email account. If Roland asked about the message to her sister, which he probably wouldn't, she'd say she had changed her mind and would send it from her own account tomorrow.

Hamish came into the media room as Elaine was about to leave for lunch. "Good work, Elaine. I bumped into Roland on his way back to our block. He says he feels a migraine coming on and is going to lie down. What did you do to him?"

"Nothing, really. I just encouraged him to bore the pants off himself while looking over my shoulder at pictures of dogs. Anything else I can do to help?"

"Not at the moment, but I need to consult with Joe at some point. Do you know where he is?"

"No. I haven't seen him since early this morning. What about lunch?" Elaine asked.

"I'm not that hungry, I'll skip it."

"Really? Oh, and by the way, you don't need to worry about sending my email to Alexandra. I found a way to get a message to her."

+++

Elaine felt tired after lunch and decided to go back to her room for a nap. As she went into her unit, she met a stony-faced cleaner on his way out. She opened her own door and choked on the throat-grabbing reek of bleach. The cleaner's attempts to remove her paintings had resulted in a filthy, fuzzy, greyish mess on each wall.

Elaine pushed her window open as far as it would go and then looked in Miss Latimer's room. Betty hadn't removed the wing chair yet. Elaine hauled it across the corridor and used it to wedge her own door open and create some air flow, then she went back into the old lady's room and fell asleep on her bed.

She was woken by someone shaking her shoulder and opened her eyes to see Betty glaring at her. "Why's my aunt's chair in the hall, and why are you sleeping in her bed?"

The woman was so objectionable that Elaine couldn't' resist the urge to be facetious. "I was playing at being Goldilocks."

Betty sniffed loudly at the end of Elaine's explanation, clearly unconvinced. "Well, if you would kindly leave my aunt's room now, I have some more things of hers I want to collect. I can't take the chair now, but I'll be back for it another day, so don't you dare touch it again. It's an antique, I'll have you know. Now help me bring it back in here."

They manoeuvred the chair back into Miss Latimer's room, then Betty held the door open for Elaine to leave. "Oh, the funeral will be on Sunday, by the way. Ashley said you should speak to her tomorrow and she'll give you details of how you're getting there."

The smell of bleach had abated somewhat, but not enough. Elaine decided to take her blanket and towel down to the kitchen and use them in place of a mat to do some more Pilates. She opened up her desk drawer to get out her Nexus and consult her crib sheet of Pilates exercises, but the tablet was gone. She searched in her wardrobe, under the mattress and inside the bed, but it wasn't anywhere. Someone had taken it… but who, and why?

Chapter 21

Saturday 21 April

Elaine walked over to the central building with a slight residual headache from the smell of bleach. She had breakfast alone. While she was eating, Roland came past her table bearing a tray, then veered off and sat down as far away from her as possible. It would appear that he couldn't face another dog evaluation session, which was just as well, as neither could she.

Hamish did not appear at all, but she found Joe at the seating area a bit later. "Hi," she said, "I'm glad you're here. Everyone else is avoiding me."

Elaine recounted the events of the previous twenty-four hours to him. "I suppose Betty might've taken my tablet," she said, "but I can't see why she'd bother. It's much more likely that one of the staff took it. Anyway, I'm going over to the admin block now to learn the arrangements for Miss Latimer's funeral tomorrow, and I'll try and find out about my tablet at the same time."

"That must be one of the world's most rapidly arranged funerals," Joe said. "I wonder where they're having it. Presumably somewhere off the premises, as Miss Latimer was never officially here."

"I had assumed it would be in the chapel here, but now I think of it you're probably right. In that case, maybe I should do a runner," Elaine said only half-jokingly.

"Don't even contemplate it, Elaine. How far would you get

with your vision, and no money?"

"Well, I'm not quite as blind as you and Hamish seem to think. Nor am I totally incompetent. In fact, I am pretty resourceful."

"Be patient, Elaine," Joe said, patting her knee. "Would you just take it for granted that we've got your best interests at heart?"

Elaine brushed his hand aside, and sighed loudly. "Patience is not my strong point, never has been. Look, don't preach any more and tell me your news."

"Well, Lyndsay got me a new battery for the GPS jammer, but Hamish reckons it'll be complicated to jam the tag's signal without being detected. I'm leaving the technical details to him, but we'll know at curfew tonight if his solution has worked. I usually get a regular pulse in my tag if I'm not indoors by nine p.m. If that doesn't happen tonight, the jammer will be working and I'll come over and see you."

"Good, something to look forward to," Elaine said. "Was Lyndsay not suspicious about you needing a battery?"

"Obviously I couldn't say what it was for, so I told him a friend had a tablet that needed a new battery. They're about the same size and shape, and he wouldn't know what a tablet battery looks like. They're ancient history for a lad his age."

"I see," Elaine said, getting to her feet. "Not one of your more inspired lies, Joe. It seems that your little boyfriend guessed whose tablet it was and grassed me up to the authorities, who sent someone to look for it. Never mind, I'll find out what happened and deal with the culprit. See you around nine p.m., I hope?"

Joe sounded surprised. "So, you still want me to come

over?"

"Of course, why not?" Elaine shrugged. "We're both in need of distraction."

+++

Elaine waited for half an hour in the corridor before Ashley opened her office door, waved her in and scanned her ID card. "What's your issue today?" Ashley asked.

"I was told you wanted to see me concerning Miss Latimer's funeral," Elaine said. Ashley looked completely blank, so Elaine prompted her. "Violet Latimer. She stayed in the room opposite mine in Unit 1, Block 3, South-West Section. I'm room 5, so hers must have been room 2."

Ashley consulted her monitor. "Oh, yes. The deceased is undergoing Incineration tomorrow and before that there is to be a religious post-Closure Ceremony."

"Exactly, a funeral. That's what I've been asking about."

"Yes," Ashley said, checking her screen again. "Be ready at three p.m. tomorrow. Two guards will call for you and accompany you to the ceremony and back. Try to dress appropriately."

"Don't worry. I'll wear my sable coat, and the black veil."

"Excellent," said Ashley, apparently oblivious to sarcasm. "Is there anything else I can do for you? Would you like a coffee?"

"No coffee, thanks," Elaine said, "but I have a question. A tablet has been stolen from my room. It's a Nexus 7." Ashley looked blank again. Elaine couldn't decide if the woman was being deliberately obstructive, or was just plain stupid. "It's a mobile computing device. Like an iPad, sort of. Do you remember those?"

"Mobile computing devices are not allowed here," Ashley said. "Where did you acquire contraband of this type?"

"I've had it for about ten years. I brought it in with me. Hell, Ashley, you were there. You scanned the bag it was in."

"I very much doubt that," Ashley said. She opened a drawer in her desk, and produced Elaine's tablet. "Is this the device you are referring to?"

"Yes, that's it. May I have it back, please?"

"Absolutely not. As I said, these devices are forbidden here. You can't have it back until after your Exit Date."

"I'll be dead then, Ashley."

"I meant that your next of kin may have it back."

"Have a heart, please, Ashley," Elaine said. "All it's got on it are a few old files, and my entire photo collection."

"Well, you won't need your photos where you're going," Ashley said. "Sorry, no can do. Now, I've got lots of other people to deal with." Ashley walked to the door and held it open until Elaine accepted defeat and left. Ten minutes later she remembered that she'd meant to find out who had told the staff about the tablet.

Without Hamish, Joe, Miss Latimer, or even Roland for company, Elaine was at a loss as to how to spend the day. Force of habit took her to the northern entrance of the central building, but she didn't go into the media room. She couldn't face another game of Spider Solitaire, and she had tried in vain many times on other occasions to make sense of the tiny buttons on the TV remote. Instead she turned left and went down the corridor.

The games room was empty as usual, so she carried on to the VR room. A list taped up beside the door showed names, categories and Exit schedules for people who had booked the room. It seemed to be fully booked for the next two days. If her guess at the time was right, Veronica, ('T', nine days to go) was in there now. A sudden high-pitched scream from the other side of the door caused Elaine to leap backwards in shock. Presumably Veronica had just bungee-jumped off the Victoria Falls Bridge. Either that, or she was being pursued through the flooded streets of New Orleans by giant alligators. Elaine rather hoped it was the latter.

She retraced her steps and went in the other direction past the entrance. For once, the door of the chapel was unlocked. Elaine pushed it open and went in. She was astonished by what she saw. The walls were pure white, broken only by a sort of dado rail made of vibrant blue mosaic tiles, reminiscent of ones she had admired on a visit to Morocco many years before. A large stained glass window in an abstract pattern was set into the back wall. The sun was shining through it and casting red and blue shapes onto the black marble floor and the blond wood of ten pews arrayed in five rows. The same wood had been used for a plain lectern and a low, unadorned table in front of the back wall. An open cabinet against the same wall held what appeared to be half a dozen rolled up prayer mats.

Moved and calmed by the beauty of the room, Elaine slipped into a pew, closed her eyes and bent her head. She addressed a silent prayer to she knew not whom or what, asking for Alexandra's safe return and her, Joe's and Hamish's successful escape.

Behind her, the door opened and closed again and footsteps approached. Elaine opened her eyes and saw a man carrying two polystyrene cups walk past her. He laid the cups on a pew diagonally opposite hers and sat down.

Elaine couldn't restrain herself. "Excuse me," she said, "but I don't think you should bring hot drinks in here. The wood is so beautiful, it would be a shame to stain it."

"I entirely agree," he said, "but these are not actually hot drinks." His voice was mellifluous and vaguely familiar.

The man stood up, and moved towards her, his hand stretched out for shaking. "Rupert Mortimer," he said. "Humanist celebrant. Haven't we met before?"

The navy blue silk cravat tucked into the neck of his pale pink shirt clinched it. "Yes, I'm Elaine" she said. "We met at a pre-Closure Party for two amazing women a couple of weeks ago."

"Of course, Olivia and Rose," he said. "That's right. We did meet, Elaine. I'm surprised you're still here."

"Oh, I've still got another twelve days to wait. Administrative problems. I'll have waited thirty days in total by the time my Exit comes."

A look of concern crossed the celebrant's face. "My goodness, that seems very inefficient. Not to mention downright callous."

"Indeed. So what brings you back here, Rupert?"

"The girls," he said, glancing at the polystyrene cups. "It was typical of Olivia, of course. I've known her since childhood and she was never any good with paperwork, but I would have expected Rose to get that sort of thing right."

"I'm sorry, I don't follow you," Elaine said.

"No, I'm not making myself very clear, am I? Rose put Olivia as her next of kin on the consent form, and Olivia forgot to fill in the section about where her ashes should go. They've been keeping them for collection all this time, and finally got in touch with me. I expect I will think of a good place to mix and scatter them once I've come to terms with the idea."

"I see," Elaine said, feeling rather guilty that she'd hoped she might wangle a cup of coffee out of this encounter.

"And while I was here, I thought I'd pop in and see the chapel again. It is superb, don't you think?"

"Absolutely," Elaine said. "You know, it's the first time I've seen it. It's usually locked." She hesitated briefly, wondering whether Rupert could be trusted. "This may seem a bit odd, but I wonder if I could ask you a couple of things. Outside, perhaps? We could have a brief walk in the grounds." Rupert looked surprised but agreed. "Don't forget the ashes," Elaine said.

"Ah, yes, of course. Would you mind taking this one, that's Rose I think, while Olivia and I open the door for us?" Elaine stifled a fit of inappropriate laughter and followed Rupert out of the chapel.

Elaine waited until they were out of earshot of any windows before beginning. "I wondered if you knew anything about where Closure takes place and what happens to people afterwards? I mean, obviously they're cremated, but where and …."

"My goodness, hasn't this all been explained to you? Olivia was very thoroughly briefed before her Closure."

"Not yet. I think I'll get an Exit Interview next week, so maybe they'll explain it then. I'm just rather anxious and confused about it at the moment."

"Understandably so, my dear. Olivia told me the Closure rooms are all underground. Apparently there's a big complex of tunnels below the facility. I believe the PCI, that is the Post-Closure Incinerator, is down there too."

"I see. So they don't conduct funerals in the chapel? Only, pre-Closure ceremonies."

"I believe so, but it could be on a case-by-case basis," Rupert said. "I'm terribly sorry, I'm afraid I have to go now. I was given a visitor's pass for an hour only. But it was a pleasure to meet you again."

"You too," Elaine said, wishing he could stay longer. There was something comforting about Rupert's presence.

"Hold on, can you take Olivia for a moment?" Rupert passed the other cup to Elaine, pulled a wallet out of his jacket and extracted a business card from it. "If there's anything I can do to help, do get in touch. I am a person-centred therapist as well as a celebrant."

They carefully exchanged the cups for the card.

"Thanks," said Elaine, "you never know," and put the card in her jacket pocket.

+++

Shortly after nine o'clock, there was a tap at Elaine's bedroom window. She rushed outside to let Joe in. Obviously, the GPS jammer was working. "Great," she said once he was in her room. "Does this mean you can stay the night without being detected?"

"We'll see," Joe said. He looked strained and more serious than she'd ever seen him before.

"What's up, Joe?" Elaine asked. "What's happened?"

"Only what I told you yesterday. There were sixty or so of us in our blocks two days ago. Now there are less than fifty, and I'm wearing a badge that gives me just five more days to go. It focusses the mind in a direction I'd rather avoid."

In the excitement of meeting Rupert and her irritation about Joe and Hamish's secrecy, Elaine had temporarily forgotten about the plight of the Indigents. "I'm not surprised you're feeling tense. The number on the badge really brings it home to you." Elaine said. "I know what will cheer you up. I've always found the best cure for anxiety is sex. It stops me thinking entirely."

"Slow down, Elaine. There's also the question of Hamish's gizmo to keep in place." Joe removed the rug that habitually covered his legs from the knees down. The left leg of his jeans was rolled up to just below the knee and his lower leg was enclosed in a bizarre metal mesh cylinder sealed at either end with silver foil and duct tape.

"What the hell is that? It looks like some kind of calliper," Elaine said.

"Hamish improvised a Faraday cage out of the loose grille from the extractor fan in his kitchen, and the foil that came out of the dope box. It's a bit Heath Robinson, but it seems to work."

"I'll take your word for it. Science was never my forte. So that's what Hamish has been up to. He's been ignoring me entirely."

"Well, like me, he's worried that the Pemberton woman has got it in for you, and he's trying to keep you out of trouble till we go," Joe said.

"That's pretty pointless. It seems that most of the staff have it in for me. Ashley has confiscated my tablet and refuses to give it back. I didn't find out who told her about it, though."

"I'm sorry. Was there anything incriminating on it?"

"Other than a few rather embarrassing photos Gary took of me, no."

"Who's Gary?"

"He was my last boyfriend."

"I see," Joe said, frowning at Elaine. "What happened to him? Couldn't he have looked after you a bit better so you wouldn't have landed up in here?"

A jolt of anger set Elaine's heart racing. "One, I am not a pot plant, or a kitten, or yet so old that I need to be looked after, Joe. Two, he died about five years ago after a vascular event brought on by a surfeit of Viagra."

"You're kidding me."

"Unfortunately not," Elaine said. "You see, we used to go wild water swimming together and …"

Joe laughed. "Well, no doubt all that cold water would have a detrimental effect on anyone's erectile capacity."

Elaine was gazing, unfocussed, out of her window. With the way the light was hitting the window, Elaine could see smears on it and the marks of her fingers on the inside of the glass where she'd pushed the window open. She moved over to the window, pulled the sleeve of her top down over her hand and began rubbing at the marks. "So, I just swam for fun, but Gary was very competitive about it. One Saturday he came third in an event which he had expected to win. He seemed to feel his masculinity had been compromised and spent the rest of the weekend proving to me that it hadn't. I didn't discover he'd been taking pills until it was too late."

"At least the poor bugger died happy," Joe said.

"It's wasn't funny, Joe," Elaine said, her back still turned. "Why do you have to make jokes about everything?" Elaine heard the creak of Joe's wheelchair and wondered if he was leaving. Instead she felt a light kiss at the nape of her neck and Joe took her by the shoulders and turned her to face him.

"Oh, have you changed your mind?" Elaine said, a smile gradually creeping up from her lips to her damp eyes.

"I have. It's a better way to die than in the bowels of the Exit Facility. Just be careful not to dislodge the cage."

Chapter 22

Sunday 22 April

Elaine slept a deep and dreamless sleep and woke up to find Joe had gone and had left her a note scribbled on the back of a Scrabble score sheet – 'Confab around 10.00 @ p. shed? Burn after reading!' This was followed by an emoji of a winking face with its tongue stuck out. Not having any matches, she contemplated and then rejected the idea of eating the note. Eventually, she tore it into four pieces and flushed it down the toilet, feeling more than a little ridiculous as she did so.

Elaine ate breakfast alone, savouring the fact that she felt physically relaxed and pain free today. Her biggest worry for the moment was what she could wear to Miss Latimer's funeral. Her happy state of equanimity did not last long.

"Hi guys!" she said, sitting down beside Hamish on the wooden bench when she arrived outside the potting shed. He and Joe had were silent and the atmosphere felt as chilly as the weather had been since last week's storm.

"Right," Hamish said, "I think it should be quiet enough here on a Sunday, but let's keep this snappy just in case. Joe and I had a tentative plan, but we obviously need to revise it in the light of what's going on now. We can't let all the Indigents vanish overnight without doing something to help them."

"Count me out of any heroics," Joe said. "I feel sorry for my fellow inmates, of course, but I'm not jeopardising my own chance of freedom for their sake."

"What are you suggesting, Hamish?" Elaine asked. "That we should organise a mass breakout with all the Indigents? Would that even be possible?"

"All I know is that I couldn't live with myself if I turned a blind eye while innocent people were being executed."

Joe snorted. "You won't even get a chance to live with yourself, Hamish, the way you're thinking. Either you'll be shot in the course of a half-baked mass escape attempt or you'll be offed according to the timetable, which your badge says is in fourteen days."

"Look, we don't even know they are being executed, do we? It's possible they're being transported to another venue overnight," Elaine said.

Hamish was unconvinced. "Then why assign Exit Dates?"

"I see your point, Hamish, but wouldn't it be logistically difficult to execute and dispose of so many people in one go?" Elaine continued. "We know the system is already overburdened, because that's why your and my Exits were delayed. And I heard the Administrator complaining on the phone that the second PCI hadn't been completed yet."

"What's a PCI?" Joe asked.

"It stands for Post-Closure Incinerator," Elaine said. "I discovered yesterday that there's one underground, as are the Closure rooms. I don't know where the other one's being built. Presumably there's an exhaust pipe or chimney or whatever you'd call it that protrudes above ground. If we'd been monitoring that, we could perhaps tell if the PCI has had a higher throughput than usual."

"I looked into that a while back" Hamish said. "It seems incinerator emissions are not perceptible either by sight or smell unless something has gone wrong with the equipment."

Joe was shifting in his chair impatiently. "Right. So can we just drop this issue, Hamish, and focus on getting ourselves out?"

Hamish stood up and paced up and down, his hands thrust deep into the pockets of his trousers, and his shoulders hunched. "The pair of you don't seem to care that people who didn't choose this fate are being gassed, or worse, beneath our feet every evening."

"I don't think either Joe or I said that, Hamish. But we don't have proof. Anyway, we'll be more use to them on the outside. We can call in a human rights group to investigate."

Hamish scratched his beard. "Hmm, yes…"

"Personally, I'm not interested in being a whistle-blower," Joe said. "I'll leave that to you two. But Elaine's right about being more useful once we're out. Besides, we can't involve another forty people when our plan hinges on the fact that our escape won't be detected until the following morning."

"Oh, so you have got a plan," Elaine said. "I was beginning to wonder."

Hamish sat down again on the bench and sighed loudly. "OK," he said. "You're right. I've been thinking with my heart instead of my head. But in that case we have to bring the date forward. If people are being executed, we can't wait until they've all died before we expose what's going on. How about tomorrow evening?"

"That's too much of a stretch," Joe said. "We both still have preparations to make, and you're not a hundred per cent sure about the system on the northern perimeter yet, are you? Do you know where they'll be taking you for the funeral yet,

Elaine?"

Elaine shook her head. "All I know is that I'm being fetched at three o'clock."

"Right, I'm off," Joe said. "They serve our breakfast even later on a Sunday and I'm ravenous. We can reconvene after Elaine returns."

Hamish and Elaine watched as Joe wheeled himself away towards the Indigents' blocks. "He's an odd chap," Hamish said. "Do you think we can trust him?"

"As long as we're helping him to save his own skin, yes, absolutely."

"I hope you're right. He certainly doesn't seem to care about anyone else's. Still, he should be competent, at least. Apparently he was in the SAS when he was younger." Hamish paused for a while, as if uncertain how to continue. "You do realise he's not actually disabled, don't you?" Hamish asked.

"Yes, I've known for a while," Elaine said, keeping her voice and face neutral. "So, are you going to explain the plan to me now, Hamish?"

"No, I'm not. I know you're angry, but think about it, Elaine. All it would take is for the administration to decide you were transgressing the limits again, and they might give you a shot of truth serum, or arrange a faster Exit."

"That goes for you, too," Elaine said. "OK, forget it for now. What size of shirt do you wear?"

+++

"Is that what you're wearing?" Brendan asked, looking Elaine over from her trainers to Hamish's charcoal grey polo shirt. He and his companion had swapped their orange uniforms for identical navy blue suits.

"I came equipped for a short stay, Brendan. I wasn't expecting social occasions," Elaine said. She shook her badly rumpled jacket and slipped it on.

"Well, it'll have to do, I guess," Brendan said. "This is my colleague Stewart. You'd better behave yourself, Elaine. Just because we're in suits today doesn't mean we're not prepared for any funny business." He patted his right pocket and scowled.

"Walk ahead of us up that path," Stewart said, pointing to the path that led north past the Indigents' blocks. They walked as far as what Elaine had called 'the hiding tree' and then turned left up the path where she had seen Joe and Siobhan chatting together.

"I haven't been up this way for ages," Brendan said. "I always go out the south gate."

"Well, I live in Dourmouth, so this is closer for me," Stewart replied. "Hey, you. Stop there!" Elaine continued walking. "Stop, I said!" Elaine paid no attention. "Stay there, Elaine. I thought you said she was half-blind, Brendan, not deaf."

"Well, she's old. She's probably a bit deaf too."

Elaine stopped, pleased that her ruse had worked. They'd talk more freely if they thought she couldn't hear them.

"Stay close to us as we approach the gate. Don't leave the path," Stewart said.

Brendan scanned his ID card over a post set to the right of an ordinary-looking metal gate, which opened and swung inwards. He stepped through the gap, followed by Elaine, with Stewart at the rear. Elaine was surprised to notice that the fence on either side of the gate was a simple affair consisting of three horizontal strands of thin wire. It looked like it wouldn't keep a dog in or out of the premises, far less a determined intruder or would-be escapee.

They walked about ten paces along the path in single file then Stewart suddenly shouted. "Hey, Brendan, whoa there! Scan again before we go on."

"Sorry," Brendan said, scanning his pass over another sensor mounted on a post beside the path. "Like I said, I haven't been this way for a while; I'd forgotten about the second sensor."

"Yeah, well, that's the important one," Stewart said. "Hold your pass there till we're through."

Elaine glanced to her left but could see nothing but another post that might have had a sensor mounted on it. There was nothing visible to go through; nothing that could have caused Stewart to get jittery.

"Keep moving, Elaine," Brendan said. "We haven't got all day. Go ahead of us again, and stay on the path."

The path wound down a steep slope towards the river. The embankment to either side of it was dotted with trees and carpeted with fallen leaves interspersed with swathes of vibrant bluebells. "Could I pick some of those to put on Miss Latimer's coffin?" Elaine asked, indicating the nearest patch of flowers.

"Don't push your luck. It's not the frigging teddy bears' picnic, Elaine," Brendan said. "Get a move on."

Elaine continued down the path, which descended even more sharply and then emerged from the trees in front of the little single-span stone bridge she had seen at a distance from the lawn behind Hamish's block. A pale sun had broken through the cloud cover and bathed the golden stone walls and yellow-grey cobbles of the bridge in light. Elaine quickened her pace, feeling light-hearted and hopeful as she set foot on the yellow brick road of the bridge.

"Hey, there!" shouted Stewart. "Not so fast."

Elaine stopped and turned. "I'm sure I was told to go faster a few seconds ago."

"Cool it, Elaine," Brendan said. "Stewart's got a short fuse. Just walk at a normal pace over the bridge, a few steps ahead of us."

Elaine did as she was told, while moving slightly closer to the parapet in the hope of getting a glimpse of the water.

"It's nice here," Brendan said. "D'you reckon you could swim in the river?"

"We used to do it all the time when we were kids," Stewart said. "The lads from the village jumped off the bridge to impress the girls. It's quite deep in the middle."

"Cool," Brendan said.

"Effing freezing more like it," said Stewart.

Elaine reached the other side of the bridge. The path continued for a few yards and then forked. She stopped and the two guards caught up with her. "We want the right fork," Stewart said. "The crematorium's about two hundred yards further on. You, walk between us now. When we get there, try to stay out of conversation with anyone. If it can't be avoided, just explain that you were a friend of the old lady's in the … ehm … care home, and we're your nephews. Got it?"

The chapel was not as beautiful as the one in the Exit Facility, but still light, simple and pleasant. Elaine and her companions sat in a row of seats at the back. The rest of the congregation consisted of Betty, a tweedy woman in her fifties, and a frail old lady in a wheelchair accompanied by a uniformed nurse. The minister had clearly never met Miss Latimer, but made great play of the fact that she had been a parishioner of his father's in Inverdour. The tweedy woman gave a eulogy – she turned out to be a former head girl of Miss Latimer's and spoke with enthusiasm of the old lady's leadership style and track record as a headmistress. Finally, the tiny, unprepossessing coffin was carried off on a conveyor belt between two maroon velvet curtains. It looked like Betty had gone for a cardboard coffin, for reasons of economy rather than ecology, Elaine suspected.

With so few mourners, escaping the line-up was impossible. "Stick to the script, OK?" Brendan said.

Elaine duly offered her condolences to Betty, the head girl and the old lady, then was nabbed by the minister. "Perhaps you'd like to sign the Book of Remembrance," he suggested.

"Yes, definitely," Elaine said, an idea coming into her head. Brendan kicked her ankle and scowled. Elaine responded with a shrug and a look that she hoped conveyed that she had no option but to comply.

Elaine rehearsed what she could write while waiting in line behind Betty and the ex-head girl. *May God forgive her and rescue the innocent who are imprisoned opposite*, she wrote in demotic Greek when her turn came.

The minister glanced at the book. "Oh, that's unusual," he said. "Are you Greek?"

"No, but I converted to the Greek Orthodox Church when I lived in Cyprus." Elaine stuffed her right hand in her jacket pocket and crossed her fingers to excuse the lie.

"How lovely, my dear. I studied a bit of ancient Greek on my

Theology course, but I'm pretty rusty now. Let's see what I can make out."

Elaine stiffened with fear. She wanted her message to be read, but not under the watchful eyes of Brendan and his pal.

"Well, that word's easy." The minister was warming to his task. "That's God, of course. And this one here – ath – o – something, let me see, is it ath-o-ous? Does that mean innocence, or the innocents? I'm afraid I don't remember much."

"You're doing fine," Elaine said, improvising rapidly, "but let me help you. It says *May God forgive her, for blessed are the innocent*."

"Amen," the minister replied, beaming. "I couldn't have put it better myself."

Brendan was shifting nervously from foot to foot as Elaine walked up to him. "We should get back," he said, "but we need to find Stewart. He went for a smoke."

As Brendan and Elaine stepped out of the door of the crematorium, two black vans with smoked glass windows came up the drive and turned into a side road that led round the back of the building. They looked identical to the vehicle that had taken Elaine to the Exit Facility. They were followed by a black limousine that drew up in front of the building. Nicola Pemberton, her usual navy suit replaced with a black one, got out of the car and hurried towards the entrance, her heels clacking on the marble flagstones. She stopped by Brendan. "We had a flat tyre, most inconvenient. Have I missed the ceremony?"

She then noticed Elaine, who had been standing slightly behind Brendan. "What is going on? I left strict instructions with Ashley. Why are you standing around out here? And where is the other guard?"

"He had to answer a call of nature, Miss." Brendan jerked a thumb towards Elaine. "And she didn't see the vans; she's almost blind."

"I have to pay my condolences now, but you haven't heard the last of this, Brendan. Report to my office at ten o'clock tomorrow, along with whichever slacker is on duty with you now." She gave Elaine an icy look and went into the church.

The walk back to the Exit Facility took place in silence. As they crossed the bridge and headed up the steep escarpment, Elaine noticed stern signs in severe lettering facing back towards the river: 'State Property. Keep Out.' 'Trespassers Will Be Prosecuted'. At the top of the hill, just before the post where Brendan had scanned his ID card, other large, garish notices read: 'Danger. Do Not Proceed Beyond this Point' and 'Stop! Danger of Death'. The three-strand wire fence looked as innocent as it had on the way out, but she gave it a wide berth now, just in case.

+++

Elaine caught up with Hamish at dinner and they met Joe at the shed as dusk was falling. "Well done, Elaine," Hamish said. "You've confirmed what I suspected. The wire fence is just a notional perimeter; it's the covert fence beyond it that's important."

"I didn't see another fence. Just a sensor on either side of the path," Elaine said.

"There's a whole line of posts with sensors on them beyond those, but probably too far off for you to spot," Hamish explained. "And it's covert because the sensors emit waves that you can't see, but which detect any movement by people or things crossing between them. Any images they pick up will be relayed instantly to the control room."

"I see," Elaine said, "but where's the danger? There were heavy-duty danger signs facing down the hill before you got to the sensors..."

"We suspect there's more to the fence than just monitoring movement," Joe said. "A capacity to administer some kind of shock that could kill, or at least stun"

"Nasty, "Elaine said. "That would explain why the guards got anxious on our way out. Anyway, I think you're right about Indigents being terminated. Why else would there be vans arriving at the crematorium?" She explained the message she'd left in the Book of Remembrance. "Probably about as much use as a message in a bottle, but …"

"… it appealed to your Famous Five fantasies," Joe said.

"Look who's talking! What about instructions to burn messages after reading them?"

"Huh?" Hamish said. "What are you talking about?"

"Nothing important, Hamish," Elaine said. "So when are we going? Joe's got three days left, and I need to be back home before my daughter gets there."

"There are still some details to firm up. I'll need your tablet tomorrow, Elaine. I downloaded some data on covert fences onto it."

A feeling like a bayonet being thrust into her guts hit Elaine. "I hope you're fucking joking, Hamish! Why didn't you tell me? If I'd known you'd kept that kind of data on it. I'd have found a safe hiding place! Ashley confiscated the tablet two days ago."

Hamish groaned and buried his head in his hands. "Oh God,

Elaine, I'm sorry. I should have told you, it slipped my mind with all the other stuff going on. I did encrypt the data before saving it, but if the IT security team run checks… "

"… we're all dead," Joe said, then began manoeuvring his wheelchair. "I can't believe you did that, Hamish." His mouth clamped shut in a tight line. "I'm going to my unit. Let's just hope the techies get distracted by the saucy photos before they get to the incriminating bits. Our lives depend on it, at this point. I'll see you guys tomorrow."

"I bloody well hope so!" said Elaine.

Chapter 23

Monday 23 April

Elaine slept fitfully, waking at every sound from inside or outside the block, terrified that guards were coming to take her away to the tunnels where the Closure rooms lay. It wouldn't be a merciful Exit now, Nicola would choose the cheapest and nastiest method in her arsenal.

Elaine finally woke to the sound of tapping at her window. Her heart racing and her legs shaky, she got out of bed and moved to the window. It was Joe. Elaine left her unit and went round to let him in at the main door of the block. "Shit, I thought it was the guards coming for me," she said. "What's the time?"

"Early, I don't know exactly. Look, in the light of Hamish's revelation last night, we're going ahead as soon as we can, and hoping they don't bother examining your tablet, or not for a while at least. And Hamish reckons he can pretty much remember the information he needs."

"It all sounds a bit haphazard."

"Yep, not what we'd planned, but what else can we do? I need you to do something for me. You'll have to remove my tag."

"But why? You've disabled it."

"Trust me, it's necessary."

Elaine glared at Joe. "No, I've had enough of trusting you and Hamish after what I heard last night. Tell me what's going on."

Joe paused before answering. "You're right, Elaine, it's not fair to keep you in the dark. This is the plan. D'you remember Pete, the locksmith and ex-con in my block?"

Elaine nodded.

"Well, he's going to act as a decoy. My chip will be re-enabled and taped onto my wheelchair. We'll disable Pete's tag using the gizmo Hamish made with the cage and the jammer. That way Pete can move freely without setting the siren off before he gets near the perimeter. He's going to shove my wheelchair through the wire fence at the west end of the embankment. It's steep there so the chair will roll on down the hill. When it goes through the wire fence, it will trip the alarm and floodlights will come on, illuminating that area and attracting the guards. As the wheelchair is made of metal, it will also break the circuit of the virtual fence for a few seconds, at which point we can go through the detection zone without registering on the system, or getting hurt."

"I see," said Elaine. "So your wheelchair goes down the slope and into the river, and the guards search for you there, never thinking that you can actually walk or that an escape has been carried out further to the east?"

"That's right," Joe said, grinning.

"And the tag will be on your chair, still giving out signals, but they may not be able to get at it immediately since it'll be night and the river is quite deep," Elaine continued. "It's good, unless Hamish gets the timings wrong. But why would Pete do that and not want to escape with us?"

"He's really ill with chronic emphysema and gets no palliative care. He's the only person in the Indigents' blocks that is actually looking forward to exiting."

"Well, the man's a saint. Let's just hope he's got enough

breath to do the job. And how am I meant to remove your tag?"

Joe reached into the pocket of his flying jacket and took something out of it. "You'll have to cut it out. Pete made this prison version of a scalpel." Joe handed the shiv to Elaine. It was a razor blade that had been partially embedded in the shaft of a yellow biro by means of melting the plastic.

"Christ, Joe, this thing is hideous." Elaine shivered, turning the object over in her hands. "I don't think I can do this. Can't you ask Hamish?"

"I did, but apparently he faints at the sight of blood. C'mon, I'm sure you can cope. Didn't you slaughter your own chickens when you lived in bucolic bliss in Cyprus?"

"No, Andreas did that. I gutted fish."

"Perfect, it's exactly the same thing. Just a small incision, then remove the innards, or chip in this case. Oh, and you have to do it while the cage is still on, apparently, and then wrap the chip in tinfoil afterwards."

"Great, nothing too complicated or messy, then," Elaine said, feeling her stomach start to heave. "It sounds like a nineteenth century gynaecologist carrying out obstetrics under a modesty sheet."

"I have something from the redoubtable Siobhan," said Joe, fishing in his other pocket. He extracted a quarter bottle of pale rum. "Disinfectant, painkiller and reward rolled into one. What more do we need?"

"Bandages," Elaine said.

Elaine brought two clean dishtowels from the kitchen, which Joe nicked with the shiv and tore into strips. She then gathered up the standard issue towels from the five empty rooms in her

263

unit, laid them over her desk, and propped Joe's leg up on it after taking off his shoe. She wiped the blade of the makeshift scalpel with rum and swabbed the skin around the tag. Joe took a swig of the rum and passed the bottle to Elaine.

"Later," she said and pulled back part of the silver foil and inserted her hand inside the metal grille. "I can barely see what I'm doing through this gadget without getting pissed as well."

The incision was easy, but the chip had embedded itself quite thoroughly in the flesh of Joe's calf in the weeks he had been wearing it. It took some minutes of gouging at the edges of it before Elaine finally dislodged it, retching as she did so. Joe had shut his eyes and swore profusely between gulps of rum. Elaine held the chip, slick and slippery with blood, and wrapped it in silver foil from the end of the cage. "Can the cage come off now?" she asked, swallowing the bile that had risen in her throat.

"Yes, if the chip is wrapped up." Joe opened his eyes. "Fuck, I'm bleeding to fucking death."

"I'm sorry," Elaine said. "It wasn't as simple a job as you'd expected."

She eased the cage down over Joe's foot and wrapped towels around his calf, pressing hard to stop the bleeding. By the time the flow had eased to an ooze, all five towels were soaked through. She peeled them back gently, poured some rum over the wound and wrapped it in the improvised bandages. "I hope those will suffice," she said. "Keep your leg up on the desk for a bit longer while I clean up. Then I'll have some of the rum."

Joe shook the bottle that was still clutched in his right hand. It was empty. "Sorry, darling, can't have you drinking before breakfast, can we?"

Elaine couldn't contain her revulsion any longer. She went into her bathroom and just had time to close the door before she was violently sick. She rinsed her mouth out and washed her hands. "Sorry about that" she said as she went back into her bedroom.

"That's OK, not the worst thing I've been through this morning" Joe said.

Elaine washed the cage and then gathered the bloodied towels into a bundle and stuffed them in a corner of her bathroom until she could think of what to do with them. She washed her hands again and came out of the bathroom to find Joe settling himself into the wheelchair, his trouser leg pulled down over the bandages.

"Have you stopped bleeding?"

"More or less. I'm going back to my room to lie down. I think it will be better to keep my leg horizontal for a while. Thanks for doing that."

"My pleasure," Elaine said automatically. "No, actually it was horrible, but you know what I mean. Make a speedy recovery. I'll tell Hamish the mission has been accomplished."

Elaine kissed Joe lightly on the lips, put the foil-wrapped chip in his pocket, tucked the cage under his blanket and opened her bedroom door to let him wheel himself out.

+++

Without the Nexus, Elaine didn't know what time it was, but she guessed from the position of the sun that it was somewhere between nine and ten o'clock. She still felt queasy but hoped food might settle her stomach and give her strength for what was to come. As she was heading to the central building she saw a figure moving towards her from the copse.

Shit – was it a guard? The gait and stature resembled Brendan's, but he wasn't in uniform.

"Hey, come over here," he called. It was Brendan.

Elaine approached him, her heart thumping too hard again. Brendan was wearing jogging trousers and a hooded top and his shoulders were hunched. He held something out towards Elaine.

"The fucking bitch fired me," he said. "Go on, take it. It's yours isn't it?"

Elaine was too surprised to speak, but reached out and took her tablet from Brendan, stunned and grateful.

"It's not like I was the one who naffed off for a fag yesterday, was it?"

"No, certainly not, it wasn't you," Elaine agreed.

"Right. But the bitch didn't fire Stewart, did she? She said I've got too big a mouth for this job and yesterday was the last straw."

"I'm sorry, Brendan. That's most unfair."

"Too right it is." Brendan turned his head and spat on the grass beside the path. "And that other bitch Ashley didn't stand up for me at all, even after I'd gone and got your tablet for her. Mind you, Christ knows what she wanted it for, since it doesn't work."

"It probably needs charging. The battery runs down fast."

"Really?" Brendan brought his face closer to Elaine's and looked at her looked suspiciously. "Somebody told me you'd got a new battery."

"Yes, well I did, but I haven't put it in yet. I'm not very good

266

with that kind of thing."

"Whatever. Anyway, keep it somewhere safe. And Ashley can go fuck herself."

"Thanks, Brendan. What will you do now?" Elaine asked.

"Go back to my old job as a bouncer, I guess. At least you get to do the bossing around and you meet plenty of birds." Brendan grinned and gave her a theatrical wink.

"Well, best of luck then, Brendan. Thanks again."

Elaine felt almost dizzy with relief; if the Nexus 7 had died, then probably nobody had examined it yet. She dithered over taking the tablet back to her unit, or leaving it in her jacket in the dining hall vestibule. Both were risky, but she chose the latter option. Her appetite fuelled by optimism, Elaine piled her plate with everything on offer bar the blood pudding.

"Wow, you're hungry," Hamish said, eyeing her tray as Elaine sat down beside him. He looked tense and drawn and was pushing a piece of fried egg round his plate listlessly.

"I've got two bits of good news, that's why," Elaine said. She reported the successful outcome of her operation on Joe, omitting the gorier details, then described her encounter with Brendan.

Hamish relaxed visibly. "Thank God. I've been feeling awful about leaving that data on your tablet."

"So you bloody well should, Hamish. But I really think it's OK. It sounds like Ashley shoved it in the drawer and forgot about sending it for examination. Or maybe she just didn't get round to it as Nicola was away."

"How long will it need to charge?" Hamish asked.

"Ages. Six hours at least."

"OK. So let's all meet around four p.m. at the shed, then. Bring it with you." Hamish popped his final piece of egg on a triangle of toast, munched it noisily, and left Elaine to finish breakfast on her own.

She returned to her unit and searched the other rooms for anything that might be of use. Someone had cleared out Dorothy's room. The beautifully arranged best sewing basket had gone, as had the second-best one. Only a beige jumper with holes in the elbows remained, forgotten on the top shelf in the wardrobe. Elaine left Miss Latimer's room for last. The other three proved to be totally empty of anything personal.

Betty had done a thorough job of cleaning out Miss Latimer's room, and only the wing chair remained to be collected. Seen without its occupant, it was an ugly, cumbersome piece of furniture, but it held fond associations for Elaine. She patted the seat cushion affectionately, and heard something rustle as she did so. Elaine lifted off the cushion and traced the noise to half a dozen cellophane toffee wrappers that had slipped down the side of the cushion. She also found two paperclips, a couple of small coins and a £20 note that had been folded into a small square.

"Thank you, Miss Latimer. Rest in peace," she said, pocketing the money and binning the rest.

Inspiration for hiding the tablet while it charged came to her in the kitchen. She checked out the floor-level cupboards, but these were largely empty. Even the most cursory search would reveal the tablet instantly if she put it there. But she noticed that the flimsy hardboard back of the cupboard to the right of the fridge bellied inwards slightly, perhaps warped by damp. Elaine gently pulled the small free-standing fridge away from its position under the worktop. There were two sockets in the wall behind it, one housing the plug for the fridge, and the other unused. As she had suspected, there was a slim gap between the wall and the back of the cupboard on the right. Elaine slid the Nexus 7 into the gap, plugged the charger into the free wall socket and replaced the fridge.

Elaine went into her own bathroom to wash her hands and was confronted with the bundle of blood-stained towels. A hunt in the cupboard that housed cleaning equipment yielded a black bin bag, so she put the towels in that and placed it in the communal bin in the kitchen. Five minutes later, a dozen scenarios having crossed her mind, Elaine retrieved the bag, brought it back to her room and stuffed it in the back of her wardrobe, thinking she could find a place to dump it near the potting shed later. She lay down for a nap; the start to the day had been grim, but things had taken a turn for the better with her tablet back and twenty quid in her pocket. There was light on the horizon again.

+++

"I've been thinking," Elaine said to Joe as they all sat outside the potting shed. Hamish was absorbed in scanning through the files he'd encrypted and saved on Elaine's tablet. "The sensors on the virtual fence send data to the control room about anything that passes through, don't they?"

"As I understand it, yes," Joe said.

"So it doesn't just detect movement, but can tell exactly what it is that is moving?"

"I think so, but Hamish knows more. Why?"

"Well, if it relays images of what is going through it, then won't it be obvious that your wheelchair is empty? In which case, it will still work as a decoy and break the circuit, but it won't fulfil the purpose of distracting attention and resources for a long time while we make our way to somewhere safe," Elaine said.

"True," Joe said. "Hamish, did you hear what Elaine said?"

"Yes, I was just checking some facts as you were speaking. Assuming that the system is as, or more, sophisticated than the one Roland thinks it is, then it can detect shapes and some materials as well as movement. So it will recognise hidden explosive material on an intruder's body, for example."

"Then Joe's wheelchair is clearly going to look empty, isn't it?" Elaine asked.

"You're right. And you're right in saying that won't prevent us getting out, but it could mean that they realise almost instantly that a trick has been pulled," Hamish agreed. "So, what do we do?

"Oh, you want my ideas now, do you?" said Elaine.

"It's not worth getting huffy now, Elaine," Joe said. "I think I'm going to have to give up my leather jacket. I'll hate losing it, but if it makes it look more like I'm in the chair…"

"I agree," Elaine said. "Especially if we stuff it with something that makes it look like there's a body inside the jacket."

"What, though?" Joe asked.

"I just happen to have five unwanted bloodstained towels in my unit. And a beige wool jumper that could perhaps be shaped vaguely into a head. Would wool and hair come up as similar materials, Hamish?" Elaine said.

"Frankly, I've no idea, the files I found don't go into that much detail, but maybe. Anyway, anything's probably better than sending an empty wheelchair down the slope."

They spent the next hour refining and rehearsing the plan. Elaine and Hamish would have preferred to leave that night, but Joe was in pain from the improvised surgery and could barely put any weight on his left leg, so they agreed to postpone till the following evening. The guards changed shifts at five past nine, just after the Indigents' curfew, so they would time the decoy event with Pete to coincide exactly. Sunset would be twenty-five minutes before that, but whether it was really dark by then would depend on cloud cover. Elaine, Joe and Hamish would be in place in the copse beside the north gate before that. With luck, the sky would be overcast and they could creep to the wire fence unseen, then crawl through it and be in place to dash through the covert fence when the wheelchair broke the circuit.

"There's a ten-second gap after an alarm is triggered and before the system resets automatically," Hamish said for the fifth time. "That's ample for three of us to get through. It doesn't matter if you cross on the path or to the side of the path, but we'll leave the path to you Elaine, so the ground is easier since you don't see well in the dark. OK, got that?"

"Yes, Hamish, got it," said Joe and Elaine in unison for the fifth time.

"And remember, if we get separated, cross the bridge, take the left fork in the woods, and hole up there in the cover of some trees or bushes. We'll find you, Elaine."

"Yes, Hamish, thank you, I'll be fine. I've been down that path and over the bridge only recently, remember."

Elaine and Hamish dined together in a tense silence broken only by inane comments from Elaine any time someone passed their table. They parted outside the main door and Elaine returned to her room and retrieved the bin bag of bloodied towels from her wardrobe, added Dorothy's old jumper and walked over to Joe's unit. She tapped on his window and he swung the window open and grabbed the bag from her.

"Good work, Elaine," Joe said. "Are you OK?"

"Well, kind of nervous, you know," she answered, keeping her voice low. "I don't suppose you'd like to come round a bit later, seeing as how we both need to relax?"

"No, a good night's sleep is more important," Joe said, whispering too. "And my leg still hurts like hell."

Elaine bit her lip. "Fair enough. See you tomorrow then, Joe."

She made her way back to her unit, thinking that a good night's sleep was the last thing she'd get in these circumstances, and reflecting – not for the first time in her life – on the fact that despite their reputation for being endlessly up for it, men were often far less interested in sex than women were.

Chapter 24

Tuesday 24 April

Contrary to her expectations, Elaine slept, but it was not a refreshing sleep. She dreamed constantly – inane, fragmented dreams – and woke at seven o'clock, tetchy and unrested. She did Pilates for an hour, persuading herself that it would help her stamina and agility. She ripped the metal buttons off her denim jacket because Hamish had stressed that they couldn't cross the covert fence with anything metal on them. She stared at every photograph on her tablet and committed it to memory; this couldn't be taken across the fence either. Had she had a hammer she'd have smashed the device to pieces – if she couldn't take her photo collection, she didn't want anyone else looking at it either – but that wasn't an option.

A shower did little to soothe her frazzled nerves and churning guts, but she was at least clean when she made her way to the central building, sidling into the dining hall fifteen minutes before the breakfast service ended.

"Are you all right, Elaine?" Siobhan asked, sounding genuinely concerned. "You're looking a bit peaky."

"I'm fine, Siobhan," Elaine lied. "And I'd like to say thank you for all your kindness to me while I've been here. You're like a ray of sunshine in this place."

"Why thank you," Siobhan replied. "Oh, have you got your appointment at last? I'll be right sorry to see you go, Elaine."

"Thanks," Elaine said, wiping her nose on the sleeve of her

jacket. "Yes, I'll be going shortly. So thanks again, and perhaps I could have just one more rasher of bacon ..?"

She made her way to a nearby table, tears clouding her vision, and realised she'd sat down two places away from Roland. Surprisingly, he greeted her warmly. "Ah Elaine, just the person I wanted to see. Hamish tells me you're an artist. I hadn't realised before."

"Well, yes, of sorts," Elaine said, wondering what this was leading up to.

"Oh, you don't have any cutlery," Roland said. "Let me get some for you."

He leapt to his feet and returned with a plastic fork, knife and teaspoon for Elaine. "So, how did you get on with the puppy for your niece?" he continued. "Chosen yet?"

"Ehm, no, still in negotiations, but we're getting there," Elaine said. "Your help has been invaluable."

"Not at all, not at all," Roland said. "Glad to be of assistance. And, well, I don't want to be presumptuous, but I thought you might be able to offer me a little help in return."

"Of course," Elaine said, hoping that the bacon, scrambled eggs and toast she was consuming might settle her stomach and stiffen her resolve, rather than reduce her to gut-wrenching indigestion.

"Excellent!" said Roland. "You see, it's to do with the dogs' home I've endowed. I'd like them to have a painting that they can put in the entrance hall in memory of me. Of course, the artist's name will be the most prominent, but I'd like the plaque to mention that I was the donor. The problem is that I'm not very knowledgeable about art."

Elaine accompanied Roland to the media room after

breakfast and spent an hour on his internet account looking out potential pictures that he could buy. His taste ran to the kitsch and sentimental, while hers favoured abstract representations or images in which the dog was a minor feature in the iconography. Eventually, Elaine bowed to Roland's wishes and chose the least lurid of his favourites, thus netting an artist she hoped was poor and needy a cool £10,000 for their efforts.

"Deeply grateful for your help," Roland said. "I'll just sort out the financial aspects now."

Elaine left the media room and headed up the path she'd taken on the day that Ashley had spiked her. It was odd how every corner of the Exit Facility was redolent with memories. She'd hated it here in one way, but in another she'd been more connected with other people than she had been in the outside world. Did she really want to leave? On the other hand, if she didn't leave on her own terms tonight, she'd leave in a permanent fashion within the next nine days. It was hard to comprehend how life had come down to this binary choice.

She continued through the kitchen gardens and took a right up to the potting shed. Neither Joe nor Hamish was there, but when she peered in through the still dusty window of the shed, the memory of Joe was there, creeping up behind her and looking at her arse. "Enough, Elaine," she said to herself. "Go back to your unit and get some more sleep."

+++

Elaine woke up feeling somewhat calmer. Her tablet – denuded of photos, but still telling the time – showed her that it was ten past four. She lay in bed for a while longer, rehearsing what she had to do later that evening. She'd already removed all metals from her person. She had ditched the coins, but she had £20, Miss Latimer's cheque book and a business card from Rupert, the civil celebrant. *Probably all nigh on useless, but you never knew. Dark clothes.* She had her black jeans, Hamish's dark grey polo-shirt and her denim jacket. There would be ten seconds to get through the covert fence after the alarm sounded. She should keep to the path and take the left fork after crossing the bridge.

She got up to use the loo, then returned to her bed to think some more. Ten minutes later she got up and peed again.

Hell, this was not good. Was it just nerves or a UTI? Where were Joe and Hamish? Why hadn't she seen them all day? Had they cooked up a plan of their own and abandoned her? Surely not – she was the one who was offering to fund them if her paintings sold; they wouldn't abandon their benefactress, would they?

Elaine got up, used the loo yet again, then dressed and left her room. As always, she felt a pang as she looked at Miss Latimer's door, knowing there was no longer a welcoming soul behind it. She rifled in the drawers in the kitchen and found a small plastic bag, then returned to her room and put the £20 note, Miss Latimer's cheque book and the business card in the bag and tucked it into the inside pocket of her jacket. Seconds later she used Miss Latimer's Parker pen to write her own name on the back of a Scrabble score card. Beneath this she wrote 'next of kin' and added Alexandra's name and email address. She added this note to the plastic bag and returned it to the jacket pocket. She hid her tablet in the gap behind the kitchen units and left the Parker pen in the desk drawer as a gift for the next inhabitant of Room 5, Unit 1, Block 3, South-West Section. Stifling an upwelling of sadness and fear, Elaine left her unit.

Hamish was in the dining hall, staring at a plate of fish and chips that he seemed to find alien and unappealing. Elaine sat down opposite him with her vegetable lasagne. Her appetite was no heartier than his, but she thought she should eat now as they might not find another meal for a while.

"Everything OK?" Elaine asked. "No hitches?"

"OK so far," Hamish hissed. "How about you?"

"Raring to go," Elaine said, feeling it was her duty to set a good example and keep Hamish's morale up. His face was pinched and it was taking him ages to chew and swallow each mouthful of fish. "What do we do to put in the time until sunset?"

"Sssh!" Hamish looked around the dining hall nervously.

"There's nobody in earshot," Elaine said. "Unless you're wired for sound, that is."

She meant it as a joke, but Hamish choked on a piece of fish, dropped his plastic fork on the floor and dived under the table to retrieve it. He took a while coming back up.

"What the hell are you doing, Hamish?"

"Checking for hidden microphones," Hamish mouthed at her when he emerged.

Elaine rolled her eyes. "Look, we need to do something to occupy ourselves for a couple of hours," she said. "Media room?"

They couldn't think what to do once they got there. Hamish suggested watching a soap opera, but Elaine wasn't keen, so they tried a reality show. Hamish even raised a small chuckle while he watched Elaine watching the screen.

"Why are you laughing, Hamish? Are you laughing at me?"

"Well, the expression on your face is funny. You're sitting there with your mouth hanging open, looking utterly bewildered."

"I am bewildered. Is this meant to be entertainment? Why would anyone want to watch a bunch of plug stupid people humiliating themselves?"

"That's what reality shows are about, Elaine. Have you never seen one before?"

"No. I've told you already, Hamish. I've never had a TV. Anyway, this won't do. Can you find something else?"

Hamish hopped channels until Elaine suddenly shouted at him to stop. "Wow! Yes! How appropriate – it's Gloria Gaynor. I will survive!"

"Yes, we all hope to, Elaine, but don't shout about it just now." Hamish stood up abruptly, removed his jacket and hung it over the screen of the feedback machine.

"OK, but turn the sound up a bit, please. Wow, it's an omen. Just what I needed!"

Elaine leapt to her feet and began boogieing around the media room, singing along when she remembered the words. Hamish looked on, mirroring the expression Elaine had been displaying while watching the reality show.

"What is this programme, Hamish?" Elaine asked breathlessly.

"A disco revival programme, it seems – 'Disco Daze Revisited'. Original footage and videos from the 70s and early 80s," Hamish read from the TV guide he called onto the screen. "Do you want to hear more? Not my style, but if it makes you happy ..."

"Great!" Elaine shimmied across to the other side of the media room, shaking her booty to *Lady Marmalade*. Hamish went over to the monitor he usually used and swiped his ID card. He sat in front of the monitor and then, finding nothing to do on it, drummed his fingers on the table, resolutely out of time with the music.

"Come and dance!" Elaine called, shaking her shoulders towards Hamish. "You'll feel better."

Hamish stood up and shifted awkwardly from foot to foot for half a minute, then sat down again in front of the TV. Elaine flopped down beside him, out of breath, but elated. Hamish got up, looked at his monitor, and returned. He spoke quietly in her ear. "We've got a bit of time left before we move up there. You can go first, ten minutes before me. Joe will be waiting for you."

"What happened to the weed, by-the-way?" Elaine asked. "Did you and Joe smoke it all yourselves? We could use some right now, it might relax you."

"Joe used it for bribes, in exchange for information."

"And the band played believe it if you will," Elaine said.

"I don't think so. The presenter said this is the Pointing Sisters and *Jump*," Hamish said.

Elaine laughed. "Don't you know that expression? It's an old-fashioned way to say someone isn't telling the truth. In other words, Joe probably smoked it himself."

"Well, you could be right. Whatever. It doesn't matter now," Hamish said. "Oh, I know this song! It's from Grease, isn't it?"

"Well, right era, but the wrong film. *Saturday Night Fever* actually. The Bee Gees and *Staying Alive*. I'm going to dance again. Listen to the words, Hamish."

Elaine flopped down beside Hamish at the end of the track. "Did you listen?"

Hamish nodded.

"See – it's an omen again! When we smoked the weed we were singing songs about death and someone tried to break out and died. This time we're listening to songs about survival and we're going to break out and we're going to stay alive."

Hamish didn't react, so Elaine jumped up, stood in front of him, framed his face with her hands and looked into his eyes. "We're staying alive, Hamish. Put that in your brain and keep it there. I have faith in your plan."

Elaine left the media room ten minutes later, still buoyed up by the music and dancing. It was only a few minutes after sunset so there was enough light for her to find her way through the kitchen gardens easily. Joe was already in the thicket that included the hiding tree. He put his arms round her and hugged her. "Gosh, your heart's really thumping, Elaine. Are you nervous?"

"No, that's because I spent the last hour dancing."

"What, waltzing with Hamish in the gloaming? How romantic!"

"Hardly. No, boogieing on down in the media room to a disco revival broadcast on TV. Hamish didn't join in. You smell different, Joe. And you feel a bit scratchy. What are you wearing?"

"Pete's tweed jacket. I had to abandon the flying jacket, remember?"

"Of course. That was nice of him. He's doing a lot for us."

"Well, I gave him the last of the weed in return. The poor guy's got Exit in three days anyway, so he doesn't need his jacket any more. Hey, you're still wearing your lanyard and ID card."

"Shouldn't I be? Hamish didn't say anything about that in the plan."

"Well, I've put mine on the dummy on my wheelchair. I don't know if our cards would trigger an alarm, but it seemed better to have it there. It backs up the story of it being me going through the covert fence in case the sensors do read them."

"Shit. I haven't got time to go back and hide mine," Elaine said. "I can't drop it here. If they find it they'll realise too soon that I've gone through the fence."

"Well, if all goes well, there's no reason for them to look for anything in this area. Their search will be focussed on the section of fence and embankment to the west."

"But it might beep or emit a signal or something." Elaine's confidence was ebbing rapidly. "I can't believe neither of you thought to tell me this. In fact, Hamish had his with him too – he put his monitor on with it."

Joe pulled Elaine further into the darkness of the trees and put his hand over her mouth. "Sssh, someone's coming," he whispered in her ear.

It was Hamish. They conducted a hissed altercation about the ID cards, then agreed that they should embed them in the ground close to the roots of the tree. They balled up the two lanyards and threw them as far as they could into the undergrowth. Hamish was muttering to himself, "How did I miss that? I'm a fool, a bloody idiot."

"Shut up, Hamish," Joe said. "We're wasting time. We should be through the wire fence by now."

Fortunately there was no moon. They walked up the path towards the three-strand wire fence. "Keep well away from the gate. It's got sensors on it," Hamish said. "Crawl through or under the wire. It isn't alarmed or electrified. Stop two metres or a bit more before the posts with the sensors that make up the covert fence."

"I can't see the posts with the sensors in this light," Elaine whispered.

"Fuck! OK, stay beside me," Joe said. Hamish was busy counting under his breath.

Elaine dropped to the ground and slid under the lowest wire of the fence, then crawled on down the slope beside Joe. Hamish was further to the left, on the opposite side of the path. Joe put out an arm to signal to Elaine to stop.

"OK," Hamish hissed. "I figure we've got about a minute until the wheelchair goes through and all hell breaks loose off to the left. After that, we've got ten seconds while the circuit is broken to get through the covert fence. Elaine, you should go through on the path itself, as the surface will be smoother and you won't see hazards on the ground. Got it?"

"Yep." Elaine began counting too. She had got to forty-seven when a blue-white flash rippled across her vision from left to right in front of her, accompanied by a terrifying sizzling and cracking noise. A second later a siren went off and floodlights snapped on, illuminating an area about fifty metres to their left. Elaine scrambled to her feet and stumbled, her right hip shooting pain at the most inopportune moment. She swayed, Joe caught her then pushed her forwards. She lurched downhill and landed on the path, regained her balance and limped ten steps down the path. Suddenly the blue-white light flashed again, followed by the sizzling noise and a scream of agony. Elaine stopped and turned. Joe was on the ground, writhing and groaning. Elaine hobbled back up the slope towards him as a second siren went off, and more floodlights snapped on at the top of the hill above them.

"What is it, Joe? Are you hurt?"

She knelt down beside him. She couldn't see much, but she was aware of a smell of singed wool and burning flesh.

"Forgot the fucking pin in my elbow," Joe gasped.

"It's not the time for bullshit now, Joe. Get up and run."

"Can't, I'm in fucking agony. I'm burning up from the inside. Metal pin from a bike accident as a kid. Fucking fence, I was two seconds too late."

Hamish arrived, panting, having run back up the path. "Move! Before it's too late."

"Joe can't, he's injured."

There were whistles blowing now, and the sounds of guards shouting, coming nearer. "Go, Elaine!" Hamish hissed.

"I can't leave him, it's my fault." Elaine was crying.

"Get the fuck out, Elaine," Joe said. "You've got a daughter to go to."

The smell, like roasting pork turning to crackling, was stronger now.

"I'll do what I can, but go now," Hamish said. "Hole up in the woods on the other side. Take the left fork. You'll be safe over there."

"I'm sorry, so sorry," Elaine said to Joe, and turned down the path, stumbling blindly, terror and horror and guilt churning inside her. She kept to the path, feeling it beneath her trainers more than seeing it, and managed not to fall. Behind her she could hear the voices of guards shouting and Joe swearing, but it seemed no one had spotted her yet.

She entered the area of trees and bluebells that she remembered from her trip to the funeral, and slowed down slightly. Still nobody was pursuing her, but there was no sign of Hamish either. *What the hell was going on?* The floodlights were still focussed on the two areas at the top of the hill, but she thought she glimpsed lights from the other side of the river as she ran towards the bridge. When she had got halfway over the bridge there was no longer any doubt, there were lights ahead of her, as well as behind. *This wasn't right. Where was Hamish? Had he betrayed her after all? Had he been caught with Joe? Were there guards in front as well as behind her?*

Elaine stopped and leant on the bridge's parapet. A green light appeared to be flashing on and off ahead of her. *Or was it just her eyesight playing tricks on her?* She moved her head around trying to locate the light in a section of her vision that wasn't pixelated. Yes, there was a light and it seemed to be coming closer.

Suddenly she remembered Brendan and the other guard discussing the river. "The lads from the village jumped off the bridge to impress the girls. It's quite deep in the middle," Stewart had said. She hadn't come this far to be caught in a pincer movement and dragged back to the Exit Facility. Elaine kicked off her trainers, climbed up onto the parapet and jumped. She hit the water clumsily, feet first, but didn't touch bottom – Stewart hadn't been wrong about the depth of the river. She bobbed back up to the surface and floated for a bit to test the strength of the flow. Joe was right; she had a daughter to go to, and paintings to sell. A life to live. "I will survive!" she said to herself, kicking out in a slow but confident crawl. Then Elaine shut her mind to anything but the rhythm of her strokes and the gentle pull of the current drawing her downstream to freedom.

Chapter 25

Tuesday 24 April

Some time later, a time that was hard to judge, that felt like an hour but was probably far less, Elaine began regretting her rash leap into the river. Her clothes, waterlogged, were slowing her down and the chill of the river was making her movements increasingly slow and lethargic. It was five years since she'd last swum; now the five extra years she'd lived and the lack of intervening training showed her just how out of practice she was. Plus she'd never gone wild swimming without a wetsuit before. *Should she have taken Hamish at his word and run on towards the lights on the other side of the bridge? Maybe they'd been beckoning her, not hunting for her... If only Hamish hadn't got so bloody secretive in the last few days... As for Joe, after all the warnings Hamish had given, how could he have forgotten he had a metal pin in his elbow? Maybe that was a side effect of telling lies to everyone; if you span that many yarns and believed them all, at least temporarily, yourself, maybe your brain stopped distinguishing between truth and fantasy. Maybe a barrage of self-created untruths just wiped out your memory of what had really happened...* A wave of nausea hit Elaine as she thought of the high price he'd paid for that memory blip.

A tug on Elaine's right leg caused her heart to jump. She turned her head back and saw she had floated into a patch of reeds and kicked out to free her foot. She couldn't afford to worry about Joe and Hamish right now. She needed to concentrate on her own survival. *She'd be all right, she'd manage. She always managed, didn't she? She'd managed through forty years of declining eyesight and ongoing poverty. She'd managed to support herself and a child and a no-user of a husband. She'd managed to*

paint works of art that had just sold for £18,000 each. She had
survived the Exit Facility with her sanity intact, and had managed
to break out of it successfully. She'd bloody well manage to survive
this swim and get back home too.

The river seemed to be widening out now, maybe into an estuary. The current pulled more in the middle, but Elaine didn't want to get carried out to sea; she'd drown within minutes if she did. She forced herself closer to the bank on her right; sooner or later the shore must curve south, and south was the way home. She started counting her strokes aloud to keep herself focussed until she realised the extra breath required for that was making her even more tired.

At last, the darkness to her right was relieved in the distance by a series of evenly-spaced lights – streetlamps, maybe – and a dancing irregular light far closer to where Elaine was. She dragged herself even closer to the shore, put her feet down and touched bottom with her toes. Another couple of strokes and she could stand up. She trudged towards the shore, feeling sand beneath her feet. When the water reached only to her knees, she dropped onto all fours and crawled towards the flickering light, tasting salt on her lips; the river had debouched into the sea and she was on a beach. Elaine crawled further up a gentle incline, and collapsed as she reached dry land. She lay face down, arms outstretched, belly flat on the sand like an exhausted turtle that has struggled through breakers to lay its eggs on a tropical beach. She shut her eyes and drifted into sleep.

"Fit the fuck! It's a wifie!" a rough male voice said. Elaine turned her head to the left, opened her eyes and saw a pair of trainers and ragged-hemmed jeans barely four inches from her face.

"Look, she opened her eyes!" another man said.

"She's nae deid, then," the first man spoke again.

"I'm not dead," Elaine said. "Just cold, bloody cold and wet."

"Let's get her over to the fire" the second man said. The two men bent over her, exuding a reek of alcohol, stale sweat and dirty clothing. They flipped Elaine onto her back and dragged her over to the flickering light, which turned out to be a small bonfire. The second man pulled a half bottle of something out of his anorak pocket, unscrewed the lid, wiped the neck of the bottle on his T-shirt and handed it to Elaine. She struggled to a sitting position, tool a gulp and nearly choked. It was whisky, of sorts, vile-tasting but full of kick. She hoped it wasn't home-distilled – that stuff could make you go blind and she had problems enough in that department already.

"Thanks" she said when she had stopped coughing, "that'll warm me up, and the fire too."

"Fit the fuck were ye deein in the waater?" the first man asked, reaching out and taking the bottle from Elaine. "Long story," she said, to give herself time to think of one. "And far's yer sheen?" the man persisted.

"Sorry, what?" Elaine said. She'd followed the rest of the man's questions, but this was stretching her comprehension.

"Och, Dod, gie her a break, for fuck's sake," the second man said. "Speak proper English. You can dee it fine when you try."

"Aye, richt. Ye'd ken, seein' as yer a fuckin' Weegie. Davey!"

Davey rolled up his sleeve, revealing a heavily tattooed forearm, and bunched his fist. He shook it under Dod's nose, then roared with laughter, grabbed the bottle, and took a swig before passing it back to Elaine. "Dod's asking about yer shoes. And how come you were in the sea."

"Oh, my shoes," said Elaine, who had come up with a vaguely plausible cover story. "They must have fallen off in the water. I don't remember. I was terribly upset, you see." She took another gulp of the fiery whisky and passed the bottle on. "My husband and I came up from Edinburgh for a few days' holiday. We were staying in a rented place near the river with another couple, who were celebrating their wedding anniversary. We all had too much to drink and the wife didn't feel well so I took her to her room and put her to bed. I guess my husband thought I'd gone to bed too, because when I got back downstairs I heard him speaking loudly to the other man and saying he was going to ask me for a divorce so that he could marry his secretary. He said they'd been having an affair for the last three years. I was so shocked, I just ran out of the house and down to the waterside. I must have slipped on the jetty in the dark, because the next thing I knew I was being carried away down the river."

Davey and Dod looked at her, saying nothing. After a while, Davey broke the silence. "Aye, that'll be right" he said, passing the bottle to Elaine again. Dod intercepted the bottle before Elaine got it to her lips. "She's had enough already," he said to Davey, then looked Elaine straight in the face. "Div ye nae ken it's a sin tae try an commit suicide?"

Elaine stared back, her eyes suddenly full of tears. She began shivering uncontrollably; the front of her jeans from the knee down were now steaming gently with the heat of the fire and one shin was throbbing unaccountably, but the rest of her was still chilled and wet. She put a hand on the sand and levered herself upright. "I should be going. Thank you for your help."

"Far ye gaun?" Dod asked.

"I've got a cousin in the town," Elaine said. "I expect she'll give me a bed for the night."

"Dinnae be daft," Davey said. "You're no in a fit state to go anywhere."

"Aye, and there's nae buses till the morn." Dod looked at Davey and jerked his head to one side, indicating that they should speak privately together. The two men moved away from the fire and held a muttered conversation that Elaine couldn't hear. They returned, kicked the dying fire into embers and doused them with sand, then led Elaine towards a dilapidated Victorian bandstand on a strip of grass behind the beach.

"Is this where you sleep?" Elaine asked, putting her hand on the rail and preparing to mount the steps to the bandstand.

"In full view? No way," Davey said. He took a small screwdriver out of his pocket, inserted it in a crack between two planks at the base of the bandstand, and prised them out. "The bedroom's in there. After you."

Dod produced a small torch and shone it into the gap so that Elaine could see. She crawled in under the bandstand, to a space about a metre high that smelled of mould, damp earth and more unwashed clothing. "Look, take your wet jacket off and hang it there." Davey shone the torch over something sticking out of an upright beam. Elaine couldn't make out much in the dim light, but it felt like a large nail. "You take my sleeping bag, I'll be all right with my jacket."

The three of them arrayed themselves on the ground, head to toe alternately, like a tin of sardines. Elaine vaguely contemplated the risk of being raped or strangled in the night, then dismissed both fears. In her experience, danger was more often well-groomed and dressed in nice manners and a smart suit. Dod and Davey had shown her nothing but kindness and humanity so far; she had no reason to believe they would try to harm her.

Chapter 26

Wednesday 25 April

Elaine woke to the sound of a helicopter thrumming overhead. A pale grey light was filtering through the cracks between the planks that formed the base of the bandstand. To her left, Dod lay snoring, looking like a large blue caterpillar in his sleeping bag.

Davey was awake and kneeling in front of a small Primus stove with a tin can on top of it.

"Morning. Tea? Or I've got instant coffee," he said, waving a small tin at her. Memories of Joe and his Nescafé bribes flooded Elaine. *God, she hoped he was still alive, though she doubted that he could be. They must have caught him.*

"The coffee, please, if you can spare it. You're well set up here, you and Dod."

"Aye, it's no bad. Beggars cannae be choosers. The hostel was cleaner, right enough, but that's been shut down."

"The homeless shelter here in Inverdour? Why?" Elaine said.

"Austerity, cutbacks, the usual shite."

The usual shite, perhaps, Elaine thought. *Or maybe because a final solution was being enacted not so far from here.* The helicopter was throbbing overhead again, heading north as far as Elaine could tell without being very sure of her bearings.

"Your husband must be able to pull a lot of strings," Davey said. "That's a police chopper, not a search and rescue one. Looking for you, or your dead body, I suppose."

"I guess so," Elaine said. "I should go, I don't want to get you and Dod into trouble."

"So tell me the truth, then. What have you done?"

Elaine hesitated. It might be safer for her if she insisted last night's story was true. On the other hand, he and Dod might be safe here for a while but, sooner or later, they could be rounded up and taken to an exit facility too. Davey seemed like a resourceful bloke, so he could probably be trusted to get himself and his pal out to a safer, more remote place. Deciding to trust him, Elaine sketched out the role of exit facilities and her own escape as succinctly and rapidly as she could.

"So, I need to get out of here fast, you see. Hopefully the authorities will think I drowned, or went across the bridge at Dourmouth and am somewhere further north by now, so I might be OK going south. Is there a bus into town from here?"

"Aye, every hour on the hour, but you'll stand out a mile if the chopper comes over again. Nae sheen, as Dod would say, and your jacket's still wet."

"And no bus fare," Elaine said. She picked her jacket off the nail and checked in the inside pocket. The plastic bag containing the £20 note, the chequebook and the business card was still there, the contents only slightly damp. "Here," she said, offering the £20 note to Davey, "this is for you and Dod. If you've got any change I could use for the bus that would be great."

"Is that all the money you've got?"

"Yes, but take it, please. I'll manage. Just a bus fare – that's all I need."

Davey rummaged in a plastic bag and produced £2 in small coins. He gave the change and the £20 note to Elaine.

"No, Davey. Keep the note."

"Shut up and take it back. You need it more than me."

"OK, then, Davey. Thanks. You're a hero. Look, this is my address and my daughter's number. If you or Dod ever need help, get in touch. But if anyone is questioning you, eat the note fast!" Elaine gave Davey the next of kin note she'd prepared yesterday, thinking again of Joe and his joking injunction to eat the note he had left her.

Davey bundled up Elaine's jacket and put it inside his anorak while she slid her bare feet into Dod's trainers and put on his hoodie to hide her hair. Then she and Davey crawled out of the hole and onto the grass.

"Try and walk like a man," Davey said as they headed for the nearby public toilet. "If you do that and keep the hood up, you should pass if they come over in the chopper again."

There was no one in the gents apart from them, which was lucky as Elaine looked awful but would certainly not have passed for a man if seen face on. They used the toilets, had a cursory wash and part-dried Elaine's jacket under the hot air hand dryer. From there they walked as casually as possible to the bus shelter.

"You're walking like you'd pissed yerself," Davey said. "Did we no get there in time for you?"

"Shut up, Davey. I'm just trying to keep the trainers on. They're about four sizes too big for me."

There was no one at the bus shelter either. They waited until Davey saw the bus coming down the esplanade, then Elaine took the shoes and the hoodie off and put her jacket on.

"The bare feet are a bit weird, aren't they?" Elaine said.

"Nae borra, hen. They'll just think you're doing a walk of shame," Davey said. "Good luck."

"Thanks for everything Davey. Say goodbye to Dod from me." The bus pulled in and Elaine got on, her bus fare clutched in her hand.

+++

Elaine got off the bus in the main street of Inverdour, from where it would be about a ten-minute walk to Linda's house, assuming her cousin hadn't moved away in the meantime. With little but dead relatives in common, she and Linda had been equally guilty of letting communication fizzle out.

Amused by Davey's walk of shame notion, Elaine attempted to strut like a hungover reveller brazening out her shoelessness until she caught a sideways glimpse of herself in a shop window. She looked like a bag lady who had lost her bags, her shoes and her marbles. Finding shoes was clearly imperative.

A block further on, a cheap fashion store was advertising a spring sale; with luck, she might find a suitable, sensible pair of shoes for £20 or less. Elaine went down to the shoe section in the basement and encountered hordes of women tottering around, shackled at the ankles in shoes that were clamped together into pairs with thick, tagged, plastic cord. Elaine grabbed a pair of trainers and elbowed her way to a circular bench. Piles of discarded shoes, both those on sale and those temporarily removed by bargain hunters, littered the floor like molehills. Most of the women were too absorbed in their search to notice Elaine's filthy feet, but one tutted loudly and shuffled as far away from Elaine as she could. The trainers didn't fit. Elaine squinted at the label – they were two sizes too small. Clearly, they'd been put back on the wrong rack. She fought through the melee to the size 6 area again, only to see the last pair of trainers being snatched by the woman who had tutted at her. Elaine returned to the bench, thinking she might find something in her size in one of the reject piles. As she sifted through fettered court shoes and sandals, a woman cried out, then crashed headlong over a pile of shoes, her feet still attached at the ankles. Other shoppers went to help. Elaine spotted a pair of navy plimsolls that looked big enough in a nearby pile. She grabbed one but its partner remained in the pile – not new shoes, then, a shopper's own pair. They fitted perfectly. Elaine stood up and moved away from the bench. People were still milling around the fallen woman, offering help or complaining to the shop staff. Casually, Elaine sauntered out of the shop with the plimsolls on her feet and Miss Latimer's £20 note still intact in her pocket.

The square was as Elaine remembered it – elegant granite Georgian houses on three sides, and a broad tree-lined road on the fourth. Linda's house was on the side opposite the main road, but Elaine couldn't remember the number, so she tried all the doors, starting from the north end. The fifth door had a large 'For Sale' notice above it, and was opened by a woman sporting an expensive-looking silver perm, tailored slacks and a Liberty print blouse. For a moment Elaine thought her aunt Charlotte had risen from the dead.

"I'm not buying anything, and I already support several charities," the woman snapped.

Elaine stuck her foot in the door to prevent Linda from closing it. "Linda? It's me, Elaine. Your cousin."

"My goodness, so it is." Linda looked Elaine up and down, disgust etched on her face. "You look like a tramp. What trouble have you got yourself into now, Elaine? And what are you doing on my doorstep?"

"I was rather hoping you'd let me in."

"It's not convenient. I'm on my way out shortly."

"Come on, Linda, please. I need your help."

"You always need help. Where were you when Gordon passed away and I needed help?"

"Oh no! I'm sorry to hear that, Linda. I didn't know Gordon had died. Why didn't you tell me?"

"Of course I told you. You just didn't give a damn."

"Could we perhaps discuss this inside? I'm sure you don't want the neighbours hearing our family gossip."

"Oh, alright, then. But you can't stay." Linda opened the door fully and ushered Elaine through to the kitchen at the back. She seemed to relax a little once they were indoors, and gave Elaine Earl Grey tea with a slice of lemon, and a chocolate and ginger biscuit. A world seemed to separate this tasteful kitchen from the Exit Facility and the bandstand on the beach, but the 'For Sale' sign outside indicated that all was perhaps not well in Linda's world either.

"So what happened with Gordon?" Elaine asked. "Honestly, you never told me."

"Heart attack. Three years ago," Linda said. "It was all very sudden. Well, for me it was sudden, at least. He told me he'd been going for regular check-ups, but apparently he never did. Typical Gordon, he hated doctors."

"I'm sorry," Elaine said. "It must have been an awful shock for you."

"I fell apart. The children weren't here at the time; Susan was gadding about in the Far East, and it took ages to even find her, and Tim was on a business trip in the States. They got back for the funeral, of course, but I had to make all the arrangements myself. It's possible I forgot to let you know." Linda glanced at the clock on the kitchen wall. "Oh, it's after eleven o'clock. Will you have a sherry? There's time for one before I go off for my lunch do."

"Thanks, but not now. I wouldn't mind another biscuit, though," Elaine said. "And how are the children? The last time I saw then was at Aunt Charlotte's funeral, and that must have been about twenty years ago."

"Tim's an investment banker, doing very well for himself, I must say. Susan, well … Anyway, why are you here? You look like a beggar, to be frank."

"I had an accident," Elaine said, having decided the truth would be far too much for Linda to handle. "I came up on the train for a funeral in the crematorium at Dourmouth," she said. Funerals seemed to be high on the agenda today. "It's a very pretty area, so I went for a walk in the woods after the service. You may not remember this, but I have vision problems and I just walked smack into a low hanging branch. I must have been concussed and may have been wandering around for a while, because I woke up this morning sleeping under a tree, with my shoes gone and my handbag lost." Linda looked stony-faced, so Elaine tried a question on her. "What day is it today?"

"Wednesday, of course."

Elaine put her hand to her mouth theatrically.

"Wednesday! But the funeral was on Sunday! I've lost more than two days out of my life."

"Was nobody with you?" Linda asked.

"No, I came on my own and didn't know any of the other mourners."

"Well, you should see a doctor and check you're fit to travel home. I can't have you staying here. You know what happened the last time."

"That was about forty years ago, Linda. Surely you're not still upset?"

"I certainly am. Gordon and I were newly married. It was terribly embarrassing for me to have my cousin pick up some hippie bloke with dreadlocks, drag him back here and then break the sofa bed! Gordon was appalled."

"OMG," a voice behind Elaine said. "You're my disreputable Auntie Elaine!"

Elaine turned round and saw a tall, striking girl standing in the doorway from the hall. "Susan, I guess. You look great. It must be twenty years since I last saw you."

"Yes, at Granny's funeral. I was only about seven, but I remember you vaguely. And Alexandra. How is she?" Susan sounded genuinely interested.

"Well, I hope. I haven't seen her for three years. She's been working in Hong Kong, but she stopped off in Goa on her way home."

"Oh, cool, I just love Goa!" Susan said.

"She's due back soon. In fact, if this is a Wednesday, she'll be back in a week exactly."

"Then you're no doubt in a hurry to get home and have everything ready for her," Linda said. "Look, I have to leave soon, but if you'd care to clean up a bit in the downstairs lavatory, I can give you a lift to the station on my way to the lunch."

Mother," Susan said. "Is that a sherry you're having? It is,

298

isn't it? In which case, you should not be driving. I'll take you to the club, Elaine can have a proper shower upstairs, then I'll drive her to the station."

"Certainly not, I've only had …"

"You're not driving after drinking, Mummy. We've discussed this before."

Linda caved in surprisingly fast and went to touch up her makeup and fetch her bag and jacket. Susan led Elaine upstairs to a luxurious bathroom with expensive bath oils and foams, shampoos and conditioners and skincare products arrayed on glass shelves.

"Perhaps you'd prefer a bath?" Susan suggested, and Elaine accepted gladly. She hadn't owned a bath tub for years, and the shared one in the Exit Facility had been far from appealing. "Take you time. I'll be about half an hour. There's a robe on the back of the door you can use." Susan emptied half a bottle of l'Occitane bubble bath into the tub and turned the hot tap on full. "Enjoy" she said, gave Elaine a cheery wave and left.

Feeling cleaner than she had for a month, Elaine had wrapped herself in the robe and was examining a cut on her leg when Susan returned. "Would you like to lie down, Elaine?" she asked. "You look pretty tired, and Mum won't be back for three or four hours."

"Thanks, but I need to leave. What I would really appreciate now is something to eat and a fresh T-shirt, if that's not too much to ask. I also seem to have a cut on my shin. Have you got some antiseptic, by any chance?"

"Of course," Susan said. "Gosh, I'm so excited to really meet you at last. You've been a kind of legend in the household, at least since Dad felt I was old enough to hear the sofa bed story. Let's have a look in my wardrobe."

They selected a T-shirt for Elaine and Susan offered her two pairs of knickers from an unopened multipack, then went downstairs to make scrambled eggs on toast. As Elaine was eating, a helicopter flew overhead and she paused mid-chew.

"There's a lot of police about today," Susan said. "Probably connected with the break-in at the research facility in Dourmouth. IT's funny to think that you had your accident there. Normally nothing ever happens in Dourmouth for about a hundred years at a time."

"A break-in, at a research facility?" said Elaine, astonished at this version of events.

"Yes, I heard it on the news on the way back from dropping Mummy off. Can't think why anyone would want to break into a chemistry lab, can you? Apparently they make chemical weapons there. Or that's what people around town say."

"Good God, "Elaine said. "Has the government no scruples nowadays?" She wiped her toast over the plate to pick up the last traces of buttery eggs. "That was delicious. Thank you. So, tell me more about you and your mother. I'm sorry to hear about your father. I'd have come to the funeral if I'd known about it. How have things been since his death? I couldn't help but notice that the house is up for sale."

"I know, it's awful, isn't it?" Susan replied. "Mummy's just terrible with money. Daddy left plenty, apparently, but she had never needed to manage money and she's got through most of it in three years. Not that I can talk really; I'm terrible with money too. It runs through my fingers like water."

"I thought your brother was an investment banker. Couldn't he help?" Elaine asked.

"You'd have thought so, but between you and me, Tim is a total shit, and tight as a duck's arse, excuse my language. He's the one insisting that Mummy has to sell the house and downsize and he's going to manage the money from now on. I don't really trust him. Have you heard about these exit facility thingies?"

"I have indeed."

"I'm worried he's going to pack Mummy off to one so he can keep the money from the house."

"It's not that easy," Elaine said. "I mean she'd have to sign the papers herself and she seems to be in full possession of her faculties. But if any suggestion like that is made, don't let her sign anything without reading the small print."

"Well, that's always sensible advice," Susan agreed. "I got my fingers badly burned that way. I ended up taking out a mortgage I couldn't possibly afford and the flat was finally repossessed. Oodles of money down the drain. Anyway, are you feeling better? I wish you could stay, but Mummy will kick up a fuss. Shall I take you to the station now?"

"There's a friend I'd like to visit for a few days. I need to recover from my accident before going home. Could I possibly use your landline?"

Elaine rang Rupert Mortimer and asked if she could stay for a couple of days. He seemed surprised to hear from her – no doubt the story of the so-called break-in had reached his ears too – but agreed to put her up as long as she could make her way to him discreetly.

"Thanks, I found my friend and I can stay with him, but I need to make my own way there. He lives near Glen Almond. Can you look up how I could get there on public transport?"

Susan tapped rapidly on her smartphone and made a face. "Impossible. No public transport at all."

"Damn."

"I'll drive you. It would be fun, and we can get to know each other better on the journey," Susan said.

"But won't your mother object? She's not very fond of me."

"I'll use Tim's car. It's in a lock-up garage while he's away and I know where the keys are kept. Why don't you hang out in my room till after I bring Mummy back? She usually has a nap when she gets back from a Conservative Club luncheon so she needn't know you're here. I'll sneak out and fetch his car, then drive you down to Glen Almond."

The plan seemed feasible, so Elaine enjoyed a nap until Susan woke her, barely concealing her giggles, and indicated they should sneak down the stairs together. She opened the front door with a flourish and indicated the car parked outside. "Isn't it glorious?"

The car was a scarlet Porsche 911; glorious indeed, but not quite what Rupert had intended when he suggested a discreet arrival.

Chapter 27

Wednesday 25 April

T he scenic route will take about three hours, or we can go down the A90, which will be faster," Susan said. Elaine chose the former, thinking there would be less chance of police checks if they were still searching for her. "Good choice," Susan said. "There are fewer speed traps on that road."

Susan drove at high speed, but with great panache and confidence, chattering all the while about her boyfriend, her travels and her inability to hold down a job for any length of time. "I've got a very low boredom threshold," she said, taking a corner so fast that the rear of the car span out and the tyres squealed. Elaine recited a silent prayer in Greek, her language of choice on the rare occasions she felt in need of divine assistance. Between terror at the prospect of being caught and returned to the Exit Facility, and the fear of landing upside down in flames in a ditch, her breathing had become fast and shallow and her palms were hot and sweaty.

The entrance to a village loomed and Elaine suggested tentatively that Susan should slow down. "Shame," Susan said. "Don't you just adore this car? It moves like a dream." She finally slowed down as a speed bump came into sight.

Elaine spotted a small chemist's shop up ahead and asked Susan to stop outside it. Miss Latimer's £20 note could be invested in some hair dye that would disguise her for her onward journey after hiding out at Rupert's house for a couple of days. "I'm just going to buy some hair dye," Elaine said. "I don't want Alexandra to see me looking like this." She tugged at her uncombed hair, indicating her fading burgundy tint and a quarter inch of grey growth.

There wasn't a great deal of choice in the shop, but Elaine took her time to make her choice, glad to have solid ground under her feet for a few minutes. She glanced outside the shop while waiting to pay and was horrified to see that a police car had drawn up immediately behind the Porsche. *God, no! Were they onto her?* Elaine's heart started racing alarmingly. An officer got out and approached the driver's window of the Porsche. *Would Susan keep her mouth shut if asked if she had seen a badly-dressed fugitive? Or was she being booked for speeding?* Elaine surrendered her place in the queue to an elderly man and went to examine the rack of flu remedies, from where she could peer discreetly out of the shop window.

Susan had got out of the car and was handing something to the policeman, her licence presumably. She was standing very close to the officer and tossing her long blonde hair while he examined the object then gave it back to her. Susan then took something out of her bag and moved even closer to him, leaning forwards with one hand to her mouth, her head close to his and her bust jutting. *Ah, the old flash some cleavage and ask the officer for a light trick!* Elaine grinned to herself. Susan clearly believed in making full use of whatever assets you had. The policeman retreated rapidly to his own car, reversed and then pulled out and drove off. Elaine paid for her hair dye, left the shop and slid back into the passenger seat of the Porsche.

Susan was doing up the top button of her blouse. "Did you see that, Auntie Elaine?" she dais. "Didn't I do well? I got rid of him pretty fast."

"What was he asking you about?" Elaine said. "Speeding?"

"No, actually not. He wanted to know if I'd picked up a hitchhiker. Specifically a female hitchhiker in her sixties, who might seem confused, or dishevelled."

"And what did you say?" Elaine asked, trying to keep her panic from her voice.

"I said I wouldn't dream of picking up anyone who was badly-dressed – they might ruin the leather upholstery. Then I flashed a bit of tit, and he left." Susan grinned. "It's funny, though. His description might have fitted you when you turned up at our house this morning, Auntie Elaine." Susan examined her perfectly manicured fingernails and then cast a sideways look at Elaine.

"Well, of course I was confused. I told you what had happened in the woods at Dourmouth. Ehm … I don't suppose I could have one of your cigarettes, could I, Susan? I'm feeling a bit nervous. You're a very good driver, but I'm not used to being driven so fast these days."

"I'm sorry, I don't have any cigarettes. I don't smoke."

"But didn't you ask the policeman for a light?"

"Oh, that fag's just a prop. I've had it in my handbag for months now. It'll be horribly stale."

"I'm not fussy, I'll smoke that."

"Not in the car, no way. Tim would have kittens if he came home and found his beloved Porsche smelling of smoke. Get back in and I'll take you to a quiet spot off the main road and you can smoke it there."

In silence, Susan drove them out of the village, a mile or two along the road, then swung the car onto a forestry track. The car bumped and swayed, its low-slung chassis scraping the earth, but Susan didn't seem to notice. She stopped abruptly, grabbed something from the glove locker, jumped out of the car and came round to Elaine's side. She yanked the passenger door open and stood a few steps away from Elaine, waggling something at her.

"What's that?" Elaine asked.

"A packet of Dunhill cigarettes," Susan said. She stuck a hand in her trouser pocket, extracted something else and waggled it as well. "And a lighter."

"Oh, so you lied," Elaine said. "You do smoke."

"Yep, I lied. And you're lying too. C'mon, Auntie Elaine, spill the beans and you can smoke as many fags as you want. But not in the car." Susan backed away, dangling the cigarette packet and the lighter in front of her like little puppets.

Elaine laughed and got out of the car. Susan had seemed like a bit of an airhead at first, but she was proving herself to be smart as well as kind-hearted. For the second time that day, Elaine spilled the beans, replacing her elaborate lies with the truth.

+++

They arrived at Rupert Mortimer's white-painted, harled house just outside Glen Almond around seven in the evening. Susan drove too fast up the drive in order to have the pleasure of hearing the car's tyres crunching in the gravel.

Rupert came out to greet them, presumably alerted by the sound of the Porsche before Elaine and Susan had time to ring the doorbell.

"Welcome, Elaine. Is that what you call a discreet arrival?" he said.

"Well, in this neck of the woods, a Porsche probably blends in better than a beat-up old Ford," Elaine answered quickly, not wanting Susan to be offended.

"That's true, I suppose. Elaine, come indoors. And you, young lady, will you come in for some tea?"

"This is Susan," Elaine said. She thought she should probably say more by way of explanation, but her head was swimming and she suddenly felt cold and shivery now she was out of the car.

"Thanks, but I'd better get back," Susan said to Rupert. "Mummy will freak if she discovers both I and the car keys have gone." She turned to Elaine and held out her arms. "If you ever need a chauffeur again …" she said.

"Thank you very much, Susan," Elaine said, hugging her niece. "You've been a lifesaver. I hope we meet again soon."

Elaine walked into Rupert's house and was shown into a warm room lined with books. Seconds later, she passed out on the carpet.

Chapter 28

Friday 27 - Saturday 28 April

Elaine opened her eyes and saw light flooding through a net curtain into a room she didn't recognise. The light hurt her eyes, so she shut them again and nestled deeper into the bed. The sheets were soft and scented with lavender, reminding her of waking up at her grandmother's house where she had spent weekends as a small child. She had no idea where she was, but it smelt and felt safe, so she decided to sleep a little bit more.

She woke again to the sound of a door being pushed open and a male voice saying "How's she doing?" It sounded familiar, but Elaine couldn't place whose voice it was. She kept her eyes shut.

"She opened her eyes about half an hour ago, but only briefly," another man answered, his voice coming from near the foot of the bed. "Otherwise no change. Her temperature's as high as ever."

"I'll crush some more paracetamol and put it in water," the first man said.

"I think it's gone beyond that, Rupert," said the second voice. "She's had a high fever for thirty-six hours now, maybe more. That's no ordinary flu. She needs to be seen by a doctor."

Rupert. Sheldrake, maybe? She'd read some books of his, way back when, but Elaine couldn't imagine why she'd be lying in his bedroom. The same went for Rupert Everett, even though she was a big fan and would love to be sleeping in his spare room.

"I told you, I'm prepared to provide a safe place for you both to stay for a little while, but I can't have the village doctor coming here. I don't want it getting out that I'm mixed up in this business," said the first man. "I have a lot of wealthy and influential clients and I can't afford to lose their trust. You've no idea how much the upkeep on this house costs."

"I'd have thought that, as a humanist, you'd put a person's life and welfare above business." The rebuke from the second man was delivered quietly but firmly.

She'd got it now. The first voice belonged to Rupert Mortimer, the humanist celebrant. She'd come to his house after escaping from the Exit Facility. Elaine opened her eyes again, winced at the pain the light caused, but pushed herself up on one elbow and turned in the direction of Rupert's voice.

"You're absolutely right," she said. "I've had a little rest and I feel fine, so I'll be off. I don't want to get you into trouble." She attempted to sit up and put her legs on the floor, but the room swayed and swirled round her, and she sank back down again. "Fuck, my head hurts. Could I have that paracetamol you mentioned? Then I'll go."

A figure in a grey sweater moved to the head of the bed. He looked a bit like Hamish but he didn't have a beard.

"Hi Elaine," the figure said. "You're not going anywhere just yet. You need medical attention." Elaine recognised his voice. It was Hamish. *He was alive!*

"What the hell are you doing here, Hamish? Are you OK? What happened to your beard? And where's Joe? Did he get away?" Her questions were plentiful but her own voice sounded weak.

"I'm fine, but you're not. You've had a high fever for a couple of days. Please just lie down again, Elaine. I'll get a doctor to look you over and I'll explain everything once you're better."

"Don't be so bossy," Elaine protested, but the light hurt her head so much that she shut her eyes again. "What do you mean by a couple of days? I only just got here a little while ago."

"I'm afraid not, Elaine," Rupert said. "You got here on Wednesday and it's Friday now."

"Could I use the landline, Rupert?" Hamish asked. "I'll get a doctor from the organisation, someone discreet."

"Oh, very well. In the evening, then. And make it low key," Rupert said. Elaine felt too ill to argue.

As Hamish left the room, Elaine wondered silently if he had said nothing good about Joe because there was nothing good to say.

+++

The next time Elaine woke, the room was suffused with a rosy evening light. Hamish and a woman she didn't know were sitting by her bedside.

"Hello, Elaine," the woman said. "I'm Felicity, I'm a GP. How are you feeling?"

Elaine sat up cautiously. "Better, I think. My head's not pounding or swimming any more."

"I'm glad. And your temperature is down to 38, which is good. Hamish says it was much higher before. I'd like to ask a couple of questions. You have quite a deep scratch on your shin. When and how did you get that?"

311

"I haven't the foggiest," Elaine said. "I noticed yesterday that my leg hurt, but I don't recall scratching it or cutting it. I think it was yesterday. What day is it today?"

"Friday," Hamish said.

"Have you been anywhere that might have been contaminated by the urine of rats or other rodents? A river, for example?"

Elaine looked at Hamish.

"It's OK, Elaine," Hamish said, "you can tell Felicity anything. She's one of us."

"Yes, in a river, a rather sluggish one. And then I spent a night underneath a bandstand. I didn't think to check it for rats."

"I see. That confirms my suspicion. I think you may have contracted a bacterial infection called leptospirosis. Your symptoms match that diagnosis. I'm going to put you on an antibiotic drip for a couple of days." Felicity dived into a large black bag and produced a metal frame which she screwed onto the bed head and attached a bottle and drip to it.

"No, I don't like taking antibiotics," Elaine said. "I'll get over this on my own."

"I warned you, Felicity," Hamish said.

"Listen, Elaine. If untreated, leptospirosis can develop into Weill's disease, a serious bacterial infection that can cause meningitis, jaundice, and/or complete kidney or liver failure."

"That sounds vile," Elaine said.

"You must be feeling a bit better if you're making awful puns," Hamish said. For the first time since she had woken up, he was showing a little of the guarded affection he had sometimes displayed to her in the Exit Facility.

"So, I don't need the antibiotics if I'm already getting better."

"Do you really want to risk meningitis?" Felicity asked.

Elaine suddenly remembered the sheer terror that had gripped her after two children in Alexandra's nursery school had contracted meningitis. All the children in the class had previously been taken to church and given communion from the same unwashed spoon. She had lived in fear for a week thereafter that her daughter would develop symptoms. It wouldn't be fair to inflict a similar dread on Alexandra now that they were about to meet again. Elaine rolled up the sleeve of the burgundy silk pyjamas she was wearing – Rupert's presumably – and offered her forearm to Felicity.

"OK, then," she said, "bring the drip on."

"Good," Hamish said. "That's a wise choice. We need you fit and well as soon as possible."

"What's with the 'we' and 'us' Hamish?"

"I'll explain everything, I promise, but now I'll see Felicity out and then I'll bring you up a cup of tea."

+++

Elaine woke up, desperate to pee and with a slight pain in the back of her left hand. The pale grey light seeping through the curtains allowed her to see the IV cannula that Felicity had inserted last night. *Shit – the bloody antibiotic drip! How was she meant to find a loo and get to it when effectively chained to a bed? And what if it wasn't antibiotics she'd been given, but some kind of sedative or psychotropic drug? She only had Hamish and the hitherto unknown lady doctor's word for it. And why did Hamish keep going on about 'the organisation' and 'we need you' and all that crap?* She really didn't know if she could trust him any more.

The IV cannula was firmly taped to her hand and the thought of ripping it out was only marginally less disturbing than the memory of excavating an electronic chip from Joe's leg. She'd have to free herself at the other end of the contraption. By judicious wriggling, Elaine managed to sit up and then unclamp the portable metal stand from the headboard. She slid out of the bed cautiously, avoiding a full cup of tea that somebody had left on a little table beside the bed. Elaine made her way to the door and opened it. A dimly-lit carpeted corridor stretched away to her right. Holding the clamp and drip bottle aloft in her right hand and feeling like the Lady with the Lamp, Elaine edged her way along the corridor in search of the bathroom. She put her ear to the first door and heard breathing through it. The second door was almost vibrating with the stentorian snoring that was going on behind it. The third door yielded the sound of intermittent peeing and murmurs of "Bugger" and "Oh, for fuck's sake."

Elaine knocked gently on that door. "Occupied, engaged, bathroom not free," said a man with a resonant voice in a perfect RP accent. "Use the downstairs loo."

"I can't, I'm desperate. And I don't know where it is," Elaine hissed back.

"Bloody hell. Oh, very well. Just a mo."

Elaine heard another short trickle, followed by the sound of the toilet flushing and a tap running. She clenched her thighs until the door opened.

"Thank goodness," she said and squeezed past the figure standing in the doorway. She began plucking at the drawstring of Rupert's pyjamas with her bandaged left hand, getting the cannula stuck in the waistband.

"Do you need some help?" the man asked in an amused tone. "Not easy to get those pyjamas off, I know from experience. Especially when you're impersonating the Statue of Liberty."

"No, don't make me laugh, it'll be fatal," Elaine said. "Yes, I need help. But you can hold the drip, I'll manage the pyjamas. And shut your eyes."

"I'm a gentleman, I wouldn't dream of doing anything else."

Elaine got the cord undone with her free right hand, yanked down Rupert's pyjamas and the knickers from Susan, and sat on the toilet.

"Thanks. What a relief. I'm sorry about this."

"No problem, Liberty Statue lady. We're all in dire straits here. I wish I could still pee like you can." The beautiful voice, with its perfect elocution, sounded vaguely familiar to Elaine.

"It's because of the wretched drip," Elaine said. "You know, I rather fancied myself as Florence Nightingale."

"Definitely not. Not prissy enough. Oh, and I appreciate it if you avoid any puns about drips."

"Duly noted," Elaine said, wiping, flushing and hauling her borrowed clothing up. "You can open your eyes now, and we can shuffle over to the washbasin together."

The handsome, elderly man holding her drip bottle opened his eyes and smiled at her. "By all means. Let's do a two-step." And then the voice and the startlingly green eyes connected in Elaine's memory.

"Oh, my God!" she said. "You're Hugo Earle. How embarrassing! I saw you play Hamlet when I was sixteen and I fell madly in love with you."

"Of course you did, darling," he said, filling the basin, mixing the hot and cold water carefully for her. "I was gorgeous in those days, but now *Age with his stealing steps hath clawed me in his clutch.* Anyway, you were probably lovely then too. But, as you no doubt know, I have always batted for the other side." he

Elaine nodded, too embarrassed at peeing in front of a national treasure to think of anything to say.

"Careful now, you don't want to get those bandages soaked. Just twiddle the fingers of your left hand in the water... That's it, and here's a towel. Shall we go downstairs and have something to drink? Rupert's snoring far too loudly for me to get back to sleep."

Elaine and Hugo made their way downstairs in tandem, and into a cosy French country cottage-style kitchen. Hugo clipped the metal bracket for Elaine's drip onto the shade of a wall-mounted lamp and pulled out a chair.

"Don't go forgetting you're hooked up and making any sudden moves, now. Rupert paid a fortune for that lampshade. Now, what'll you have?"

Elaine spotted a bottle of malt whisky on a dresser. "I don't suppose I could have a wee nip of that?" she asked, indicating the bottle.

Hugo raised one eyebrow, reminding Elaine of one of Joe's favourite mannerisms. *Perhaps Joe had been an actor as well.* The thought had crossed her mind before and it would account for his facility in assuming whatever personality fitted his needs at the time.

"Whisky on top of whatever's in that IV bottle?" Hugo said. "No, I was thinking more along the lines of herb tea, or cocoa."

Elaine asked for coffee.

"It'll keep you awake and make you widdle, but it's your choice," Hugo said. "Everything makes me widdle these days. So, what's your affliction?" Hugo filled a kettle and switched it on.

"I have lepto something-or-other, which can cause meningitis. But I don't think it's contagious. You get it from rat's pee, apparently. Sorry, just can't get away from the subject of widdling tonight."

"So it seems," Hugo replied. "My problem's not contagious either. Not that it could affect you even if it were. What an irony! Rupert hates illness, and he's ended up with two patients on his hands."

"So why are you here, then?" Elaine asked.

"Rupert and I go back a long way. We were lovers years ago, close friends for decades, then intermittent lovers again. He didn't want the media getting wind of the fact that I'm ill and badgering me, so he offered to take me in. He reckoned a house tucked away in the countryside would be well away from paparazzi. Which is why he was a little disconcerted when you roared up the driveway in a scarlet Porsche, followed by a 'purely routine' visit from the police a few hours later." The tone of Hugo's voice made it clear that the police visit had been anything but routine. "And then your friend Hamish turned up the following day. It's been like Piccadilly Circus around here."

"Oh, God, I'm sorry I've broken your peace like this," Elaine said. "I had no-one else to turn to. I'll leave as soon as I possibly can."

"Oh don't do that, darling. We're having far too much fun together." Hugo poured water into two mugs. "It's instant. Do you want milk or sugar in it?

"No, it'll be fine as it is. Many thanks," Elaine said, taking a mug from him. "What did the police say, by the way?"

Hugo laid his own mug on the table and sat down. "I don't know exactly, Rupert dealt with them. We can all discuss what to do about your situation later. In the meantime, I'm curious to know your side of the story. Tell all." Hugo leaned back in his chair, stretched his long thin legs out in front of him and put his hands behind his head.

Elaine took a deep breath and began to tell her story once again.

Chapter 29

Saturday 28 April

By the evening, Elaine's temperature had stabilised around 37 degrees and she was considered well enough to dine downstairs with Rupert, Hugo and Hamish. The sky was still light outside, but someone had drawn the curtains across the large picture window, presumably to screen the guests from any prying eyes.

Hamish showed Elaine to a high-backed, tapestry-covered chair and attached the metal frame for her drip bottle to it so that she could eat with ease. Rupert ladled chilled cucumber soup into four bowls, added a swirl of single cream and a pinch of fresh dill to each, and handed the bowls round.

"My speciality," he said. "I hope you like it." Elaine sipped slowly, savouring the delicate flavour of the first home-made food she'd eaten for nearly a month.

They ate in silence until Rupert put his spoon down and dabbed at his mouth with a navy blue napkin. "So, you've met Hugo, I hear," he said to Elaine. She smiled and nodded. "Now, I'm sure you and Hamish appreciate that I hadn't really expected to be helping two fugitives from the law. I'd like to be able to do more for the pair of you, but my primary concern is Hugo's health and privacy." He glanced at his friend and erstwhile lover, who put out his hand and patted Rupert's forearm reassuringly. "Accordingly, can you tell me what your plans are, Elaine? Hamish? I'm not asking you to leave instantly, but … "

"I'll clear and bring in the next course," said Hamish,

gathering up the soup plates and leaving the room.

Rupert looked at Elaine questioningly.

"Well, first of all, I'm really sorry for the inconvenience, Rupert, and I am extremely grateful for your help. I didn't know I would fall ill or I wouldn't have come. As to why Hamish is here, I have no idea at all. He doesn't seem to be who or what he purported to be when we were in the facility. As far as I'm concerned, we can go our separate ways. I feel a lot better, and I need to get home to my flat in Edinburgh before my daughter arrives, so I'll leave tomorrow. If you could just get me to a bus, I've got a bit of money and …"

She was interrupted by Hamish returning to the room carrying a vast shallow dish of paella that he placed on mats in the centre of the table. Hugo cut chunks of crusty brown bread and passed them round.

Hamish must have heard the last part of Elaine's speech, because he looked at her steadily, "There's no need for you to go anywhere alone, Elaine. In fact, there's no question of it. You'd last an hour or two at most before a convenient accident shut you up forever. We're in this together and I've got plenty of friends behind me."

Elaine gritted her teeth. Her rising anger fought with her good manners and her desire to be polite towards her hosts. "Not this crap again, Hamish, please! Don't do this, don't do that, leave it to the men, leave it to the fully-sighted people. I got myself here, didn't I?"

Hamish sat down with a large sigh. "Yes, but there was no need to jump into that damn river, there were people waiting to help us in the woods beyond the bridge. I told you to turn left into the woods and wait."

"So what about that green light in the woods? I thought that was people from the Exit Facility, or a drone trying to trap me in a pincer movement or something." Elaine accepted a bowl of paella from Rupert and smiled her thanks, then turned back to Hamish.

"Those were the friends, Elaine, trying to show you the way to safety."

"Well, it would have helped if you'd told me to expect bloody green lights ahead of me. I did the only sensible thing in the circumstances."

"You panicked, Elaine."

"I did not. Who are you anyway? You and your mysterious organisation that conjures up secret doctors in the middle of the night."

"I'll explain later."

"No, explain now, Hamish. I've had enough of being patronised."

"Excuse me, Elaine," said Hugo in a soothing and mellifluous tone, "but I agree with Hamish here. Clearly the two of you have a lot to discuss together, so why don't you do so over liqueurs after dinner? In the meantime let's enjoy our paella, and I have made my speciality, Belgian chocolate mousse, for dessert. And while we're eating, do let me tell you the story of the time I was working on a film with Peter O'Toole in Rome. We got into a hell of a lot of scrapes, I can tell you!"

+++

Before Rupert and Hugo retired to bed, Elaine had persuaded Rupert that a thimble-sized portion of an Italian digestif couldn't possibly interact badly with the antibiotics, and was now sipping it in homeopathic doses while attached

321

by the IV cord to one of the bookcases in his study. Hamish sat in an armchair at right angles to her, shifting uncomfortably from buttock to buttock and toying with a tumbler of whisky.

"Right, Hamish, spill the beans! What is this organisation you keep talking about? And what were you really doing in the Exit Facility?"

"OK, I have to admit I wasn't entirely honest with you, Elaine. I work for the UK branch of an international human rights organisation, Warriors for Justice. We got wind of irregular activities at British exit facilities – ours isn't the only one, you know – and I was sent under cover to investigate rumours of various so-called 'undesirable' groups being sent to facilities and then disappearing."

"So you were a mole?"

"Of sorts, yes."

"What about all the stuff about your Mum, and Parkinson's, and having no money, and doing time for computer fraud? Was that just pure bullshit to make me feel sorry for you?"

"Certainly not! Come on, Elaine, you know I was very fond of my mother. How could I have lied about that?" Hamish's voice broke slightly. Either he was a far better actor than Elaine could ever have imagined, or he was telling the truth.

"No," he went on. "That was all true; it just added veracity to my cover story. And I owe you a lot. I couldn't go in with any electronic devices due to my hacking offence. Your tablet was a lifesaver. Not just for finding the hash – that was just a bonus. But it meant I could set up a little more potential backup in case of emergency than I let on to you or Joe. That's why I kept trying to get you both to do things my way. I had a bit more input on the facility's security systems than I could tell you and Joe about."

"Why not? Didn't you trust us?"

Hamish hesitated before answering. "It's not that I didn't trust you, Elaine, but I really wasn't sure about Joe. He was a bit of a slippery character, you know."

Elaine sat silently, staring at Hamish. Clearly Joe had not been the only slippery character she had teamed up with in the Exit Facility. In fact, Hamish was really the slippery one. Joe at least had not made a secret of his multiple personas to Elaine. She felt foolish and betrayed.

"Do you really expect me to believe that you put your own life at risk to enter an exit facility and investigate breaches of human rights? Only possible breaches at that. That's completely crazy."

"No more crazy than a perfectly healthy woman signing herself into an exit facility just because she's run out of money."

"How dare you, Hamish, you fucking sanctimonious prick?" Elaine's voice was rising, and she made an effort to speak calmly. "For a start, I am not perfectly healthy. I am partially-sighted. That may not mean much to you in real terms, so let me help you. Imagine filling in a one-page form with boxes to tick or to complete with your credit card details or tax number. That would take you, what – five minutes, ten at the most? I would need half an hour and two magnifiers to do the task, and even then would still make mistakes. It's a pain in the bloody arse being so slow and useless at the simplest of tasks. And in that state and at my age, it makes finding paid employment almost impossible. I wasn't down on my uppers because I was profligate or workshy or stupid if that's what you've been thinking."

Hamish interrupted her, keeping his voice calm too. "Of

course I wouldn't think that. And I'm sorry, Elaine, I know I shouldn't have said your choice was crazy. It's just that you seem to cope so well most of the time that I tend to forget you don't see like other people do."

Elaine was not prepared to accept this olive branch quite yet. "Secondly, I have a daughter and I believe very strongly that it's a parent's duty to provide for their offspring. Since she doesn't have anything from her father, that is my role. You know all this already, Hamish. Of the three of us, I was the one who wasn't hiding anything or making things up." Elaine glared at Hamish.

"I know," Hamish said, his voice low. "What more can I say, Elaine? Everyone has different motivations and I accept that mine may seem crazy to you. I apologise for not being strictly honest with you. Like I said, I would have been if Joe hadn't been involved. I never trusted him and, as it turns out, I was right not to, but for the wrong reason."

They sat in silence for a while, staring into their drinks and avoiding each other's eyes. The memory of Joe writhing in pain and the smell of his burning flesh were horrible for Elaine to recall.

Hamish was the first to speak. "How can someone forget that they have a metal pin in their arm? Now that's crazy, especially after I warned you both so many times about wearing or carrying anything metal when going through the fence."

"I know. I've asked myself the same question a dozen times. The only conclusion I can come to is that Joe had reinvented himself so many times that he sometimes forgot what was really true and what was not. He didn't have a scar on his arm to remind him, so it may have been put in when he was a very young child. Don't blame yourself for that, Hamish. You gave us plenty of warnings about the danger of metal. I'm as much to blame as anyone else. I stumbled against him while trying to get onto the path and that lost him a couple of seconds while the circuit was broken. "

Elaine paused before asking the question she had to ask but whose answer she dreaded. "What happened to him after I left? Did you see?"

Hamish sighed deeply. "I tried dragging him further down the hill a bit, but he was in too much pain. He begged me to leave, so I did. I saw them carrying him back into the facility. God only knows what happened after that. I feel terrible about leaving him to his fate, but …" Hamish removed a tissue from his trouser pocket and dabbed at his eyes.

Elaine could think of nothing more to say. She'd abandoned Joe too. She hoped he'd died rapidly, that he'd not been tortured and questioned. Or maybe he'd been given emergency pain relief at first, and then Closure? They'd probably never find out.

"What's next then, Hamish? What is it that you and your organisation want from me?"

"Your testimony. You're the prime witness to what went on, apart from me, and obviously, by nature of who I work for, I am biased. But I also want to help you. As I said at dinner, they may well engineer an accident, or something. It's all too plausible that a partially-sighted person could walk in front of a moving car."

"Look Hamish, all I want to do is get back to Edinburgh, see Alexandra, and put my paintings up for sale. And who are "they" anyway? I know the police were looking for me, but it seemed pretty easy to throw them off my scent. So it's not MI5 or anyone heavy-duty like that, I guess. You and the GP got here without any incidents, didn't you?"

"Yes, that's true. To be frank, we are not sure how much of the whole operation at our Exit Facility was sanctioned by the government, and how much was Pemberton overstepping her remit. I do know that our break-out was reported on the local news as a break-in and ..."

"Yes," Elaine interrupted. "I heard that on the radio at my cousin's house. It seems like most people in Inverdour think the facility's a chemical research lab. Do you know any more than that?"

"Only that nothing has been reported nationally regarding the facility. But in this case no news is not good news." Hamish got up and moved to a bookcase where Rupert had left a bottle of malt whisky for him. He topped up his glass and added a splash of water from a jug while Elaine looked on jealously. While Hamish's back was turned she tipped her shot glass on its side and licked that last sticky drops of digestif out of it.

"I'll take the risk," Elaine said. "I'm pretty sure I can make it. I'll disguise myself. That reminds me, I bought some hair dye to do just that."

Hamish sat down again and took a large gulp of his whisky, for courage perhaps, then said "We have a plan that should keep you safe, and win public sympathy for our cause."

When Elaine didn't reply, he tried again. "The cause, I mean. The cause of saving homeless people, poor, innocent underdogs and outcasts of society from a needless death."

Elaine still said nothing.

"Come on, Elaine, you cared about that when we were in the facility. You wanted to help the Indigents."

"I did," Elaine said. "I still do care, to an extent, but now

326

they're an abstraction. The poor homeless person I cared about the most didn't make it out, at least not in one piece. I'm finding it very hard to process that."

Elaine was sitting close enough to Hamish to see a red flush rise from his neck to his cheeks. He took another gulp of whisky and coughed, then wiped his mouth on the sleeve of his jumper.

"I'm sorry, Elaine. Did you ... ehm ... have feelings for Joe?"

"I'd rather not go into that, Hamish."

Elaine turned Hamish's words over in her mind. She thought of Dod and Davey, and the unquestioning help they had given her when she'd washed up on Inverdour beach. She thought of Pete, who had gladly risked punishment by helping with their escape plan. "OK, Hamish, you've succeeded in lighting a small glimmer of altruism in me. I don't promise anything, but tell me what your plan is."

Hamish looked up from his whisky and smiled at her. "Thanks, Elaine, I really appreciate it. So the idea is this, and it's not just mine; Hugo has a lot to do with it too. We'll use the power of the media for us, instead of against us. We'll give a press conference, you and me, and get public sympathy for you in particular. Hugo thinks you have charisma and can win people over. He's offered to coach you. And if the public and the media are fired up and like you and feel sympathetic to the cause, there's no way any government agency will target you. It would be too obvious, too likely to provoke outrage. After all, this isn't Russia. What do you say?"

Elaine was flattered by Hugo's confidence in her but couldn't help but see holes in the plan. "I say bollocks, Hamish. I think there are too many risks."

"Not as many risks as there would be if you snuck out of

here with a tenner in your pocket and hoping some cheap hair dye will serve to disguise you."

"Yes but I'm no public speaker. What if a celebrity dies on the day we hold the press conference, or an earthquake kills thousands in Japan and therefore nobody gives a shit about us and our homeless people?"

"That would be unlucky, but unlikely to affect us. The organisation has contacts with exactly the right press people to drip-feed this to beforehand. And remember it's not just the homeless issue. Dorothy and Miss Latimer were lied to and exploited as well. That could happen to any member of the general public if we don't put a stop to the way the facilities are run."

Elaine felt weary and confused. "OK, Hamish, let me sleep on it. I'm too tired to discuss anything more now. Can you help me get this bloody drip bottle off the bookshelf?" She stood up carefully and Hamish unhooked the drip bottle and frame and handed them to Elaine. "Oh, and one more thing. How did you find me here?"

"As soon as we realised you had jumped off the bridge, the organisation sent people to stake out your flat in case you or Alexandra, or the authorities, showed up there. You didn't, but an unmarked black van spent twenty-four hours outside your tenement. No one went into or out of your flat. So I knew you weren't in Edinburgh. You'd told me about meeting Rupert at the chapel in the facility, so I thought I'd give him a try."

"I don't think I told you his name or his address."

"You didn't, but how many humanist celebrants work with the glitterati and live within hitchhiking distance of Inverdour? It was child's play to find you. And if I could do it …"

"Point taken, Hamish. I'll think it over and give you my answer tomorrow. But I'll need protection for Alexandra too."

"Of course," Hamish smiled and held the door open for Elaine.

Chapter 30

Monday 30 April

The drip had been removed the previous evening and Elaine was feeling much better. She and Hamish had discussed his plan in finer detail the day before. Now they were in the study again, having a second cup of coffee after breakfast. The large French window gave onto a back garden, far from the street, and Rupert had felt it was safe to leave the curtain half open. Through the glass, Elaine could see the sun shining brightly.

Rupert and Hugo had taken his car just after breakfast and headed for the hills to go walking. They were taking Olivia and Rose's ashes with them and planned to scatter them in a valley in the hills. Elaine longed to get out of the house and go for a long walk too, but Hamish was having none of it.

"We've been through this before, Elaine," Hamish said, "we can't put you or the press conference at risk by letting people in the village see you. You'd stand out a mile – everyone here wears tweed skirts and green wellies …"

"… Including the men?" Elaine interrupted. "Sorry, being facetious. But that's a point. What the hell am I going to wear to a press conference? I've got nothing but two T-shirts, one of which is yours, my old jeans and a scruffy denim jacket with no buttons on it. Do you think your Justice Freedom Fighters would run to buying me a suit and blouse and bringing them here?"

"It's Warriors for Justice," Hamish said. "I don't think that would be a good idea. You'll look more the part in your own clothes."

"I don't need to look the part. I'm not playing a part, Hamish. I am being me and am going to stand up there in front of the cameras and tell what happened and what I heard and saw. That's it. But I will feel more confident if I look halfway respectable."

"I'll ask the press team what they can do," said Hamish, making a note on his phone. "But there's a hell of a lot to organise. We're aiming for Thursday and that's really soon."

"What date is that?" Elaine asked.

"The third of May."

"Holy fuck!" Elaine said. "That was my scheduled Exit Date. Where did the time go? Didn't we break out a week ago?"

"Eight days ago, actually," Hamish said. "But you were sick for a lot of that time. Is there a problem?"

"There certainly is. Alexandra's due to arrive in London on the night of the first. That must be tomorrow if Thursday is the third. Then she plans to come north by train some time on the second. If we leave the conference till the day after, she'll get to my flat and freak out when I'm not there and she sees the letter I left. And you said the flat is being staked out, so she could be at risk."

"That's true. I'll get the logistics team to work on that. It will be quicker and easier to arrange support for Alexandra than to rearrange a whole press conference. Do you know what her flight number is?"

"No, she didn't tell me. But there can't be that many flights from Goa getting into a London airport late tomorrow night. Will you arrange for someone to meet her?"

"Not exactly. I think that might alarm her, don't you? But someone can trail her and make sure she's safe. From the airport to wherever she stays that night, then onto the train and up to Edinburgh on Wednesday. Do you have a friend who could meet her there, and break the whole story to her gently?"

"Not off the top of my head, Hamish, but I'll think about that. And there's another thing. What about Joe? If he's still alive, the sooner we nail Pemberton, the better a chance he has of survival."

Hamish sighed and rubbed his temples. "Elaine, remember our aim is not to nail Pemberton, as you put it, but to expose the fact that injustices are going on and the government is complicit, to a greater or lesser extent. I wish you'd stick to the script."

"What script? I am not standing up there and spouting whatever you want me to say, Hamish. As I said a few minutes ago, I'll bloody well say what I know and you can put your own spin on your narrative."

"I was speaking metaphorically, Elaine."

"Good. Hugo had me doing speeches from Shakespearean heroines yesterday to improve my diction and projection. It was fun, but that's all the working from scripts that I'm prepared to do."

Hamish sighed again, but did not comment.

"So let's talk about the date," Elaine continued. "Can we bring it forward to the second?"

Hamish's phone pinged and he looked at the message that had come in.

"Not now, I'm afraid. That's the press team saying the venue is confirmed for the third. It's a hotel in Stirling, a good central location. We'll kick off at two p.m. in the conference room. You and I are booked to stay there that night."

"And what will happen after that?"

"That depends on how well it goes. If we generate lots of interest and big papers and networks pick up the story, you'll be safe to go back to your flat and be reunited with your daughter. There will be official investigations, possibly a trial. You may well be asked to do in-depth interviews or chat shows, if you want to, that is."

"It sounds stressful," Elaine said.

"Just focus on preparing for the press conference for now. None of the rest may happen if that doesn't go well."

"Fear not, Hamish," Elaine said, rising to her feet. *"My tongue will tell the anger of my heart, or else my heart concealing it will break."*

"I beg your pardon, Elaine?"

"I told you I was working on Shakespeare speeches with Hugo yesterday. I think that one's from *The Taming of the Shrew*, but you can look it up on your phone. I'm off to practise my voice exercises in my room."

+++

Dinner that evening was a subdued event. Hugo and Rupert had returned late from their walk, having stopped off on the way back for a pub lunch. Hugo had insisted on doing the planned coaching session with Elaine, but had cut it short, saying that an excess of fresh air had made him feel sleepy. He hadn't felt up to joining them for dinner, either.

"Is Hugo OK?" Elaine asked Rupert. "I feel bad about him

helping me if he doesn't feel up to it."

Rupert sighed. "He's a law unto himself, Hugo is. If he decides he wants to do something, no fire, flood or tempest will stop him. I had planned a nice five-mile circuit for our walk, quite long enough for a man in his eighties with health problems, you'd think. But he was enjoying himself and insisted that we extend the walk. We must have done at least eight miles – far further than I wanted, and I'm fifteen years younger than him."

"You look tired too, Rupert," Elaine said. "Leave all the dishes and things and Hamish and I will clear up. I'm sorry I wasn't able to help until now. That wretched cannula …"

"I know, my dear," Rupert interrupted. "It's perfectly understandable. Thank you. And there's something else. I have a funeral service to conduct tomorrow, over on the west coast. I'll be home in time for dinner, but can you fend for yourselves during the day? The fridge and the freezer are well-stocked."

"Of course," Elaine said. "In fact, why don't I cook for the four of us tomorrow night? I'd enjoy that. I haven't cooked for over a month."

"I'd appreciate that, that sounds wonderful," Rupert said, getting to his feet. "And now I wish you both good night."

Hamish and Elaine gathered the plates, glasses and cutlery and took them into the kitchen. Elaine looked round at the detritus; clearly Rupert was in the category of creative but messy cooks. She began stacking used pots, pans and utensils on the side of the sink.

"Hold on," Hamish said. "I've been helping for the last week or so and learned there's a method to this. Rupert likes the glasses washed by hand in very hot water and everything else

335

goes in the dishwasher."

"A dishwasher! Wow! I haven't used one of those since I was a kid. So, will you fill that and I'll wash the glasses?" Elaine spotted a pair of rubber gloves beside the sink and pulled them on.

"I think you've got the better deal there," Hamish said with a smile, "but never mind. I've checked Goa flights into London. The only night one gets into Heathrow at eleven thirty p.m. Have you had any more thoughts about what we do when Alexandra gets to Edinburgh? Or about when she'll arrive?"

"Yes. She'll be staying with an old friend somewhere in Islington tomorrow night. If I know Alexandra, she'll be wired after the journey and she and Maria will sit up chatting for at least a couple of hours."

"OK, so she should be at Maria's place by one a.m. on the second, I guess," Hamish said.

"That seems about right. Then they'll talk till three at least, so I doubt she'll wake up before eleven. She might make it to King's Cross by one."

"That's fine. We'll have a WFJ member tail her from Heathrow to the friend's flat, then return around noon the following day – it's better to be on the safe side."

"Thanks, I appreciate that, Hamish. But it doesn't leave room for any last minute changes of plan. Would it be possible to watch her friend's flat from the moment Alexandra arrives to the moment she leaves? Alexandra may be super-anxious about me and head off to the station sooner than I think."

"I'll see what we can do. I'll let the London office know." Hamish made a note on his phone, then stuck it in the back pocket of his jeans. "And what about when she reaches Edinburgh?"

"I've had an idea," Elaine said, distractedly soaping the same wine glass for the third time. "I think her second cousin Susan would be up for meeting Alexandra at the station. She brought me here in a Porsche from Inverdour and she seems to like driving. Would WFJ pay for her petrol?"

"Of course."

"Great. I think she'd do it for a full tank of petrol and a carton of Dunhill cigarettes. God, I'd kill for a fag now!"

"Probably doing you good not smoking," Hamish said. He wiped his hands on a piece of kitchen towel and removed his phone from his back pocket. "What's her phone number?"

"Oh shit, I have no idea," Elaine hit her forehead with her hand, forgetting it was covered in soapy water. "She drove me here, but I was in such a state when I arrived I never thought to ask for her number. What an idiot I am. We could ring her mother's house, I suppose. Can you find that number out?"

She gave Hamish Linda's name and address, but she wasn't listed anywhere online. "She's probably ex-directory," Elaine said. "Typical! What now?"

"I could go up there and ask Susan in person, I suppose. It's a bit of a long shot, though."

"Won't that be risky for you, Hamish? Whoever might be looking for me could be looking for you as well."

"Right, I'm going to make some enquiries with WFJ people in the Inverdour area, and with HQ, I'll get back to you. Could you deal with the dishwasher stuff while I'm doing that? I'll be in the study if you need me."

Elaine joined Hamish in the study about forty-five minutes later. He was talking on the phone in an uncharacteristically animated fashion. "Yes, great, that sounds good. … Yes, that would probably be best … Fantastic! … See you in Stirling on Thursday."

He tapped his phone off and beamed at Elaine. "All sorted. I will be taken up to Inverdour early tomorrow and I'll make contact with Susan and see if she can meet Alexandra off the train at Edinburgh on Wednesday. If I can't get hold of Susan, or she doesn't want to play along, the person going up on the train will intercept Alexandra and explain the situation. But that's a fall back. We hope Susan will help."

"I hope so," Elaine said. "They haven't met each other for about twenty years, but I think the story would be better coming from someone Alexandra knows vaguely rather than a complete stranger. And if Susan agrees to help, please make it clear to her that Alexandra mustn't come looking for me until after the press conference. Otherwise, she could put both me and herself in danger."

"Will do. I'm sure Alexandra will believe it all more easily from a relative," said Hamish. "And I need something from you to help Susan believe that I am genuine."

"A photo of me?" Elaine suggested, going to the sideboard and pouring herself a slug of whisky from Rupert's decanter then topping up the glass from a jug of water. "Oh dear, we've rather punished poor Rupert's whisky. I'll need to send him some when – or if – I get some money for my paintings."

"Don't worry. The organisation is taking care of it – a case of his favourite malt is being delivered tomorrow."

"Oh, that's nice!" Elaine said, raising her eyebrows at the precise moment Hamish took a photo of her with his phone.

"Hey, let me see that" Elaine grabbed Hamish's phone and held the screen close to her face. "I wasn't ready. Oh, no way! I look ghastly. Delete that instantly!"

Hamish retrieved his phone and took another six photos of Elaine before she voiced approval of one of them. "Yes, show Susan that one and if she's still not convinced, tell her I told you not to ask about the sofa bed."

"Not to ask about the sofa bed? What sofa bed? Why?"

"Long story, Hamish, I'll tell you another time." Elaine felt perversely happy that, for once, she was withholding information from Hamish instead of the other way round. She sat down on the sofa and cradled her whisky. The thought of a day spent in Hugo's company was also a pleasure to look forward to. That would take her mind off the anxiety of how Alexandra was getting on and what would happen after she arrived in Edinburgh.

"So when shall we two meet again?" she asked Hamish, the thought of Hugo having led her into Shakespearean terrain again.

"When the hurly burly's done," Hamish answered immediately, surprising Elaine. "Except it will actually be just before the hurly burly starts. A member of the WFJ press team will fetch you here early on Thursday and drive you to Stirling. I'm not sure who at the moment but I'll get word to you so you know who to expect. I'll meet you in the hotel there. As you know, the press conference starts at two, but if you are there earlier you can check in, rest, sort yourself out, and we can go through the running order again. Are you OK with all of that?"

"Absolutely, everything's clear," Elaine said. "Just take care up in Inverdour. We've made it this far; we wouldn't want to lose you now." She stole a sideways look at Hamish, in his usual position on the armchair at right angles to her. He looked rather pink, but was sporting a big smile.

They sat in companionable silence finishing off their whiskies, then crept upstairs to their respective bedrooms so as not to wake Rupert and Hugo.

Chapter 31

Wednesday 2 May

Elaine woke with the first light of dawn, feeling anxious and unsettled. She knew where she was in terms of space – Rupert's spare bedroom – but had no idea of where she was located in temporal terms. It struck her for the first time in however long she'd been at Rupert's that she had swapped one form of incarceration for another. Admittedly, Rupert's house was far more comfortable than her room in the Exit Facility had been and the food was in a class of its own, but she still had no freedom of movement. A song from her school days suddenly popped into Elaine's head and she sang it softly to herself, pulling the bedcovers over her face so she didn't disturb anyone. *One more day to go, one more day of sorrow, one more day to go and we'll be free tomorrow.* Immediately afterwards she felt guilty. Rupert had been incredibly kind and generous to her, and she had had fun while at his house. Especially yesterday, when she and Hugo had spent most of the day together, polishing her speech and delivery, then watching old films on TV with the sound down and making up their own dialogue as they went along.

One more day to go. Now she felt oriented in time again. The press conference would be tomorrow and if that went well, she would be free again. *So where was everyone today?* Hamish had rung the house last night to say that he'd met up with Susan and she was willing to drive down to Edinburgh and meet Alexandra, and that a WFJ operative was in place at Heathrow, waiting for her flight to get in. So, if all was well, Alexandra would be safely installed in Maria's house in Islington now. Reassured to an extent, Elaine checked the small alarm clock on her bedside table. It was six fifteen in the morning. She tossed and turned for a bit, then finally fell asleep again.

"Have you heard any news today, Rupert?" Elaine asked after lunch as she cleared the table. Her host usually listened to the radio while he was cooking, and he had cloistered himself in the kitchen for several hours that morning while preparing their lunch.

"Just the usual stuff – political squabbles, public spending cuts, protests and police crackdowns. I don't know why I bother really. Was there something in particular you wanted to know about?"

"No plane crashes?" Elaine's voice shook slightly and she noticed Hugo turn to look at her quickly.

"No, not that I've heard of," Rupert replied, absorbed in dabbing at a spot on the tablecloth with his napkin.

"Rupert dear, I think Elaine is concerned about flights from India. Alexandra was coming in last night, remember?" Hugo said. "Poor Elaine's been like a cat on hot bricks all morning."

"Good Lord," Rupert said, "so sorry, I'd entirely forgotten. No, there was nothing on the news about plane crashes or missing aircraft. I say, do you remember that awful incident in ehm – 2015, was it? Or maybe 2014, when a Malaysian airplane…"

Hugo coughed loudly. "No word from Hamish, then, Elaine?"

"Not since last night and that was before her flight was due to land. She should actually be heading for King's Cross right now to catch a train."

"I'm sure there's nothing to worry about," Hugo said. "I

expect she just slept in this morning. It must have been a long flight."

"Yes, probably that's it," Elaine replied. "I think the flight was about fourteen hours, but I still don't understand why Hamish wouldn't get in touch just to tell me she's here at least."

Rupert finally gave up on the stain and switched his attention to Elaine. "Cheer up, my dear. No news is good news. How about coffee in the study and a game of chess?"

Elaine shook her head; there was no way she could concentrate on chess in her state of agitation.

"No? I'll tell you what then. Why don't I put you through your paces today and we'll let Hugo have an afternoon nap. I may not be a famous actor, but I have plenty of experience in talking to groups of strangers."

"Thank you," Elaine said, "that would be useful." *He could teach her a trick or two and it would help to take her mind off a phone that remained stubbornly silent.*

The landline finally rang around ten p.m. Rupert answered it, then passed the receiver to Elaine. Hamish's voice sounded distant and disjointed. "Terrible reception … out here … wilds … everything OK?"

"We're fine. What about you, and where's Alexandra?"

"Didn't ….. texts … Josh."

"You're breaking up, Hamish. What texts?"

"… Josh. He sent half a … Rupert. Hold on. … can't … a bloody thing … outside."

"It's a terrible line, but I think he said something about texts to you, Rupert," Elaine said.

"Hello, Elaine. … better?"

"Only marginally, Hamish. Listen, I'll ask questions, you answer. Is Alexandra OK?" Elaine listened, repeating out loud what she understood from Hamish so that Hugo and Rupert could follow the conversation. '… She's frazzled? I'm not surprised after that journey…. No? Razzle? … Oh, she's on the razzle. … With Susan? … Cool. What about tomorrow? … Guinness? Why would I want Guinness? … Oh, I see. Innes, tomorrow morning. OK…. What? … Oh, Hamish, I can't hear a word now! I'll see you tomorrow."

Elaine put the receiver back in its cradle and turned to Rupert and Hugo. "Jesus, you'd think we lived in the nineteenth century from the quality of that call. Un-bloody-believable. Anyway, Alexandra seems to be in Edinburgh with Susan and I think they've gone out on the town together. He said something about texts and Josh, or maybe it was that the texts were tosh. Did you give your mobile number to Hamish, Rupert?"

"Come to think of it, perhaps I did," Rupert said. "Actually, I've no idea where my phone is. I remember I had it at the funeral yesterday, because I rang you afterwards, Hugo."

"Try your coat pocket," Hugo suggested. He went to the sideboard and poured himself a small whisky and water, and one for Elaine.

Rupert was gone for a good fifteen minutes. He returned with a mobile phone in one hand and a charger in the other, and plugged them into a socket on the skirting board. "I'll have a whisky too," he said.

A couple of minutes later the phone emitted several loud pings. Rupert knelt on the floor to read the messages while the phone continued charging.

"23.45, yesterday. The eagle has landed.

00.30 Target at friend's flat.

11.57 Target departing friend's flat.

13.35 Train v busy but all well.

18.40 Arrived Edinburgh target with friend.

20.00 Target and pal in pub.

20.57 Target and pal in second pub.

21.30 Third pub, fifth round.

22.37 Targets have purchased wine from supermarket. Are waiting for a bus. Overheard them saying they're going to the flat. I need sleep. Good night, Josh."

Rupert put the phone on the floor and stood up, bracing himself on the end of the sofa to do so. "Sorry, Elaine. I should have thought to check."

"It's OK," Elaine said. Relief that Susan and Alexandra had met up and that Susan's distraction techniques had been so successful overcame her annoyance with Rupert about not checking his phone. "All's well that ends well. Where did you find it?"

"In the bathroom cabinet behind the extra toothpaste stash. Don't ask; your guess is as good as mine."

"Well, like Josh, I'm off to bed," Elaine said. "It seems I'll be collected tomorrow morning by a man called Innes. Good night to both of you, and I'll see you in the morning."

She went upstairs, changed into Rupert's pyjamas and got into bed, thinking it would be strange to be outdoors again the next day. Still Innes was a reassuringly practical-sounding name and she felt she would be in safe hands with him. Elaine fell asleep imagining a burly bloke with big hands and a bushy ginger beard driving her in a bulletproof jeep to Stirling.

Chapter 32

Thursday 3 May

Elaine woke to a pale light filtering through the curtains of Rupert's spare bedroom. She stared blearily at a figure sitting on the other bed.

"Hi Elaine, really pleased to meet you. I'm Ines, from the Warriors' Press Team." It was a woman's voice.

"Huh?" Elaine said. "What day is it, what time, and who are you? I was told a guy called Innes was picking me up?"

"It's the third of May, the day of the press conference. And it's nine a.m., so you don't need to rush. And, as you can see, I'm female. My name is Ines, with the stress on the second syllable, not 'Innes'."

"Cool, got it," Elaine said. "Excuse me, I need to pee."

She headed to the loo on the upper floor and met Hugo emerging from it.

"Good morning, my dear," he said. "Are you ready for your big debut today? I'm sure you'll be marvellous."

"Thank you," Elaine replied, jiggling slightly on the spot. "If I am, it's thanks to you. I had so much fun with you and Rupert, and I've learnt a lot. And now, if you don't mind …"

"Of course," Hugo said, standing back to let Elaine into the bathroom.

When she returned to her room, Elaine found Ines sitting on the bed clad in a slinky grey and black matching bra and pants set. She was wiggling her ankles to free her legs of the camouflage print cargo pants she had been wearing.

"Ehm, er, hello?" Elaine said, her mind racing. "Shouldn't we be getting on? I mean, there's not that much time. Plus I'm not, well, you know, ehm, how should I put it? You seem very nice and all that, but …"

Ines had freed her feet from the trousers at last. She picked them up, shook them and held them up for Elaine to see. "We're changing clothes, OK? At least we are if they fit. Do you like what you see?"

Elaine gulped, still unsure whether the question referred to the cargo pants or the woman who had lately shed them. "Yes, they're great," she managed at last. "And what about the lingerie? Are we swapping that too?"

"No way," Ines said. "This set is Boux Avenue – it cost me a bloody fortune. Just the outer gear." She reached behind herself on the bed and held up a dark khaki T-shirt and a waist-length black bomber jacket. "OK?"

"I guess so," Elaine said then, sensing more enthusiasm was called for, "they're nice and you've caught my style quite well. But why are we doing this?"

"If anyone's watching the house, they'll have seen a woman in these clothes going in, and hopefully will assume it's the same woman coming back out. Also, Hamish told me you wanted new stuff. I didn't think a suit was quite the image we want to put over, so I went for something casual, but at least not shabby."

Elaine nodded, feeling vaguely resentful that her life was being taken over in this way, but at the same time aware that she should be grateful.

"Your English is very good, Ines," she said. "Have you lived here for long?" It was the kind of backhanded compliment that had driven Alexandra mad when she first moved from Cyprus to the UK.

"My Dad's Spanish and my Mum Scottish," Ines said, "so I grew up totally bilingual. And I've lived here for about five years now."

Ah, a half-and-halfer, just like Alexandra! Elaine warmed to Ines a little bit. She wriggled out of Rupert's silk pyjama trousers and took the proffered cargo pants. They were a little too long, but otherwise a perfect fit. She turned them up once at the ankles, then smiled at Ines.

"I like these. Will you want them back once the press conference is over?"

"No, we bought them for you," Ines said. "Hamish seems to have done a surprisingly good job of guessing what size you'd take. Try the T-shirt and jacket now."

Elaine turned her back and slid out of Rupert's pyjama top. She reached under the pillow for her bra, which she had shoved there one day when the under wiring was digging into her. For the first time since she'd got here, Elaine wondered who had undressed her after she'd collapsed in Rupert's study. She hoped it hadn't been Hamish. At least whoever it was had left her underwear on, and the knickers had been new ones from Susan. The bra was a disgrace though, shabby and discoloured. Elaine wriggled into it quickly and put on the T-shirt before turning round to show Ines the result.

"You look great in that," Ines said. "The colour really suits you. I didn't have much to go on, as Hamish just said your hair was red, but it works really well with that kind of burgundy colour you have."

"That reminds me," Elaine said. "I bought a hair dye on my way here. It's a dark shade, almost black, but I thought it would cover the red and the roots that are coming in as well. I never got to use it though, as I had a cannula in my hand for days. Maybe you could help me with that? Have we got time?"

"It depends what kind of dye it is."

"Oh, just a simple box dye from a chemist's. It's called Easy-Peasy, or Dye-so-Eezy, a brand name something like that." Elaine scanned the room, trying to remember where she'd last seen the white paper bag the chemist had put her purchase in. "Hey, Dye-so-Eezy could be a brand name for an exit facility, don't you think?" Elaine giggled at her own joke. Ines didn't seem to find it very funny, or maybe her English was good but not up to getting bad puns. Elaine then spotted the chemist's bag on the ledge below the ornate mirror on the wall opposite the bed. "Look there it is," she said pointing.

Ines leapt to her feet and retrieved the bag and offered it to Elaine.

"It's OK, you open it. You'll be able to read the small print better than I can. Could you check how long you have to leave it on for?"

Ines opened the bag, pulled out the box and then made a strange choking noise. Elaine looked at her and noticed her shoulders were heaving. Suddenly it seemed she could contain herself no longer and Ines burst into hysterical laughter. Elaine felt miffed that her pun had fallen on stony ground but a packet of hair dye had reduced Ines to hysterics. "What's up?" she asked. "What's so bloody funny?"

"It's not … it's not …" Ines stopped to bring her laughter under control. "Sorry … not hair dye. The brand name is

Kwik-n-Eezy but the product is suppositories." She began laughing again.

Elaine grabbed the packet and examined it. It bore a picture of a dark-haired woman with a fatuous smile that could just as easily convey pride in her shiny hair as relief that her constipation had been satisfactorily dealt with. "Shit, I've done it again!" she said and suddenly burst into tears.

"Literally shit!" Ines said, then noticed that Elaine was crying. "Hey, what's wrong? Here, I'll get you a tissue." She pulled a tissue from a box on the bedside table and offered it to Elaine. Elaine pressed her face into the tissue, then reached out a hand for another one. She felt like all the tears she hadn't cried for Joe, or for herself and for her humiliation, had welled up together and might never stop.

Another six tissues later, the flood abated and Elaine turned a tear-stained face to Ines. "Sorry, I don't quite know where that came from. I'm forever making mistakes with products. The previous time it happened I bought flaked almonds thinking they were grated Parmesan cheese. I don't usually cry about it, though."

"It was an easy mistake to make. They don't usually put pictures of people on suppository packets, as far as I know," Ines said. "And you've been under terrible stress, plus you're probably a bit nervous about speaking in public. I hope I didn't offend you by laughing."

Elaine shook her head.

"You've got to admit it is quite funny though, better than almonds for parmesan."

Elaine smiled wanly, hoping Ines would drop the subject soon. She got off the bed and went over to the mirror and peered at her roots, tugging on her hair to see them better. The slight pain this caused grounded her. "What do you think, Ines? Are the roots really bad?"

"No, they're hardly visible, not even a centimetre yet. But if you'd feel better, when we reach Stirling I can nip out and get you something to touch the roots up and blend them in. I'll bill it to WFJ."

"Good plan," Elaine said. "What about these?" She picked up the packet of suppositories and looked inside. There seemed to be dozens of the things in it. "Any use to you?"

Ines hesitated then said "Well, you never know, I suppose. Just a few, for emergencies."

Elaine pulled out a strip of six suppositories and gave them to Ines, feeling smug that she'd found the younger woman's Achilles heel, then instantly guilty for her uncharitable thought.

"I'll put the rest into Rupert's medicine cabinet in the bathroom, then I'll go down and say goodbye to him and Hugo," Elaine said. "Have I got time for some breakfast?"

Ines pulled out a large tablet out of a small rucksack she'd laid on the floor and consulted it. "Yes, but only a quick one. We need to be out of here by ten thirty, then it's about a half hour's drive to Stirling. Check-in for your room at the hotel is any time after eleven. You can have a nap then, or a shower, and we can sort your hair out for you."

"Will you come and eat too?" Elaine asked.

"No, I've had breakfast, and I was told to disturb your host as little as possible. I'll wait up here, and I've got arrangements to check." Ines held the tablet up and tapped on it as she spoke.

Elaine took the suppositories box to the bathroom and went

in search of Hugo and Rupert. They were still in the kitchen, eating croissants and reading newspapers.

"Ah, new togs, I see," said Rupert. "Here, help yourself to coffee, it's a fresh pot."

"You look very fetching in them, my dear," said Hugo. "But why the puffy eyes? You haven't been crying, have you? Surely you're not suffering from stage fright after all my excellent tuition?"

"Thereby hangs a tale," said Elaine and told them the story of the suppositories. It sounded funny even to her this time round, and she was gratified at making both her benefactors laugh.

"I have to leave soon," she said after her second croissant. "So I'd like to thank you both. Rupert, I know it's been an awful imposition, but you've been very patient and incredibly kind. How can I ever thank you?"

"A painting would do nicely, once you've got yourself settled and this is all over. I hear your work is worth a bob or two these days," Rupert said.

Elaine was flattered. "With pleasure, Rupert. I'd love you to have one. And Hugo, thank you again for all you've done for me. It was an honour to be taught by a …"

"National treasure?" Hugo suggested.

"I was going to say by an actor of your stature and talent, actually."

"Bah, leave the accolades out, I've heard them all before. My pleasure entirely. You took my mind off my own troubles. Now, go off to Stirling and slay them. I know you can do it. I won't say goodbye, as I hope we'll meet again."

"Me too," Elaine said, aware that they both knew that might not happen. Hugo stood up and held his long arms out to her and Elaine wrapped hers round his thin body and buried her face in his jumper. Then, on an impulse, she went round to the other side of the table and hugged Rupert as well.

"Thanks again," she said, then headed back upstairs to the spare room.

As she entered the room, Ines appeared to be struggling to pull a pinkish grey bathing cap over her short dark curls. "Can you help?" she said. "It's really hard to get this thing on." On closer inspection, the object turned out to be a wig with a frill of fake grey hair surrounding a bald patch. Elaine held the wig tight on Ines's forehead while she pulled it over her hair and tucked her curls in under it. Elaine realised Ines was now wearing her own scruffy jeans and a large, shapeless grey jumper. "Oh, you're being Hamish!" she said.

"That's right. Will I pass at a distance?" Ines dipped into her rucksack and produced a pair of wire-framed glasses.

"I guess so," Elaine said. "But will you be able to drive with Hamish's glasses on?"

"No, they're not his. It's just plain glass in the lenses."

"Good, because I can't, for obvious reasons. Stand back a bit. Yes, I think you'll pass as Hamish if nobody looks too closely…"

"It's really only till we get out of the house and on the road, and at the other end of the journey. OK, have you got all your stuff? What about your old jacket?"

"I'll ditch it," Elaine said. "It's beyond repair with the buttons gone." She transferred Miss Latimer's chequebook, the change from her ill-fated chemist's purchase and a couple of tissues into the pockets of the cargo pants, and put on the new black bomber jacket. It fitted like a dream. Then she gathered up the T-shirt from Susan and looked around for Hamish's polo shirt.

"If it's that ghastly greyish top you're looking for, I'm wearing it under the jumper," Ines said. "I thought it would bulk me up a bit. Sorry, that was rather rude."

"No problem, I don't like it either. It's Hamish's, so you'll be right in character. But can you pack this one in your rucksack for me, please?"

"Sure," Ines said. "Is that all you've got?"

"Yep. I travel light. Shall we go?"

Chapter 33

Thursday 3 May

A boxy-looking white SUV was parked on the drive. Ines held the door open and Elaine scrambled into the front passenger seat. She settled down low into it, feeling nervous and too visible. Ines got into the driver's seat and swung her door shut.

"Seat belt, Elaine, please. And you can sit up properly. The windows are smoked, so we won't be seen now."

"Cool. I'll take this off then." Elaine removed the baker's boy cap Ines had insisted she put on before they left Rupert's house. It was bad enough getting into clothes someone else had been wearing, but she drew the line at wearing another person's hat. After years spent delousing Alexandra's hair when she was at school, Elaine didn't take chances on that kind of thing. Ines looked squeaky clean, but you never knew.

"Fine," Ines said, "just pop it back on when you get out of the car at the other end. OK, let's go."

They drove for some minutes in silence. Nervous about what lay ahead, Elaine searched for a conversational opening. "The last car I rode in was a Porsche," she said. "This one seems very quiet in comparison."

Ines turned briefly to look at Elaine, giving her what Elaine thought might be a withering glance. "A Porsche – really? Well, the difference in sound is not surprising. This is an electric vehicle. WFJ never use anything else. We may not campaign on green issues, but we still care about the environment, naturally."

Feeling that she had perhaps just been put down, even if subtly, Elaine gave up on the idea of calming her nerves with chit-chat and counted down the distance to Stirling with every signpost they passed on the A road. Ines drove confidently, but kept within the speed limit and checked the rear view mirror regularly. They were about fifteen miles from their destination when Ines put an indicator on, accelerated rapidly and overtook a slow-moving van, then almost immediately swerved left again and turned down a slip road. A robotic voice from the dashboard said "Keep on the main road. Do not turn off. Keep straight ahead." It continued chastising Ines until they reached a lay-by about half a mile down that road where Ines pulled into it and sat scanning the cars coming up the road behind them in her wing mirror.

"What's wrong?" Elaine asked, her heart thudding with shock.

"Just checking," Ines said. "I didn't like the look of a car that was on our tail, but it hasn't followed us so that's OK." She leant over to an instrument on the dashboard and pressed a few buttons. "I'll reset the satnav to guide us in from this route. You're not a Yoda fan, I take it?"

"No," Elaine said, baffled by the question, "funk or soul are more my kind of thing."

Ines shook her head and pressed another couple of buttons. The rest of their journey was guided by the reassuring tones of Billy Connolly issuing from the satnav. After twenty minutes more, they turned off onto a ring road and then into a small, pleasantly-landscaped business park. They pulled up in front of a two-storeyed modern building with a canopy over the entrance. Ines cut the engine and took a folded paper out of the glove locker and gave it to Elaine.

"This is your booking confirmation. Check yourself in while I go and park round the back, then I'll bring my stuff to your room if you don't mind. I'll need to change again. Hey, don't forget the hat!"

Elaine removed the hat as soon as she entered the hotel foyer, which seemed to be empty of guests. The receptionist took her confirmation and handed her a key card. "Here you go, Ms Tarrant," she said. "You're on the first floor, room 109."

Elaine opened her mouth to protest that her name was Treasoner, not Tarrant, and then shut it hastily when she realised this was an alias.

"And your colleague, Mr Redditch, is in room 110."

Hamish, Elaine presumed, realising she'd never actually known what his surname was. She walked up the stairs opposite the reception desk and along a corridor to room 109 and let herself in. She threw Ines's hat on the nearest bed and hung the new bomber jacket in the wardrobe, then used the loo and washed her hands and face. She then searched the room for a clock, but found none. Of course, nobody needed them these days when everyone, except her, carried phones. She was contemplating phoning reception to ask the time when there was a gentle knock at her door. Elaine opened it a slit and peeped out. Two versions of Hamish were standing in the corridor. Elaine stood back and one version pushed past her into the room and dumped a rucksack and a small travel bag on the luggage rack then began tugging at his temples.

"Thank goodness," Ines said as the wig came off. "That thing was hot and itchy." Elaine automatically scratched her own head then hoped this was merely the power of suggestion.

"Glad you got here safely," the real Hamish said, smiling at Elaine.

"You too, Hamish. It all went well, thanks to Ines. What news have you got? That was a bloody awful line last night."

"It's always terrible there," Hamish said. "I once had to stand on top of a garden table to get any signal at all. Anyway, I think you know as much as I do. Alexandra and ..."

Ines interrupted. "Can I change in your bathroom, Elaine?"

"Sure," Elaine said, still focussed on Hamish. "Thanks for arranging the business with Susan. I guess you don't know if the girls are coming here?"

"No, I don't. I told Susan about the press conference, of course, and that Alexandra shouldn't contact you before it. But I left it up to her to decide if they will come here. I hope that's OK."

"Of course, Hamish, and thank you so much for making the journey up to Inverdour and persuading her to find Alexandra. I really appreciate it, and I won't forget that you did that for me." Elaine threw her arms around Hamish and hugged him. He patted her awkwardly on one arm and drew away, a pink tinge on his cheeks.

"No problem, Elaine. It was a pleasure, and Susan needed no persuading. She thought it sounded like an adventure and was delighted to get some expenses for the trip."

The bathroom door opened and Ines came out clad in a silver jumpsuit. She dropped Elaine's old jeans and Hamish's polo shirt on the bed and took her tablet out of her rucksack and glanced at it. "It's nearly ten to twelve. We need to get moving, Hamish. I'll check in, then go down to the conference room and start setting up. Elaine, I'll see you downstairs at half past one. The show starts at two."

"What about my hair?" Elaine asked. "You said you'd pop

out and get something for the roots."

"Shit, so I did," Ines said. "Sorry, I didn't realise the hotel would be this far outside the town centre when I said that. Maybe Josh or Krystal could stop off. Hamish, what do you reckon?"

"I got a message from Josh ten minutes ago. There are roadworks on the motorway up from Edinburgh and they're behind schedule."

"Double shit. Elaine, I'm really sorry, but no can do. Here, take this, it may help a bit." Ines pulled a gold and cream pot of something out of her rucksack and handed it to Elaine, grabbed her luggage and headed out the door. As she left, Elaine saw the acronym W f J emblazoned in huge black letters across her back.

"Wow!" Elaine said as the door banged shut behind Ines. "Great outfit, and a very formidable lady."

"May I?" asked Hamish, indicating a fake leather armchair in the corner of the room.

"Of course, Hamish". Elaine sat down on the bed where Ines had dumped her jeans.

"That's our uniform, actually," Hamish said. "We have to wear it on all official events, like this, or at protests. Hey, is that my polo shirt? I was wondering where that had gone. I'd rather wear that than the silver suit any day. I feel like a headless astronaut in it."

"Yeah, I get that," Elaine said. "Why silver, I wonder?"

"You wouldn't believe the problems the colour of the jumpsuits caused. We wanted it to symbolise justice, but no matter what colour marketing came up with, there was always one country in the world where that colour meant death or mourning or fertility or imprisonment or something inappropriate. And nobody except me liked grey. So I'm stuck with it. Just don't laugh when you see me later."

"I promise."

"You were OK with Ines, I hope. Some people find her a bit brusque, but she's extremely competent and intelligent. I think she's got three different law degrees."

And a cruel sense of humour, Elaine thought, but bit the comment back. "So how come she's doing a lowly job like driving me to a venue?" she asked instead.

"I think I mentioned before, we're an organisation with a pretty flat hierarchy. Everyone turns their hand to different tasks, as required."

Hamish's phone pinged and he looked at it. "That's Josh and Kristal arriving shortly. I'd better go down and meet them and help them unpack the van. Why don't you stay here and rest? But no walks."

Shit – Hamish had read her mind. "Not even just round the hotel grounds?"

"No, Elaine. We've come this far safely. We're going to make news, and then you'll be safe to do whatever you want. Look, I'll try and get up here around one and we can have lunch together in your room. If not, order whatever you want from room service."

"I have no way to tell the time, Hamish."

"It's on the TV screen, look there … bottom right corner. No? Too small I guess. And black on grey."

Elaine nodded. "And you know I can't use a remote. I'd probably set the fire alarm off by accident."

"I'll see what I can do, Elaine. Trust me. I'll catch you later."

Alone and confined to barracks once again, Elaine paced the room. Eight strides from wall to wall between the beds, ten from door to window. She went from side to side and back and forth ten times. A hundred and eighty paces and she reckoned that had wasted less than four minutes. Another eighty-six to go until she was required downstairs and this wasn't the way to pass them. She opened the drawers in the dressing table, hoping for a pen and some hotel notepaper to draw on, but there was none. A room service menu bound in fake leather was, predictably, illegible to her. She could read only one box in the centre of the right hand page, which said 'Hot Dish of the Day' in large, bold letters. A handwritten card had been glued into the box below the title. Elaine took the menu over to the window and held it sideways to the light. By judicious squinting and peering she finally made out the words 'vegetable lasagne'. Double shit, as Ines might say.

Elaine returned the menu to the drawer and picked up the pot of hair product Ines had left for her. It was heavy – a glass container, not a plastic one, and had a gold lid. The body of the pot was cream-coloured and the name of the product was inscribed on it in fancy gold lettering. It appeared to be called 'Kerouac', a name Elaine found highly inappropriate. She very much doubted that the author of *On the Road* had given a damn about hair products, and this gloop was way too heavy to suit a peripatetic lifestyle. Maybe it was some kind of wax, with the name deriving from the Greek word *keri?* That would make more sense. She opened the pot, sniffed it and prodded it gingerly. The consistency seemed more like something between a gel and a mousse. She scooped some out, rubbed it between her palms as she had seen Alexandra do, then ran her hands through her hair and tried to tease it upwards. This resulted in nasty, sticky clumps of hair that drew further attention to her grey roots. *Damn, now she'd have to wash it.*

Elaine was pleased to find that the bathroom was well equipped with a robe, towels, shampoo, conditioner and shower gel. She could have a leisurely shower and that would pass some of the time and, hopefully, help her to relax.

Elaine sang every Beatles song she could remember while doing two shampoos and a thorough body wash. She was applying conditioner and moving on to Abba hits when she became aware of an insistent knocking sound. She turned the water off and heard knocking again, accompanied by the sound of someone humming the tune she had just been belting out at top volume. Elaine hadn't bargained on an audience when she had left the bathroom door open and now felt like a total idiot. She stepped out of the shower, threw on the hotel bathrobe and opened the door to the corridor slightly. Applying her left eye to the gap, she saw a silver jumpsuit and decided it was safe to open the door fully. A young man with glossy blue-black hair and an artfully placed mauve streak in his floppy fringe was standing there grinning. He looked exactly like a K-Pop star Alexandra had had a huge crush on about five years before. He looked at Elaine's hair dripping gobbets of conditioner onto her cheeks and neck, and broke into a pastiche of Elaine's last song:

"There is something in your hair tonight, it's not quite right, Elaine-oh!"

Elaine burst out laughing, her embarrassment dissolving, and stood back to let him into the room. "OK, you know who I am. And you are …?"

"Josh," he said extending his hand to Elaine. "I'm happy to meet you."

"So am I," she said. "You kept an eye on my daughter last night and the night before. I can't thank you enough for that."

"No worries," Josh said. "It was easy enough, at least until the final pub. I wasn't drinking cos of being on duty today, and there's only so much lemonade you can put away in one night."

"How was she? Did you speak?" Elaine sat down on the bed that wasn't strewn with clothes and gestured for Josh to sit beside her. "How does she look now?"

"We didn't speak," Josh said. "I'd been told not to approach her unless I thought there was any danger or if her friend didn't show up."

"That's Susan, her cousin, well, second cousin really."

"Alexandra looked tired. She slept nearly all the way from London to Edinburgh. Then she seemed excited, very animated, a bit hyper maybe. I know Susan was going to explain where you had been, so I guess that's understandable."

"Yes, I expect she was absolutely livid. And how does she look these days?"

Josh looked at Elaine, his perfectly groomed eyebrows drawn together into a slight frown. "Have you not seen her for a while?"

"No," Elaine said, "not for about three years in the flesh. Virtually, about six or seven weeks ago over a bad internet connection."

"Oh my God, that's ages!" Josh said. "She looks great – she's got a fantastic tan and her hair is chestnut with blonde highlights. It could do with a trim, but whose hair doesn't. And talking of hair, Ines sent me up here to help with yours. Show me what she left with you."

Elaine gave Josh the pot of Kerouac hair care and he

wrinkled his shapely nose. "That won't do, it's for longer, curlier hair than yours. You basically want to hide the root regrowth by fluffing your hair up a bit, right?"

Elaine nodded.

"Cool. I've got something in the van. So why don't you pop back into the shower and rinse the conditioner off and I'll go and get it."

Half an hour later, Elaine was clean and dressed in her new clothes and Josh had dried her hair and made it stand up enough that the burgundy tips obscured most of the grey. He chatted easily throughout the process, telling Elaine about his early childhood in Hong Kong, his family's move to the UK, his first career as a hairdresser and his subsequent transfer to activism after his pro-democracy uncle had disappeared overnight in Hong Kong.

"Do you know that Alexandra was working in Hong Kong until a few weeks ago? Her visa was revoked after she took part in a demonstration."

"You're kidding me! That is so weird! I hope I get to meet her properly and talk. Is she coming to the press conference?"

"I have no idea. I was hoping you could tell me, but you didn't talk at all, you said."

"That's right. At one point, in the second pub I think it was, I got the impression she'd noticed me and might come and confront me. But then her cousin said something that made her laugh a lot and the moment passed."

I'll bet she noticed you, Elaine thought to herself. In a pub full of Scottish men, Josh would shine like a bonfire on a dark night.

"OK, let me look at you," Josh said, standing back to survey

Elaine from head to toe. "Hair's the best I can do with the stuff available, trousers good, top OK, the jacket's great." His gaze travelled over Elaine's stolen second-hand plimsolls, but he was tactful enough not to comment on them. "Are you nervous?" he asked.

"A bit."

"You'll be great, I'm sure of it." Josh pulled a phone out of a pocket in his jumpsuit and it pinged as he looked at it. "That's Hamish. He says you should order something to eat up here if you want and he's sorry he can't join you. I need to go down now. You've got twenty minutes till the team briefing starts. I'll see you downstairs."

"Thanks for your help, Josh. I'll see you in twenty."

Elaine opened the mini bar and helped herself to some crisps and peanuts, then started counting the minutes down again.

Chapter 34

Thursday 3 May

The conference room was larger than Elaine had expected and the array of chairs, their rows alternately upholstered in yellow or purple, was daunting. Elaine looked down at the jazzy, faux tartan purple and yellow carpet and felt suddenly nauseous. Maybe the crisps and peanuts had been a mistake. She sat down abruptly on a purple chair in the front row, staring at the long table behind which Hamish and Ines were conferring and at which she would soon be speaking.

"Hi, I'm Kristal", a voice said. Elaine turned to see a young silver-clad woman with a mass of curly red hair standing beside her. "I'm on tech today. Do you prefer a fixed mic, or a lapel one?"

"It's the first time I've done this," Elaine said. "What do you suggest?"

"It depends. If you're reading from notes, the fixed one is better. If you prefer to wander about a bit when you're talking, then I'd suggest the lapel one."

"I'm partially-sighted," Elaine said, "so I can't read. I'll be talking without any notes. I think I'd feel better with the second option."

"Great," Kristal said and suddenly bent in towards Elaine, who flinched. "Sorry, didn't mean to make you jump. I just wanted to fix this on your jacket." Kristal held up the microphone in explanation.

"It's OK, my fault," Elaine said. "Do it now. I'm feeling a bit nervous about this whole thing, I must admit."

"That's normal," Kristal said. "Josh nearly threw up the first time he spoke in public."

"I can relate to that. In fact, do you happen to know where the ladies is?"

"See that double door you came in through? Back out there and it's the second door on the left. Do you want me to come with you?"

"I'll manage, but thanks for the offer."

"No problem. I need you back here in five minutes for the sound check, though."

Elaine found the ladies easily and dashed into the nearest cubicle, her stomach churning with nausea. She leant over the pan, braced herself on the cistern and dry-heaved, bringing up nothing but a little bile. She tried again with the same result. Elaine straightened up and leant against the wall, waiting for her heart to stop racing, then went to the row of basins, splashed cold water on her neck and wrists and rinsed her mouth out. She must have been more than five minutes as she could hear Hamish and Ines's amplified voices from the corridor outside the toilets.

"Are you sure about this Hamish? She seems pretty flaky to me. We don't want this whole thing to backfire," Ines was saying.

"I'm positive, Ines. I stand by her abilities a hundred percent" Hamish replied, "And she's been mentored by a great actor and a sought-after celebrant. Trust me."

Elaine coughed loudly to signal her presence, entered the conference room and strode toward the long table, bolstered by Hamish's confidence in her. "Thank you," she mouthed at him while sitting down in the seat to his left. She checked her lapel microphone had not been dislodged, then said "I'm good to go for the sound check. Perhaps a little less volume, Kristal? I could hear Hamish and Ines while I was out in the corridor." She glanced towards Ines in the seat beyond Hamish, hoping she was blushing, but it was too far away for her to tell.

"Right, running order," Ines said. "I'll open with an overview of the legal background to the introduction of assisted dying. Not in massive detail, as there is a summary and links to further reading in the press packs Josh will be handing out. Just enough for the journos to get an idea of the framework in which the exit facilities are, or should be, operating. Over to you then, Hamish, for a description of your undercover mission, what you discovered, and the escape. Then it's Elaine's turn. You've been through what to say with her, haven't you, Hamish?"

"Many times," Elaine said. "And you can address your questions directly to me Ines. I may be half-blind but there's nothing wrong with my hearing."

"Questions, yes, good point." Hamish broke in hastily. "After each section, or all at the end? What do you both think?"

"A few after Ines's speech, I would suggest," Elaine said. "They need to be clear about what the law does or doesn't allow in order to understand how unacceptable some of the practices in there are. The rest at the end."

"OK, happy with that," Ines said, surprising Elaine.

Kristal joined them and stood at the opposite side of the long table. "The sound is fine now, and the video camera is set up and checked. What about a roving mic for question time? I thought that might help Elaine."

"Why? The hall's not that big and she tells me there's nothing wrong with her hearing." Ines said.

"True, but how will Elaine know who to speak to when she answers a question? I can't help cos I'll be filming, but Josh could take the roving mic to the questioner and stand beside or behind them, so she knows what direction to look."

Wow! That's really understanding. "Good idea," Elaine said. "Let's give it a go."

"Can you come over here a minute?" Kristal waved and called to Josh, who was assembling roller banners with WFJ logos on them and distributing them around the room. A few attendees had already drifted in and seated themselves in different rows. Kristal explained her plan and Josh walked over and stood behind the furthest away journalist. Elaine could see no details, but his silver form stood out clearly against the clamour of the coloured chairs. Elaine gave Josh he thumbs up and grinned at Kristal.

"Clever plan! Thank you," she said.

Kristal grinned back. "That's OK. I used to work as an enabler for a vision support charity, so I know a trick or two."

A lull ensued as the room began to fill up and a low buzz of conversation replaced the silence. Ines tapped on the desk with a ballpoint, while Hamish tugged incessantly at the collar of his jumpsuit. This kept creeping up his neck, confirming his image of himself as a headless astronaut. Elaine had felt better after the rush of anger triggered by the remark she'd heard Ines making, but now the adrenaline was ebbing and anxiety and nausea were creeping back. At last Ines stood up and tapped the water jug on the table with her pen and waited until the conversation had died away.

"Good afternoon and welcome," she said. "My name is Ines Garcia and I am a member of the Warriors for Justice UK team. You can find my contact details in the press pack you have been given. You have been invited here today to discuss alarming information we have discovered about exit facilities as part of an undercover programme of surveillance carried out by Warriors for Justice UK. WFJ have sought to open a discussion with government for a long period now about the ethical minefield and general inhumanity of exit facilities. Unfortunately, our efforts to make this discussion more public have been spurned at several junctures. Therefore, we decided to take direct action and launched a covert surveillance mission some months ago to bring the issues we have been warning about more clearly into public consciousness. For the purposes of complete clarity, I will start by outlining the legal framework within which the exit facilities were set up and are operated. My co-speakers, Hamish Redditch and Elaine Treasoner will then tell you about their experiences inside one of those facilities. Hamish is a Warriors for Justice undercover agent and Elaine is an exit facility escapee who is today coming out of hiding and breaking her silence." Ines paused while a broad muttering rose across the room. Elaine realised all the faces in the chairs were now looking up, directly at her. She was glad she couldn't make out more and stared down at her hands, fidgeting, while Ines continued. "If you have questions concerning the legal aspects, I will take those after my introduction. Please leave any other questions until after both Hamish and Elaine have spoken."

"As you will no doubt know, the law allowing assisted dying was passed five years ago. As in most European countries that allow similar practices, this was confined to the terminally ill and required signatures by two different doctors before a patient would be accepted for what is sometimes known as a timely and dignified death. This law also stipulated the establishment of dedicated centres, to be known as exit facilities, where these patients would be assisted by medical experts, rather than placing this duty on GPs or hospital doctors. What is less well known is that a secondary piece of legislation, which went through Parliament late one Sunday evening, was passed eighteen months ago. This introduced the novel concept of self-referral to an exit facility. You will find a short summary of each law in your press pack, by the way, along with links to relevant reference materials. Clearly, not all groups in society were made eligible for this service …"

"Just as well, or the Samaritans would be out of a job," a loud voice shouted from the back of the room. About half of the audience sniggered at the joke. Ines waited until any laughter had died down.

"Indeed," she said. "In fact, the service was made available to very specific groups in society, namely only to those who are over the age of twenty and who are non-taxpayers. By non-taxpayers, I am referring mainly to the elderly and those who do not have work, either for reasons of disability or due to lack of training or employment opportunities. Of course, some other criteria need to be met, principal among which is a certificate of mental health proving that a client, as they are referred to, is of sound mind when making the application to enter an exit facility. You will hear more on that topic from my co-speakers but I would like to point out that the service is free to any people who meet the criteria I have outlined. Warriors for Justice is clear that the voluntary side of this service is being abused. It is possible that in some exit facilities, it is being used as a covert eugenics operation. In addition, we have discovered that some people are in exit facilities without having given their consent. I will now take questions if you have any."

Someone in the middle of the room raised a hand and Josh

ran over to give them the microphone and stood in place behind them.

"Jackie Thomas, *Edinburgh Evening Mail*, so what you're saying is that the government has passed an obscure law that allows it to bump off the most vulnerable members of society and thus cut the social security budget? Have I understood that correctly?" a woman said.

Ines replied clearly and deliberately. "As a trained lawyer and a Warrior for Justice, it is not my place to infer the motives of the government in this or any other issue. It is my job to lay out the facts. To reiterate, the facts are that this service is free, that only non-taxpayers over twenty-five are eligible for it, and that a certificate of mental health is required. I should perhaps also mention that the exit facilities are actively promoted to this target audience."

Ines pressed a button and a screen behind Elaine lit up. She turned round to glance at it and saw with a chill that it was a blown-up version of the pamphlet that had been delivered to her flat just over a year ago. A myriad of questions ensued from the floor and Ines spent the next ten minutes dealing with them, then handed over to Hamish.

He spoke for about ten minutes, outlining the concerns and suspicions about homeless people disappearing off the streets that had led him to volunteer for an exit facility in order to investigate from the inside. He spoke of meeting Elaine and Joe and the roles that they had played, of their decision to break out when it appeared that the Indigents were being exterminated, and then touched briefly on their escape. Not surprisingly, he steered clear of the issue of the weed they had unearthed.

When he finished speaking, several hands went up in the audience, but Hamish reminded them to save their questions until after Elaine had spoken. Elaine got to her feet, her heart racing, and immediately felt hemmed in by the table in front of her. The others had spoken from behind it, but Elaine moved in front of the table, narrowly avoiding tripping over one if its legs, and stood there. They were a mass of blurs, some pink, their faces turned to her, others brown or black or blonde, their heads bent over tablets or notepads, she assumed. She grounded herself as Hugo had taught her and breathed in from her diaphragm.

"Good afternoon, ladies and gentlemen," she said. "My name is Elaine Treasoner." She waited for a heckler to comment on her unusual name, or for someone to ask how it was spelt, but no reaction came. "Today is the third of May," she continued, "and this is the day that I am meant to die."

An audible gasp went up from the audience and a wave passed through them; Elaine could see the different hair colours being replaced by a ripple of pinkness as heads were raised to look at her. Several flashes went off, making Elaine blink, but she kept her internal focus. She had their attention now, no doubt about it. Elaine felt a rush of energy and a warm feeling that radiated from her solar plexus out towards her extremities. She filled the space at the front of the room with that energy and scanned the audience, Rupert's words in her head: *it doesn't matter that you can't see them; just look at each person briefly as if you were making eye contact and they will feel like you are speaking to them*. And then she spoke.

She spoke like she had never spoken in her life before, with passion and confidence and fluency. She spoke of her arrival at the Exit Facility, her delayed Closure, the people she had met, the lies and hindrances the administration had thrown in her path. She spoke of Joe and Miss Latimer and Dorothy and of the fate of the Indigents. She spoke of her paintings. Finally, she became aware of Josh standing a few rows back and off to the side, making exaggerated thumbs up gestures at her, and deciding perhaps she had spoken enough.

Hamish's voice broke in. "Thank you, Elaine. We will now take questions." Elaine returned to her seat as Ines answered another legal question "Did I talk too much?" she whispered to Hamish. "Not at all," he whispered back. "You were brilliant, totally amazing, in fact. I knew you would be."

The next question was for Elaine and it was one she had had to answer many times before, in different forms: "How come you managed to get a certificate of mental health to enter the Exit Facility? I would have thought the very fact that you were suicidal would have mitigated against that."

Elaine leapt to her feet again. "Firstly, the certificate of mental health was issued by an official who worked for the Exit Facility Intake Office I attended. No questions were asked of me, no health records were checked. It was basically a rubber stamp." Another gasp went round the room. "Secondly, I refute the notion that I was, or ever have been, suicidal. I made what I consider to be a rational choice, based on my financial circumstances and prospects. I am partially-sighted and so I cannot actually see any of you properly, but my guess is that at least thirty percent of you have elderly parents who are in care, or are likely to need care soon. To me, the choice of a dignified death that would leave a small inheritance for my daughter was infinitely preferable to a slow, lingering death in a care home that would also bankrupt my offspring."

"Derek Milner, *The Stirling Clarion*. Why go to all the trouble of breaking out?" another person asked. "You could have sat tight and been quietly offed today." A murmur of protest arose in the room; seemingly several people found this question offensive.

Perhaps worried that the question would upset Elaine,

377

Hamish decided to answer this one. "I think Elaine made it clear that neither she, Joe, nor I could stand by and do nothing while people who were there against their will were being exterminated. In addition, the administrative procedures where Dorothy Brown and Violet Latimer were concerned clearly breached their human rights."

"Alyson Currie, *The Scottish Feminist*. Do you have any proof of these allegations?" another journalist asked. Elaine and Hamish had discussed this issue at Rupert's house, aware that they had no evidence to back up Joe's claim that the Indigents were being executed. They had already decided that their best tactic would be distraction until evidence could be gathered.

"Actually, I do," Elaine said, getting to her feet again. She paused for dramatic effect, then pulled Miss Latimer's cheque book out of a leg pocket in her new cargo pants. She moved in front of the table and held it up for the reporters to see, and was met by another round of flashbulbs going off. "This rather old-fashioned object is a cheque book that belonged to Violet Latimer. As I told you, she was under the impression that she was housed in a care home, not in an exit facility which would, as she was there voluntarily, have been free. Now, as I said, I am partially-sighted, and I need some help." Elaine walked along in front of the first row of journalists, and chose a middle-aged woman with a friendly-looking face. "Would you be so kind as to read the second last stub in that cheque book?"

"N. Pemberton, March fees, £3,000," the journalist read aloud.

"Thank you," Elaine said. "And I will remind you all that the name of the administrator in the exit facility Hamish and I were in was Nicola Pemberton." She retrieved the cheque book from the journalist and sat down among a hubbub of voices and the flashing of several cameras.

Ines stood up and tapped on the water jug with her pen until silence finally fell again. "Thank you all," she said. "We have come to the end of our allotted time for this press conference. If you have further questions for Elaine, Hamish or myself, or if you would like to set up private interviews with any of us, please contact my colleague Josh," Ines gestured to where Josh was standing near the double doors, "who is managing the diary for us today." More cameras flashed and several reporters stood up and shuffled along to the end of their yellow or purple row before heading towards the exit.

Ines, Hamish and Elaine all stood up and gravitated towards each other at the front of the long table. Ines held out a tumbler to Elaine and filled it from the water jug. "You were incredible, Elaine, thank you. I'm really sorry I doubted you. You clearly have a great talent for speaking in public." Elaine grinned at Ines, pleased by the apology more than the compliment. She was about to respond when a huge clamour arose at the double doors.

About a dozen journalists were trying to leave while two female voices were raised in protest. "Stand back and bloody well let me in!" one said. "It's urgent, let us through!" said another. Each sounded familiar, but Elaine could not make them out clearly against the background grumbling of the reporters who were trying to leave the room. Suddenly two figures were ejected inwards from the cluster at the door that was pushing to get out. A tall broad-shouldered girl strode towards Ines, Hamish and Elaine, followed by another, blonder one of roughly the same height, each wearing large dark sunglasses. They were accompanied by top notes of over-applied expensive perfume that didn't quite cover the base notes of stale alcohol.

"What the flaming fuck were you thinking of, Mother?" the first girl yelled and slapped Elaine hard across the cheek.

Elaine staggered backwards and was caught by Ines as a lightning storm of flashes lit up the room, the journalists who had not yet departed rushing to the front of the room to get close-ups of this family drama.

"Hello, Alexandra," Elaine said, "It's rather a long story."

Epilogue

18 months later

Elaine got out of bed, put on her dressing gown, had a pee, then went through to the kitchen to heat up leftover coffee from yesterdays' batch in the cafetiere, switching on her new laptop as she passed through her living room. By the time her coffee had heated in the microwave, the laptop was fired up and ready to go, a fact that never failed to please her. She scanned through her morning emails; these included the usual offers for products she didn't want to buy; and a slew of messages asking her to talk to various organisations about poverty, homelessness, disability, assisted dying or macular degeneration. There was a short email from Hamish sending greetings from his holiday in Cornwall, though she suspected he was more likely to be on a mission in the Yemen.

She binned the promotional emails and stuck the others in her 'to be dealt with' folder and moved on to one entitled 'YaY!!!' This was from Susan and was written in her usual effervescent style – over-punctuated, peppered with acronyms and emojis, and much of it misspelled. None of that mattered though, as Susan was a powerhouse of brass neck and energy who had taken Elaine's paintings to hitherto unknown heights of sales and popularity. Her niece was worth every penny of the commission Elaine paid her, and she, along with Alexandra, had persuaded her to replace her paints, brushes and canvases and get back into the studio.

Hungry after a late night of painting, Elaine was on her way back to the kitchen to make breakfast when her phone rang. She hesitated, aware that only Davey, Hamish or the Warriors for Justice ever used that number and she wanted peace and food before she faced the business matters of the day. Then it crossed her mind that this was still Alexandra's emergency point of contact for her, and she picked up the receiver. It was Davey.

"Hiya, Elaine. I didn't wake you, did I?"

"No, it's OK, Davey. I've been up for a while, but I did have a late night in the studio last night."

"Aye, I ken. I saw the light on up there." Elaine smiled ruefully to herself; not much passed Davey's eagle eye. She wondered what life would be like in the improbable event that she ever got a new boyfriend.

"So, what's up Davey?"

"There's this bloke here says he knows you and wants to see you. Tall, suntanned, and he's only got one arm."

"What's his name?"

"He says he's Joe. He won't give a surname."

A jolt of electricity caused Elaine's heart to thud, then travelled down to her abdomen.

"Ehm ..." she said. "Well, I think you should ehm ..."

"Tell him to piss off?" Davey suggested.

"No, no, it's OK. I'll see him, but not immediately. In half an hour."

"So what the hell d'ye want me to dae wi him till then?"

"Give him the tour, Davey. The dormitory, the classroom, the hydroponics, you know the drill."

"Well, if you're sure." The doubt and suspicion of the

stranger's motives were redolent in Davey's tone.

"Thanks, Davey." Elaine put the phone down and ran to the bathroom for a shower. As she hastily washed and shampooed, her emotions veered from hope and excitement to guilt and dread. *If this really was Joe, how would he react? Well, there was only one way to find out.* She rushed into the bedroom, dressed and hastily dried her hair. *If this really was Joe, she wanted to look good.* Elaine put on her favourite pair of earrings.

Bang on time, the doorbell rang and Elaine buzzed the visitor into the stairwell. She waited behind her flat door with her heart thumping, listening as his footsteps came rapidly up the stairs. She opened the door before he had time to knock and found a tall, well-dressed man in an expensive-looking russet-coloured overcoat worn open over a black roll-neck jumper and black jeans.

"Joe?" she said, unsure if her eyes were playing tricks on her in the dimly-lit stairwell.

"Who else? Don't tell me you're even blinder than the last time we saw each other!" It was definitely Joe's voice.

"Thank God," Elaine said. "I thought you were dead." She bit her lip to stop herself from bursting into tears.

"Apparently not," Joe replied. "Aren't you going to invite me in?"

Elaine stood back to let him into her narrow hallway, then gestured towards the door into her living room. She followed him into the room, where she could see him better, and looked him up and down. He was deeply tanned, which suited him well, and his silver hair was short, but well-cut. The left sleeve of his coat seemed strangely limp from the elbow down, and the cuff of it was tucked into his pocket.

"You look well, but different," she said.

"Yes, sporting a different disability these days," Joe said and indicated his left sleeve with his right hand then flashed the wry smile she had seen so many times before.

"I didn't mean that. I meant, ehm, sophisticated, well-groomed ..."

"C'mon Elaine, there's no need for flattery," Joe said, removing his coat one-handedly and slinging it over the back of her sofa-bed and dislodging the throw Elaine had bought to disguise its faded upholstery. "Hey, I recognise this from your saucy photo collection. Is this the sofa where old Jerry pegged out in ecstasy?"

"Gary, not Jerry," Elaine said, blushing. "Yes, it's the same one. I haven't got round to replacing it yet." She picked up Joe's coat and rearranged the throw. "Sit down, the throw's clean. What can I get you? Coffee? Tea?"

"Haven't you got anything stronger? Whisky? Gin?"

"It's eleven o'clock in the morning, Joe!"

"So? That wouldn't have stopped the Elaine I used to know." Joe winked.

"OK, then. Coffee first, booze after." Elaine hung Joe's coat in the hall, made a fresh cafetiere of coffee and brought it into the living room with cups and a plate of biscuits.

Joe was looking at her portrait of Alexandra in her graduation robes. "This must be the much-beloved but ever-absent Alexandra, I guess," he said. "Where is she now? Absent again? Or in another room?"

"We don't live together, Joe, and there's only one other room in the flat. She's absent because, a, she'll be at work now and, b, she moved in with her boyfriend a couple of months ago."

"The Hong Kong activist? He made it out?"

"No, not that boyfriend. Josh is an activist, too, but he's with Hamish's lot, as is Alexandra now. She also teaches the literacy classes that I offer here at the shelter."

Joe frowned as he picked up a biscuit and bit it in two. "It's going to take me a while to digest all of this." Elaine glanced at the biscuit, wondering to herself if Joe had suffered damage to his stomach as well as his arm.

"No, not the biscuit, of course," Joe continued, "your life and how you live it nowadays. Your guard dog in the building opposite told me that you're quite in demand for public speaking gigs these days, and that your paintings are selling well now, but I don't get why you're spending your money on literacy classes and a shelter for rough sleepers."

"Don't you, Joe? I'd have thought it was obvious."

Joe shook his head, and poured himself more coffee.

"Because of you, Joe, of course. The other Indigents too, but I never knew them. And Davey, whom you met, and his pal, Dod. I met them after I escaped. Hamish and I tried to fight what was going on in the exit facilities through legal channels, but we got nowhere. The government inquiry's apparently still going on, but I think it'll be swept under the carpet and forgotten about when a new scandal comes along. So, knowing what you had lived through on the street, I'm trying to improve life for homeless people as best I can, in a small but practical way."

"Wow! You're quite the altruist these days, Elaine. Hamish must have got at you."

"And you're just as cynical as ever, Joe."

385

"I have good reason to be." Joe raised his left arm to show Elaine; the sleeve of his jumper was pinned up to just above the elbow. "Wait till I tell you what I've been up to."

"I want to hear your story, Joe, but there's something else I need to say first." Elaine put down her coffee cup and looked directly at Joe. "I thought you'd die back there on the slope outside the facility, either from your injury or because the guards would shoot you. WFJ tried to trace you, but they couldn't find any information, so we assumed you had really died. And it was my fault. If I hadn't stumbled and nearly fallen, you wouldn't have wasted the time you needed to get through the fence. Instead you pushed me through and saved my life." The tears Elaine had been holding back began to course quietly down her cheeks and she looked away. "That's the other reason I'm helping street people – it's a way of giving back and assuaging my guilt."

"Oh, for fuck's sake, Elaine." Joe crossed the room to a side table with a box of tissues on it, pulled two out and handed them to Elaine. "I pushed you because you were in the bloody way, not because I wanted to rescue you. You surely know I'm not the heroic type. Plus, who was the utter prat who actually forgot he had an ancient metal pin in his arm? You can't blame yourself for that."

"No, I suppose not." Elaine dabbed at her eyes with the damp tissues.

Joe reached out with his good arm, shifted closer on the sofa and pulled Elaine into an embrace. She cried for a minute or so more, wetting the soft fabric of his jumper.

"Right, that's enough," Joe said. "Where do you keep the whisky? The sun's over the yard-arm, as Miss Latimer's beau would have said."

Elaine sat up. "Hardly. It can't be much after midday."

"Yes, well, this is Scotland in November; it'll be dark soon, therefore definitely drinks time."

"Fair enough," Elaine said. A small whisky might bolster her nerve and see her through whatever horrors Joe might recount. She brought a bottle of Glenfiddich, two glasses and a bowl of cashews into the living room. As she did so, the phone rang again.

"Are ye all right, Elaine? Is that bloke still there?" Davey asked.

"I'm fine, Davey, thanks, Joe's an old friend. You don't need to worry."

"Christ, he's like a mother hen, or a jealous lover, that man," Joe said. "Does he fancy you?"

"No, he's gay, I think, but not out. He's just very protective of me because I was on the run when we first met. And I've given him a job. Turns out he's great with plants, so he's been experimenting with hydroponics and growing food indoors. I don't know much about it but he grew a great crop of tomatoes in the summer. Anyway, cheers! Here's to survival!"

"I'll second that," Joe said, clinking his glass against hers. "To physical and sartorial survival!" He looked at the damp patch on his jumper where Elaine had wept on it.

"D'you want to take that off and I'll hang it up to dry? I can lend you a sweater of mine."

Joe grinned at her. "Ah, the old Elaine who ripped my clothes off is not dead and buried after all! I was beginning to get worried about you!"

Elaine grinned back, blushing again. "Certainly no cause for worry. But I want my bedtime story first."

"OK, here we go," Joe said, draining his whisky in one go and reaching out for the bottle. "Do you mind?"

Elaine shook her head.

"Well, when they scraped me off the embankment with a burning arm, they took me to the hospital block and shot me full of morphine. A couple of days later, I woke up with my left arm amputated just above the elbow and was told that I didn't exist, and never had done so. My role was to answer Pemberton's questions about your and Hamish's intentions after your escape. The careful granting or withholding of serious pain relief ensured my acquiescence. I told her the little I knew, in dribs and drabs to keep her interest going and myself alive. The rest I just made up; I'm good at guessing what people want to hear, and telling them it."

"Yes, I've noticed," Elaine said.

"She expected something dramatic to happen quite soon after you and Hamish had gone, but the pair of you disappeared for about ten days. This made her uneasy as she didn't know what moves to make. I think the normal Exit Facility business continued while she was waiting for developments. She was bloody stingy with the morphine supply then, I can tell you."

"D'you know what happened to the Indigents that were left?"

"No idea. They may have been executed, but her problem with that would have been the lack of cremation facilities to get rid of bodies en masse. Or maybe she packed the vans and had them driven to some remote part of the Highlands where they couldn't survive without food or water and dumped them there. I was never allowed out of the hospital block so I knew nothing about anything that was going on."

"When Hamish attended the initial hearing, he was told that there were no alleged Indigents at the facility when the IGIO arrived, and that there never had been any. Neither people nor records of them existed," Elaine said.

"What's IGIO stand for?" Joe asked.

"The Internal Government Inspection Office. Sort of auditors cum investigators whose function is to make a show of asking questions then do a good whitewash job, as far as I can make out."

"Ah, those fuckers," Joe said. "I met a couple of them. Nicola kept me well doped-up when they questioned me. She claimed I was a paranoid schizophrenic with delusions. They arrived after your famous press conference. What took you and Hamish so long to blow the whistle?"

"I was ill for several days with some ghastly infection you get from rat's pee. Don't ask how, I'll tell you another time. So Hamish and I were hiding out until I was well enough to speak at the press conference."

"I owe you thanks for that, Elaine. Pemberton actually showed me some clips from your speech – she was so enraged that she was almost spitting fire. If you hadn't described me and my plight with such detail and passion, I think I'd have been quietly offed. She didn't want me to testify at the hearing, but at the same time she needed to be able to produce me if necessary as you'd made an ancillary hero in the drama."

Elaine poured herself another whisky while she thought. "If only I'd known that before! I've spent months feeling guilty about possibly causing your death, but I actually helped to keep you alive! I'm so glad!" On impulse, Elaine gave Joe a brief but firm hug. "So glad!" she said again.

"Everything went tits up at the hearing, though, didn't it?" he said.

"Yes. I wasn't allowed to testify. They said my impaired vision made me an unreliable witness. WFJ and I wanted to call you as a witness but the IGIO said you had never existed. After that it was only Hamish's word against Pemberton's. We realised it was stitched at that point. We did get her for defrauding Miss Latimer, as I had proof. It was a hollow victory, though. I think the petty fraud proved a handy distraction from the real issue of the Indigents. But at least she's in jail now."

"No she isn't," Joe said.

"What? Of course she is!" said Elaine taken aback. "I saw videos on social media of her entering the prison with handcuffs on."

"They may have filmed her going in, but she didn't stay there. I know – I had to live with the bitch for nearly a year."

Elaine gasped. "With Pemberton? Explain!"

"Nicola cut a deal with the government. She was released, with a decent sum of money, a new identity and a new nose. They must have been grateful that she'd done a good job of burying evidence of the Indigents and providing a handy smokescreen with the fraud, as you said. I was released from the Exit Facility into her custody. I got new clothes and a new identity, but no prosthetic arm, unfortunately. We provided cover for each other, nothing more. And fought a lot. I slept with a knife under my pillow in case she tried to murder me in the night."

"Fuck! Are you serious?" Joe nodded and Elaine stared him, shaking her head in disbelief. "And where did this domestic hell take place?"

"In a small village in Sicily. I did a lot of drinking, she did a lot of hill-walking, which kept her out of the house, thank God. But it all came to a tragic end about a month ago. Did you hear about the British couple who were lost in a boat during a storm off the coast of Sicily? A retired professor from a provincial university and his much younger wife."

"I vaguely remember hearing something about that on the radio in the studio one day. His body washed up on the beach, but hers and the boat were not found. Is that right?" *Could this actually be true? After all, this was Joe she was talking to.*

"Almost. But it was Mrs Wilcox, formerly Pemberton, who washed up on a beach near Agrigento. The good professor is drinking whisky with you now, though not in that persona, which is lost at sea. I told you I was from an Italian family. That was true but, more specifically a Sicilian one. In Sicily, family is very important, and there are lots of people who are very competent at problem-solving when a family member needs help. Let's leave it at that, shall we?"

"Did you deliberately persuade Pemberton to go to Sicily with an accident in mind?" Elaine asked, scrutinising Joe's expression for clues.

"Absolutely not. She chose the venue for our quasi witness protection retreat. She'd been there on holiday as a child and loved the island. For me it was sheer luck, the only piece of good luck I've had in twenty years. Apart from meeting you, of course." Joe raised his glass and toasted Elaine.

Elaine ignored the flattery and asked another of the dozen questions that were flying round in her head. "How did you get back here and into the country when you're meant to be dead?"

"I have a passport," Joe said. He went into the hall, where

Elaine had hung his coat, and returned with a maroon object in his hand. He gave it to Elaine, then brought her the magnifier that was sitting beside the box of tissues. It was an EU passport, issued in Italy six months previously. In the name of Giuliano Mangioni. The photo was of Joe, the birthplace was a province in Sicily and the year of birth was only two years after hers.

"A forgery, I presume?"

"No, it's genuine. My parents changed my name to Julian Murray after they immigrated to Britain. I thought Julian sounded like a sissy when I was a kid, so I called myself Joe instead, and it stuck. A relative in Sicily helped me get a copy of my birth certificate and the passport application was easy after that."

Joe broke the silence that ensued. "So that was the story you wanted. What about the tour of the rest of the flat you promised?"

"Not now, maybe later. As you said, there's a lot to digest."

"In that case, let me provide you with something more tangible to digest. I have money as well as a passport these days. I'll take you out to lunch."

"Good plan, Giuliano Mangioni, I accept. And you can be my plus-one this evening. I have complimentary tickets to see Hugo Earle at the theatre."

"Great. *Andiamo.* And you can still call me Joe."

Elaine grabbed her jacket, took Joe's good arm and they stepped out of the flat together.

THE END

Acknowledgments

I would like to express warm thanks to Heather Pearson, who persuaded me to keep writing when I was feeling discouraged. She and Konstantina Scott-Barrett Braoudaki are also due many thanks for their invaluable editorial input. I am very grateful to Max Scratchmann for his expert help in typesetting and designing the book and cover.

I also express my gratitude to Hara Davis, Murdoch Morrison, Emily Simeoni and Bill White, who read and commented on the manuscript. Finally, Mary Gladstone and the late Helen Lamb, both formerly tutors at Edinburgh University, were also instrumental in providing guidance and encouragement in the early stages of writing this book.

Fiona Scott-Barrett
Edinburgh
September 2021

Printed in Great Britain
by Amazon